DREADFUL BEAUTY

By

L. M. RAPP

Atoll Publishing

First paperback edition April 2022

Translation by Luke Owain Boult

ISBN 978-965-90195-0-2 (paperback)
ISBN 978-965-90195-1-9 (ebook)

www.lmrap.com

TABLE OF CONTENT

To Aryeh, Noa, Daphna, and Ori

CHAPTER ONE

The sudden burst of sunlight stirred Neria from her sleep. She groaned, turned over on her stomach, and covered her face with the sheet. She knew what was to come yet she refused to let such thoughts linger.

After opening the shutters, Ellane started to tidy away the clothes scattered across the room. She busied herself like a frightened animal, the rustling of her cautious movements soothing Neria like a lullaby. Just as she was drifting back to sleep, the slave whispered her name. The faint sound was enough to wake the girl from her slumber, but she remained still. The timid, hesitant call came again. There was a time when Ellane would have shaken her by the shoulder or kissed her on the forehead. A light kiss, somewhat apologetic, but boldly asserting a forbidden fondness. These subtle signs of affection had disappeared ever since the incident. They had been replaced by a heavy void. Neria was, at times, surprised by just how much weight such emptiness could have, like an ever-present boulder on her back. After a moment of silence, Ellane repeated her litany of whispers. Neria bolted upright and yelled, "Can't you see I'm trying to sleep, you stupid woman?"

The slave's figure cowered. Her eyes widened. Just before they were concealed behind her eyelids, Neria noticed moisture marring their tranquil azure. Ellane bowed, a lock of white hair falling on her forehead, "Forgive me, Miss Neria. Lady Nephalie told me that..."

"I know what my mother said."

Arhel's eyes had also been blue, but a dark, grayish shade, quite unlike Ellane's almost transparent pupils.

"I'm sorry. I shouldn't have lost my temper. It's because of the execution."

"I know, Miss Neria."

The slave lifted her face for a moment and gave a feeble smile to convey forgiveness that she could never possibly deny. Neria stiffened at the thought of her father learning that she had apologized. Fortunately, neither of them would ever tell him about it.

"Bring me my breakfast."

Ellane left the room. Neria was not hungry but had seized upon this excuse to gain a few moments of respite. She let herself fall back onto the bed and closed her eyes. The sound of birdsong blew in with the scent of jasmine from the half-open window. The heat would soon make the air unbreathable, but for now, a gentle breeze caressed her arms and face. She thought of various ways of getting out of the burdensome chore. An embroidery work to finish? Feigning an illness? A rash that would render her so disfigured that her father would refuse to let her out in public? Perhaps he would allow her to stay at home if it were as punishment. Neria's thoughts went round and round, trapped in the confines of her skull. She did not understand why her father forced her to attend these plebeian spectacles.

Ellane reappeared, carrying a plaited olive wood tray that she placed on the bed. Neria sat cross-legged, sighed, took the cup the slave handed her and smelled the infusion... mint and white poleo with a hint of lavender. She sipped it. Just the right temperature; its warmth comforting rather than scalding. Ellane knew her tastes well. She knew the tastes of every member of the family. Everything she touched bordered on perfection. A decapitated egg sat in a ceramic bowl, the top of its shell removed to reveal its firm white and smooth yolk. Three dates bulged and glistened on a fig leaf. Neria bit into one, but, repulsed by its sweetness, put the half-finished fruit down.

Ellane took a blue tunic out of the trunk and laid it at the foot of the bed.

"Why do you live here with us?"

The slave froze still.

"I've often wondered why. You're the only female Chimera living in the city."

"There may be others like me living in hiding, Miss Neria."

"Perhaps. But still... How did you end up here?"

"Thanks to your father. It is a long story."

"Tell me. I won't tell anyone else."

The slave smoothed out the fabric of the tunic.

"I don't want this one. Get me the yellow one."

"But Miss Neria..."

"With the gold belt and that coral bead necklace. Quickly!"

"Are you sure? Your father..."

"I'm sure."

Ellane began to fold the dress with a calm elegance out of place in a slave.

"What does flying feel like?"

"I beg your pardon, Miss Neria?"

"Well, you could fly before. What was it like?"

The woman held the dress to her breast with an unreadable expression on her face.

"It was wonderful."

"Tell me about it."

"Not now. You're going to be late."

How had her father managed to hide a female Chimera under his roof? And why take such risks? Neria knew that she would not be able to extract any more details from her but resolved to try again later that evening.

The egg mocked her with its congealed yellow eye. A stare like that of the barn owl she had seen just a matter of days earlier in the cool of the night. She had looked up and seen it perched on the branch of an oak tree, so very close. The bird had watched her for a few minutes before turning its flat phantom face away and taking off to the skies, nonchalantly beating the air with its great white wings. How would it feel to fly? What would it feel like to have your wings cut off? Like the phantom pain of an amputated limb? Regret for no longer being able to soar towards the sky? Neria had suddenly felt nostalgia for unknown lands. At that moment, she wished she could have followed the bird's example and gone.

Neria put on her long tunic and clasped the coral bead necklace around her neck. The Balou Tipol Manual encouraged the use of muted colors. Well-raised girls should reserve red for their family circles. The color attracted too much attention at public gatherings. Irritated by Ellane's worried glances, Neria dismissed her. She proceeded to carefully fasten her belt to highlight her waist and raise the hem of her dress, revealing her

4

ankles. She fixed her hair and placed a veil over her brown curls. After strapping on her leather sandals, she sat herself down on a chair. The twittering of the birds softened the muffled sound of the preparations she could hear from downstairs. Neria got to her feet when she heard her mother calling her. Hasty steps announced her arrival, eyebrows creased and mouth pursed.

"They're waiting for you to leave... Why are you wearing that necklace? Why do you have to be so stubborn, Neria? Take it off this instant."

"No."

"What will people say?"

"They'll be jealous, especially the ladies, I think..."

"You don't think. If you only knew... this is no time to be drawing attention to yourself. At least hide it under your veil. Hurry up! Your father's getting impatient."

Neria rushed after her mother, ran down the staircase and burst into the living room with a smile on her lips. A haze of spice from the kitchen filled the house, making her nauseous. The others were waiting for her. Elinor, beautiful in one of her favorite blue tunics, wore an immaculate veil. Adamek had, of course, dressed in white to imitate his father.

"Any reason why you're late?"

"I didn't realize the time."

"You know how I value punctuality."

"Yes. Sorry."

As Valterone approached her, Neria lifted her eyes and tried to maintain a calm expression and an air of innocence. He raised his hand as she held her breath. His hand falling again, he smiled. This smile worried Neria more than the looming threat of being struck.

"Let us leave. We have delayed for too long."

Surrounded by walls that protected their privacy, the residences of the More-Than-Pure were concentrated in front of Supreme Square, where the Temple stood. Neria turned around. Only the flat rooftops of the family residence could be seen from the square. Her mother, a frail solitary figure, raised her hand to wave goodbye. Exempted from public appearances since Arhel's death, Nephalie would be waiting for them at home. With the help of Ellane and the servants, she would put the finishing touches on the preparations for the reception. Paz and Anaëlle would join her at a later time.

Valterone, dressed as ever in white, walked forward in long strides. Adamek, of similar stature, seemed to have difficulty keeping up with his father. The strides of the family's eldest son made him look like a horse in a dressage competition. The girls, dazzled by the harsh light, hurried along, trying not to fall behind. Their leather sandals slapped against the flagstones. This early summer heat had already become unbearably intense as the sun shone in a blue sky speckled with debonair clouds of white. The heatwave would last for five months, with minor variations that would fluctuate between two temperature levels: barely tolerable and outright infernal. Neria glanced over to her sister and noticed her pinkening cheeks and a veil of moisture on her upper lip and forehead. Her pale skin could not withstand the heat. Neria was always amazed to notice she had any sort of defect, however small it was, and derived a guilty pleasure from it. Yet there was also a certain fondness or hope that she perhaps vaguely resembled her sister in some way, in spite of Neria's curly hair, dark complexion and hooked nose.

As the custom required, they circled the Source three times, with Neria opening her veil and exposing the necklace that adorned her neck with its ruby luster. The bystanders threw glances in her direction. The women did not seem envious, but rather surprised, even critical. As for the men... Neria felt herself blushing. She decided to ignore them, in the same way that she avoided contemplating the dark waters of the Source. She adjusted the veil on her forehead to partly conceal her face.

They walked toward the Temple. Its three terraces of decreasing size, piled one on top of the other, leaned against a rocky peak that towered over the building, as if the earth's entrails had given birth to an architectural protrusion or, on the contrary, had pierced the human structure to punish humanity for its arrogance. Neria would have preferred to wander on street level, among the fine goods stalls of the Grand Hall, which served, except on feast days, as an indoor market. Its stone walls, pierced with narrow openings, would have protected her from the heat. In accordance with their rank, they took the Cardinal Staircase, located to the west and perpendicular to the building. Neria dreaded the ascent of the hundred and fifty steps that led to the First Gate. Three majestic outer staircases, the north, the south and the west, joined in front of it and provided access to the roof of the Grand Hall, the Sublime Terrace. Neria eventually arrived soaked in sweat, with a red face, labored breath, and burning calves, the price to pay for her status, and passed under the stone arch following Elinor.

The guardian priests, responsible for opening and closing the three Temple Gates, stood on either side of the First Portal. The eldest carried large keys, attached to his belt by a crimson cord. They bowed as Valterone approached, who returned their salutations without stopping. He continued to the area reserved for the More-Than-Pure and their families, just at the edge of the parapet, but immediately left his children to talk to some of his acquaintances. As they settled on their bench, Draz joined them and sat as usual beside Elinor, in the place left vacant by Nephalie. Neria asked herself for the thousandth time why they had not yet married. Their long engagement had become something of a joke and, at twenty-one years old, Elinor now passed for an old maid.

The More-Than-Pure occupied the first row. Other dignitaries had taken their seats behind them, rich merchants, military men, a few priests. They spoke among themselves, happy to prance around in their finery, to boast of their children and to spread rumors. Neria replied to a friend with a smile, then turned her head away. She felt too ill for mindless prattle. The gaping mouth of the Source opened in the center of the esplanade, which was swarming with people. Neria gazed at it — she was not at risk from this distance — and remembered the first time the visions had appeared.

After several days of bad weather that had confined them indoors, their mother was annoyed by the children's unruly play and hoped that a little exercise and a change of scenery would calm them down somewhat. She had taken advantage of a break in the weather to take them shopping. They went to the market in the Grand Hall, but the bright spell was short-lived. By the end of their shopping, black clouds had gathered again in the sky and icy gusts of wind swept through the square, ruffling their hair, and shaking their clothes like sails on a boat. Neria remembered the joy she had felt as she stood witness to the force of nature and its potential for destruction. When Nephalie stopped to speak to a neighbor, she seized the opportunity to let go of the hand holding onto her and walk away.

"Stay away from the Source!" her mother had shouted to her. An unnecessary warning. Neria had been afraid of the black waters for as long as she could remember. Children played a game of chase. With their feet bare and dressed in grayish rags, they seemed indifferent to the cold and to the opinions of passers-by. Their dirty faces lit up with beaming smiles. Neria, who could never have imagined being among these destitute wretches crawling with vermin, had not been able to take her eyes off the group.

Until she noticed a call. She had already felt a feeling of expectation emanating from the Source, but on that day, this presence had grown into a demand. Neria had approached the water as much as she had dared to and let her gaze sink into it. At first, she had only seen the reflections of clouds, then there had been glimpses of faces: her family, her friends, familiar landscapes. She watched them for a while, enraptured by this magical transformation, oblivious to what was going on around her. But, little by little, the images became less innocuous, and scenes of suffering emerged. Woken from her trance by Arhel tugging at her cloak, she ran away. Since that day, the Source had tarnished her childhood outings with its noxious air. As soon as Neria left her house, she could feel its malignant presence following her down the city's alleyways. Several months after this incident, she had gathered the courage to ask her brother — in a blasé tone, as if she could not attach any less importance to the question — if he had ever seen the pictures in the black water. His expression confirmed her fears. She claimed it was a joke, just a story a friend had told her. Arhel looked at her in that piercing way he would at times but had not pressed her any further on the matter.

From this distance, on her bench among the privileged, Neria could not discern any images on the surface of the Source and felt safe. All around the pool, some passers-by were going about their business, but the majority now awaited the beginning of the spectacle. Silence gradually descended. Valterone took his place next to Adamek. He cast a distant gaze on his children before he sat down, like a final inspection of his troops. Neria could see in his expression he had noticed the necklace. She resisted the desire to cover it with her veil and turned her attention to the high priest, standing on his pedestal. At his signal, the audience rose, and the ceremony began. Down below, younger priests perched on platforms echoed his voice. The congregation recited their praises like all the faithful in the land of Gashom:

"Born from the bowels of the earth, we yearn for exaltation..."

"We are the link between heaven and earth..."

"Blessed be thou, Asoas, show us the way to eternal purity, send the Savior unto the earth, the Liberator who shall lead us to an enraptured future..."

The air shook with their chants. Neria, carried away in spite of herself by the zeal of the flock, was surprised to find herself voicing her exaltation aloud.

"Blessed be Elatek, thy emissary, who shows us the way of righteousness..."

"Burn the cesspit with thy fiery breath, blind our enemies

with thy flaming anger..."

"Let them die, let them perish, let them suffocate in their putrid pestilence..."

At the end of the prayer, a troop of soldiers made their way through the congregation and formed a protective ring around the Source. Insurgents had tried to free the prisoners in the past. Despite the ineptness of those ill-fated endeavors and the moribund condition of the rebellion, the More-Than-Pure took precautions to ensure the solemnity of their justice.

The crowd roared. Two men escorted out a repulsive woman. They propped her up, dragging her along. She did not struggle and seemed to accept her fate. Neria saw red patches, tufts of hair and perhaps even scales on her inflamed skin. Bulbous protuberances disfigured her temples and her bloated legs labored her movement. At this point, it was impossible to tell what kind of monster she would become. A few weeks earlier, she had thought she was safe and was still part of the community. Neria wondered how such a disgusting creature could have dared to hide in the city. Chimeras, with their deceitful and malicious nature, would remain ever unworthy of the trust of Humans. Neria thought suddenly of Ellane, submissive and honest, that Ellane with her many talents. Her extraordinary gifts had distinguished her from the others and had encouraged Valterone to keep her.

The people shouted with glee or jeered at the prisoner. The most daring of them risked the ire of the guards and threw rotten fruit at the condemned. Neria did not dare look away out of fear of her father's scorn. Seized by nausea, she focused on her breathing. The pained feet of the monster were dragging on the ground. Neria felt a great heat and fanned herself with a side of her veil. The executioners stopped in front of the rim surrounding the Source. The Chimera raised one leg, leaned on the uneven stones and, propped up by the two men, climbed up onto the edge.

Neria hoped that the criminal would not struggle. She abhorred those pitiful spasms, those pathetic attempts to escape an inevitable death. But this one accepted her fate. The executioners pushed her forward and backed away hurriedly to avoid any splashes. She fell, disappearing as if sucked into quicksand. A few feeble ripples, then nothing. The Source devoured its victims like an ogre. But who was the real ogre here? Those unfathomable waters or the Humans who used them to dispose of their condemned? Neria's throat tightened, a wave of heat overwhelmed her. She was afraid of fainting or worse... What punishment would she face if she defiled the Temple grounds?

"Are you feeling okay?"

Sweet Elinor... So obedient and caring. She didn't ask for much, really, just a little affection.

"But what are you wearing? Are you crazy? If father finds out..."

"He saw."

"You're going to get in trouble!"

"I need to get some air. I won't be long."

Neria ignored her sister and left. The public was still discussing the anatomical curiosities of the monster and rejoicing in its death. Neria had the sudden sensation of seeing her reflection in a distorting mirror. In no rush, she moved towards the Transcendental Staircase that led to the second floor.

She climbed the first step and waited. Reassured by the hubbub of the conversations that continued without interruption, she continued her ascent. If anyone noticed her, she would tell the truth, that she had wanted to get some fresh air. But no one in the crowd of dignitaries was interested in the strange behavior of such an insignificant girl. She reached the shadow of the Sovereign Gate, cooled off for a moment, turned around, leaned against the wall, and took in the view. She could still hear the incessant cackling. Vividly colored clothes studded the terrace like precious gemstones. Valterone, like a white sun, stood dominant among them with his stature and his presence. Beyond the parvis lay the tapestry of the streets of Alipaz. Beyond that still lay the sea, both magnificent and malevolent.

A decade had passed since the last sea monster attack. After breaching the protective nets, tiger sharks had swarmed onto the beach and into the city. They slaughtered thirty-five people and then left, taking the remains of their victims with them.

Neria shivered in spite of the heat, turned her back to the sea, advanced towards the Superior Terrace and stopped in front of the Sanctuary of Asoas the Glorious. Elinor and Neria had been admitted to this holy place only on rare occasions, a place mostly frequented by men. Their father usually went there accompanied by Adamek. She clearly remembered its stately antechamber with six arched windows, which led into the Chancel. Adorned with pilasters and recesses, the Chancel was illuminated by several narrow openings in the upper part of the walls and by the Clarifying Fire on its stone pedestal. The opulence of the ornaments, the magnificence of the clothing of the priests, and the gold and silver holy artifacts that glistened in the half-light had dazzled Neria. After the ordeal of the many steps, she had been rewarded by the privilege of being comforted by cool water, the fragrance of incense, and shimmering flames in the intimacy of the house of Asoas.

This time, Neria did not dare enter. She skirted the Chancel and approached the balustrade. From this point, the highest in Alipaz, higher still than the walls that protected it and domineered only by the great rock against which the Temple leaned, she could freely admire the two peaks that flanked the eastern road, the so-called Two Sisters. The two peaks were crowned with buildings. They had served as sentry posts in the distant past when the forest reached the sea and wild hordes attacked the city. They were no longer needed and were falling into ruin. The Little Sister's post resembled a fortified farmhouse, the Big Sister's a tower. To Neria's eyes, the Big Sister, slender with its top crowned with battlements, represented Elinor. The other, the Little Sister, was stocky and banal, reminding her of herself. At their feet, the Yatir River meandered, languishing and lazy, crossing through fields before flowing into the city and into the sea. Beyond the Two Sisters, a mysterious world began, a world that neither Neria nor Elinor had ever gone near.

"What are you doing here?"

With her heart pounding, Neria turned to the stranger, an emaciated priest with thin lips twisted into a spiteful grin.

"Answer me! Why aren't you saying anything? Such stupidity. Don't just stand there dangling your arms, you're defiling the sanctity of our Temple. I'm taking you to the guardhouse."

The excuse of wanting to take in some fresh air would not

be enough. Neria imagined the shame she would feel if she had to go back down like some common criminal accompanied by this middling nobody. Her father's reaction...

"The Divine Valterone, my father, gave me permission to come to admire the Sanctuary and the view."

"The Divine Valterone? But he knows very well that..."

"I was just about to leave. No need to see me out."

Neria walked away as proudly as she could.

"Wait, I'll come with you."

She heard the hurried steps following her but continued on her way. The priest, now groveling, smiled to her with a foul grin.

"I've always wanted to meet the Divine Valterone, such a wonderful man..."

"Don't even think about it. You'd only disturb him."

"But why not? This is the perfect opportunity."

"I advise you not to get on his nerves when he's in conversation with his friends. The executions may seem like a bit of fun for you, but I assure you that my father takes them very seriously. They are more than a cleansing ceremony; they are a crucial opportunity for this city's leaders."

"But..."

They had reached the Sovereign Gate. She stopped and looked him straight in the eye: "Trust me. Coming with me now will only end in trouble."

He must have sensed the sincerity of her words, revealed as an expression of disappointment spread over his face. She had not lied. Bearers of bad news were by no means immune from

Valterone's anger.

"See you soon, I hope."

"Yes. Sure."

She began to descend the stairs. She would have liked to mimic the serene immobility of the stone and melt into it but forced herself to maintain the same regal rhythm as when she had begun. One step and then another… The crowd had started to disperse. She could see her father talking to another More-Than-Pure. From time to time, he turned away from the speaker. He seemed preoccupied. As long as he did not raise his head… One step and then another…

Elinor, blue and white as a summer sky, with her widened eyes and mouth half-opened, had seen her. She snapped out of her amazement and came to meet her. The two sisters arrived at the bottom of the stairs together.

"What were you doing up there?"

"Just needed a bit of fresh air."

"On the Superior Terrace?"

"Whyever not? You think it's right we're not allowed to visit it?"

"You're mad."

"Don't tell anyone I went."

"What do you take me for? I'd rather not get us in trouble. But you might want to think about the consequences of your actions…"

"Shut up, he's coming."

"Where have you been?"

"I needed some air, so I found a quiet spot in the shade."

"Where do you think you are? A picnic?"

"I'm sorry, I didn't think…"

"Exactly. You never think. And that necklace… Well, I suppose you won't be my problem for too long, but don't think that this conversation is over. Come on. Inside. Our guests are waiting. And cover up that ridiculous necklace!"

CHAPTER TWO

A naëlle ran to greet her aunts as soon as they crossed the threshold of the door. Neria lifted her up and spun her around. Comforted by this burst of innocence and her fragrance of tart peach, she squeezed her in her arms. She kissed her rosy cheeks, reassured by the sight of her cheerful face and golden curls. How could Adamek have fathered such a lovely child?

"Newia! Let's play!"

"What did you call me? Newia?"

"No, Newia!"

"Ah, I see, *Newia*."

"No, Newia! You're being silly!"

"Ah, I see! Neria, right?"

"Yes! You dunno your name?"

"I'm not as smart as you."

Paz joined them. The spirit of the young woman had faded over the years of married life. She looked tired and tense. After exchanging pleasantries, she tried to convince her daughter to come and finish her food, but Anaëlle, happy to have found a playmate, refused to yield and Paz reluctantly allowed her to do as she wished.

Disgusted by the stench of food, Neria skirted the low tables laid out for the meal and led the child towards the quietest corner of the room. They settled themselves down on cushions, got out a deck of cards, and started a game of War. Neria was distracted by Anaëlle's babbling. How old was she again? She seemed precocious for her six years, she understood the numbers and made few mistakes. The frustration she felt with each of her defeats did not last long and she savored each of her victories, even the smallest. She would slam her cards down, menacingly, before she took her spoils with a triumphant air. Neria, who had long lost this passion of childhood, this hope that the best remained to come, suddenly felt very old. Bile reflux burned her throat like acid. Executions were not good for her. Or was it that cake she had bought the day before from a street vendor? At the moment when she rejoiced that her absence at the table had passed unnoticed, a call rang out.

"Neria! Come here!"

She got up leisurely.

"Hurry up will you!"

Neria was not too worried. Her father would not dare tell her off for her behavior in front of all the guests, trying to foster the image of the perfect family. He would later, there was no doubt. He and Zelimo sat in deep armchairs and watched her approach. Dirtied plates, strewn with scraps of food, lay on the table.

The two men had very different physiques. Maturity suited Valterone's charm: black eyes, rimmed with thick lashes, with an expression softened by the outline of crow's feet, thick hair, well-defined lips, nestled in a brown beard, barely whitened by time. Good food had enlarged his figure without overburdening him, maintaining his athletic stature.

Small and lean, Zelimo's eyes were minuscule and his ears

too large, for which he tried to compensate by wearing a goatee. While Valterone always dressed in white, Zelimo adorned himself in bright colors and kept himself informed of even the smallest details in the latest fashions. Most notable, however, his plain face came alive with a captivating energy when he spoke. He had exceptional oratory skills, which were useful for his role as "Builder of the Humans" and he hypnotized crowds whenever he was given the opportunity. The people adored him and swallowed every one of the sweet words that left his mouth.

Neria could not find a chair to hand and remained standing in front of them.

"Zelimo was asking about you."

"Ah yes? Thank you."

The old family friend looked her up and down in a way that repulsed her.

"Tell Zelimo what you do, what your interests are."

"Well, I enjoy sewing."

"Do you like cooking?" asked Zelimo, in a honeyed tone.

"Um, no, not particularly."

"Whatever's the matter with you, Neria?" Valterone grew annoyed. "You're normally much more talkative than this."

"Never mind, it doesn't matter! She's young, she'll learn."

They looked at each other and burst into raucous laughter. Neria felt herself turning red. Ellane appeared, bending down to take the dirty dishes away and raised her face for a moment. Her expression gave Neria the strange feeling that she pitied her, that the slave felt sorry for her mistress. The two men spoke among themselves. Neria was no longer listening to them, simply nodding and smiling. She spotted her mother, a platter of honey cakes in her hands, watching the conversation from a distance. Everyone already knew what Neria had just realized. The More-Than-Pure had to propagate their perfect genes and consequently practiced polygamy. This time, Neria had been chosen to participate in the communal effort. She had to call upon all her strength and her years of education to remain standing upright, nodding with a friendly air. When they finally dismissed her, she walked out to the patio, crossed it, and reached the large oak tree. The leaves rustled, with the hubbub of the reception barely audible.

Seized by violent nausea, she doubled over. When the attack passed, she wrapped her arms around the tree trunk and rested her forehead on its bark. Tears glistened in the corners of her eyes. She had to calm her nerves before joining the others. Someone might come to check on her. She walked away and took the path leading to the stable. Her hand spread open, fingers outstretched, she caressed the shrubs along the boundary wall. She crouched down, picked up a few mint leaves, crumpled them up, and then brought them to her mouth. Their familiar scent comforted her. A few more minutes and her dignity as a perfect young woman would be restored, as told by the Manual.

Only the children and the servants, especially Bobka, who divided his time between the vegetable garden and the stable, used this service path. In this part of the garden, her favorite, Neria could imagine she was in a forest, far from Alipaz and its intrigues. Large solemn trees surrounded and protected her. Out of habit, she softened her steps, trying to silence them, just like when she used to play her game of sneaking up on the groom-gardener and his remarkable sense of hearing. Through the wide-open stable doors, she could discern a grotesque creature in the half-light, a caricature of a Human, clutching onto the neck of a horse. A powerful jaw with thin lips revealing the teeth of a predator, small eyes sunken into protruding sockets, a low forehead, a stubby nose, a stocky body, bow legs. Coarse brown fur covered its skin and wretched rags hid the scars of its severed wings.

Suddenly, its large, pointed ears twitched, wrinkles creased its forehead adorned with two short horns, and the creature raised itself up to enthusiastically currycomb the mount.

"I did it this time."

"You've got to be kidding. I heard you from the vegetable garden. I was just thinking. Liber's hoof is worrying me. I think it's starting to get inflamed."

Neria noticed traces of sweat moistening his hairy face. Did Gargoyles have feelings like Humans? Not exactly, without a doubt. Rather more like those of a dog. Dogs felt pain and joy in a crude but undeniable way. Otherwise, they could not form a bond with their masters. But their affection lay mostly in the promise of food and the comfort they took from their obedience. If he could, Bobka would leave the family.

"You were thinking, you said?"

"Yes, I was…"

"I wanted to tell you that… well, if you need help, if you need to talk, you can come to me."

"I know. Thanks."

He stopped grooming Liber's croup and turned to her. His arms fell back to his sides. He hesitated before his lips tightened in a faint smile.

"Everything's fine, Miss Neria, don't you worry. But don't waste your time with a beast like me. Go back to the house, your parents must be looking for you."

Neria felt the urge to insult Bobka. She tightened her fists. Years of frustration poisoned by the discovery of her father's designs had been triggered by this moment of pure rage, which had just been waiting to be released.

"You're a liar!"

The Gargoyle took a step back.

"Everything is not fine. If you don't feel like talking to me, then I'll leave you alone. Good luck with those hooves," she hissed before turning away.

Anger had eased her pain and she felt she had the strength to face her family and their guests. If her father thought the deal was done, he was quite mistaken.

No one seemed to have noticed her absence. Elinor and Draz were still chattering away in a world of their own, with the characteristic selfishness of lovers. But why was her sister still waiting to marry him? It was all clear to Neria now. Her sister had landed a prize of great value: a young man, certainly a little bland, but not unsightly, the offspring of a More-Than-Pure and, on top of all that, single too. Draz's father, an ally of Valterone's in the struggle for power, had rejoiced at the engagement. And now, people gossiped. Neria noticed that Zelimo's wife had cornered Nephalie. What did they think of this arrangement? Had the first wife resigned herself to sharing her husband's affection? Did she feel jealousy or relief? And her mother? Why hadn't she warned her? Valterone, in the center of a group of men, seemed at ease. The others laughed at his jokes. A herd of goats fascinated by the flash of a knife.

Neria made her way towards the table, waited for a servant to pour her a cup of tea, and took a sip. The brew calmed her upset stomach. Someone, however, was pulling at her tunic. Anaëlle had found her and, it was an obligation, a higher duty, an incantation of fate, they had to finish their game. Neria granted the little girl her wish. She gazed in admiration at her and once again grieved for her childhood years. People seemed happier before. In any case, they had been better liars. Anaëlle had a few years of peace ahead of her, and then she would slowly learn the truth about the world in which she lived.

The girl had put the game away in two neat decks. Her mischievous smile made Neria wonder whether she had cheated. After all, why not? The skill would prove useful to her later in life. Neria sank into the cushions. She wanted to be back in her room, to sleep, to recover her strength. Why had her father sold her off like this? She deserved so much better than Zelimo. She was young, perhaps not as beautiful as Elinor, but still pretty. And the daughter of one of the most powerful men in the city... The dull game soothed Neria. She no longer shared Anaëlle's enthusiasm about the outcome of a game of War, but she pretended to, voicing her dismay, or expressing her joy depending on the circumstances of the game. That was enough to satisfy Anaëlle who, Neria was sure of it, had slipped the best cards into her own deck during the break in the game.

"Tell me, you've not cheated by any chance, have you? I don't remember my hand being so bad."

"No, I haven't! I just put 'em away. I put your deck hewe and mine hewe. See? I didn't cheat."

24

"Well, don't get cross, I believe you."

Arhel's death had tarnished the family's reputation. Elinor had been lucky; her father had concluded their engagement before the death.

Neria was feeling worse and worse. Although she had not eaten anything all day, even the thought of food made her nauseous. She stretched out her aching limbs, touched her forehead with the back of her hand, and found she had a fever.

"I won!"

"You destroyed me."

"Again! Let's do it again!"

"No, I'm tired."

"But playing doesn't make people tiwed!"

Anaëlle set about collecting the cards and then tried her hand at building a house out of them. Two cards at a steep angle, two more beside it, a third duo for the roof. She stuck her tongue out between her lips, which tightened with the effort. Neria looked around her. The satisfied guests continued with their conversations, clumped in scattered bunches. Elinor and Draz, vapid and predictable, took advantage of the occasion to gaze lovingly into each other's eyes and whisper to one another in a nauseating way. Nephalie was valiantly performing her role as hostess. Valterone was still parading among the guests. Zelimo stared at her. She felt her cheeks flush.

"I've changed my mind. Let's play again."

"Oh, neat! Wait, I'll set it up."

"Here, I'll help you."

"No, I know how."

The cards were slipping out of her clumsy little hands, but the child persisted, picked them up, separated them into two decks that she then tried to put back together again. Neria refrained from intervening.

"Finished! Now I give them out."

"Give me that, I'll be quicker."

"No, I can do it."

Anaëlle focused and carefully placed the cards down one by one.

"One for you, one for me, one for you... Oops, that one slipped. I'm..."

"Anaëlle? Anaëlle? What's the matter?... Answer me."

With her limbs rigid, her eyes opened wide, the child looked in front of her, an expression of terror on her face. Afraid of drawing any attention, Neria called to her in a quiet voice while Anaëlle still seemed to be cut off from the world.

The thud of a vicious slap followed by the fall of a body to the ground interrupted the conversations. Adamek shouted, "I told you not to speak to me in that tone!" Amid the commotion and the screams, the men tried to calm Adamek down while the women came to Paz's aid. Neria held Anaëlle, who had begun to sob in her arms.

Every couple has its arguments, but Adamek lacked the good taste to settle them in private. The incident had shattered the carefree atmosphere. The violence of her elder brother did not surprise Neria. She had often experienced it herself. But the behavior of the child worried her. Had she foreseen the aggression? Or was it just a coincidence? Anaëlle broke free and ran to her mother. With Nephalie joining them, the three of them slipped away upstairs. Adamek had also disappeared. Neria, accompanied by her father and her sister, posted herself at the entrance to see off the guests.

Zelimo approached her. His broad grin revealed stained teeth.

"Neria, say goodbye to our friend Zelimo."

Taken aback, she looked at her father.

"He's a talented man and one I very much admire."

"Goodbye, thank you for coming."

"See you soon, my dear."

He patted Neria's skull like the neck of a mare before allowing his hand to casually slide down, brushing her hair, her cheek, her neck, her collarbone, and her breast. Neria returned his smile in spite of the filthy lingering trail that this hand had left in its wake. When could she put an end to this nightmare, leave these people behind, go to bed and finally sink into the unconsciousness she so desired? A throbbing headache had joined her earlier discomfort, but before returning to the refuge of her room, she decided to see her mother first. She went up the stairs, knocked on the door, and opened it. A whispered conversation immediately stopped. Paz lay sprawled on the bed, Nephalie sitting beside her. Anaëlle was playing with a trinket by her feet.

"My brother doesn't deserve you. I'm sorry. Did he hurt you? Does it still hurt?"

"My arm hurts. I twisted it when I tried to break my fall. A stupid reflex. But it'll pass, don't worry about it."

A red mark lingered on her cheek, threatening to turn blue.

"Does this happen often?"

"No, it's only happened a few times... when he overdoes it. Your father gives him so many responsibilities and his work really gets to him."

"I'm very familiar with my brother and his fragile temper."

"That's not what I mean..."

Paz's voice trembled. Anaëlle clambered onto the bed and cuddled up with her mother.

"I'd leave him if I were you."

"You speak with the inexperience of youth."

"You're not that old."

"Yes, but I do have more experience."

"I can believe that. Living with Adamek must be quite a character builder. Are you sleeping here tonight?"

"No, I'm going back home, he'd rather I stayed there. But Nephalie convinced him to leave Anaëlle for the night."

The child wrapped her arms around her mother's neck and tightened her grip to the point of throttling her.

"Careful, I can't breathe with you doing that."

"I love you and wanna sleep here with you."

"Sweetheart... You know I love you... but we've already talked about this. You'll be staying at your grandmother's for the night and I'll come to get you tomorrow."

"I don't want to."

Her chin trembled, with tears threatening to break free. Neria hastened to change the subject.

"Something's been bothering me about what happened earlier."

Paz, who until then had been lying on her back, turned to her sister-in-law. Her face was contorted by a wince of pain. Neria felt the worried concern of the two women focus on her and sensed that they would rather she stayed quiet.

She told them about the fit earlier and her suspicion. Anaëlle had foreseen her father's actions.

"What do you think?" she asked her. "How did you feel when..."

The child looked at her mother.

"It's nothing, I know all about these fits," interjected Paz. "I've even talked to the doctor about them, and he reassured me they'll pass when she grows up."

"Don't worry about it. These troubles of hers, they're to do with her nerves, they won't last."

Anaëlle, returning to her game, rolled a long wooden bead necklace around her arm. Neria detected a sorrowful air about her.

"You're hiding something from me."

"Not at all!" insisted Nephalie. "Why would we do something like that?"

"Because it's a habit in this family. When were you going to tell me about your plans?"

"What are you talking about?"

"Father's decided to marry me off to Zelimo, hasn't he? I've had to put up with such obvious insinuations that you won't even need to bother with the announcement."

Nephalie lost herself gazing at the bracelets on her wrist. She grasped one and twirled it around.

"Your father's fond of the idea. I'm still trying to talk him out of it."

"You could have told me about this before. I would have liked to have been prepared."

"I didn't want to worry you and I was hoping he would change his mind."

"Have you set the date yet?"

"Not really. In three or four months probably."

Neria clenched her jaw. She had very little time to find a solution.

"I'd rather die than marry that old fossil."

Nephalie nodded in acquiescence.

"Don't you have anything to say? I expect you'll be willing to help me get out of this nightmare."

"I will. Just... it's not going to be easy. You know what your father's like when he sets his mind on something."

"I'm not his daughter for nothing."

A faint smile lit up Nephalie's face.

"I know you've got spirit, but I doubt it's going to be enough to get you out of this mess."

An embarrassed silence descended. Neria understood that the two women wished to resume the discussion that she had interrupted. Despite this, Nephalie asked, "Are you alright? You seem tired."

"I must have eaten a bad cake from a street vendor."

"I've told you a hundred times, don't buy food outside. You have everything you need here. Healthy food, made from fresh produce..."

"They looked really good."

"Go ask Ellane for some herbal tea for an upset stomach. Maybe a little soup? Take Anaëlle with you."

"I wanna stay with mommy."

"Is that all? My father wants to sell me off to the highest bidder and you send me on my way with a bit of herbal tea?"

"I assure you that if I could, I would have chosen a different husband for you. But, believe me, not everything is about you, and I have other problems to deal with. So, do me a favor, take Anaëlle and bring her to Ellane. I want to take care of Paz; she's also been going through a difficult time."

"I don't wanna leave mommy."

"Sorry, sweetheart. You need to get used to the idea from now on that no one will ever ask for your opinion."

Neria had always had a reputation of being a troublemaker, reinforced at the age of ten by her rebellion against her tutor. That morning, like every morning, Rona had told her to learn two pages from Balou Tipol's *Manual of Good Manners* by heart before falling asleep in her armchair with a book on her lap to give an illusion of attentiveness in case anyone made an unexpected appearance. Arhel's quill scratched on the paper, the faint noise annoying Neria. Her brother's arithmetic exercises had seemed much more interesting to her than her insipid manual, whose words slipped through her numbed brain without leaving any imprint behind.

"A young woman should know how to brighten up her home, but it will suffice for her to know just enough to enliven a conversation. She should not put herself in the forefront; a real lady makes use of subtle suggestion. She should wait for her parents' guests to address her first and on no account should she attract attention in a rude and provocative manner."

The Manual and sewing, that's all her education had consisted of. Bemused and outraged by her plight, Neria had initially contented herself with appealing to the tutor. Failing to get a reaction from her, she had torn off a corner of a page, fashioned it into a small pellet, and then aimed it between her eyes. The pellet had ricocheted off her shoulder and landed on the tiling. Arhel put down his quill to sit back and watch the scene unfold. After several failed attempts, a projectile hit one of her bulging cheeks. Rona had stirred a little but soon fell back into the mists of her blissful stupor. Sound effects unexpectedly accompanied the spectacle, which made the children laugh so much it hurt. Neria continued her ballistics experiments but had realized the obvious. Not even a rain of pellets would disturb Rona from her slumber. She consequently resumed calling for her, gradually increasing her volume until she was screaming.

She smiled at the memory of Rona's bewildered expression when she had awoken. Her confusion hadn't lasted long and soon turned to fury.

"I hope you have a good reason for disturbing my reading!"

"I want to do arithmetic exercises like my brother."

"Stubborn girl. We've been over this a hundred times. Those exercises are for boys. Well-raised girls don't go around acting like tomboys. I've had more than enough of your silly questions. Now come here!"

Clutching onto a metal ruler, she had risen from her chair like a knight pulling himself up on his steed before slaying a dragon.

"No."

"How dare you? Come here this instant, you little brat!"

Rona had sputtered in her frenzied fury. This spray of spittle had disgusted the now-furious Neria. She had picked up the Manual and then thrown it against the wall with such a force that the old book had torn, its pages scattering all over the floor. After having examined the damage for a moment, her tutor tried to catch the delinquent. The more agile Neria had evaded her without any difficulty, maneuvering to always keep the table between them. Her pursuer had already started to lose her breath by the time Nephalie's entrance interrupted the chase.

"Rona, I trust you have an explanation for this ridiculous behavior."

"It's Neria, she's intolerable. But, as the Great Star is my witness, I love this child. It's her ingratitude, that's what it is. After all that I've done for her..."

"Rona!"

"Well... Neria out of nowhere demanded that she do arithmetic exercises like her brother and threw the Manual straight at my face! I'm very lucky I avoided it. I trust you realize I could have been seriously hurt!"

"That's not true you dirty liar! I didn't throw it anywhere near you. If I'd wanted to hit you, I would have!"

In the end, Nephalie had dismissed Rona. Despite the reprimands and punishments, her parents had felt a certain pride in her without daring to admit it. Valterone, who admired strength of character and likely saw that he and Neria were alike, had nevertheless not given in—he thought that the Manual was enough for a girl's education — and Nephalie yielded to his decisions.

Once she was alone in her room, Neria thought to herself that a better person would have agreed to serve the interests of her father, of her family, of all of Humanity, and would have worked enthusiastically to spread the genes of the More-Than-Pure. Her mother had been right to imply that she had a difficult and perhaps even selfish nature.

She filled the enamel basin, dipped her hands in the water, and washed her face, neck, and chest to clean away any traces of the disgusting hand. She considered a more thorough cleansing but felt too tired. Her gaze fell on the umber vase on the table. Once a week, Nephalie cut hawthorns from the flower garden. She arranged them in these small ceramic vases and then scattered them in the house like an echo of the world outside. Neria delicately held the stem of a flower and plucked off the petals one by one, saying, "She loves me, she loves me not…" She then gently shook the flower, scattering the petals that fell to the ground like rain. Yellow traces of pollen were left on her fingers. Carried away by a wicked glee, she tore the bouquet apart. She whirled around the room in her quest for destruction. Corpses of white, gold, and green littered the tiles, the trunk, the chair, the bedsheets. Her ammunition exhausted, she grabbed the vase that seemed to taunt her, then decided to spare it.

She approached the window, opened it wide, and sat down on the ledge. Her feet dangled in the air. She thought of Adamek, of how he got out of all the trouble he caused by being the eldest son. Since their wedding, the brute had worked to destroy the young woman he had been lucky enough to marry. When they had been children and Adamek had hit them, their parents did not tell him off or, if they did, they only did so a little.

On the day he had beaten Ellane, Neria had been shocked by a detail to which they did not seem to attach much importance. The incident had occurred shortly after Rona's departure. That same afternoon, encouraged by the sweetness of the fall air, they had gone out on the patio to play a racket ball game. Arhel had often missed the ball. With her advantage of being two years older, Neria had cursed at him as he ran, with red cheeks and brown curls stuck to his forehead by sweat.

Adamek had joined them. Without saying a single word, he had grabbed his younger brother and, despite his struggles, snatched the ball out of his hand. Without thinking, she had thrown herself in his direction and hit him with all her might. To her astonishment, she had managed to throw him off balance and they both fell down, him underneath and her on top. The exhilaration of this success had been short-lived. Adamek had straightened himself up, slammed her down on the ground, and twisted her arm. She had felt a sharp pain shooting through her elbow and shoulder.

"Ask for forgiveness or I'll break your arm."

Arhel had rushed to her aid. He pushed and pulled at his big brother, without managing to shake him off. Neria had been considering surrender before she had heard Ellane's voice. Adamek had let Neria go, throwing himself on the maid and striking her. He had repeatedly pounded at her with his fists while, curled up on the ground, she had protected her face with her arms. He had then stood up and kicked her as he screamed. Blood had streamed down Ellane's forehead. Her torn dress had revealed two old scars, long and blistered, on her bare back. It was then that Neria had learned that she was not Human.

Servants came at last with Nephalie on their heels. The children had run towards their mother.

"Mom, Adamek's killed Ellane!"

"Go to your room. Wait for me there."

In the bedroom, Arhel had slid to the floor. Snot had run down from his nostrils to his lips, threatening to seep into his open mouth. Neria had taken out a handkerchief from the wooden trunk.

"Blow your nose. Men don't cry."

The sobs had intensified.

"I can cry if I want to... It was awful..."

"Take the handkerchief anyway. There, that's good... No, not like that. Blow... just blow..."

She had sat down beside him and put an arm around his shoulders. The explosion of violence had shocked her, but not as much as the discovery of Ellane's true nature. This woman who had raised her had lied to her. She was an impure Chimera, a flying creature with its wings severed, a miserable slave with a faded beauty. Yet Neria had believed that Ellane had truly cared for her... Had it all been a farce? How had her father been able to keep a female Chimera in his home when the law forbade even their presence within the city walls? Neria had asked Arhel if he had known. Between his tears, he had purported to have known and said that that he didn't care, that he liked Ellane anyway.

Seized by a sudden impulse, she had run to the window and flung it open. A jay, annoyed by her racket, squawked before flying away. The air had been filled with the sweet scent of honeysuckle. She had sat on the ledge, swinging her legs in the air. Arhel had joined her, slipping himself into the narrow space beside her. She had felt the warmth of his body pressed against hers.

"Don't lean over, you could fall."

She had put her hand around his shoulder as a precaution. The ground had seemed to be a considerable distance away. Dizzy with vertigo, she had looked up to see the setting sun reddening the sky and the clouds.

She had later overheard a conversation between her parents.

"Aren't you shocked by what he did?"

"Not terribly. I've done worse, you know."

"You seem to even be proud of him for it."

"It's a relief, I would say. I was afraid that Adamek was weak, sentimental. That he took after your side, you see? I'm glad he's finally showing some character. As for Ellane, she's got nothing to complain about. She's had a good life these past few years."

"He beat her in front of Neria and Arhel! After attacking them too, by the way."

"They might as well get used to it. It's character building. We must keep the Chimeras in terror. And for that, we need strong, uncompromising Humans who can do their duty without hesitation."

"Until when?"

"How can you still ask such a question? We will have no peace until we have eradicated those monsters from the face of the earth. You're too sensitive. If you'd been educated differently, you'd see things in another light."

"I doubt it."

"Ah, you and your good heart…"

As a consequence, Adamek had never been punished for beating Ellane, and when the time came, he had married a charming young woman. But deep down, he was still the same little boy who liked to break his toys.

Neria knew that she would not be able to bear the sight of Zelimo every morning… not to mention the confinement during the nights… nor could she give birth to his children, however genetically perfect they were. Despite her vertigo, sitting on the windowsill gave her a sense of freedom. If she were to jump, the chances of her death would be small. She would be in a great deal of pain, handicapped for life. Would that be enough to call off the wedding?

If she wanted to kill herself, she would have to leap from an even greater height. From the top of the Temple, perhaps. She imagined the scandal that would follow. Using the most sacred place in the city to commit such a heinous crime. But she would no longer be there to suffer the blame or the consequences. Her father would finally understand that he had pushed her too far. She savored this idea for a few moments before abandoning her perch and closing the window.

CHAPTER THREE

A flash of light awoke Neria. With a dry throat, aching limbs, and a fever, she blinked and saw Ellane armed with a lamp, studying her face.

"What are you doing? What's the time?"

Without offering an explanation, Ellane continued with her inspection, going down her neck and arms before lifting the sheets to reveal her feet. The slave clearly no longer knew her place. Neria was already annoyed enough that she woke her up in the mornings, but now she was starting to do it at night too, without even offering an explanation.

"Turn over on your stomach."

"No way."

"Show me your back."

"Since you're here anyway, go get me some water, I'm dying of thirst. Maybe one of your herbal teas…"

"How do you feel?"

"Not good. Let me sleep!"

To Neria's great relief, Ellane left her, but she returned all too quickly, preceded by Nephalie. She too brought her lamp close to Neria's face, studying her forehead, her eyes, moving down towards her neck.

"What's wrong?"

Nephalie continued her examination without saying a word.

The luminous halo slipped over her arms, legs, and feet. She firmly pressed on Neria's shoulder to tip her onto her side before uncovering the nape of her neck and moving aside her nightgown. She put her lamp on the bedside table and sat down on the bed.

"You've contracted Nymphosis."

"It can't be! You're wrong."

"You've got the symptoms, that reddening around your eyes, down the middle of your face, all along your body, those purplish spots on your arms, legs, and back. Get up. Ellane, go and get Anaëlle ready."

Without saying a word, the slave walked out of the room as if it were the most natural thing in the world.

"Why Anaëlle?"

"You were right, she's a Dreamer."

"But how's that possible? Were we adopted?"

"Of course not. I'm going to get you some clothes, yours would draw too much attention."

Neria was left with a thousand troubling questions, but Nephalie had already gone. She pulled off the sheets and placed her feet, flawless in form and perfect for their purpose, on the cool tiles. She remembered the monster that had been executed that very morning, deformed and lame. Its swollen, aching legs had been unable to carry it. Soon, Neria would resemble that haggard creature. She struck the bed with a fist of rage. What good was it being the daughter of a More-Than-Pure? Nephalie returned carrying a pile of rags. Neria wondered if they'd been the clothes of a servant or Ellane's. A shiver of revulsion ran down her spine. Nephalie handed them to her, telling her to hurry up. Hurry up for what? To go where? What else could possibly await an infected person other than the depths of a black hole?

Neria put on the clothes, which had an unexpected smell of lavender. Nephalie fixed a veil around her daughter's head and adjusted her belt. She then took a knife covered with a leather sheath out of her purse, which she carried tied to her waist. She fastened it to her daughter's belt, hiding it under the folds of her coat.

"Take this to remember me by. I hope it'll protect you."

"I wouldn't know how to use it."

"You will if you have no other choice."

Then she listed her instructions. Neria struggled to listen, but her mother pressed her and forced her to repeat them, making sure that she had understood every last word.

"Find an old, abandoned shack on Shazilo Street. You will know it from the others by the traces of blue paint on its shutters. You will see a wardrobe leaning against a wall. Push it and you'll find a secret alcove. Hide inside it and put the cabinet back in its place. Someone will come to find you. Do you understand? Don't do anything stupid. Hide there and wait."

Neria did not recognize this determined individual as her mother, a woman who had been devastated since Arhel's death and had walked through life like a shadow.

"I've never gone outside on my own."

"You won't be on your own. Anaëlle's coming with you."

"Anaëlle?"

"Pay attention Neria! Anaëlle can't stay here either."

"So we're going to hide."

"Exactly!"

"And then what?"

"A man you can trust will come to find you and help you leave the city."

The city's surroundings, which had seemed so attractive up until then, synonymous with adventure, suddenly seemed threatening and filled with deadly traps.

"Leave the city?"

"Neria!"

A cry like that of an enraged beast. Neria recoiled. Nephalie seized her by the shoulders.

"You must survive! You are going to get through this, and you are going to survive. And one day, we will meet again. Do you understand me?"

"Yes, don't worry, I understand."

The mother hugged her daughter for a moment and then released her. They went out on the landing. A halo of menacing light emanated from Valterone's room at the end of the corridor. There was no telling if he was asleep; he was known to sometimes work well into the night. To reach the back staircase they would also have to pass the servant quarters, filled with light sleepers who had unknowable loyalties.

They abandoned the idea and, with their sandals in hand, took the main staircase. They crossed the living room, with the weathered wood of the furniture, brushed by the glow of lamplight, glistening in the darkness. Ellane was waiting for them in the kitchen accompanied by Anaëlle who, with her rag doll hung at the end of her arm, red eyes, and a look of terror, watched the adults in silence. Neria stifled the urge to comfort her. She strapped on a canteen and shoulder bag that the slave had prepared for her and then put on her sandals. With her heart beating, she held her breath while her mother lifted the latch for the front door. The friction of the metal seemed to echo throughout the house and the door creaked on its hinges. Nephalie went out first. One after the other, they stepped into the service passage. Their lamps shone like bonfires. Valterone would only have to look down to see them. When they reached the small door in the perimeter wall, Neria grabbed her mother's arm and whispered, "What about the guard?"

"I've paid him off."

Nephalie put her key into the lock, opened the door, and pushed her daughter out. Neria turned around. She would have liked to kiss her one last time, but she was left with nothing but a closed door. One moment, she had been enjoying the security and comfort of her family home. The next, she was left helpless in a deserted square. An oil lamp rested in Neria's hand. A clay container, filled with a greenish-yellow liquid. A wick, coiled within its heart, snaked up to the groove that guided it into the open air. A flame danced on its tip, a paltry defense against the darkness of that night, one of those gentle nights that often follow the heat of the day. The moon watched her with a wry smile.

Neria suddenly felt she was going to collapse, crumpling like a sheet that had fallen to the ground. Without the warmth of the hand curled inside hers, she would have indeed done so. She remembered the last time she had seen Arhel's hand, crimson and reaching out of the covers. Who knew what the disease would do to her? But before she succumbed to it, she would save Anaëlle.

She breathed in, then out, and took a step forward. Her aching limbs strained at first, but after a few minutes, she was walking briskly, her head bowed like a servant, the child in tow. First, she had to find the secret passage her mother had told her about and cross the wall of the High District without going through the ever-guarded gates. She came to a dead-end and saw the dried-up well and a withered pistachio tree lined with shrubs of rosemary leaning against the perimeter wall. It concealed a narrow, low opening. She went in first, crawled into a tunnel bereft of cobwebs and emerged behind an olive tree, also surrounded by shrubbery. Crouching down, she peeked between the branches. No one was there. She called to Anaëlle in a hushed voice, the child joining her. They emerged from their cover and arrived on the street. Before long, they had made their way to an impoverished part of town they had never been to before. The hovels were huddled together, separated here and there by narrow, randomly arranged passageways. The first on the left... The second on the right...

"Hey there, little lady! Where are you off to in such a hurry?"

Three guards had concealed themselves in a nook to drink to their hearts' content.

"Lady Yarine's sent me on an urgent errand."

She hoped they would be too drunk to do anything and turned away. She tried to maintain her composure, a technique that had worked for her that morning. Yet heavy footsteps came ever closer behind her before her arm was seized by a coarse grip.

"You've got more than enough time to come give us a little cuddle."

One of the guards looked at her, a yellow smile spread across his brown beard. He reeked of alcohol and nauseating filth. She tried to pull away from him, but his grip tightened.

"Stay still or we'll give you a good hiding. It'll go better for you if you don't put up a fight, believe me. Leave the kid here and come on."

The two others approached.

The lamp fell and shattered. Neria took out her knife and stuck it in the arm restraining her. The guard howled in pain and let go of her.

"You're going to regret that you whore."

The guards now surrounded her. She threatened them with her bloodied weapon. She couldn't believe she'd been so stupid not to have stabbed him in the stomach. Her assailant barely seemed bothered. She spun around, Anaëlle clinging to her clothes. The girl was sobbing.

One of the men drew his sword, "Drop the knife or I kill the kid."

Neria's hand trembled. The knife fell on the dusty ground with a dull thud.

"Run, Anaëlle, get out of here!"

The wounded guard threw himself on her, seized her elbow, slipped behind her, and choked her with his good arm. The child, small and spirited, ran away. Just as Neria thought she was going to make it, the man with the sword grabbed her mid-flight. Neria struggled, hitting the arm that choked her. His hold tightened. Her mouth gasped but the air would not come, and her movements weakened. Suddenly, the guard holding her let out a yowl of pain and released her. She collapsed, heavily panting gulps of air on all fours. Her assailant lay there with his throat slit. The coarse, black-nailed hand that moments before had clamped down on her arm now clawed at the earth. The corpse's glassy eyes stared up into the starry sky. His red tongue in his gaping mouth, his fleshy lips, his fat cheeks swallowed by his beard... like a giant sea urchin washed up from the sea, his insides hanging open. A shrill cry rang out and she covered her ears.

A monster, half-man, half-beast, had ripped open another guard and had now set its sights on the third. The remaining guard was still holding Anaëlle hostage and keeping the beast at bay with his sword. While the tiger and guard danced their macabre dance, Neria, still on all fours, fumbled for her knife. She grasped its hilt, ran towards the soldier, raising her weapon, a wild howling in her throat. The monster took advantage of the diversion to pounce on its adversary. Neria sheathed her knife, picked up the child who had fallen to the ground, and fled, pursued by screams of agony.

Despite her terror, she managed to follow her mother's instructions and arrived at the place she had indicated, exhausted. Anaëlle was no longer crying. Neria put her down and indicated to her that she should stay quiet, putting a finger to her lips. The peaceful street seemed to be in a deep sleep, its inhabitants unaware of the horror that had taken place just a few feet away. They moved through the shadows of the slums and soon reached a hovel with faded blue shutters.

"Stay here."

"No, I don't wanna be on my own."

"Okay. But if there are any problems, go run and hide in the lane behind the rosemary bush. I'll come get you there."

The dwelling had an even more wretched air than the others around it. Neria raised the latch of its coarse wooden door, which slid open on its hinges. They entered the hovel. Before the door shut, they caught a glimpse of a table and three chairs, one of them toppled over on the ground and, leaning against the back wall, a dilapidated wardrobe. They stood still in the darkness for a moment. There was a musty smell to the dust-ridden room. Anaëlle sneezed.

"Shhh!"

"I didn't do it on purpose!"

A faint sound of paws scratching against wood suggested the presence of mice or rats. With Anaëlle still clutching onto her tunic, Neria moved towards the wardrobe. Her arms outstretched, she slid her feet on the bare earth floor. They reached the piece of furniture. Neria leaned against its side and pushed. Little by little, she managed to clear a large enough gap for them. She hesitated for a moment, seized by dread at the idea of going into this black hole.

"We have to hide, wait for the nice man who is going to save us. Gwanny said so."

Neria gave an unseen nod in agreement and caressed the child's soft hair. She then pulled away the hand clutching onto her tunic and took it in hers. She went into the narrow space first, sideways. Anaëlle followed her inside. They could stand upright in it. Neria found a handle fixed to the back of the wardrobe. She pulled at it, but it hardly budged. She considered leaving it as it was.

"Gwanny said to put it back."

"I know."

Neria took hold of the handle with both hands and pulled. The wardrobe moved back with excruciating slowness. After having returned it to its original place, she looked around her, unable to see anything. Exhausted, she slumped to the floor and leaned against the wall. Anaëlle snuggled up against her.

"It's all right. We made it. I'm sorry you had to see that... Some people are bad, others are kind, like the man who's coming to get us. Here, have some water."

The idea of this man, ready to brave the greatest of dangers to rescue them, was enough to make her want to cry. Only the scratching of paws with clawed nails disturbed the silence. Neria, who had to show a good example, held back the desire to scream and throw herself against the wardrobe to get out of this claustrophobic hatch. With a trembling hand, she opened her canteen.

"I'm afwaid."

At these words, Neria burst into tears and Anaëlle soon followed suit.

"Me too, I'm also scared... but the hardest is over... and we're together..."

The critters that populated the nooks and crannies of the house were its true owners, the only legitimate inhabitants of this hovel. They, on the other hand, would soon leave it. When their tears dried, Neria felt a terrible fatigue. She lay down on the filthy ground and encouraged Anaëlle to do the same. They fell asleep, taken away by the deep and irresistible sleep of youth.

Neria suddenly awoke and bolted upright. Her heart beat in her chest. A painful throbbing radiated from her limbs and skull, screams resounding in her ears like the rallying call of a conch shell. She placed her hand over the child's wide-open mouth.

"Be quiet, I'm begging you!"

Anaëlle struggled. With her free arm, Neria grabbed hold of her and clung her against her body, stopping her legs from kicking.

"I'm here, everything's okay."

As soon as these words left her mouth, Neria realized just how stupid they were.

"The Guards will hear you."

The shouting stopped, replaced by trembling and tears.

"What happened? Did you have a nightmare?"

"Mommy killed Daddy."

"How?"

"She got a knife and hit him."

Neria did not have time to ask for details. Voices were approaching. The front door opened.

"I'm telling you I heard someone crying."

"Can't you see there's no one here?"

"Look! The dust's been moved. Someone's swept it over to cover up their tracks."

"Who do you think you are? You've joined the Watchers now, have you? I've been patient with you so far to honor the memory of my aunt, rest her soul, but be warned, if you get on my nerves again, you'll be joining her."

With the sound of dwindling footsteps moving away, Neria knew that one of the men had left. Yet she thought she could hear the breath of the one who had stayed behind through the wardrobe. She jumped in surprise when he started to move again. He picked up the fallen chair, spun around, and muttered to himself, "It's not my problem if he doesn't believe me. I'm not going to do his job for him."

When the door slammed shut, the child and Neria remained still, one curled up in the lap of the other. The subtle activity of the vermin reassured them and Neria allowed herself to breathe more freely.

"Tell me what happened."

In a monotonous almost indifferent tone, Anaëlle described her vision.

Paz had been lying awake in bed. Adamek stirred in his sleep and a light snore drifted from his mouth. Without even lighting a lamp, she got up. She knew the place like the back of her hand and guided herself by touch like a blind woman. Her fingers crept along the walls. The moon illuminated her pale silhouette as she passed a window. When she reached the kitchen, she opened the cutlery drawer in the cabinet and took out a large knife with her right hand. The blade shone with a subtle glint. Paz then retraced her steps. At the foot of the stairs, she lifted her nightgown with her free hand and climbed back up to the room, before hesitating in front of the bed. Then, as if seized by a sudden fit of inspiration, she struck Adamek in his throat with all her might, once, twice, and stepped back. With the pleading expression that his wife had worn when he beat her, he garbled incomprehensible gibberish, his hands clasped around his throat. Life left the formidable figure in flowing brooks of red. Paz removed his soiled garment. The thin cloth fell to the ground with a silky rustling. She washed in the basin, put on clean clothes, and ran away.

Anaëlle began to cry again. She tried to hold back her tears but to no avail. Neria took her in her arms, then almost let her go and moved away at the fear of the risk of contagion. But she decided against doing so. It would be too late for such precautions. She couldn't find the right words and they remained in silence for a while. Anaëlle made the most of an all too short respite; she had lost her childhood and had perhaps lost it a considerable length of time ago, ever since she had first witnessed the beatings.

Neria felt terrible for the relief that had come over her. She had not liked her brother, but her indifference at the thought of his death had been a surprise.

The heat, now uncomfortable, forced them apart. They drank, then ate a little.

"Your visions... do they always come true? You've got to be wrong sometimes."

"No, never."

"Where did Paz go?" asked Neria before realizing the indelicacy of her question.

"I don't know. I woke up."

The child started crying again.

"Your mother would want you to be brave. It's okay to worry. But you have to put those feelings aside, be strong so that one day you can find her."

Neria felt miserable. Anaëlle had lost both her parents anyway since she'd had to leave the city. You never get over death. It follows you everywhere you go every single day. Neria knew it. The tragic and tender memories of those final months before Arhel's death still haunted her like an aching wound. The obligation of secrecy had kept the images new and vivid in a box that still remained shut. She remembered the night she had seen her younger brother for the last time.

After having contracted the ferruginous plague, Arhel had been kept isolated for a week. Neria had been forbidden from visiting him. No one was allowed to enter his room except Nephalie, who left it with a blank look, tired, but recovering her strength to face Valterone. A tense silence reigned in the house, interrupted from time to time by their violent arguments. That night, curled up in her bed, Neria listened in to their echoes.

Unable to sleep and pushed to the limit by anxiety, she had thrown aside the covers and placed her feet on the icy tiling. She had grabbed the shawl folded on the chair and had wrapped herself in it. On the landing, the sounds of the argument immobilized her for a moment, but the desire to see Arhel had compelled her to overcome her fears. With her heart pounding, she rushed to her brother's room. A pungent smell seized her throat; various spices had been burned to purify the air and repel germs. The only source of light came from the brazier, which exuded a gentle heat. Neria had made out a shape on the bed, wrapped in a blanket. Curly hair protruded from within, a somber stain on the immaculate pillow. The girl had called out to her brother in a quiet voice. She approached him when he didn't react. She told herself that she would not touch him, that she only wanted to see him.

The noises of the suddenly heated argument had startled her. She had rushed to the door and looked through the doorway. Valterone had scaled the stairs four by four, followed closely by Nephalie. Neria had gone back on her steps, opened a trunk, and found it filled to the brim. Her fists clenched, she had scanned the room in search of a hiding place. With no other recourse, she had crouched in the darkest corner, covered herself with her shawl, and wrapped her arms around her knees. Valterone had burst in with a crash. In two steps, he had reached the bed before snatching up his son, still wrapped up like a chrysalis in his shroud. A small hand had slipped out, inert, reddened, and emaciated. Nephalie had hung on to her husband's arm and screamed, "Just leave him to me! I'm begging you!"

"Shut up, you stupid woman! You know what will happen to us if he stays here."

She had clutched at Arhel, who had groaned. Valterone had struck her hard, forcing her to stagger back. After seeing this, Neria had jumped up and ran towards her brother, but a powerful blow had stopped her in her tracks. She had struck the ground and lost consciousness.

Neria had woken up in bed with a throbbing headache and the taste of blood in her mouth. The silence in the house had alarmed her. When she had tried to go outside to investigate, she had found her door locked. After walking aimlessly around the room, she had gone back to lie down. Sleep must have crept up on her because she had been awoken by her father's arrival. She recognized that expression she had feared so much: the clenched jaw, the narrowed, black eyes. She had moved back, feeling the icy touch of the wall against her back. He had leaned towards her and had grasped her by the shoulders. His nails had sunk into her flesh. His face too close, his breath foul. He had punctuated his speech with abrupt jerks.

"Your brother is dead... A daughter of a More-Than-Pure... cannot indulge in her emotions... You shall remain locked in this room... until you are presentable... Do you understand?"

She had nodded. He had let go of her, looked at her with disdain, and added, "I forbid you to talk about this."

CHAPTER FOUR

Burning up with a fever, Neria sporadically awoke every now and then, taking a few sips from her canteen before offering it to Anaëlle, who shook her head. She insisted and asked her if she had eaten anything, but lost consciousness without hearing her answer.

She snapped out of her stupor with the sound of the wardrobe scraping against the floor. She straightened up, found the child's hand in the darkness, squeezed it, and opened her eyes as wide as she could to make out the details of a dark silhouette in the doorway. A metallic clatter, a dazzling flame. A man with a wrinkled face, white hair, and a scowl stood before them. He stepped past Neria, squatted beside Anaëlle, brought a small flask to the lips of the child, drinking from it this time without hesitation. Still in silence, he took her in his arms and, before leaving, indicated to Neria with an authoritative gesture to wait for him. Kneeling down in the flickering light of the lamp that he had left behind, she picked up their belongings. Her heart was beating far too quickly but she tried to remain calm. Her mother must have chosen this wretched individual to not draw any attention to them, throwing off the guards. She would never have made the mistake of picking anybody incompetent for the job.

The old man soon returned. He pointed to his small flask and asked in a husky voice, "Do you want to go to sleep?"

She shook her head. He pinched the flame between his

fingers, suddenly extinguishing it. Neria did not hear him leaving the shack. She got up with difficulty, guiding herself by touch. A rough hand took her by the elbow and led her towards the door. The sea breeze caressed her sweaty skin in the alleyway as the moon still laughed in the starry sky. She clambered onto a cart filled with varied miscellany and lay down on the spot indicated to her by the old man. He covered her with a dusty rug.

She was suffocating. Sweat ran down her back and under her armpits. She looked for an air pocket to breathe without the rough fabric clogging up her nostrils. Everything had happened so fast. Where was Anaëlle? Had he hidden her in the cart? The cart rattled along. The sound of the wheels on stone slabs signaled that they had left the slums and come onto one of the main roads. Whatever could the time be? The silence indicated it was either very late or very early. Was the monster still lurking somewhere? Was it going to attack them and then rip them asunder as it had done to the guards? She should have warned the old man.

Neria heard fragments of voices. They stopped. Jaded guards asked the man a few questions, which he answered with just as much apathy if not more. The cart set out again and they crossed the city walls. Neria remembered the road she had gazed at from the top of the Temple, the one that meandered by the feet of the Two Sisters and forked off with innumerable offshoots. She thought of Ellane who would soon be getting up to help in the kitchen, of Elinor, the luckier of the two sisters, of her mother who would either come up with an explanation for her absence or not, of her father who would send the guards in search of her as soon as he learned of her disappearance. Would he feel a guilty relief like she had felt when she heard of Adamek's death?

She fell asleep, waking up every so often, tortured by pain, heat, and thirst. She hoped that Anaëlle was not suffering and still under the influence of the sedative. And that she was in the cart with her. She should have followed her. Why had she ever trusted a stranger? She had to find her. She could hear nothing but the monotonous sounds of hooves and wheels on stone. They were alone on the road. No one would see her.

She caught a glimpse of a blue sky before a cane came crashing down on her skull.

"Stay still!"

"Is Anaëlle okay?"

"Stay hidden."

The cane struck her shoulder.

"Stop hitting me and answer!"

"She's fine. If you move again, I'll knock you out."

Neria repositioned the rug as best she could. The blows had given her new pains while also reviving her old ones. She had exchanged the mood swings of her father for those of this vagrant who dared to order her about. The walls of Alipaz pursued her, wanting to swallow her up, imprison her and turn her into an unspeaking stone, present yet invisible. Like a pebble on a path kicked up by an absent-minded foot, spinning off to the side, her momentum exhausted, forgotten, only to be kicked away again by another. Neria swore to herself that she would never feel this powerless ever again. For her survival's sake and for Anaëlle, she had to learn as soon as possible to cope without her family, then get rid of this old man, and find somewhere peaceful to live. And to heal.

The quickening pace of a group of horsemen added to the monotonous rhythm of hooves. A patrol of five men rode alongside the cart.

"You there, peddler, have you seen any travelers passing by on this road? Did you see two captives? A young woman and a child?"

"Two cargo convoys passed me by. I did see a young lady in one of them. She didn't seem to be in any trouble."

"Where are you going?"

"I'm heading for trade in Opheck market."

"What's in your cart? Are you hiding anyone?"

The guard struck a few objects with the end of his spear, sending them tumbling down in a cacophony of metallic clanging and the clatter of broken pottery. The others burst out laughing.

"Woe! Have mercy on me, brave soldiers, a poor old man struggling to earn his keep. Here you are! It's an excellent wine from Karcar. It'll give you strength for your mission. Take an amphora. Take two."

"You've got four… Do you want us to go thirsty?"

"Please, sirs! Take them all."

"That'll do for now."

With a loud thump, he triggered another avalanche.

The soldiers left and the echo of their merrymakingmerrymaking faded away. The man began to arrange the still salvageable trinkets. Neria heard him grumbling,

"Damn scrap! I hope you choke on the wine, and it kills you, with your bellies distended in agonizing pain. May your descendants curse your names, may no one plead on your behalf with Asoas the Benevolent..."

He got back into the cart and resumed his journey. From time to time, faster carriages and riders passed them by. The cart swerved. Judging from the bumps that shook her, Neria realized that they had left the main road. She dozed in spite of her discomfort, rocked by the jolts. She woke up as they stopped. Dazed, she freed herself from the rug and raised her eyes towards the large trees leaning over her bedside. The old man, standing in the middle of his merchandise, took the still sleeping Anaëlle out from a barrel. Before Neria was able to get any closer to him, he had jumped off the cart, the child in his arms. He laid her down on a patch of grass, slipped his arm under her neck, and lifted it before bringing the flask to her lips. The child whimpered a little, opened her eyes, looked around, then closed them again. He encouraged her to drink with a gentle voice. Although the liquid dripped down her chin, soaking the collar of her dress, the movement of her throat showed Neria that at least some of it had found its way inside her unconscious body.

Carefully, she got down from the cart and joined them. Her limbs trembled, her head spun, a taste of decay polluted her mouth. She sat down next to her niece and stroked her hair. She was sleeping the artificial sleep, intense and raw, of men overcome by alcohol, men she had sometimes seen slumped over in the dark corners of alleyways.

"Drink this."

Neria took the flask that the man held out to her and brought it closer to her mouth. It gave off a potent odor.

"No, thank you. I don't feel very well. Just a little water, please."

"No. No water. Drink this."

"I'm telling you I can't."

She recoiled. A rugged brute had replaced the elderly white-haired man and was now giving her an unpleasant look. Neria brought the flask to her mouth, swallowed a gulp of a thick, bitter, and viscous liquid. To her great surprise, the potion seemed to calm her troubled stomach and, suddenly gripped by an intense thirst, she drank until the Peddler stopped her.

Although the dilapidated cart seemed to be overflowing with worthless bric-a-brac, its strength would be obvious to a keen observer, as would the good health of the donkey pulling it. The man wore a grayish-beige tunic over darker pants. A carefully folded brown wool coat lay on the seat. He settled Anaëlle down on a rug, took the donkey by the bridle, and set off without saying a word. Neria snapped out of her drowsiness and hurried to catch up with them. They followed a narrow path through vegetation that grew thicker and obstructed their progress. The donkey and its master, panting with effort, combined their energy to hold the cart steady. As the slope became steeper, they pressed on through the thicket of branches towards a babbling brook and stopped when they reached the bank. The man congratulated his animal, then, with unexpected gentleness, picked up Anaëlle, and laid her on the ground. She opened her eyes and closed them at once. Exhausted, Neria let herself fall by her side.

The red skin, as if scalded, on her feet reminded her of Arhel's hand on the day of his death. She looked for the outline of deformities but could not find any. Her skull and back were torturing her. She ran her fingers over her face and forehead, shivering when she felt the lumps that had grown there.

The Peddler walked up to a rock face and pushed aside the plants that covered it. They had concealed the entrance to a cave. He brought the cart inside, unhitched the donkey, and threw some saddlebags on its rump. After closing the curtain of plant life, he approached Anaëlle and tried to get her to wake up. The child's limp body collapsed as soon as he let go of her. He put her back down. He made a harness using a strip of cloth, wrapping her in it and hoisting her onto his back. His careful movements reassured Neria as if the man's dexterity would have a positive influence on their future. He then moved away without saying a word nor looking back. With the very last of her strength, she got up and followed him without a word of complaint. They crossed the brook and went deeper into the forest. At dusk, they bivouacked in a clearing, presumably created following the death of the uprooted tree that lay in its center. A stream babbled below. Reassured by signs of Anaëlle's awakening, Neria collapsed and fell straight into a deep sleep.

In the days that followed, she awoke every now and then, sometimes burning, sometimes freezing. The pain and fever kept her in a constant daze that soon made her lose track of time. The man quenched her thirst and fed her with the viscous liquid. She would have preferred to ignore that insistent hand that shook her shoulder, that wanted to impose its nebulous designs on her. She would have welcomed death without a second thought and understood why the mutants did not try to escape. Anaëlle appeared to her at times like a painting, her outline blurred. Neria felt relief in the depths of her sickness from knowing she was alive and resigned herself to her impotence to help her. She was tortured by unbearable pain, from the top of her head to the arch of her back, making it nigh on impossible to use her arms. When she ran her hand through her hair, she felt it break away. It slumped to the blanket in a lifeless mound like a dead cat.

Every morning, the old man brought her water for washing with and yelled at her to get up. One day, when she was feeling a little better, she made the mistake of looking at her reflection: bald, her face red, bloated, unrecognizable, her ears shapeless, her eyes watering and sunken in their sockets. She screamed, dragged herself to her bed, and collapsed. Alerted by her scream, the Peddler appeared. She wailed, her face hidden in her arms.

"What's the matter?"

"Leave me alone. I want to die."

"All the risks I've taken to save your life have been worth it then, have they?"

"I'm a monster! What's the point of living when you look like this?"

"Don't complain. How many innocent people in the same condition did your father put to death?"

"They were lucky."

"You're going to wash and change your clothes. You stink."

"You don't understand. I want to die. Clean or dirty, it doesn't matter! I'm not moving."

He walked away. Anaëlle looked at her with a worried expression. Neria buried her face in a blanket and sobbed.

Returning from the brook, the Peddler poured the contents of a cooking pot full of icy water over her. She screamed.

"Get washed and get dressed. I'll go pick some fruit."

"You ignorant yokel. One day I'll…"

He turned back to her.

"Fine, I'll get washed."

Anaëlle stood, motionless, an expression of disgust on her face.

Neria squatted, plunged her hands in the pot, and splashed water on her face.

"Don't worry, I didn't really want to die. I hope I don't frighten you?"

The child said nothing.

"That thug has just pushed me over the edge. I've been wallowing in my misery, but I'm still the same deep down. Just much uglier. As soon as I feel better, I'll look after you, we'll go somewhere quiet. You still trust me, don't you?"

"Yes."

Neria repressed the desire to beg this child, who lied and turned her face away, not to judge her. She knew that in her place, she would have behaved in an even more abhorrent manner. In her waking moments, Neria could see the bonds forming between the other two They played, laughed, went foraging, and cooked together. The girl even pronounced his name with ease.

"Mataw, look at this funny pretty flower I found for you… Mataw, I want to help you, I know how to light a fiwe… '

Matar. This name echoed like an avalanche of pebbles

rolling down a mountainside, like the promise of bad news.

The fever finally subsided and, one evening, Neria got up without having been told to do so. Matar had cut branches off the dead tree and had arranged them in a bundle. The water was being warmed in the cooking pot propped up on stones above the fire. Anaëlle, with her hands in a pot, was washing roots while Matar was cutting up a small bird. The smell of charred feathers still hung in the air. The child spoke nonsensically to an imaginary audience. Sometimes, a more pressing question obliged the man to answer. Neria approached and waited for a pause in the continuous string of words.

"Have you seen any transformations before?"

"Yes."

"Will I ever be normal again?"

"You're Valterone's daughter, a monster by definition."

The Peddler's scornful expression made her pause for a moment, but her curiosity won in the end.

"Is there any way I'll get my looks back?"

"No."

"Because…"

"I don't know. Shut up."

"But I…"

"I'm telling you to shut up."

The girl turned away and headed for the brook. Everyone hated Chimeras and she had to get used to it. She crouched down on a rock, noticed a leaf drifting away, jostled by the current. She didn't want to envy her niece, always so lovely… so human… but the difference in their treatment seemed unfair.

Anaëlle's defect, her strange power, was not visible. Neria spent a moment dreaming up various punishments that she would inflict on the Peddler one day, before returning to the camp.

They had not waited for her to begin their meal. She grabbed the full bowl they had prepared for her. She picked up the wooden spoon and tasted the concoction, a strange kind of stew that Matar made on a daily basis, following the same primitive recipe with different ingredients depending on what he could find. In Alipaz, they would have refused to even touch this broth and would have fired the cook. Still standing, Neria gulped down her portion and asked for more. There wasn't any. Even if the quality of the food were poor, Matar could at least have made enough of it so she wouldn't go hungry. She put down her utensils and approached the area she used as her bedroom.

"Go do the dishes."

"What?"

"You're feeling better so help with the chores."

"I haven't done any housework before."

"All the more reason for you to do it."

"I won't demean myself with that sort of work. I'm not your maid!"

Anaëlle watched this exchange with a serious, responsible, almost adult demeanor.

"I see. The service is not to your ladyship's liking. I am not your slave, and you will no longer be receiving meals at my expense. If you want to be fed, you will have to get to work."

With a smile on his lips, Neria watched him take their

bowls to go and wash them.

"I'll come too, Mataw. I like doing dishes."

"I think it's mainly playing in water that you like."

"I can do both."

Neria decided not to wait for their return and moved away from the camp to observe their surroundings. Scattered like clues, subtle modifications to the fauna and flora revealed the strangeness of the place. The different colors of the wings of the butterflies, the strange blended species of trees, an oak whose branches bore needles of pine, a cypress with red fruits like apples. She considered picking them but didn't know if they were edible nor did she want to appear to have yielded to the Peddler. Her appetite had grown since her sickness and the hunger was getting to her. She drank an enormous amount of fresh water from the brook in the hope of calming the pleas of her stomach. She would have liked to go back to the camp but did not want to face the disapproving looks of the old man and perhaps those of Anaëlle as well. She got up, wandered around the camp's surroundings, and lay down on a bed of fragrant leaves that crunched with her every move, pricking the bare skin of her arms and neck. She nodded off to sleep. At dusk, she returned to the fire. Matar and Anaëlle paused their game of dice for a moment. She walked past them without a word and settled down for the night. The hours drifted away one by one in a silence punctuated by the rumbling of her stomach. The following evening, the smell of broth and the sounds of chewing broke her will.

"Fine. I want to help."

Matar filled a bowl with gruel and handed it to her. She

wanted to savor it, but after a few mouthfuls, she forgot her resolve and hurriedly devoured the meager portion.

"Your bad temper coming back proves you're getting better. Tomorrow we'll hit the road. I want to put as much distance as possible between us and your father's gang of murderers."

"He would have found a better way to keep me alive."

"You're an idiot. Or at the very least naive."

Despite her anger and urge to make Matar take back what he'd said, she kept quiet for a few moments and imagined Valterone's reaction. She remembered the last execution, the defeated look of the young woman, her feet scraping against the stone slabs. She had witnessed her ordeal without suspecting that she might be the next to suffer it. Yet her father loved her in his own way. And as a More-Than-Pure, he had the power to save her.

"Where are we going? Where are we anyway?"

"In Barham Forest."

"The cursed forest?"

"Is that a problem? Were you planning on showing off your new look on the road?"

Neria had to get used to the idea of becoming an outcast. She thought of her mother and Ellane, the only people she could trust. They had proved their love by risking their lives to save her. A submissive wife and a despised slave. She had misjudged them.

The following day, Neria did as Matar said without protest. She took care of the dishes, shook and folded the blankets, and helped to load up the donkey. Onyx hated her. Whenever she approached him, he pricked up his ears, and looked as if he were about to bite her. She considered him similar to his master, with his dimwitted face and smug pout, and even his spiteful grin. His beautiful eyes, too intelligent in an animal with such a dull coat, bothered her. She had caught the Peddler whispering sweet nothings to this beast of burden on several occasions; his white hair mingled with the gray coat, his hazel eyes, with a disconcerting stare, sought out the large dark eyes of the animal, concealed like those of a sacred dancer. Of course, Anaëlle loved the donkey. She spoke to him in a sing-song voice, the kind she normally reserved for her doll. She would scratch him on the withers and if she dared try to stop, he would nibble her on her back, as she put it. She would burst out laughing and carry on cuddling him. They never grew bored of this tiresome game.

Matar perched Anaëlle on the animal's croup. He held the tether in one hand and his iron-tipped cane in the other. Neria followed them at a respectful distance to avoid being donkey-kicked. As they went along, it became more humid, and the flora became more diverse. Neria recognized the few trees that were familiar to her like old friends. Some were made up of two species. The strangest were adorned with extravagant colors and came in unusual shapes. She noticed specimens with purple, orange, or blue trunks, covered with unusual leaves. An incredible variety of creatures were flying, crawling, and jumping around them. The air resounded with whistles, cries, and clicks. The forest seemed to vibrate with wild, untamed life, radiating a frightening beauty. In spite of her fatigue, she felt a strange elation take hold of her as if the spirit of nature took her in its bosom.

She yelped as a monkey spider landed on her shoulder.

"Can't you just stay quiet? You're always looking for attention."

Although Matar grumbled about the irrational nature of city dwellers when confronted with such harmless creatures, the body of the monkey spider was terrifying to the uninitiated: far too many legs and bristles. The grimacing face did not help either.

"Which animals should I watch out for?"

"Your father's agents. Shut up and try not to draw any attention to yourself."

"How long will it take us to get to our destination?"

"At this rate? Three days."

"Have you planned any breaks?"

"No."

Neria let her mind wander. An idea had been bothering her since the night before. Had her parents lied about Arhel's death? Had he contracted the Nymphosis and not the ferruginous plague as they had claimed? She could not blame her mother for hiding the truth from her to save Arhel. Neria had not attended her brother's funeral but had visited his grave several times. Perhaps her own death would be staged, and another body would be placed in her grave.

They passed through a grove of giant rose bushes, with thorns like stakes, flowers bigger than a human skull, and a heady aroma. She could not resist the temptation to caress a white petal, smooth and soft to the touch.

Perhaps Arhel had fled Alipaz and was living in this forest or in some far-away land. One day, she would meet her changed brother and recognize him at first sight. She imagined him transformed into an Angel, with large wings and pale feathers like Ellane's before the amputation. But no matter how hard she tried, she could not change his boyish face. He would be fourteen now and look so very different from the eight-year-old boy she had last seen. Maybe he had turned into a Centaur. The More-Than-Pure, who only tolerated docile Chimeras, had purged them from the city; it wasn't easy to control an intelligent creature that weighed half a ton. After one had kicked and killed a More-Than-Pure, the Council had published a decree prohibiting the use of Centaurs. Neria thought it had been a shame. She remembered having seen some drawing carriages and had considered the sight magnificent. And if Arhel had become a Dryad? The most mysterious of the Chimeras. They avoided cities, hiding in their sacred forests. If that was the case, maybe he was living right here.

Several feet further on, a flash attracted Neria's attention, and she stopped, curious to find the cause. In a rapid writhing movement, a snake coiled itself around her ankle. She shook her foot to get it off, but the animal tightened its embrace. Desperate to follow the old man's advice, she held back a cry and, without losing her composure, bent down to pull the reptile off. Another seized her by the waist and, with a jolt, pulled her off the track. No matter how much she resisted, it dragged her toward a smooth tree trunk. Hundreds of tentacles, taking the place of this hybrid creature's branches, twisted around her in a gruesome dance. On the end of each one was a disturbing blue eye, fringed with long black lashes. Some of them simply watched as others coiled around her body, carrying her. At the base of the trunk, an opening seemed to grow larger. She thrashed out. The appendages retracted like horns of a snail and spread out once again. Neria screamed. Her cry was strangled silent by a tentacle wrapping itself around her neck. The more she struggled, the more the tree tightened its grip.

When she finally saw Matar coming into her field of vision, her relief was so intense that she could have hugged him. She let out a frightened screech.

"That's some weird fruit."

At this, Anaëlle burst into a shattering peal of laughter. The Peddler uttered a mysterious, monotonous chant to which the tree responded in a hoarse, cavernous voice, its vibrations spreading to the end of its tentacles. The tentacles dropped the girl to the ground and reluctantly released her. She staggered away.

A few minutes later, she spoke again, "Is this forest haunted?"

"It's inhabited."

"This tree… What would have happened to me if you hadn't spoken to it?"

"Nothing. It was just curious, that's all. But there's no telling when it would've let you go. It doesn't have the same understanding of time as we do."

CHAPTER FIVE

With the donkey by his side and the tether in his hand, Matar advanced in an agile, swift, and silent manner, carrying a sleeping Anaëlle on his back. Tired of riding the donkey, Anaëlle had managed to inspire pity in the Peddler. Neria had noticed the old man's brief smile and contented expression when the girl had unhesitatingly slipped into his arms and had rested her head on his shoulder. Neria trailed behind. She yearned for a camp, a hearty meal, and sleep. The sky had reddened, night would not be long. One step, then another, and another. Her thoughts lulled to the rhythm of the walk, a nonchalant haze in a foggy mind. She felt she would doze off at any moment. After all, horses could sleep well enough on their feet.

Suddenly, some powerful force tore her away from the ground and swept her up to a dizzying height. She screamed. Branches whipped against her as a monster gripped her by the ankle. Her screams silenced in her throat. She stopped struggling, realizing that the alternative to this grip was being let go to crash down in a free fall. She swayed like a rabbit with a broken neck. Suddenly, the monster released her. She would be dead soon. She crashed through branches, snapping them with the impact. The monster caught her again, the sudden stop in the fall nearly ripping her head off. They resumed their erratic flight. She felt she was going to crack her skull open at any moment, her fear stopping her from breathing. Cliffs were getting ever nearer. The monster propelled her against the wall. Just as she was about to hit it, she plummeted through a curtain of vegetation, firing through like a missile before crashing on the floor of a cave.

She wheezed with an effort subdued by sharp pains in her ribs. Hideous creatures with bodies covered in thick fur surrounded her. They cackled, revealing long, sharp teeth. Their huge ears twitched. They stirred the air with their leathery wings, scratching at it with their hooked claws. She refused to go down without a fight. Her hand closed around a rock as her captor came forward, with a malicious smile on its face. She threw her improvised weapon with all her might and the beast yelped in pain. Blood flowed from the wound on its forehead. Its companions burst into laughter. She drew her knife.

"You're crazy! What's wrong with you, lady?"

"Come any closer and I'll kill you."

The laughter grew louder.

"This is what I get after all I've done for you? You should be thanking me, I saved you a long walk."

Neria suddenly realized that these creatures reminded her of Bobka, in a similar manner to how real bears resemble children's toys.

"You almost killed me!"

"Not at all. I'm a master at flying with a burden, expertly so."

"A burden?"

"Considering your weight and the distance covered, I think I've actually set a new record. Right?"

The others agreed enthusiastically. Cries, whistles, and cheers echoed around the hall. Her captor was given a few congratulatory slaps that would have easily knocked over a small cow.

A gray-haired individual stepped forward.

"Don't be afraid. Forg was only joking."

Seeing her puzzled look, the individual added, "We mean you no harm. We think very highly of Matar and the friends of our friends are always welcome in our home."

Neria did not wish to enlighten them about the quality of her relationship with the Peddler.

"Don't get any closer! Nobody comes near me until Matar arrives."

"We'll leave you be. Get some rest."

The monsters kept their word and, weary of the spectacle, returned to their duties. Neria was in a large hall hollowed out into the rock. Cave carvings that expressively depicted scenes from everyday life were scattered over its walls. At first, she had thought them primitive, like childish scrawls, but on closer inspection, she could see Gargoyles, animals, and plants, accurately and evocatively rendered, interwoven in a harmonious whole. An enormous gong stood in front of the wall opposite the entrance, and Neria wondered what it could be used for. She observed the incessant landings, astonished by the ability of the Gargoyles to avoid one another in spite of their chaotic flight. They must have started their journeys from elsewhere. She then examined her limbs, which were streaked with red lines. Blood oozed from a series of gashes while her knee was adorned by an unsightly graze. A dull pain still pulsed from her extremely tender neck and shoulders. She pulled down on her sleeve to hide the tuft of coarse hair that was growing above her elbow.

The elder Gargoyle was tending to her abductor's wound. A female appeared. She held a bowl in her hands, an appetizing smell wafting from it. She put it down on the ground before Neria and instructed her in a powerful voice, "Eat." Her figure was every bit as imposing as her male counterparts, even with the addition of her feminine curves. Neria gulped down the delicious meal then leaned back against the wall. She felt dizzy from the droning activity of the hive, but the spectacle distracted her from the tedium of waiting for Matar to finally arrive, before he was winched up and dropped down like a bundle.

"Forg, one day one of your jokes is going to end very badly."

"She's got no sense of humor that one! She almost knocked me out."

Matar burst out laughing and turned to Neria, "I've got to admit I enjoy your bad temper when I'm not on the receiving end of it."

He left to greet friends who came over to meet him. Pats on the back, enthusiastic head rubs, and cheerful smiles punctuated the reunions.

Only Anaëlle was treated with some consideration. Placed on the floor of the cave like a jewel lain out on a precious garment, she let herself be admired by the Gargoyles and turned around with a delighted look on her face. When she grew tired of the attention, she remembered her aunt and ran to snuggle in her arms.

"Mataw told me evewything was fine, but I was still

fwightened. I'm so glad I found you, I'll nevew leave you again."

"I was really frightened too. Did you hear me scream?"

"You've gotten really vewy ugly, you know. But I decided to love you anyway."

"Thank you. It's good that you're making a compromise. You don't really have many other options."

The female Gargoyle asked them to follow her. They accompanied her through a succession of tunnels as poorly lit as the stomachs of a cow. Neria guided Anaëlle, who clutched her hand.

"I can't see anything."

Neria wondered if the fits of prescience had affected the child's vision. After many winding bends, their guide led them into a magnificent hall lined from the ground to the ceiling with a myriad of stalactites and stalagmites. Passages tracing between the formations divided the area into various harmonious spaces. No rock frescoes competed with this natural splendor, although the wall of the entryway was dotted with rough-hewn alcoves. A pool of water embedded in the rock sparkled. A small number of bathers washed and relaxed in the dim light, alone or in groups of two or three. The hostess removed a lamp from an alcove. After lighting it, she offered it to Anaëlle. The child, at first dazzled, then surprised to be entrusted with such a responsibility, took it with both hands. Amazed by the beauty of the place, she set off to explore it. From another recess, the Gargoyle took out some soap and large patches of fabric that she gave to Neria. Then she moved away a few paces to undress.

Neria, daughter of Valterone, More-Than-Pure, Steward of

the Peace, hesitated to wash in the company of creatures worth
less than cattle in Alipaz. She may as well have been bathing
with a cow or a dog. And then there was the matter of the fleas.
She could imagine her father's reaction to the idea. Blood would
have been spilled, wings would have been ripped off, or worse.
Yet these Gargoyles did not resent her. Did they know who she
was? It didn't matter. She was now living off the charity of
strangers. A vagrant, diseased and deformed, with no family nor
friends.

Anaëlle was talking in a hushed voice with two of the
bathers. She seemed to be good at adjusting to all of these
novelties without prejudice. Or close to it. She had overcome
the separation from her mother and the probable death of her
father, but the metamorphosis of her aunt had nevertheless
repulsed her. Neria felt as if she was melting away, as if she was
flowing like a stream which, instead of flowing into a more
powerful river, divides into a multitude of minuscule gullies
until it disappears. She found it difficult to accept these changes
with no preparation. You don't erase years of education in an
instant.

She walked towards her niece as if in a dream. Even though
her face prepared onlookers for the worst, she was afraid of
revealing her hideous body. The indifference of the females
lounging in their baths reassured her. They were enjoying a
moment of relaxation as a family or among friends and only
afforded her a few curious glances. Neria could not have
imagined a situation like this in Alipaz, where washing was
considered a shameful duty that everyone had to perform behind
closed doors.

The water shimmered among the rocks with a tempting and

ominous lapping. Its transparency reassured Neria. She called Anaëlle, took off her clothes, hung them on a stalagmite, and invited the child to do the same. Then, without waiting any longer, she immersed herself in a sudden motion. Water concealed the hideous blisters that disfigured her body and, after the initial shock had passed, its coolness soothed the swelling. Neria helped Anaëlle wash. Shivering and blue, the child then got out of the pool and wrapped herself in a towel. Neria lathered the citrus-scented soap and touched her aching shoulders and nape of her neck. She scratched a patch of scales on her forearm - they tormented her like gnawing insect bites - and saw that they fell off, carried away by a light current. She laid her head on a rock and allowed herself to be swayed by the waves. The water, made even colder by her stillness, blurred this treacherous, cumbersome body of hers. She exhaled and sank to the bottom. She wanted to be forgotten there enveloped by this oscillating mass, her deformity hidden, her pains soothed, her body supported and caressed. The discomfort turned all too quickly into suffering. She rose up, broke through the surface of the water, and breathed in. Less than a couple of feet away, the Gargoyle was watching her.

"Out, now."

Thick hairs covered her muscular anatomy. Only her breasts and hips differentiated her from a male. She moved with confidence, her leather wings sagely folded on her back.

Neria reluctantly complied. Water slid down her skin and dripped onto the smooth stone. She dried herself off. The Gargoyle took the rags, carried them away, and returned with a pile of clean clothes: tunics, pants made of soft fabric, and large jackets.

"My name's Neria, what about you?"

"Imri," she answered with a grimace that she wore in place of a smile.

Neria had, in a question, exhausted her conversational ammunition and found she had nothing else to add. They left the baths to go down some more corridors. On the way, they passed Gargoyles, some hurrying and some nonchalant, often playful, sometimes brooding, and ever rowdy in groups. The larger tunnels led to other, narrower ones, pierced by passages obscured by sturdy wooden doors. Imri knocked on one of them and opened it. They entered a spacious room that served as a dormitory. Their guide indicated two straw mattresses to the newcomers. Neria and Anaëlle collapsed on them in a state of bliss and fell asleep immediately.

A silhouette armed with a broom moved in the half-light. Anaëlle had disappeared. Neria, still dazed by her sleep, pushed back the light covers and got herself up.

"Excuse me, can you show me the way out?"

"This isn't an inn."

Neria recognized her guide from the day before. She pointed out her bedding and the ceiling to her - five straw mattresses were hung up there on wooden rails - then gave her the broom.

"Where's the child?"

"Don't worry about her. Matar came to get her while you were sleeping."

Matar had hated her all along for some reason she didn't understand and was going out of his way to keep them apart. Why hadn't Anaëlle waited for her? Neria felt that they should at least be able to rely on one another. The heat suddenly seemed unbearable to her and she looked for a window to open. The holes piercing the upper walls didn't seem to be connected with the outside, yet a gentle current of air and an unclear light crept into the room. In this strange place, time was transformed into an elusive, amorphous substance. She could not tell whether it was day or night and when Imri told her the hour, she was surprised she had slept so long.

Neria put herself to work. The sooner she finished her chores, the sooner she could join Anaëlle. She shook her bedding and hung it up. The sweeper, who had left for a moment, returned with pails of water. Together, they wielded their brushes and mops with the zeal of great Amazons in battle. Neria, bare feet in a puddle as she mopped, thought to herself that being unsightly and hairy were not synonymous with squalor. Their task completed, they went once again to the baths, then towards a refectory and kitchen that smelled of freshly baked bread. Imri, a former Human from Roguelle, had chosen to go to Gork's Corrie after her metamorphosis.

"There's no better place to learn how to use your wings than here. If it was my fate to have them, I'd rather use them to go and see the world. City Gargoyles are such a bore."

At the end of their meal, Imri, who had been given the responsibility of acclimatizing the newcomer, led her to a hall buzzing with activity. Dazzled by the intense brightness, Neria squinted and, preceded by Imri, approached the great opening pierced in the wall. She paused to admire the sunset, clung to the stone wall, and looked down. She was standing on the edge of a cliff at the foot of which herbaceous plants grew. Farther on, the forest grew ever larger, and, towards her right, a river snaked away down below.

Imri held Neria in her arms. She initially believed this to be a mark of untimely affection but realized her mistake when she launched her out into the void. Still entwined, they plunged towards the ground at full speed. Neria closed her eyes. The Gargoyle spread her wings and changed trajectory. Neria opened her eyes. In a corner of her terrified mind nestled the wavering satisfaction of not having screamed. They lost altitude and flew low for a few minutes, then, without warning, Imri dropped her cargo. Miraculously, Neria managed to land on her feet but lost her balance regardless. The impact nearly emptied the contents of her stomach.

Like a grasshopper, Imri had regained altitude. She used her legs to propel herself and jumped from tree to tree. What her technique lacked in elegance, it made up for in strength.

"What do you make of getting around like that?"

Neria jumped and swiveled around. Armed with a bow and arrows, Matar stood before her.

"Efficient but uncomfortable."

"The landings leave something to be desired."

"Where's Anaëlle?"

"School."

This concept seemed so strange to Neria that she remained silent for a moment. Schools indeed existed in Alipaz, cramped, and consisting of classes packed with grubby little miscreants.

"Who with?"

"Other children and some teachers."

"What children?"

"You're worrying about who she's spending time with now? Gargoyles, of course."

"What will she be learning?"

"No idea. It's late and you've been lounging around long enough. I would have woken you earlier, but Isk advised me against it. He says sleep is essential in the early stages of a transformation. Make the most of it. You've got permission to carry on with your lazy ways."

"Are we going hunting?"

"l am. You're going to pick berries."

"I'd rather go with you."

"I didn't ask for your opinion."

"In the middle of the night? What a weird idea, picking berries in the dark."

"You'll do fine."

"How?"

"You've not been bumping into the walls in the tunnels, have you?"

"Of course not, thanks to the lighting."

"There's no lighting in the caves. Come on, I'll show you the place."

Neria followed behind him. She looked around her, covered her eyes with her hand, and was astonished to be able to make out shapes. When Matar stopped, she watched

Gargoyles busy gathering red berries on bushes with lustrous leaves. She understood her status better now: a slave who, like Ellane, would be entitled a little consideration as long as she made herself useful. She had traded the constraint of Alipaz's laws for internment with savages. She would indulge them, then find a way to escape. With Anaëlle, of course.

His mission accomplished, Matar was now moving away. Neria chose a promising site, picked a berry, and bit into its sharp, sweet flesh.

"By the way, don't eat the berries. They really do sting if you eat them raw."

For several weeks, her life had settled into a familiar rhythm and yet Neria continued to dream of an escape that seemed even more desirable to her when she was with the Peddler.

Dodge, parry, attack, parry... Ouch. Neria shook her hand to clear the pain. The light weathered oak weapons, with their smooth, slightly curved shapes, seemed harmless enough as long as they were not in the grip of the old man. Still, the offer of training - while she was still trying to come to terms with her inferior status - had pleased her. This knowledge would lead to her freedom. But she soon became disillusioned. She came out of these training sessions bruised in body and soul. Matar gave his lessons reluctantly, convinced in advance that she would fail and seeming to derive pleasure from proving her worthlessness. When she mentioned the discomfort from the bump on her back, he told her in a scornful tone not to make excuses.

The classes took place at the end of the day, when the shadows grew long, always on the same site, a discreet clearing far from the main thoroughfares. Following the methodical instructions of the Peddler, they had cleared the ground, cut the bushes, and hacked away the tall grass that risked obstructing their movements. Neria preferred the sessions when Anaëlle joined them. In these training sessions, the child injected a casual enthusiasm that seemed to help her. Whatever happened, Matar would often congratulate the child on her progress.

"Again!"

Neria tried to concentrate and follow the set rhythm, but the sword struck her once again at the base of her thumb. The sounds of her surroundings seemed to subside, masked by a throbbing pain. Her wet clothes stuck to her skin. She pulled her hand from under her arm and wiped her face with her sleeve.

"I want Anaëlle to sleep in my room. I'll take her to school and take care of her when I get home from work."

"En garde!"

She reacted, pressured by attack after attack, managing to parry a few blows before the sword made impact with her swollen knuckle. She screamed and threw her weapon to the ground.

"Pick it up!"

Trying to keep the rest of her emotional strength to avoid a fit of tears, she didn't react.

"I told you to pick it up."

Neria squatted down, stretched out her hand, and felt the polished wood. She straightened up.

L. M. RAPP

"You don't actually mean to teach me, do you? Who's ordered you to do this?"

Matar's features remained unreadable. She held his disturbingly steady gaze. "I don't take orders from anyone. Isk asked me to help you out."

Isk, the gray-haired Gargoyle she had met the day she had arrived, didn't speak often, but always smiled at her whenever they passed each other in the dining hall.

"I want Anaëlle to live with me. Thank you for helping when I was sick, but I'll take care of her from now on."

"She doesn't want that."

"I don't believe you."

"Put yourself in her shoes, a child of her age in total darkness... We live in an area reserved for visitors, for those who can't navigate in the dark."

"Then I'll come with you."

"No, you'll stay with the unmarried. You have to get used to life in this community. You might turn into a Gargoyle."

"I don't look much like them."

"Isk has his doubts too, but that doesn't change anything for now. Pick up your weapon, we're starting over."

"I miss Anaëlle. I want to see her more."

"Hurry up, we're wasting time."

Neria reluctantly picked up her sword.

"Close your eyes and relax."

"No way."

"Do what you're told without arguing for once."

Was this a kind of punishment being forced upon her? Some unheard-of humiliation? Being caned without being able to defend herself? She knew that her newfound gift - unrelated to her night vision as that had not improved any more - would not allow her to detect rapid movement with her eyes closed. She closed them anyway and brought the tip of her sword to Matar's. She followed the sequence and waited with dread for the final blow, the moment when the Peddler's weapon would move away from hers, soar up towards the sky, and crash down with astonishing speed and equal strength down on the tender flesh of her hand. When the dreaded moment arrived, something strange happened. Time seemed to slow down, and, for the first time, she managed to master the timing of her dodge. The sword had not touched her.

"You slowed down on purpose."

"I didn't. You wouldn't learn anything if I took pity on you. Let's start again. Close your eyes."

A new series of attacks followed and, as if listening to the echo of some cryptic advice she had once heard but not fully understood, the miracle happened again. Sensing the weapons, their dance, without anticipation. Not using her sight, but touch, not being caught by the sword as it flew down but letting herself be carried with the wave of its energy.

"So? Think it's going better? We'll start archery tomorrow."

Neria nodded. She wanted to speak, to describe her astonishment to Matar, to show him her gratitude, but she could not find the words. She had finally had her revenge on Rona, on all those who had confined her to a predetermined role and had limited her knowledge to imprison her.

"And what about Anaëlle?"

"I'll think about it."

As they parted, Matar added, "Practice constantly. Listen to the song of a bird, the brush of a quill on a scroll, the swish of a sword over another, as if your existence depended on it. First, well... the habit will take your mind off things. But one day it will save your life."

CHAPTER SIX

Yet another failed drop. She got to her feet, spat the dirt out of her mouth, and dusted off her clothes. Her friends were making these landings rougher than necessary to have a little fun at her expense. They would either not slow down enough, release her too soon, or let go of her too late, keeping her constricted in their muscular arms, trapped between heaven and earth. Flung forward at full speed, she was forced to run at a frantic pace to stop herself from falling head over heels. She was nevertheless grateful for the Gargoyles' willingness to serve as her means of transport. They enjoyed the journey down but dreaded the return. They hated taking off from the ground, which used up too much energy, and instead brought her back the majority of the time by following the method Forg had used on their first encounter: a plunging dive, a brutal grip, then a heroic rise. Clasped against their bodies, Neria felt them puffing and panting from the effort.

Having tried her hand at gathering, gardening, and needlework, she had still not been given the opportunity to participate in a hunt. It wasn't that the Gargoyles questioned her loyalty, but there was a lack of trust due to her incomplete transformation, her unknown origin, and her inexperience.

Gork's Corrie protected its inhabitants from the stupefying heat, which showed no signs of relenting in spite of several signs foretelling the end of the summer, like the lengthening nights and the bloom of the wild chiseler flowers. With each and every step, Neria was engulfed a little more in the humid, stifling stuffiness of the forest. She had been instructed to help with gathering strawberry-cream gourds and this prospect hardly filled her with enthusiasm. The beautiful fruit, which resembled an oblong pumpkin, would sometimes detach itself without warning from the highest branches of the gigantic tree on which it grew. During the previous gathering session, one had fallen on Neria's head and she'd only survived thanks to a quick-thinking coworker who had set her back to rights. At the end of this agonizing shift, her companions, disgusted by how syrupy she felt, had refused to carry her back. To return to the cave, she'd had to take a long walk through the sweltering forest while all sorts of insects feasted on her skin, attracted by the sticky pulp. She had pulled herself up trembling rope ladders and had gone down long corridors filled with laughing Gargoyles before finally reaching the sanctuary of the baths.

Seized by a sudden impulse, Neria deviated from her path to go down towards the river. She approached the current and watched her reflection. The protuberances on her head had faded and there weren't any horns forming as far as she could see. Her ears had grown, sharpened, as had her hearing. It was thanks to this she could discern that Matar was quietly approaching.

"What's going to come of me?"

"Well, I don't even know what's going to happen to me tomorrow, so…"

"Ha. Ha. Very amusing. You know what I mean. What will I turn into? Can Isk tell?"

"You're going to have wings… But no feathers."

"So I'm going to turn into a Gargoyle, right?"

"Maybe. Maybe not. Don't worry about that for now, you'll know soon enough."

"That's easy for you to say. I'd like to see how you'd act if you woke up one morning looking like this. I think you'd be worried."

"Who says I haven't already?"

Suddenly, the Peddler's features changed: cat-like eyes, long fangs, and pointed ears. Then all the pieces fell into place.

"You're a monster too?"

"Do I look like a monster? Am I more of a monster than the Humans?"

"It's you!"

The Peddler remained silent.

"You're the one that killed those guards!"

Although her first impression of Matar as a senile old man clashed with the dreadful image of the beast that had drained the guards of their blood, Neria had often felt disturbed, sometimes even frightened, by the peculiarity of his limber body and by the constancy of his stare, accentuated by two wrinkles between his brows. With time, the initial animosity had diminished and Neria now felt respect for her savior while the majority of the inhabitants of Alipaz would have watched his execution without a hint of sympathy.

She now felt as if she had come across a fanged baby bird and fought against a sensation of repulsion. This new world she was discovering fascinated her yet frightened her at the same time. She could not excuse the More-Than-Pure ideology, but she understood it in a way. Their ideology offered the benefit of certainty and provided a vision, perhaps one that was too simplistic but nonetheless clear, of good and evil, of what was natural and what was despicable. Neria tried to free herself from this outlook that prevented her from seeing reality in all its nuances: Matar, simultaneously old yet young, savage yet patient, fair yet unkind.

She looked up at the eternal yet fickle sky, draped with the changing colors of dusk, from the very warmest to the very coldest. With an immense metallic blue dome above her, she was dazzled by the last burst of a vermillion glare from the rocky peaks on the horizon.

"I didn't get the chance to thank you."

"You had plenty of chances. I got the impression you didn't want to."

"You hated me at first. Then I was angry with you. After that, I didn't dare."

"I see."

"So, thank you."

"It's nothing."

"Not really. I think it was rather incredible."

Neria picked up a flat stone and threw it aside to skim on the water. The stone sank to the bottom.

"Your mother told me you were different, but I didn't believe her. You and Adamek struck me as the unmistakable spawn of Valterone."

"The finest clothes and food, servants and slaves, respect and fear... But as a girl, I'd already lost. Arhel was the better of us, and if he'd lived, he would have stood up to Adamek, maybe even our father. He had two qualities you don't often find together, kindness and courage."

He threw a stone. It skimmed along the surface of the water and bounced a few times before landing on the other side.

"I'm jealous of your power of disguise, anyway. If I could go back to Alipaz, I'd reassure my mother that I've survived and found a kind of freedom here, despite this bulky and treacherous body, despite your training, and gourd gathering."

"I never want to go back to Alipaz. I never want to see a Chimera suffering ever again."

"They were threatening the Humans and had it coming."

"That's ridiculous."

"Slaves are always ready for an opportunity to rebel against their masters or attack soldiers…"

"You'd rather they surrender to their persecution without resisting? It's such audacity, isn't it, to want your freedom!"

"Chimeras have greater physical strength and special abilities that Humans need to control to survive. And they attacked the Humans first. Everyone knows that."

"Before the More-Than-Pure came to power, Chimeras and Humans lived side-by-side in Alipaz in harmony."

"And what about the savage hordes that sacked the city?"

"They've not been any real danger for a very long time, ever since the walls were built."

"What they did proves that the threat can reappear at any time."

"No one's pretending that they're perfect but there are just as many Human thieves and murderers as there are among the Chimeras."

Neria looked at him with a cynical pout. She would never have suspected that Matar could speak so much, and, in spite of their differences, she had enjoyed this exchange.

"Would you think it was fair," he asked, "if you were put to death because of your transformation?"

"My case is different. I haven't conspired against the More-Than-Pure, it's not my fault."

"And what about your brother, Arhel, was he guilty?"

"Is he still alive? Do you know something? Did you save him too?"

"No. I didn't. Your mother called me too late."

"Maybe someone else then? Look, I'm asking because I think he contracted Nymphosis. I thought Arhel had the ferruginous plague until now. But I saw his hand..."

"Nephalie didn't prepare me for this."

"Excuse me?"

He sighed and sat down beside her.

"I didn't want to tell you all this. It was your mother's responsibility."

"What happened to my brother? If you know something, just tell me."

"He was murdered."

"Who killed him?"

"Your father."

"You liar!"

Neria leaped up. Matar stared at a pebble he was smoothing between his fingers.

"I shouldn't have told you like that."

"You hate me, don't you?"

"On the contrary, I'm actually beginning to like you. Otherwise, I wouldn't have said anything."

"My father has his faults, but he would never have laid a hand on one of his children. A few smacks to discipline us, yes, but... Why lie about him? Why do you hate him so much?"

"Have you really not seen anything? The way he treats his slaves? His cruelty?"

He parried the slap before it reached his face. Neria continued to hit him, with Matar blocking the blows until he decided to put an end to their dance. The Peddler roared as a warning before pushing her back. She fell over and, shaking with her sobbing, remained lying prostrate on the damp rock.

Had Arhel seen the murderous hand approaching and realized that his own father was going to kill him? Had he apathetically accepted his death, exhausted by his illness, or had he resisted? She pushed away the visions of his murder and remembered their play fighting and laughter. Their parents would make them go to bed early when they were not yet tired. They would lie and wait for sleep before dozing off in their respective rooms but Arhel would sometimes find this unbearable. The door would creak when he opened it, a faint but distinct sound that she had learned to recognize. Then she would hear the hurried patter of his bare feet, followed by the usual question, "Are you sleeping?" She would push herself up against the wall to make room for him in the bed. Very early in the morning, she would take him back to his room still half-asleep. Their father didn't like them sleeping in the same room.

When they couldn't sleep, they would sometimes start play fighting, made all the more entertaining by the risk of being discovered. Neria could make out her brother in the bluish light of the moon, his face exhilarated by the thrill, defending himself with all his might. When he was neutralized by a fit of silent giggling, she seized the opportunity to hit him repeatedly with a pillow before tumbling down beside him. Contagious laughter often shook Arhel's frail body before he collapsed, exhausted and defeated.

She would never hear him laugh or cry again. She had believed that some Peddler had saved him, that he was living outside of Alipaz, in this forest perhaps. But he had been murdered by his own father at the age of eight years old.

The fit of tears subsided as Neria straightened herself up and grabbed a handful of pebbles. Without paying much attention to them, she threw them one by one into the river. Standing, Matar scratched his forehead, pulled his tunic, examined his sandals, took a look at the sky, and then sat down. He recounted in a calm voice the events in the distant past that had shaped his life.

"Your mother, your father, and I came from wealthy families, and we met in school. I contracted Nymphosis when I was seventeen. It often happens around that age as an extension of adolescence. My parents were concerned because there can sometimes be complications, but at that time, we just accepted the inevitable. Nymphosis can affect any of us and mutants weren't considered criminals back then.

"Nephalie visited me during my convalescence. I think she enjoyed my conversation because I wasn't much to look at. We became inseparable.

"When Elatek published his theories about Human superiority as a race, most of us just laughed. I was in love and didn't care about anything else. Your father joined the 'liberation' movement from the very beginning with a bunch of fanatics who thought they'd found the Savior. Street fighting broke out between the various factions and the situation in the country deteriorated. The wildest accusations against the Chimeras spread within a matter of hours. Some left Alipaz and others, like me, felt safe there. My whole family was Human, and my mutation was practically unnoticeable.

"Early in the morning, on the Day of the Great Deliverance, I was woken up by the sound of crashing and shouting and opened my window. The air shook with the clashing of weapons and screams of rage and terror. Entire families were lying down, entwined in a final embrace.

"My parents insisted I leave and so I crossed the walls. Inhabitants had to prove three generations of purity to escape the culls. After a ridiculous trial, my father, mother, brothers, and sister were all executed. When I returned, Nephalie had married Valterone and given birth to Adamek. I embraced the life of a traveling, sometimes useful, but unattached salesman.

"I understood why Nephalie did what she did. Amidst all the denunciations and settling of scores, she chose survival. She thought she was doing the best she could in a dangerous situation. And we were wrong about your father. We thought he was just a naive man who'd bought into some foolish ideas and would soon realize his mistake.

"Did he kill Arhel with his own hands? I don't know. He had the power to get you all out of the city, but he chose to sacrifice his son instead. Your mother never forgave him, and she's risked her life many times since then to save other people. Your family's proof that this myth of purity is all based on a lie. Two mutant children out of four. Everyone's lying about their genetic makeup, starting with the More-Than-Pure.

"Well, there you have it. Now you know the whole story. Up until now, you've just absorbed Elatek's propaganda and enjoyed the suffering of the Chimera without question. If you never contracted Nymphosis, you would've got married and spawned even more despots. I would never have thought I'd be betting on you, Valterone's daughter, Adamek's sister, and a spoiled child certain she deserves her privilege."

Following Isk's advice, Neria shook her wings, her two pointless and cumbersome extra limbs. He had given her a set of exercises, added to those recommended by Matar, that was supposed to guarantee their good development. At times, she looked behind her as if to make sure they were still there or to check that she wasn't accidentally carrying around a sly and sluggish monkey spider, hanging off her shoulders. Walnut stain in color and pliable in texture, her wings resembled those of the Gargoyles. She hoped they would continue to grow in size and strength as their insufficient wingspan did not yet allow her to fly.

At least the pains in her neck and shoulders had faded, along with the repulsive blisters whose marks still streaked her skin. Neria had watched the disappearance of the patches of scales and coarse hair with a relief mixed with unease. She didn't look like anybody else. Only her wings and pointed ears differentiated her from a Human. Her face had lost its residual childlike cheeks and had become thinner. Even with her short hair, her family would be able to recognize her without any difficulty.

She arrived at the meeting place. Instead of leaves, the bird oak sported greenish-blue feathers that quivered in the still air. Without its roots anchoring it down, it would have seemed as if it could leave the ground and fly away at will. She reached out and touched its smooth bark, traversed by unseen waves, and shuddered. Then, she sensed the shuffling of silent steps and saw Matar's moving shadow. His thin smile, which lit up his face for a moment, gave him an unassertive and uncomfortable expression.

"We're going hunting."

Since the sudden revelations he had made to her several weeks earlier, he had been experimenting with a newfound friendliness, and this novel behavior alarmed her. He handed her a quiver and a bow. When she slipped the latter around her body, she felt she was crowned, embraced by an armor that breathed new strength into her. Finally accepted, almost chosen, she felt the strange conviction that she would never again suffer from loneliness.

They set off. The pulsating calm of the forest filled Neria with joy. She smelled the air and detected an aroma of fresh earth, decomposing vegetation, and, intermittently, sweet flowers and rotting flesh. The scent of a Gargoyle? More hunters perhaps? Or maybe gatherers... Matar moved with the pace of a predator on the prowl. His eyes shone. The scent of the prey grew stronger... A scaled doe. They followed the trail, moving closer against the wind and saw the female, elegant and pale, her eyes resembling lakes of dark water fringed with long, curved lashes like reeds. She was chewing leaves, unaware of the danger. Matar encouraged Neria with a nod. She placed the nock on the bowstring, readied her bow, breathed in... hesitated...

Suddenly, a shadow fell on the animal and carried it up towards the canopy. Neria lowered her weapon, taken aback.

"Damn fool! She could have killed you!" shouted Matar.

Hysterical laughter answered him. The foliage trembled and Forg appeared, laughing, with the slain animal in his arms. Matar ranted and raved as the Gargoyle chuckled even harder.

"Don't you have any other prey to hunt?"

"Go on, admit I surprised you. Well, I'll leave you to it. I've got some game to bring back home."

In a few leaps, he reached the treetops and, weighed down by his load, took off in a chaotic flight that reminded Neria of their first meeting. Ultimately, she felt relieved. Matar was right, she would have wounded Forg... if she had not changed her mind. Dazzled by the aura that surrounded hunters, she had dreamed of becoming one of them, but had refused to kill an animal at the decisive moment. Only out of weakness. She enjoyed their meat and knew that she would later be eating the animal, butchered and cooked beyond recognition.

"Let's head back. He's put me off."

After a few minutes of walking in silence, Matar added, "He used a lot of skill to trick us like that. I think he's trying to soften you up. You might want to bury the hatchet with him."

"No way, he acts so unbearably. You've said so yourself."

He paused and turned to her.

"You hesitated."

"She was so... beautiful and vulnerable."

"You'll get used to it. Especially if you're hungry."

"Maybe I will."

"I wanted to tell you I was leaving."

Neria kept silent.

"I'm going to join the Rebels, probably back to Alipaz, and I'd like you to come with me. Not to Alipaz, of course. You'd settle down with Anaëlle in a Free City. I kept my promise and took you to safety, but now I realize you could be decisive in the rebellion. As the daughter of Valterone and a Chimera, you could expose the lies of the More-Than-Pure."

Neria found it strange that, up until that day, whenever she thought of home, the image of her new sandals that she had left behind with the rest of her possessions came to mind. She was ashamed to admit it, but she had often missed those sandals. A strip of leather at the base of the toes supported the front of the sole, with two more strips running diagonally from the middle that looped behind the ankle. The cobbler who had made them had threaded an oval wooden bead onto the outside strap, transforming them into an original and elegant design. As soon as Neria had put them on, she had not wanted to take them off. But when she returned home after a long walk, the bead had embedded its outline into her skin.

Matar held out his hand and she returned the bow and

quiver to him without daring to protest. She felt guilty for not wanting to follow him, especially now that their relationship had improved, but she had experienced enough novelty to last a lifetime. The well-worn and comfortable sandals she had now suited her; she didn't want any others. She wished she had the courage to fight for the liberation of Alipaz and its slaves, but she was so repulsed by the memory of that city that the idea of going near it seemed unbearable.

When they reached the bird oak at the edge of the forest, she spotted an owl perched on a branch, so different from the ones in Alipaz, with its body a darker blue than the tree's feathers and its face turquoise, wearing the same disdainful expression as a disappointed tutor. They exchanged a glance and Neria smiled up at it.

Like every evening, she enjoyed her breakfast as night fell. Anaëlle had hers with her school friends. The child had got used to nocturnal life, was no longer afraid of the dark, and wandered through the bowels of the cave armed with the iron-tipped cane that Matar had given her. He also taught her martial arts and found her to be gifted. Neria had feared the consequences of the dramatic events to which the child had been exposed, but her behavior had reassured her. She seemed to have forgotten her past suffering and, like a thirsty plant lavished with water, grew with increased vigor.

To take advantage of this all too rare moment of peace and to savor her fragrant gruel and slice of gourd in peace, Neria had sat down in the most isolated part of the hall. Suddenly, a hand

DREADFUL BEAUTY

struck her on the back. With a jolt, the well-filled spoon that she was about to put in her mouth slipped away from her.

"How are you, my dear?"

"Fine, until you came along."

"I've got good news. Today you start your..."

"Your what?"

"Your..."

"Go get a cloth and wipe the table. It's your fault that I spilled..."

"Your flying lessons."

"Are you sure? Will my wings be able to support me? Because..."

"And I'm going to be your instructor!"

Neria's smile froze.

"Have you got any experience? Have you taught anyone else before?"

"Finish eating and come on. We've got work to do first."

Neria hurriedly finished her meal and cleaned up before following Imri. They entered the dovecote, a beautiful circular room with many cavities where birds nested. At their arrival, a few frightened doves flew out of a round opening in the ceiling. The young women improvised masks from rags and set to work. First, they scraped off the upper layer of the still-fresh droppings, which had the most pungent odors. Underneath, the dried droppings had taken on the appearance of salt blocks that crumbled under their shovels. The hours went by in a cloud of nauseating dust. Neria's reluctance was transformed little by little into zeal, the odor did not bother her any longer and her

103

pace of work quickened. The growing heap of guano contained in its bosom the promise of beautiful vegetables, fragrant soups, and crisp salads.

Imri then signaled the end of their work, dismissing any suggestion of washing themselves, saying, "There's no point, you're only going to get dirty again." She guided Neria through the maze of tunnels before they emerged on a precipice overhanging a corrie: an islet of greenery surrounded by sheer cliff faces, an emerald embedded in stone, a miniature forest surrounded by impassable ramparts. Navigating the ledge, they reached a learning area. Assembled in an untidy line, Gargoyle children waited for their turn before jumping into the abyss. The less confident among them were practicing gliding while the others were trying out all sorts of acrobatics. Their landings, not always well controlled, were at times accompanied by tears.

"No way I'm starting out here! It's too high."

"You're not going to practice with the babies, are you?"

Neria ignored Imri's protests and went down the ledge and over to the little children's area. The air resounded with the cries and the laughter of the young Gargoyles, who threw themselves off into the void. There was a group of adults supervising, with two mothers among them, carrying their infants pressed against their hearts and swaddled in harnesses. Neria was surprised she found these grotesque creatures so delightful.

"They're so cute!"

"Stop wasting time and jump."

"He smiled at me! Did you see that?"

"Well done. Now, stop your rambling and get in line."

Reluctantly, Neria turned away from the baby and took her place behind a child. The kid looked her up and down before he called out to his buddies. They shoved each other with their elbows and looked at her mockingly.

"You could have found somewhere more private."

"Okay listen up. Keep your body straight, but not rigid. If you lean to one side, you'll turn. Be ready to run when you land. There's not much risk at this height. At worst, you'll just fall flat on your face. We've all been through this."

To reassure herself, Neria flapped her wings and managed to raise herself a couple of inches from the ground. Her turn came and she launched herself out into the void. Her stomach pushed up against her throat, the wind stopped her from breathing. Her flight lasted a few seconds, at the end of which she landed with a crash. She repeated this exercise several times, much to the amusement of her young and far more skillful companions watching on.

After several successful landings, Neria, sweaty and scratched, agreed to test her new talents from more challenging heights and the two friends set out again towards the older children's area. Imri reeled off a whole series of instructions: where to place her head, her arms, her legs, what to do if she started spinning... She interrupted her explanations when a rowdy group approached. One of the teachers was holding a lamp. Neria recognized Anaëlle among the children.

"What are you doing here?"

"I know how to do this, I come evewy day with my class."

"Come here."

"Go away, I'm busy."

"Don't talk to me like that. Why are you standing in line? You can't fly."

"You'll see, it's fun. Your tuwn!

"We'll let them go past, I want to…"

"Hey, Kloups! I'm jumping!"

"No!"

Anaëlle slipped away, ran towards the very end of the ledge and, with a tremendous leap, jumped out into the abyss — her aunt noticed how much the time spent in the forest had hardened her — then she tensed herself, spreading out her arms as if she was going to glide. Neria felt the blood rushing from her limbs. Without a second thought, she threw herself off the ledge and immediately lost control of her trajectory. She realized she would not be able to reach Anaëlle in time. Her screams of terror blended with the yelling of her niece. As she tried to soften her landing, she saw a child had dived in after them and grabbed and held onto the girl with ease. Her own crash prevented Neria from seeing their landing. Having recovered from her shock, she disentangled herself from the shrub she was hanging from and tumbled from her perch with what little remained of her dignity. The failed drops had prepared her for such catastrophic landings.

Three young Gargoyles were already hoisting Anaëlle to the top in successive leaps.

"Wait for me! Anaëlle, come here right now!"

"There's no stopping youth. Leave her be, you can see she's enjoying herself."

"What a ridiculous thing to say. She's going to get herself killed. Did you know about this? Who else knew? Matar?"

Neria hurried as quickly as she could to the summit. The little ones shook their wings and, leaping like an army of fleas, scaled the steep slope with a smile on their faces. Imri reached the top in three jumps while Neria dragged herself up behind her. In the middle of her ascent, she helplessly watched Anaëlle dive again and decided to wait to intercept her. But the little rascals carrying her managed to evade Neria. Her presence made their game all the more interesting. Bright crimson and out of breath, she finally pulled herself up on the platform and, to her great surprise, was cheered by the children. Meanwhile, Anaëlle had dived off once again. So young and she was already slipping away from her... Neria felt defeated but decided not to show it. She raised her arms to the sky, like an acrobat greeting their audience after a somersault, and took her place in the queue amidst the applause.

CHAPTER SEVEN

T he Gargoyle rushed towards the gong, grabbed the mallet suspended from one of the supporting posts, and rhythmically beat a code whose echo bounced off the stone labyrinth walls. Hearing it for the first time, the sound seemed to reverberate in Neria's throat as she swallowed her saliva and slowed her breathing to calm the hammering of her heart. Human troops were advancing to destroy the Colony.

It had all started in the middle of the resting hours, with shrieks and a sudden awakening. She had thought she was back in the hiding place behind the wardrobe and instinctively reached for the knife hanging from her waist. But instead of a leather belt, she had felt the fabric of her nightgown and realized that she was lying on the straw mattress serving as her bed, in the room she shared with her companions and Anaëlle. After Matar had finally acquiesced, the child had moved in with her and become something of their little group's mascot. Frustrated with fatigue, the three adoptive aunts had begged for a return to silence. Neria had taken the still-sobbing Anaëlle in her arms, carried her out of the room, sat down on the ground in the winding tunnel, comforted her, and listened to her terrifying story. Then they went to find Matar.

They had never gone to visit him in his cell before and finding it had proved more difficult than expected. They had wandered through the sleeping hive, waking up other irate Gargoyles, one of whom had even slammed the door in their faces without hearing their explanations. Matar had greeted them with the terrifying look he had at times, when his ferocious bestial nature showed itself on his Human face. But he had listened to their story with surprising patience and, to their dismay, had decided to go and tell Isk about it at once. The elderly Gargoyle's appearance when he opened the door had reinforced Neria's doubts about whether there was really any need to wake him. She had forced her glance on his horns to stop herself from staring at his scruffy hair, his far too thin nightgown, and his half-closed eyes. But at his urging, the Council had hastily assembled in a room where a pot of chalk, slabs of slate stacked in a corner, and a chalkboard that still bore the inscriptions from the night before gave away its normal function. Out of habit or fatigue, Anaëlle had taken a cushion before sitting down on the ground, while the others had opted to wander about the room, signifying their irritation with exclamations and sudden gestures.

Neria had believed — in fact Matar had convinced her — that the Chimeras would accept the gift of prescience with understanding. But Anaëlle had looked so young and distraught to the angry Gargoyles. Any goodwill she had crumbled as they aggressively questioned her, her answers getting shorter, and her chin beginning to tremble.

"Leave her alone! She's already told you everything she knows."

The commotion had stopped and Anaëlle had burst into tears.

"See! You've pushed her too far. Come on, honey, let's get out of here."

"You're not going anywhere."

Barz had approached her, so close that his molten breath had brushed against her face. He towered over her at his full height. Sharp fangs poked out from below his tight lips and his eyebrows furrowed beneath his mighty horns.

"Leave her alone!" shouted Matar. "Is this how you thank her for her loyalty and concern for the future of this Colony?"

"She's kept the child's powers a secret so far. Why's she telling us about them now?"

"Because we're in danger, you fool!"

"I refuse to listen to the mad ravings of a Human and her damned Chimera."

Eyebrows furrowed, jaw thrust forward, hair on edge, Matar had let out a gravelly roar that swept through the room like an icy gust of wind, while Barz's figure became taut and broad.

"Stop that this instant!"

Isk had put himself between the two beasts and flashed furious glances at them.

"Have you no shame? This little girl has shown far more maturity than either of you. Neria, calm her down, please. We'll send out some scouts to see how much truth there is to this vision."

"Scouts risk alerting the Humans."

"A risk is better than uncertainty."

Too anxious to wait with the others for the results of the scouting expedition, Neria had entrusted Anaëlle to Matar and gone to the entrance of the cave. By doing so, she had been one of the first to receive confirmation that Elatek's troops were indeed approaching. Leaning against a wall, she now watched the parade of Gargoyles who, alerted by the sound of the gong, were returning to their homes, and rushing into the depths. Armored in leather garments, warriors arrived from the opposite direction, taking up positions on both sides of the opening.

Isk had always been fair and forgiving, but how would Barz react when he realized that Anaëlle had been telling the truth? Such power could spark terror or, on the contrary, envy. Poor Anaëlle... an unfortunate child whose innocence had been torn apart by nightmarish visions... so young, so lovely, and yet so... terrifying. Noxious fumes seemed to have flooded the cave. Neria longed to feel the wind on her face like when she had jumped from the training cliff. She promised herself that, one day, she would plunge into the abyss without fear, fly over great distances, and go wherever she pleased. She turned away from the sky that sliced through the opening, headed for the entrance to the tunnels, and began to run.

"They caught Blorg and killed him. I saw his head stuck on a spike. Poor old Gargoyle."

Anaëlle slept through the commotion. Matar had fashioned a bed for her out of several cushions and was standing guard. Neria joined them.

"We shall never surrender our home!"

With these words, the furor grew, everyone there shouting louder and louder to drown out the cries of others.

"Send out the patrols..."

"Kill every last one of them..."

"Set some traps for them..."

"Leave... rebuild somewhere else..."

Isk restored silence with a wave of his hand.

"With the turncoat Gargoyles on their side, the Humans will find us within a day, maybe two. Fleeing will force us to give up everything we have, evacuating the colony and only traveling at the pace of the very weakest among us. Our wings may afford us some advantage, yes, but this well-trained army will still pursue us. If we flee, who will make sure our people have access to the right living conditions and that they can live in safety?"

After a show of hands, the Council members made their decision. Barz roared a war cry, repeated by the most bellicose of the Gargoyles. Isk watched their enthusiasm with a troubled expression. Matar shook the elderly Gargoyle by the shoulder and said in a low voice, "The Corrie gives us a strategic advantage."

"We are not soldiers."

"You may lack their experience, but you are fighting for your survival."

In anticipation of the battle to come, the Gargoyles reviewed their various strategies with a frantic restlessness. After a period of grueling work made up of contradictory missions, Neria finally arrived in her room and kissed Anaëlle on her forehead, her eyes closed and breath steady. She lay down, looked up at the ceiling, said to herself that she would never be able to relax, and then fell asleep at once. Her restless sleep, filled with banging and screaming, was interrupted when a hand shook her by the shoulder. Imri stood leaning above her.

Neria's heart beat faster.

"What's the matter?"

Imri signaled for her to be quiet and follow her. Completely awake, Neria sat up and, having noticed that Anaëlle and the other Gargoyles were still sleeping, got dressed before joining her friend out in the corridor.

"I hope you've got a good reason for disturbing me."

"I want to show you something important and, no, it can't wait."

As usual, having barely arrived at the opening, Imri jumped out into the void. Neria did her best to follow her. The sun baked her wings and pierced the fabric of her clothing. Dazzled by the intense brightness, she realized too late that her companion had already begun her descent. Neria hastily performed a passable half-turn, followed by a mediocre landing, and joined Imri under the protective boughs of the bird oak.

"I'd like to be buried here."

"What are you talking about? You're not going to die."

"It's customary for Gargoyles to tell their families exactly where they want to be buried. To mark the place, Gargoyles engrave a rock with their name on it along with some symbols that represent their life. Most Gargoyles go for an isolated, picturesque spot in the middle of the forest. But, you know me, I don't like solitude and I want to be buried here, next to the cave, my adopted home."

Tears welled up in Imri's eyes.

"Don't talk nonsense. If anyone's going to die it'll be me. You're too skilled for a Human to be able to take you down."

113

L. M. RAPP

"I don't plan on just giving up and letting myself be killed, believe me, but you never know... I'd rather be ready for all eventualities."

"So, if I ever, you know... Would you be willing to have me buried here too?"

"Of course I would. I have no problem spending eternity with you."

"As long as it doesn't happen too soon."

They climbed the tree so the Gargoyle could use it as a springboard. The feathers rustled and fluttered around them and seemed to lament the unwelcome intruders. The bird oak gave off a smell of soured milk that grew stronger as they climbed. The strange leaves tickled Neria, who could not help shooing away imaginary insects. Imri wrapped her powerful arms around her and Neria filled her lungs in the vain attempt to make herself lighter. With the Gargoyle's momentum, they dived off before regaining altitude.

The guards posted at the entrance watched them arrive with a disapproving look. One of them barked in Neria's direction, "Matar's waiting for you in the dovecote."

They held back a fit of laughter that finally resounded in the still deserted corridors.

"Why's he chosen a place like that to lecture me?"

"He doesn't want any witnesses. You should be worried. You reckon he's going to offer to clean up bird poo with you?"

"Come with me. After all, it's your fault I'm in this mess."

Imri's ears were the most expressive of her features and Neria rejoiced to see them upright and playful, all thought of death forgotten. While everyone slept and they walked the empty corridors, Neria suddenly felt filled with an energy so intense that it seemed to radiate through the amiable darkness. Imri shook her head.

"The Peddler terrifies me. I don't know how you can put up with him. Anyway, I'm exhausted, you can tell me all about your conversation later. Try not to mention me and don't wake me up unless we're under attack."

Neria advanced, silent and vigilant like when she used to play with Bobka. Since her mutation, she had improved in this regard. The circular room rustled with strenuous activity, filled with clawed feet, pointed beaks, light wings, plump bodies, round eyes, and green crests. Matar had undoubtedly chosen the dovecote due to the daylight that pierced through the ceiling. He had good night vision, but not enough for total darkness. He stood with his transformed face raised to the beam of light, his eyes closed, half man, half tiger — his look of suffering or rest — his arms dangling by his side, indifferent to the soft avian cooing that surrounded him.

"You wanted to see me?"

He was not startled as she had hoped. She thought he was in some kind of trance, but that fleeting impression soon disappeared. He opened his eyes at first, straightened his head, and then turned to Neria with exaggerated slowness.

"I had trouble sleeping," she said, "and I left for some fresh air, but I wasn't really in any danger."

"A prisoner's told us news from Alipaz. Valterone's seized power and, with the support of Elatek, he's planned a campaign of conquest. He's the instigator of this attack on the Colony."

She had become unaccustomed to going out in the middle of the day. Her skin radiated the heat taken in from outside and drops of perspiration ran down her face, back, and sides with exasperating slowness. The brightness suddenly dazzled her, and she stepped back to hide in the darkness. She could still get away, escaping the war and the gaze of others. The walls of the dovecote, like blemishes from a skin condition, gave off a stench of gangrene in which the birds wallowed like bustling rats. Neria would have preferred to have wings covered with feathers, feminine and elegant like those of these birds, but fate had provided her with these hairless, dull limbs.

She was going to show her father, who with all his stature and power had behaved like a coward, the true meaning of courage. She would stay at the Corrie and, at risk to her own life, defend the people who had taken her in.

After Matar's revelations, Neria had not been able to fall back to sleep, with the anticipation of the battle ahead having removed any hint of fatigue. She squatted down and embraced Anaëlle, kissing her plump cheek and her sweet-smelling hair. They were standing in the heart of the Corrie, not far from the training area, in a place assigned to mothers, infants, and the infirm until the end of the fighting. These vulnerable Gargoyles would be concealed behind the walls, but they were not without means in the unlikely event of an enemy breakthrough. Gargoyles learned almost from infancy how to shoot with a bow and arrow and Neria noticed at that very moment a boy of about ten years old parading with his, while a fairly large knife also hung from his waist.

"No other visions then?"

"No."

"You still don't know if we're going to win?"

"No."

"Do you know if... how I'm going to survive?"

"I haven't seen you die."

"Tell me, do you sometimes have nice visions?"

"Yes."

"Why don't you ever talk about them?"

"I don't know. They awe like dweams."

"I'd like you to tell me about them."

Anaëlle described her mother working as a cook. Neria tried to keep a straight face but found it difficult to imagine Paz, the descendant of one of the most distinguished families in the city, engaged in such a degrading task. Then she remembered the dovecote and smiled. She now understood why the separation did not seem to upset Anaëlle. The child described visions of simmering dishes in great detail: cumin stew, lemon chicken, and date-filled pastries. Neria began to salivate. She remembered a lazy summer afternoon when they had savored those flaky pastries with their soft, sugary centers. Nephalie had told Arhel off for having stuffed a whole one in his mouth.

"I've seen you fly too and even do twicks in the sky."

"Have you indeed? What did I look like?"

"A Demon. You're a Demon."

"A what?"

"And you will be vewy beautiful."

Neria burst out laughing and lifted up Anaëlle, twirling her around until she was dizzy, before they both fell down on the ground, out of breath and heads spinning. After having caught her breath again, Neria asked what Demons were like and listened with interest to the babbling of the child.

"Demons are similar to Gargoyles then."

"The wings awe."

The children were playing under the concerned gaze of the adults. Two groups that had previously been playing war games and throwing nuts at one another as ammunition were now fighting; the designated Humans refused to feign their deaths and accept their defeat. Not far from them, a father fretted over the well-being of his wife and three children, the eldest of whom was trying to get their attention with his aerial acrobatics. Against the background of the ochre walls and managed vegetation, a touching mosaic of leather wings, with the warm tones of earth and shadow, spread out in front of Neria. She imagined hers fitting into the scene like a missing piece of a puzzle.

"I've got to go."

"Don't wowwy. I'll stay with Kloups and his family."

For a moment, Neria watched the young boy who was now practicing somersaults with a boundless energy. Since her first flying lesson, Neria had been anxious about the influence of this rascal, but Anaëlle adored him, and his mother had offered her help. Neria noticed her wiping away tears shed in secret before taking the youngest of her children in her arms. She bit her lip. It was not the time to let herself indulge in her emotions. She repeated the usual recommendations to her niece, distracted by her friend's antics, kissed her one last time, and then walked away without looking back.

The Gargoyles drew strength and resolve from the karstic immobility of their fortress. Once the sound of the gong had faded, a feverish hum remained behind, with whispers, weapons brushing against rock, and bodies rustling against each other. Hairy horned faces twisted into aggressive grins, fangs protruding, nervous and flaring nostrils, clawed hands clutching maces, spears, or bows. The Chimeras were waiting. The Humans would attack in the daylight, which they preferred to the night. Anaëlle had described, in her childlike way, a slaughter that would not take place, as the Gargoyles had had time to prepare. Their plan was simple. During the first defensive phase — made all the easier by the Corrie's terrain, difficult for bipeds to navigate, and even more so for an army — the enemy troops would clash against the walls. The Chimeras would watch their pathetic efforts without moving, and then, when the weakened and demoralized Humans began their retreat, they would pursue them and destroy them to the last soldier.

Besides the wide and spacious main openings that saw most of the comings and goings, the façade of the Corrie was riddled with narrow holes, more or less natural. The bulk of the fighters were on the only side accessible to the opposing army, and Neria, along with Imri, Shorka, and Fylis, was posted at the far end in a hall that served as a storeroom. The chances that the Humans would ever manage to get there seemed very slim. Their orders were to defend their stronghold and not to venture out. Not that Neria had imagined such an eventuality. If she jumped out, her flying skills would barely allow her to survive the fall, and as nobody had seen it fit to entrust her with a weapon, she had only her knife to fight with. She was disappointed, but Imri had comforted her and convinced her that the situation would improve with time and that it would all be better after their victory.

The war preparations had awakened in Neria the memory of the three guards ripped asunder, lying in their own blood. She paced up and down, forced herself to sit for a few minutes, and then got up again. The room, with amphorae and bundles against the uneven walls, was of no interest. Her comrades displayed a feigned indifference in a heavy silence. She advanced towards the outer wall, pierced by two differently sized openings, and approached the narrower of the two. A dry heat had replaced the coolness of the night before. As is often the case at that time of year, summer was slow to give way to fall. A hazy sun crept across a yellow sky and made the familiar scenery look like the end of the world was nigh. The gusts of a bitter wind shook the trees while an herbaceous expanse rippled at the foot of the cliffs. Nature, in its brilliance, seemed to wither, dry up, and prepare for death. The Humans were later than expected. Had they got lost on the way? Had they changed their minds? The patrols had reported that the troops were marching in their direction. The deep bass sound of conches heralded the arrival of the first soldiers.

"By Asoas, they think they're on parade!"

"The only thing they're missing is an orchestra…"

An array of giant shields unfolded in a straight line. Behind each one stood an archer and a servant. Men clustered behind them and busied themselves with a mysterious construction. Five units had left the cover of the forest and were organized in a rectangular formation, protected on all sides by crimson shields with blue and yellow embellishments. As their enemies advanced like stubborn insects, the Gargoyles waited for the order to shoot. At the signal, arrows rained down and bounced off the artificial shell with the sound of hailstones. If, by chance, one of them happened to hit a soldier, the ranks immediately corrected their formation and their march continued.

"Don't lean out! They'll see you."

"At this distance? Not a chance. I won't get another opportunity to see a battle like this, so I don't want to miss anything."

Fylis, crouching on the window ledge, squirmed to watch the events unfold.

"Those woodlice don't have a chance of even getting to the walls. Their shields won't be enough."

Barz's formidable battle cry resounded its way into Neria's ears and awakened the Gargoyles from their astonishment. They left the shelter of the cave and plummeted down towards the men to shatter their shields and smash in their skulls with their maces. Shields, heads, and limbs were broken off hither and thither before they fell back into the fray. One Gargoyle lost altitude and, deadly to her dying breath, cut down all soldiers in her path. The Humans retreated, pursued by the Chimera. But the archers, protected by the giant shields, stopped the Chimera's advance, and the Chimera retreated in turn. The fighting, which had begun in a disciplined manner, broke down into terrible chaos before calming down again as each side, entrenched in their positions, regained their strength, and considered new tactics.

Suddenly, the giant shields spread apart and allowed

catapults mounted on wheels to pass. Neria had heard of these, but had, of course, never actually had the opportunity to see them in action. The machines began by first launching waste, fecal matter, and rotten food, then the corpses of Gargoyles who had fallen in battle, before finally catapulting rocks. While these rocks could not destroy the Corrie walls, they made it more difficult to defend and protected the advance of the Human infantry. The armored cohorts reorganized and trampled over the bodies strewn across the battlefield. They reached the Corrie wall, placed long and lightweight ladders against it, and then the infantrymen began their perilous ascent. They climbed with great agility, using only one hand, holding a shield above their heads with the other. Preoccupied with her duty in supplies, Neria intermittently checked to see how the battle was progressing. She saw Matar, a wild beast, forging a bloody trail with his lance and claws while Forg dived, turned, and left behind streaks of death with apparent ease. Yet to Neria, he also seemed as vulnerable as a moth fluttering among razor-sharp needles in a glaring light.

Fylis gave a cry — her hands clutched an arrow stuck in her chest — and fell to the ground. Neria rushed to her aid. Her friend had lost consciousness. She heard the dry slap of a ladder on rock, then a second, and a third. Humans, dispersed along the wall, were trying their luck on less well-defended positions. The three young Chimeras arched over, pushing back the ladder, but the weight of the soldiers climbing them was too much for their combined strength. Imri shouted, "Neria! Go get help! Hurry!"

The deserted corridors went on and on. Before she reached the entrance of the cave, the screams and sounds of fighting warned her of the magnitude of the disaster — the enemy had broken through their defenses. She picked up two abandoned weapons and set off again.

Imri and Shorka were each fighting a Human. More would be coming soon. Neria threw a spear that stuck into the back of Shorka's opponent. The second spear hurtled towards a figure coming through the narrower window. Neria positioned herself in front of the opening, clutched the ladder, and pushed with all her strength. Her features contorted, her teeth clenched, she persisted. Her muscles burned. A soldier was coming towards her. She let go of the ladder, saw a head appear, then shoulders and a torso. He brandished his short sword and moved to strike her down. She dodged his first blow, drew her knife, looked for an opening and pierced his chest. The man's eyes widened, his mouth dropped open without making a sound, and then he fell. Standing by the window, she was afraid to look away, even for a moment, for fear that the next soldier would manage to break through the fragile barrier and clear the way for a storm surge that would sweep them all away. She tried to push away the thoughts of Anaëlle crying that crept in from time to time.

At first, fear gave her energy before fatigue slowed her down. A Human took advantage of her vulnerability to leap through the opening and pounce on her. Reeling from the shock, she threw her arm forward and felt the knife sink into the tender flesh of his stomach. She felt the scream, the hot viscous blood flowing from her opponent's wound. Small in stature and thin, she felt his vital energy as he shook with a vigor made all the stronger by his youth. He lifted his hand. Within it, the glint of a weapon. She parried the blow, knocking over the soldier on his side while the huge torso of another attacker had just appeared. Neria pulled away, ran, grabbed a large stone, and struck him on the temple. He slumped and remained suspended like a blanket left to air on the windowsill. She threw off his inert body. His fall dragged along the next assailant after him and gave her a few moments of respite. She returned to the young man, still alive and wrapping his hands around the knife sunk into his stomach. He turned his sweaty face toward her and mumbled something she did not understand. She grabbed the handle of the knife and pulled. A spasm of pain shook the young soldier as blood poured from the wound. She considered finishing him off but decided against it. He would no longer pose a threat to her.

Before returning to her post, she noticed that Imri and Shorka were still defending the second window. Then she lost track of the time. After an eternity, the procession of men who were all different but made identical by their uniforms — conical helmets, red tunics, and light armor — slowed and then stopped. No one was climbing up anymore. She grabbed the rungs and pushed the ladder, which toppled over without resistance and crashed to the ground with the splintering of broken wood. The sun set on the corpse-strewn battlefield. Neria left the window once again and looked around her. Shorka, leaning against the wall, seemed to be sleeping while Imri, lying flat on her stomach, was motionless. Neria approached and called out her name.

"She's dead."

With half-closed eyes and her clothes saturated in blood, Shorka had spoken in a hoarse, feeble voice. Neria dropped to her knees. She carefully turned over the lifeless body, saw the gaping wound and her unblinking eyes. A wail left her throat, building in intensity, "No, no, no. This can't be happening!"

She covered her face with her hands, swayed for a few moments as if shaken by a gust of wind, before leaping to her feet and running as fast as possible out of the room. She found Barz and, gripped by panic, begged him to come and help her.

The mighty Gargoyle only needed one look to make a diagnosis, "This one might make it. I'll take her with me."

"And what about Imri?"

"Leave her. There's nothing else to be done."

Neria went with Barz to the dining hall, where a makeshift hospital had been set up. Cries, pleas, and the stench of blood, urine, and death welcomed them. The room seemed to have lost its color and Neria leaned against the back of a chair to stop herself from falling. Barz placed the unconscious casualty on a table, head-to-tail with another patient, before ordering Neria to follow him.

"I can't, I need to find my niece."

"Your niece is fine. The soldiers didn't get to the heart of the Corrie. You're a warrior so you come with me."

Unsettled by his words, she looked over her body for a moment, stained with blood that for the most part did not belong to her, and nodded.

As soon as he reached the exit, he took off and flew away. She approached the edge, remembered the lessons her friend had given her, took a deep breath, and jumped off into the void. She managed to stay on course but lost altitude too quickly, narrowly avoided a corpse and landed without falling over. She caught up with Barz, who was surveying the battlefield to identify the wounded, taking the Gargoyles back to the cave, and killing the remaining Humans. When Neria understood what he had expected of her, she recoiled.

"You'd rather they suffer a long death? We don't even have the resources to treat our own people, let alone our enemies... And as soon as they recover, they would just attack us all over again. Anyway, it's what they would have done to us. I'm a Gargoyle of morals, so I'll put them out of their suffering."

He gave a dismissive grunt, shrugged his shoulders, and moved away. As he methodically completed his task, she tried to concentrate on hers — sorting the dead from the wounded — but the terrified screams and cries for mercy disturbed her. Nevertheless, she continued to give first aid to the Gargoyles she found alive and told Barz or any of the others about them, who'd take them back to the cave.

At times, she thought she saw Matar lying on the cold ground and her heart froze in her chest. But no, her tired eyes were just playing tricks on her. A figure emerging from the forest caught her attention. She stepped forward cautiously at first and then ran toward him. She stopped suddenly and, after a few moments of silence, began to cry. Matar approached and hugged her. Shaken by increasingly violent sobs, she broke free and fell to her knees, kicking and clawing at the apathetic earth. When she finally calmed down, she got up and wiped her face with her sleeve. Sinister paints of earth, sweat, blood, and tears adorned her skin.

After the fighting, the Chimera had thrown the corpses of the enemy soldiers into a mass grave and had hastily dug burial sites for their own dead. All that noted the difference between them was an inscription painted on a stone. Who would engrave the rocks in accordance with tradition? Rumors foretold the departure of the Gargoyles from their ancestral home. Neria and some of her comrades buried the body of their friend at the foot of the bird oak. The tree quivered even more than usual, accentuating the blue of its feathers as if for a final homage to a life cut short too soon.

Although the Humans had been massacred to the very last one, Neria could not consider this battle a victory. When it was time to sleep, she avoided looking at the empty place Imri had left behind and kept any memories of her at bay. She wanted to hide her grief from Anaëlle, who had not felt she was in any danger at any time. Exhausted by the day's toil, she lay down beside her and fell asleep, her face wet with lonely tears.

A few days later, Isk invited Neria and Matar to visit him in his cell. His living quarters did not differ much from those of the unmarried, but he enjoyed the luxury of living alone. Neria thought his smile looked forced. His characteristic spark of mischievous youthfulness had disappeared.

"Come in, come in, sit down! Shall I get you some tea?"

With a glance, Neria looked around the cell in its meticulous cleanliness and the orderly harmony of the few objects that furnished it. A rock engraving depicting stylized animals decorated the main wall. Various weapons and tools were hung on the others, as well as an obligatory straw mattress. They settled down on a braided mat, decorated with a few cushions.

"I see you're admiring my work. Engraving takes time and attention to detail. I'd planned to devote my life to it after I left the Council, decorating all the walls... I'm afraid I'll have to postpone the project to a later date."

With slow, deliberate movements, Isk poured a carob-based drink into ceramic bowls, before offering them a plate of plump cookies that Neria thought looked delicious, although she did not dare take one.

"I wanted to thank you, Neria, for your courage in battle. Your bravery and composure in defending the colony saved us from more severe losses. I'd like to offer you this as a token of our gratitude. She would have liked you to have it."

He picked up a bow from beside him and handed it to her. Neria recognized it immediately. She ran her finger on the leather strap wrapped around the handle. She remembered how Imri had replaced the old one, damaged from use. That day, at the end of their shift, they had decided to leave their group and go to the river. Imri had gone first and, flying with a perfect trajectory, had landed on the bank. Neria had tried to follow her but had crashed twenty yards or so from her friend, before catching up with her on foot ready to face the usual mockery. But that morning, Imri had greeted her with a smile. She had taken a strap out of a bag hanging from her belt, soaked it in water, and wrung it out. Then she began to bind it around the wood, each loop taut and aligned with the previous one. Her dexterous fingers made the task seem effortless.

"What's it for? Is it decorative?"

"The strap makes the bow stronger and makes the arrows faster."

The task complete, they had lain back on a large flat rock to silently contemplate the sunrise.

"You are now part of the family," started Isk, "which will make our separation all the more difficult."

"Separation?"

"We're leaving the Corrie."

"Why?"

"We've suffered too many losses to risk another battle. Other soldiers, better prepared, will come and finish the job."

"Were there Humans living here before you?"

"No. Don't trust Elatek's nonsense, Humans are strangers to this land."

"Then you have every right to eliminate them."

"Some people think like you, but I believe we could live with the Humans if they left us in peace. We have some humanity in us ourselves. You look surprised. Don't let this exterior fool you, I may be more Human than you or Anaëlle. For thousands of years, we have all had Human blood flowing in our veins."

"I've decided to come with you."

"That's not possible."

"I don't see why not."

"We're going into unknown territory."

"That doesn't scare me."

"You won't be able to come with us. Your flying leaves something to be desired."

"We can walk. I'll go with the wounded. I'll help them, I can work now... and fight."

"It's too dangerous," Matar intervened. "I promised your

mother I'd take you to safety and I don't want to have to tell her you're dead. Besides, you're not even a Gargoyle."

"What do I care what I am!"

She reddened in anger, but tried to keep her composure, "I look like a Gargoyle, my wings are the same and my vision, my hearing... I don't understand. What's the matter with you? Oh, I see. You won't accept me because I'm different?"

"Demons have a bad reputation."

Neria's hand trembled as she placed it on the polished wood of the bow.

"How can you hate people you don't even know?"

"Some people have controversial, even dangerous customs and beliefs."

"I love Gargoyles and their customs. I want to share your fate."

"Matar thinks it's best for you to take your chances elsewhere."

"Where?"

"We'll go to a Free City. Mixed."

"What does that mean?"

"Chimeras and Humans living together."

"No way."

"There'll be Gargoyles there too."

"Not the same ones. I've got friends here, friends..."

Matar watched Neria with the same expression he gave his donkey when he refused to move, while Isk's face had taken on a vacant, tired look.

"You can untie me now."

The Gargoyles had chosen to begin their journey in the middle of the night. At the edge of the forest, Matar, Neria, and Anaëlle, gripped by a sudden chill, watched their departure. Loaded with equipment, provisions, and the child sitting on his croup, Onyx kicked up the ground with his hoof. Neria contemplated her bound wrists for a moment, then raised her eyes towards the outlines of the cliffs. An initial encounter marred by terror and a separation fogged by sorrow. She could see the top of the bird oak, at the foot of which Imri lay buried. Neria had dipped her finger in a syrupy mixture and had traced marks on the rock, but she feared the winter rains would wash away her clumsy epitaph and that soon no one would know who slept in the grave.

She had thought she would be able to forget about her father, who had gorged himself on the lives of her hosts to extend his influence of misery and seclusion. Why had he chosen to attack the Gargoyles when there were so many other Chimera communities living in this forest? He had destroyed the one place where she had felt free and would continue to pursue her until she fell back into his grasp. She had wanted to go deeper into the forest, to increase the distance between herself and Alipaz, to cling on to the friendly presence of the Gargoyles. She realized now that she had been thinking mostly of herself, if she had been thinking at all, like a fish writhing on the ground desperate to get back into the water. Her attempt to escape, her last chance, had failed. Matar had foiled her plans with humiliating ease. Despite everything she had done, she found herself back at the starting point, with the grumpy Peddler and his donkey for companions on the borders of a new world she did not wish to explore.

But rather than following a group of wounded Gargoyles into a dangerous forest, Anaëlle needed a stable, organized life that only a city could offer. She had stopped crying and was stroking Onyx's neck with her free hand, holding her cane with the other, as if reassured by the presence of this tiny weapon. The head of her doll, buried in her tunic, protruded from her collar. Icy gusts of wind shook the trees. A cloud, darker than the others, took flight as the Gargoyles drifted away and vanished like smoke carried by the breeze.

"Can I trust you? You're not going to try to run away again?"

Neria, unable to speak, nodded. After Matar had untied her bonds, she patted the donkey's thick neck and, for once, the animal tolerated her advances.

Matar pointed to a tiny black spot that was growing, "Forg's coming with us."

"Why?"

The branches of a nearby oak swayed under the weight of the newcomer as Neria feigned indifference. They had planned to travel northward under the canopy of the forest, pass Alipaz, and then fork westward to reach the land of the Free Cities. They walked in a sulky silence, interrupted from time to time by Forg's calls. He went ahead of them in an erratic flight, interspersed with frequent stops in the treetops. Neria carried her new bow on her shoulder and her knife on her belt, two mementos from loved ones. After some hours of walking, they reached a glade. Unlike the usual clearings that, caused by a fallen tree or a particularity in the soil, tended to have a wild, natural appearance, this one, with its orderly bushes and a path meandering between them, seemed tamed and welcoming. Neria stopped suddenly when she noticed the Source in its center.

Forg, who had gone ahead of them, held a bouquet in his hand. The flowers, which he threw into the black water one by one, floated for a few moments before disappearing as if swallowed up by a hungry mouth devouring them from below. After the last stalk had gone, he snapped out of his contemplation.

"We come here to honor the memory of those who weren't buried according to our tradition. My parents..."

This Source had another purpose than its role in Alipaz, yet it remained ever linked to death. Neria yielded to the temptation and gazed into the impenetrable mirror. Images chased one another, at first of Gargoyles flying in a dense swarm, Isk at their head, Barz behind, and others advancing with difficulty through thick vegetation. Then the visions changed and Alipaz appeared, decorated in red, filled with joy and sunshine. Neria became lost in the streets of her childhood, contemplating the façades of the Temple and her home, more alluring than ever, with its bright stones, its luxurious furniture, its colorful tapestries... The picture was shattered with a motion, an arm stretched out like a call for help, before sinking away, and disappearing. A scream...

When Neria awoke from her trance, Forg held her and stopped her from falling into the abyss. She tried to explain the hold that the Source had held over her since she was a child.

"What a family! A More-Than-Pure tyrant, a Dreamer, and now this! What else have you hidden from us?"

Neria caressed the soft grass, while the others stood around her. Two pairs of hooves, Forg's crooked and hairy legs, Matar's trousers, two canes... and Anaëlle's smile.

"I have visions too. At first, they're harmless, like colorful paintings, then they change... I'm worried about my mother. I saw her drown."

"And you wanted to jump into the water to save her."

"Maybe, I don't know."

"Only the Dryads know the mysteries of the Source, but we haven't seen their kind around here for a long time."

A flash of lightning broke through the twilight and interrupted their conversation. They set off on their adventure once again as the rain poured down.

CHAPTER EIGHT

Nephalie continued to stay silent. She, who in recent years had made him accustomed to her pretenses of weakness and sensitivity, had proved to be more resilient than he could ever have imagined. Too emotional in the moments that required strength and stubborn when she should have given in. But once so pretty... In their youth, only Ellane could compete with her beauty. They had both rejected him... at first...

He knew she had something to do with the girls' disappearance since she had bribed the guard to leave his post. Valterone had already forgotten the face of the foolhardy man who now lay in an unmarked grave. He looked up at the large portrait of Elatek leading Humanity to Victory and suppressed a grimace of disgust. He spent a lot of time in the Council Chamber, which he preferred to keep deserted to quietly enjoy its lavish elegance: the exquisite wooden floor, the many windows adorned with adjustable blinds, and the walls decorated with tapestries depicting the legend of Creation. And most importantly, the oval table, enormous and dark, surrounded by ten varied golden chairs, each one carved with different motifs evoking the role of the More-Than-Pure who would have the privilege of resting his posterior upon it. Indeed, the one that bore the burden of Valterone looked more like a throne than a chair.

Dazzled by the parchment spread out before him, he leaned

back and closed his eyes. No, he should not have married Nephalie, a catastrophic choice for such an ambitious man. Her parenting had been dismal, and her faulty genes had produced a mutant, a disturbed lunatic, and two idiots. Many of the More-Than-Pure had been eager to marry for a second or even a third time, but he had been hesitant. He was reluctant to recommit himself and, for the moment, preferred to settle for the occasional mistress.

His own mother had taught him the dangers of weakness and love; as far back as he could remember, there had always been arguments between his parents. Whenever they happened, he would hide under his bed and wait for them to pass. The last one still echoed in his memory. A crash of broken dishes, followed by absolute silence, had interrupted the shrieking. He would have remained cowering in his hiding place, but his mother had started insistently screaming and calling for him. Terrified, he left his dust-ridden hiding place and went down the stairs one by one. Each step took an immense effort of will. He could not remember why the servants had left that day, but they had abandoned him to face his mother all alone. She had, in her fury, broken an amphora of oil over her husband's skull and he lay in a greasy puddle on the kitchen floor, his mouth gaping open like a salted fish. His mother's size and strength had always astounded Valterone, but what she had done this time had left him dumbfounded. It was said that a fit of madness could give enormous strength and she had lost her mind. His nerve shattered, he felt a debilitating weakness and began to cry. In between his tears, he had watched the erratic pacing of the terrifying woman as she screamed and pulled out her hair. Would he have managed to escape if she had ever come for him?

His father, who had survived against all odds, had abandoned them after this incident and Valterone was left alone with this unpredictable woman. A few moments of joyful bonding had not managed to alleviate his fear of another fit of rage. He scrutinized her moods like a fisherman watches for a storm and endured without complaint the slaps and spankings which, although painful and humiliating, did not put his life in any danger. He only cried when she locked him in the cellar, devoid of all light.

A few months later, maybe a year or so, one sentence spoken in a calm tone during a chance meeting at the market had heralded the disaster to come.

"Look, Vally, it's the woman who stole your father from us."

Without saying another word, she had parted the crowd, indifferent to her son who had frozen in place. The reptile-woman had turned around, a peach in her hand, and had immediately recognized the lady coming towards her. Her smile had suddenly faded. His mother had wasted no time with explanations and had, as a greeting, thrown her fist against the reptile-woman's fragile nose. She had collapsed and brought a little girl clinging onto her skirt down with her as she fell. The girl, following a survival instinct, had hurried away from the fight on all fours to get away from the violence of the adults. Staggering, she had stood up, and had made a long harrowing whine that died away before being instantly revived. She was crying loudly with the tenacity of children of that age. Her chubby feet protruded from a plain dress stained with peach juice. The crown of flowers that had adorned her greenish head lay broken on the ground.

The reptile-woman, exhausted, had dragged herself over the litter-strewn dirt while the wronged woman had continued to lash out at her. The onlookers, who had initially howled with laughter at the sight, had then tried to stop her. The first who dared to intervene was dealt a tremendous slap before three men combined their efforts and were eventually able to separate them. Her mother had resembled a rabid beast, her eyes rolling back and forth, a sneer of hatred distorting her beautiful face. She had calmed down after the guards had shackled her wrists and ankles, letting herself be carried away like a broken scarecrow. When they arrived at the guardhouse, they had noticed the boy, with one of them having taken him to the orphanage.

Fifteen days later, his grandparents, whom he did not know, had finally collected him. They had likely saved his life because he had neither the talent to make friends nor the ability to defend himself at that time.

A few knocks on the door brought Valterone out of his reverie.

"Divine Valterone, an infantryman is requesting an audience with you."

The More-Than-Pure looked up and put down his quill. He opened and closed his right hand to relax its tense muscles before examining the intruder's impeccable attire: a short, fringed tunic embroidered with red motifs, the tall, supple leather boots, a metal circle in the middle of his broad chest, a well-groomed beard, and a conical helmet fastened onto his head. For a moment, Valterone lamented the loss of Adamek, who had been killed just as he was beginning to make himself useful. The guards assigned to the Building of Omnipotence seemed to be chosen for their looks rather than their talent.

"I haven't the time to waste, send him away."

"He's come from Barham Forest and claims to have information for you."

"You could have said that earlier, you fool! Send him in!"

The guard completed a faultless about-face, disappeared for a moment, and returned accompanied by a ragged soldier before leaving for good. The newcomer, with his back straight and marching into the chamber at a military pace, bent the knee and put his hand to his heart. A reddish residue of dye was still visible under the filth of the rags hanging from his emaciated body.

"Hail to you, Divine Valterone! Infantryman Mavom at your service!"

"I'm listening."

"Well, here's the thing. Those cowards, I mean, the Gargoyles... Well, they surprised us at night. See, it wasn't so bad at first. We fought them off. We lost a few men, of course. But our morale was holding up. Uh..."

Valterone got to his feet, moved a chair, and sat on the edge of the table with his arms crossed. The soldier did not know why, but he preferred the previous arrangement with the table between them. He felt the urge to take a step back but sensed that this would be the wrong move, a little like facing a snarling dog that is only waiting for a sign of weakness to pounce on you. The Star of Alipaz stared at him, his face unmoving. Mavom cleared his throat.

"Well... So, we were in high spirits, right, we wanted to finish them off, you see. So we got ready, and we attacked. Only, well, there were too many of them. Even their females were fighting! And they're tough. And obviously the fact they could fly gave them an advantage too. Don't forget that."

Mavom swallowed his spit and wondered once again if his chosen career was really for him. He had joined for the money and had never intended to die for any job, especially not in some foul forest teeming with filthy vermin and skulking monsters. He had tried to get away before the battle, but the officers had demonstrated little concern for his health problems and assigned him to a pompous fellow, a heavyset man who shouted orders while Mavom broke his back carrying his shield. At first, he felt protected by the oversized object. But when the monsters had swooped from the air and the dandy had collapsed, his face bashed in with a mace, he had realized that these savages, with no discipline or knowledge of military strategy, were going to slaughter every last one of them. He had consequently waited for a lull in the fighting before starting his retreat towards the trees. If his comrades had caught him crawling on all fours like a tortoise, they would have executed him on the spot. He dropped his shield at the edge of the forest and sought shelter. When he stumbled across a Gargoyle in a grove, his already shaken nerves almost gave in. He had then noticed the condition the beast was in, a strong male covered with dirty brown fur, a big hooked nose, small sunken eyes, and ears like sails on a boat. Blood was running from his skull into his mouth and his head bobbed in a daze. Mavom had finished him off, taken his weapons, a bow and a good quality cutlass, and then left.

He had later found one of those humming trees, climbing it and hiding in its canopy. He had become well accustomed with the species because he had spent many a harrowing hour in it, lying in ambush in the hope of surprising a lone Chimera. The others, who had thought he was a fool, would have done better to do likewise. The asthmatic wheezing of this strange tree had covered his own and its cheese-like smell had thrown his pursuers off his scent. From his perch, he had seen brave soldiers racing to escape the patrols of flying monkeys. If anyone other than him had survived, he had not come across them. He had spent the night shaking in unison with the giant feather duster and then waited until the middle of the day to come back down.

"Anyway, to cut a long story short… So, when the captain realized we were all going to die, he sounded the retreat. And we retreated. Well, the ones that were left. Me and my group, there weren't many of us. About ten or so. And then they came after us. A pack of wild animals! You can't imagine! We fought. The others were all killed. I finished off the last one and took his weapon. And here it is, let me give it to you."

He pulled out a large, strangely crafted cutlass from his belt, held it out while bowing, and suddenly felt the cursed forest closing in on him. Had he made a mistake by coming here? Valterone examined the object, took it out of its sheath a couple of inches, and then thrust it back in with a quick jerk. He repeated this several times and seemed to have forgotten the presence of the infantryman.

Prior to the assault, a Gargoyle they had captured had revealed some interesting information. Among other things, he had mentioned a captive human child with an unusual name. This knowledge had strengthened their resolve: their mission was not only one of conquest, but of liberation and protection of the city and its inhabitants. For if the Star's granddaughter could have been kidnapped by the rebels and their accomplices, then no one would be safe. Mavom, though not very enthusiastic about the idea of dealing with these creatures, had felt a kind of legitimate rage that had sustained him at the beginning of the fighting. The information he revealed about the child and her Chimera sidekick seemed to arouse the Star's interest and he stopped playing with the blade. The soldier felt reassured. The promotion would be coming soon, no doubt with a substantial reward.

With a speed and precision that caught Mavom off guard, Valterone drew the blade and stuck it in his belly. The weapon came out with a slurping sound and traveled in an elegant arc before slicing through the man's neck, causing him to slump to the ground. As he lay dying, Valterone crouched down and searched the dying man's rags for a piece of cloth clean enough to wipe the stained blade on. Then he called the guard. At the sight of the corpse, the guard suppressed a fleeting expression of surprise, then left. He came back with spotless clothes and was followed by an assistant carrying everything necessary to clean the chamber. Disinterested in their activity, Valterone removed his soiled clothes and washed the blood from his skin. He knew that news of the execution would spread through the building and later through the city, although he didn't mind, on the contrary. Yet he did feel that his position demanded a certain decorum and he refused to appear in public wearing dirty clothes and looking like a butcher.

He went out and took a staircase that led him, as he descended, to a more authentic reality, raw and unrefined. Each level seemed to be stripped of a layer of hypocrisy. When he arrived in the basement, guards saluted him, but he gestured that he would rather be left alone. He picked up a lamp and a key and continued to the dungeons. On both sides of a corridor, smelling of damp and filth, were cells with miserable wretches lying within, following him with their gaze. The cellars of the Building of Omnipotence served as a rather cramped prison for a city the size of Alipaz. But the More-Than-Pure did not believe in rehabilitation or incarceration as a means of punishment. Those who were sent to the prison were, for the most part, executed after a matter of days or forced into slavery. Valterone stopped in front of a cell, inserted the key in the lock, and opened the barred door. The pile of rags tossed aside in the corner awoke as he entered.

"Tell me something about Paz. Why did she kill Adamek?"

"You know very well he beat her."

"If every battered woman murdered their husband, half the men in the city would be dead. She could have asked her father to intervene and gone back to live with him. Why take such a drastic step?"

"She knew he would never change, she felt trapped, I have no idea. She didn't tell me about it."

"By the way, I have news of your granddaughter. She died during the attack on Gork's Corrie. I've decided to rename it by the way. I'm thinking of Valterone's Corrie... What do you think? But first, we'll have to clean up that dump, I can't have my name associated with such a filthy hovel."

"You're lying."

The kick flew out like a reflex.

"When are you going to understand that the time for insolence is over? And I assure you that I am indeed thinking of changing the name. Gork sounds utterly ridiculous to me, as does everything to do with Gargoyles for that matter."

He crouched down beside the figure, stroked her shaggy hair, and spoke in a deep yet tender voice.

"Look where your shenanigans have gotten you. Just give in and you can get out of here. I'll put you up in a quiet, little house, not far from Alipaz. Elinor can come and visit you. We've lost Anaëlle, but we can be grandparents again soon. How does that sound? Should I start looking for that house?"

As the torturer had held her head under the water during her last session, Nephalie had decided to put an end to her suffering. She recalled the faces of her children and her granddaughter, then breathed in. The man had thought she was putting up a fight and had pressed down even harder, but Valterone had realized at once and had restored her to life. The cold had never left her since. She, who wanted to end it all, had only succeeded in weakening herself, a slow means of escape, but undoubtedly preferable to all the torment.

She gathered her strength to free herself from the trance in which the tender voice, the caressing hand, and the dream of an almost normal existence had plunged her.

"I know nothing."

Valterone clutched a handful of her hair and bolted upright. She screamed, compelled by his strength and her pain, hanging from her husband's hand. He brought his face close to hers.

"You have betrayed your race, your country, and your family."

"I'm guilty, I know… I'm paying for the mistake of marrying you."

"You and your defective genes…"

"My genes? What will the guards think when they find out about your mutant son? You, the great champion of purity?"

"I advise you to keep your mouth shut. If word gets out that you've created a monster, Elinor will follow you to the Source. And don't worry about me, I'll be fine. Look at you, old, ugly, and stupid! You reek and sicken me."

He threw her to the ground, kicked her in the stomach, and watched her writhe in pain. After a while, she regained the use of her voice, and her speech rose from her chest like feeble gasps.

"I don't care about your threats. You already did the worst thing you could have done when you killed Arhel. I would have loved him…"

"You know what? I don't need your confession. Anaëlle and Neria have mutated, haven't they? They died during the assault on the Corrie. And if by some miracle they escaped, I will find them. One way or another, this problem will be solved while you're rotting in that cell. I have all the time in the world."

After a series of formal and amicable greetings, the two men sank into the soft cushions of the living room armchairs. Upon the low table was an ornate platter with glasses, an elegant decanter filled with scarlet liquid, and, on glazed ceramic plates, tiny cakes sprinkled with powdered sugar.

"To what do I owe the pleasure of your visit?"

"Elatek sent me."

Valterone's smile faded. This time, Berdomy had not come to reminisce about the days of their youth or to slander their acquaintances. He was acting as Elatek's emissary, and that name reduced all their years of friendship to dust.

"I have been asked by our Supreme Pathfinder to review the situation and to decide whether or not to return our troops to the capital. We have heard unpleasant rumors. Rumors fueled by the mysterious death of your son Arhel, the unexplained disappearance of your daughter and granddaughter, and, finally, the murder of Adamek by his own wife. Between you and I, these family squabbles would be less troubling if the campaign hadn't gotten off to such a poor start."

"Well, I do appreciate you bringing these issues up."

"Oh, really? Then please go ahead, I'm listening."

"Arhel, rest his soul, died from natural causes. The rebels kidnapped Neria and Anaëlle with Nephalie's assistance. As for Paz, she surely joined the insurrection, there can't be any doubt."

"Elatek will not be satisfied with these explanations."

"The rebels are targeting my family because they see me as their most dangerous foe. We must cleanse Barham Forest and the heretical cities of the degenerate creatures who continue to spread their corrupting genes and ideas with impunity. I want our region to be considered, not as a remote province, but as the bow of the ship that will spread our glorious civilization to the primitive populations. By doing so, we will expand our territory and, at the same time, solve the problem of hunger and overcrowding in the south by giving farmland and new economic opportunities to those who will move there."

"I know your plan and Elatek has sanctioned it. But you seem to have met with unexpected resistance; the assault on Gork's Corrie failed."

"Come now! Cast your informants into the Source, they are utterly worthless. The fortress has fallen to us, and the fleeing Gargoyles will be slaughtered to the last survivor."

"But they wiped out three companies! If they had counterattacked, they would have taken Alipaz."

Valterone erupted into thundering laughter that died alone.

"Sorry, I thought you were joking. We are already preparing our next conquest and, as you know, our researchers have developed an unstoppable weapon."

"I wonder if you are cut out for this task. After all, you have failed to protect your family."

"I doubt you will ever find anyone more determined. I also have more knowledge of the terrain and the parties involved."

With his pudgy hand, Berdomy picked up an empty plate, placing a few sweets on it, which he wolfed down before raving about their taste. He gobbled a few more, then poured himself two glasses of ice-cold drink, which he gulped back one after the other. Valterone forced himself to relax. A cookie disintegrated into sand in his mouth, scratching his throat before he hastily washed it down with the overly sweetened pomegranate juice.

"You always did know how to hire good help. Your cook, at any rate, is simply remarkable."

That Berdomy! Such a sycophant. But rather honest... A thief, a murderer, like all of them, but with a code of conduct. Faithful to his wife, for example. What was her name again? A chubby little blonde, with a shrill voice, a gossip. How did he put up with her? He could have done better. He had fallen in love with Nephalie too when they were young. Pathetic...

147

"Joking aside, if the taking of Roguelle is unsuccessful, your head will be the first to roll. If you fail, I can't help you. My life is more precious to me than our friendship. So..."

"I understand."

"There's something bothering me... How could Nephalie just agree to hand her daughter and granddaughter over to the rebels? It just doesn't add up."

"I have no idea. I'm beginning to think she's lost her mind."

"She must have had a reason."

He thought it was a mistake at first and was just about to call the guards back when the old woman, thin and haggard, dressed in filthy rags, smiled at him.

"My, how you've changed!"

"Ah, Berdomy... And I thought you knew how to flatter a woman. Of course, my looks leave a little to be desired, but you could have pretended. It doesn't matter... I'll be dead soon and this will all be over."

She had strained herself up to speak to him. Her body gave off such an abominable odor that it seemed to have already started to decompose.

"How can he subject you to this kind of treatment? He loved you, you're the mother of his children..."

"Don't worry, Valterone takes care of his loved ones in his own way. There'll be no sign of violence on my corpse. He'll just pretend I died of some illness, avoid another scandal, and then everything will go back to normal."

"Why did you give your granddaughter to the Chimeras?"

"I don't want to lie to you, but I won't say anything else. He knows I won't betray our secrets."

"If you just explain it all to me, maybe I can help you."

"Just stop, you're wasting your time. I've accepted my fate."

"You should've married me."

"You didn't ask."

"You knew that I loved you."

"Of course, but you never say anything."

"The competition was rather tough."

"Yes, Valterone had a way with women. I should have killed him when I had the chance, but I lacked the courage. I don't have the backbone of my daughter-in-law. See? You did well not to marry me."

A joyless laugh broke out from her throat, ending in a coughing fit.

"I have to go. I'm going back to the capital."

"Berdomy."

"Yes?"

"How did a good man like you turn out so evil?"

He purposefully dusted off his clothes. When he lifted his face, his expression had hardened.

"I live in the moment. Certain opportunities came up that I couldn't refuse. Besides, I can't stand the smell of Chimeras, all that fur and feathers…"

He left without another glance at the woman he had once loved, then went to find the guard, gave him money and instructions: a change of diet for the prisoner, a weekly bath and clean clothes, all to be kept secret from her husband. He brushed aside the man's protests with a wave.

"If he finds out, tell him you were doing as I said. He won't dare punish you."

Berdomy joined his retinue and ordered an immediate departure. He was eager to leave this city.

"It's so cold. I should have brought a shawl."

Elinor tightened the collar on her cloak, blew into her hands, and hurried along.

The prospect of seeing her mother had excited her so much that she had rushed outside without thinking. Dear Bobka — she had repressed the urge to kiss him — had offered her the carriage, but the guards had objected to this idea and insisted on the utmost discretion.

She had fled the family home, now gutted, its inhabitants torn from its entrails. Her sister missing, her mother imprisoned, and her father often absent, the responsibilities fell on her and Ellane. They both wandered aimlessly and passed each other in the deserted rooms like two forgotten ghosts.

Before leaving, Nephalie had given a few instructions to the kind, sweet, yet rather incompetent Elinor. Both a blessing and a curse, her beauty, which had won her the love of Draz, seemed to rule her existence. No one ever confided in her, her own family didn't take her seriously, and yet... they would be shocked if they were to learn the cause of their long engagement. But this stage of her life was coming to an end. She wanted to be in control of her own destiny, otherwise, she might lose her mind. Despite the danger, Draz had promised her that they would be married soon. She could no longer bear to live in suspense, dangling like an overripe fruit that could crash to the ground at any moment.

The guard in front of her went down a narrow, foul-smelling alley. Elinor's heart beat faster. Cramped, rundown hovels had replaced the simple yet well-maintained houses, and their emaciated inhabitants stared at them with a sullen look. She stood still. The second guard, smaller than his companion and friendlier too, almost bumped into her.

"What's the matter, Miss Elinor?"

"I want to go back. Come with me."

"But why? We're almost there."

"I find it unusual that my father has summoned me to such a bad neighborhood, and I won't move another step without a good reason."

"There's been an accident and your mother isn't feeling well."

"Is it serious?"

"Very. At least that's what we've been told. We're just following orders, you see."

Elinor considered leaving the soldiers and returning home alone, an unseemly course of action for a woman of her status and one that could also prove dangerous. Still, the whole situation seemed strange to her, even though Valterone had made it clear that he had discreetly settled Nephalie in a quiet, little house to save face. And what better place to hide an outcast than in this forlorn neighborhood?

The wind whipped around her neck and under her clothes.

"Would you rather we escort you home?"

"Oh, yes! Thank you!"

"Really?"

The tall, brooding one was sizing her up. A muddied stare filtered through his tired eyelids. He took her for a fickle child. "Come on, it's just two streets away. You might get us into trouble."

The friendlier of the two was smiling. His steady gaze and the lock of blond hair on his forehead made him look like a young boy. Elinor adjusted her veil, which the wind was set on ruffling.

"Let's go! Hurry up."

A few minutes later, they arrived at a decrepit hovel with closed shutters.

"Go on in."

"You're not coming with me?"

"No, but here... I'll hold the door for you."

She entered a dark room with a musty smell.

"Father?"

The door slammed shut, plunging her into darkness. She tried to open it to no avail and pounded on the coarse wood, shouting, "Let me out!"

"Don't be afraid."

"Who's there?"

She knew that voice.

"An old friend, an admirer."

"Let me out! You can't keep me prisoner like this. When

my father finds out…"

"He won't be happy at first, but he'll understand."

She clutched the handle and shook it, screaming, "Open the door! I beg of you! Have mercy!"

The man wrapped his arms around her. She turned and shoved him away with all her might. She managed to push him away a couple of inches. He seized her by the wrists and dragged her inside into the depths of the room. She struggled and they began a sinister dance in the silence, staggering and jerking, punctuated by grunts and wails. As she toppled over onto the bed, her head hit the wall and she screamed.

"Don't be afraid. A big girl like you. You'll see, you'll like it."

Suddenly, she realized who he was. He brusquely spread her legs open and pressed his pelvis against hers. She smelled the fragrance of fresh sheets and the stench of his fetid breath.

"Wait a moment, I just need a little time… This is such a surprise. No, wait, I'd be more cooperative if I just understood a little more… if I had time to get comfortable… You're treating me like the first harlot you can get your hands on… to belittle me, to humiliate my father?"

"No, of course not."

"So why not talk first? Besides, that walk made me thirsty. Bring me a glass of water."

"I'll do you one better. A good glass of Karcar to help you relax."

"Excellent idea."

Zelimo stepped away and released her from his weight.

Calm, almost detached, she followed the muffled sound of his footsteps on the bare earth. She got up, fixed her hair, and stepped forward.

"Ouch."

"Are you all right, my sweet?"

"I bumped into the corner of the furniture, but it's okay, I found..."

She heard the sound of flint on steel, then a soft glow lit up the room. An amphora was leaning against the wall. Two plates, two glasses, and a metal pitcher were laid on a narrow table. No cutlery... no forks or knives... The plates were laden with an assortment of smoked meat, olives, and dried figs. She had not believed Zelimo capable of such refinement... or such candor. She looked up at him; the shadow that crept across his features gave him a skeletal appearance.

"I've even planned some delicacies for afterward... I treasure the well-being of my future wife."

"Future wife?"

"Well, yes... I intend to free you from that indecisive Draz. It pained me so to see such a beautiful flower wither away."

"Ah yes, Draz..."

She would not be able to lift the amphora and the pitcher looked too flimsy...

"You can tell me, he doesn't like women, does he? You would have had a baby by now if I were him."

"No, no, leave it. As your future wife, I would rather serve you."

"What a charming girl! I knew we would get along."

He embraced her, kissed her on the mouth, and mashed his lips against her teeth. His tongue found its way in… She turned her head away.

"I'm not really used to that."

"I know, that Draz is useless… But you'll learn quickly, you'll see. Come on, back to bed, I can't wait anymore."

"Just a glass of wine… I need to relax… let me pour you some. Sit down, just a moment, just a moment."

He settled down with a satisfied look on his face. She grabbed the chair and swung it with all her might at his repulsive smile. He slumped backward. Without delay, she rushed over to the window. Despite her fear of seeing the two soldiers there, she opened the shutters. The house had no window panes. She heard Zelimo whining and stirring. She put her knee on the sill, pulled herself up, and jumped into the deserted alley. The soldiers had gone. They must have left to avoid drawing attention. Sounds came from inside. She started to run. To the right, then to the left past the well. She wasn't familiar with this neighborhood and was afraid of getting lost. Then right… or left. She kept running forward, but she didn't recognize anything anymore. She had made a mistake, she needed to turn back, but she didn't dare. The houses were identical in their ruin. She forced herself to slow down; two women on a doorstep looked at her in amazement. A disheveled aristocrat, alone, unescorted…

"Which way's the Temple?"

The more elderly of the two pointed a crooked finger. Elinor thanked her and resumed her march. She hoped the woman hadn't lied. Why would she? But even with her clue, after making two or three more turns, she felt lost once again. Four guards appeared on the other side of the street; she could ask them for directions. Perhaps they would even agree to escort her?

"Stop that woman!"

Elinor spun around. Zelimo, enraged and glistening with blood, had found her. A door slammed shut. The girl's head whirled from side to side, the guards ran, and Zelimo drew nearer.

The sun was setting. By now she should have been at home, overseeing preparations for her father's meal. Her miserable life in the large, empty house was coming to an end... but not in the way she had hoped.

"Elinor!"

She recognized his voice before she saw him. She turned and saw Draz coming out of a perpendicular alley. She rushed to meet him. He grabbed her hand and led her on a frantic run. The guards pursued them. Blood pounded in her ears. Draz was pulling her so hard she almost fell over.

"Don't slow down! Just keep going!"

She could hear the heavy footsteps of their pursuers. After a while, which felt like an eternity, he stopped in front of a ladder.

"Climb it!"

She could not climb; she had no strength left.

"Climb it, quickly!"

She put her foot on the first rung. He pushed her or carried her. Without really knowing how, she found herself on the roof.

He lifted the ladder and put it beside her, then they lay down together on the ground. He gestured that she would need to stay quiet.

"Calm down. I didn't want to hurt you, but I do have to think of my own interests too."

"Give me one reason why I shouldn't kill you."

"Ah, but I was going to make it right. I wanted to marry her."

"That's your solution? You idiot! She's engaged to Draz!"

"He's waited too long, that boy. He's indecisive. Or you've spoiled your daughter."

"Don't you say a word about my daughter!"

"All right, all right! It's not her fault, it's his. Well, he's waited too long and it's high time she got married. She's almost twenty-two, for goodness' sake! She'll lose her beauty, and no one will want her."

"Do you want me to strike you? There are no two like her in the whole of Alipaz: beautiful, obedient, and well-born. I would have had to sift through a crowd of suitors if I had placed a notice. So don't think you're doing me a favor!"

"No, you're right, calm down. I love her, I'm going to marry her. Instead of becoming the daughter-in-law of a More-Than-Pure, she'll be a wife of one. That's all!"

"And if I don't want you for a son-in-law?"

"But you promised me Neria."

"Neria, not Elinor!"

"Oh, one or the other, what does it matter? I have nevertheless been wronged here. I've needed to find a solution since Neria disappeared."

"Well now, Elinor has disappeared too, along with Draz."

"We'll find them."

"Do you understand the situation you've put me in?"

"Calm down, I..."

As Valterone first lunged, Zelimo threw himself forward, and his skull, like the prow of a ship, rammed against his opponent's nose. He then rushed for the door. He had made an error of judgment in agreeing to this meeting and had to join his guards waiting for him at the entrance. Valterone composed himself and grabbed Zelimo by the collar of his tunic, which tore under the strain. The latter, realizing that he would not be able to escape, turned to face his adversary. The two men looked each other up and down. Valterone's face seemed as if it were cleaved in two, the top pale with rage, the bottom, red and glistening with the blood that flowed from his swollen nose. Zelimo's cheeks were ablaze, his forehead marked with a wound that ran down to his brow.

"I've noticed your schemes, the way you ousted me, your discussions with Draz... A pretentious young man with smooth skin and white teeth... He doesn't know anything, although he may act like it..."

"You want a shoulder to cry on?"

"No, thank you. My allies are sympathetic to my plight and have their instructions. If I disappear, they will know what information to pass on to Elatek."

One night, many years before, Valterone had held his ailing son in his arms and… No one had seen anything, but Zelimo had provided the corpse of a healthy young boy.

Valterone launched at his foe, lifted him above his head, and threw him against the wall. The shock put a stop to the yelling. Zelimo toppled to the floor, then scrambled to get up as he struggled to catch his breath.

"No, don't do it, no!"

With a smile fixed on his face, Valterone stepped towards him.

"I hope for your sake that we find Draz and Elinor. I will then arrange a wedding that has been put off for too long."

After Zelimo fled, Valterone went down the stairs, out of the building, and towards the stables. The rain, coming down hard, soaked his clothes and flattened his hair on his head.

"Divine Val…"

Bobka doubled over from the punch. The Gargoyle cowered and fell to the ground.

"You filthy monster… I gave you a job… spent money… for nothing… parasite…"

When at last the fury subsided, the blows became less frequent and the Star of Alipaz straightened up. He opened and closed his bloody fists.

"You are worth less than a dog. Your wife's privileges, extra food and other luxuries, will all be cut off. I'd say she'll last two months. That's right. In two months, your wife will be dead, and you will be to blame."

CHAPTER NINE

Her wings were getting on her nerves. Not powerful enough for flight and too heavy for walking. No matter how hard she tried, Neria was still holding the others back while Forg frolicked carefree in the treetops. He had fashioned a harness similar to those used by mothers to carry their infants and had offered to take Anaëlle, immediately overwhelmed by the excitement of trying out a new mount. Forg undoubtedly had the physical strength to carry the extra weight — as he had boasted before, he had mastered the art of flying with a burden — and the first few times had gone without incident. But he then risked some acrobatics that Neria had immediately forbidden in an authoritative tone. The duo fled without looking back and when she finally found them, they bore the delighted expressions of those who've made the most of a bad decision.

When the travelers began their descent down toward the valley, Neria took advantage of the slope to hone her own technique. She would choose her points for take-off carefully and apprehensively launch herself skyward. Forg, in addition to his functions as a scout, became responsible for her training. He gave advice and masterful demonstrations, and then, perched on a tree, shouted his instructions.

"Very good. Keep going straight. Straight ahead. I said straight ahead. Turn the other way. Not that way! Are you all right? Say something! Now, there's no need to get upset, that's how you learn."

Later, while Matar was cooking with Anaëlle, Forg offered to teach Neria a new skill. She barely looked away from the arrow she was sharpening and dismissed him with a couple of curt words. But he assured her that the lesson would not cause her any physical discomfort, then was so insistent that she put down her tools with a sigh and followed him. The fire dwindled to a feeble glow. Forg sat down by the roots of an age-old tree with thick boughs and suggested she take a seat next to him. She sat with the haughty elegance she had learned from Alipaz, inspected the content expression on his hairy face for a moment, and then looked away.

Suddenly, he made a flurry of short bursts of sound that set the landscape ablaze with droplets of silver light. She recognized these sounds and had used them before, first instinctively, then by imitating the other Gargoyles, but now an unexpected range of nuance and skill was revealing itself to her. So far, she had only been able to obtain a colorless and sometimes fuzzy nocturnal image whereas Forg illuminated the scene with cold and meticulous clarity.

He proposed a game to her. She had to repeat certain sounds after him and observe what effects they had on her "vision." The exercise seemed simple enough to her at first, then became more and more complicated until it exceeded the capacity of her vocal cords. He then asked her to identify shapes around them, first trees or bushes that could be easily recognized, then elusive animals.

"What do you mean a masked beetle? You can tell insects apart too? But how did you learn all this?"

"I've had some talented teachers, but the most important thing is practice. Most Gargoyles are just happy with the basics, but repetition leads to perfection. It's the same with flying. Don't get discouraged, if you keep at it, you'll succeed in the end."

"So, you're saying my problems are because of my attitude and not me having a bad teacher."

"Exactly! You're finally getting it."

The next day, the terrain became more level and the trees more infrequent. The travelers did not pay the water any attention until it came up to their ankles. Forg, out scouting, returned with bad news. The recent rains had flooded the valley and going around it would add an extra week or two to their journey. Gargoyles generally avoided this marshland as its sparse trees offered only partial protection and the Chimera who populated it had a bad reputation.

Matar turned to Anaëlle.

"Describe the monster you saw."

"It was huge, with a big head, a hown, and shawp teeth."

"Did the place the attack happened look like this?"

"It was wet."

"Was it raining?"

"I don't know, but I don't like this swamp and I don't wanna be here."

Matar scanned the surroundings, breathing in the smells, listening to the familiar yet different sounds of the local wildlife.

"Let's go, we've lingered long enough. The sooner we start,

the sooner we'll get out of here."

They took off their shoes to wade through the icy soup of muddy water, grassy miscellany, dead leaves, conifer needles, insects, amphibians, and hybrid creatures. Bare-boughed cypresses stretched their spindly imploring arms towards the sky. Their austere figures painted a picture of sad beauty, enlivened by the occasional presence of bird oaks with feathers of fuchsia, turquoise, or mauve. The cold, which at least spared them from mosquitoes, crept under their clothes and into their bodies. As the water continued to rise, Forg instructed them, "Keep going. The water will start to go down in a hundred yards."

They distributed the cargo to lighten Onyx's load, who would continue to carry Anaëlle, but he remained stood on all fours and refused to move. Matar told them to go ahead, "He doesn't like the mud, but I'll convince him. We'll catch up with you."

While the donkey and his master negotiated, Neria looked for a moment at the foul liquid surrounding her ankles, then shrugged and carried on with her journey. She suddenly lost her footing and started swimming. The weight of her wings did not make this any easier either. Once destined for the upper echelons of society, she had somehow found herself wading through mud.

She had hardly advanced a few inches before a piercing scream startled her. Neria turned around and saw a pointed shape, like the fin of a tiger shark, moving at full speed in her direction. She threw off her cargo, swam with all her strength toward the bank, managed to get a foothold on the muddy ground, drew her knife, and waited for her attacker. The monster surfaced right in front of her, its jaws wide open, furnished with several rows of jagged teeth. Just then, Neria felt powerful arms wrapping around her, carrying her into the air. The beast, with its huge, elongated skull, tiny eyes sunken into folds of fat, a vast mouth, no shoulders, short arms, and a colossal gray horn on the top of its head, propelled itself out of water. Its teeth snapped a couple of inches from her leg. The creature gave a high-pitched shriek of frustration, then dropped back down with a splash of rancid water. Matar's arrows bounced off its thick hide. Forg left Neria on a tree and set out once again.

With a thrust, the monster glided over the marshland, striking Onyx, who lost his balance and fell. Anaëlle tumbled to the ground, got up immediately, and brandished the pathetic weapon she had clung onto. Matar, transformed, threw himself onto the beast's neck, but his claws slipped off its slimy hide, and he fell off, while Forg narrowly escaped its formidable jaws. Neria sprang from the bough where she had taken refuge and positioned herself between Anaëlle and the monster. Then with a stroke of a wing, she leaped on its enormous head and planted her knife in its tiny eye. The animal gave a shrill shriek, shook with such a force that Neria was thrown several feet away, then moved back, staggering on its short legs. A few moments later, it disappeared into the depths.

Matar took Anaëlle in his arms, Forg landed by their side, and Neria joined them. They stayed motionless, panting for a moment, waiting for movements that would indicate the return of the monster. Forg put his hairy hand on Neria's head, patting it like a horse's croup.

"You didn't do too badly. You've obviously got a good teacher."

Neria shook herself free from him.

"I didn't remember anything you said in the heat of the moment and that worked out pretty well for me."

"Beginner's luck."

"Stop messing about and let's get out of here."

"I did see another path, but I don't like the look of the plants there."

"Let's check it out. I don't want to stick around."

They gathered their belongings, found Onyx, put the all too quiet Anaëlle on his back, and moved away from the water. They came across a path that wound through strange plants. Their bulging bodies, made of a soft and lumpy greenish-gray substance, were adorned with a bright red epicenter with a yellowish top. Dendrites the color of bird droppings surrounded the fleshy masses. They varied in size between a walnut and a calf, clustered in gelatinous clumps that clung to the trunks and boughs of the trees like repugnant fruit.

"Pestilential empyemas or gaseous phlegmons," said Forg. "Even the slightest touch of their filaments will make them release a paralyzing gas before they secrete an acid that kills their prey and then feed on its putrefied corpse. It's almost impossible to perceive their movements."

"Follow me at a distance. If Onyx makes it through, you will too."

"There's a feeling of evil to this marsh," said Neria. "I'd rather go around it."

"Don't worry about these creeps. At the very worst, we'll just turn back."

"I'll go with Anaëlle then."

Neria approached the donkey, took the girl's hand, and squeezed it. She was startled, as if awakened from a bad dream.

"I want to go away fwom hewe. I want to go home."

"I know. I want to be somewhere else too, in the dining hall in the cave, or in the playground, or even on the terrace at Nephalie's house. Do you remember it? But we've come this far and there's nothing we can do but carry on."

"Let's take the long way."

"Who knows what could be waiting for us elsewhere? Were these phlegmons in your vision? Let me hold you, we'll go backward. Matar will tell us if there's any danger."

"No, I'm staying with Onyx."

She was obviously smart to stick to riding an animal that had demonstrated such a strong survival instinct during the earlier confrontation.

Still soaked and shivering from the cold, they moved forward carefully, scanning the ground with each step to make out the filaments on the sodden earth. The phlegmons seemed to contract in an insidious way like carnivorous slugs. Neria shuddered at the idea that if these creatures were to surround them, all they could do was wait for death before being ingested.

Suddenly, Onyx bent his ears and Matar shouted for them to flee. With a droning, a squadron of flying creatures swooped in; they were the size of rats, with velvety bodies, the eyes of cats, a proboscis, the feet of flies, and a black stinger. The travelers doubled back but were stung by the first wave before they could get out of phlegmon territory. The Peddler's cane whirled in the air. Neria tried to imitate him. The cat-hornets they hit gave a shrill hiss like balloons before crashing down on the ground. Their corpses piled up around them, but more were still coming. Forg defended himself with his cutlass. He twirled, performing elaborate acrobatics in the hope of losing the swarm that had completely engulfed him. The hornets relentlessly pursued him and as he flew over their heads, the others heard him cursing and shouting in rage.

Matar and Neria turned their backs on Onyx to protect Anaëlle, who fought valiantly and slaughtered her share of the vermin. But the child's courage waned, her blows became more frantic, and she eventually cowered on the donkey's back. She cried and screamed in terror. Onyx ran away, panicked by the stings. In his escape, he knocked down Neria who lost her balance, stepped on a filament, and was struck in the face by a stream of ocher gas. Blinded, she covered her face with her arms. The cat-hornets came crashing down on her. Matar coughed and cried yellow tears but continued to fight. All around them, the phlegmons erupted in a chain reaction.

Suddenly, they heard a strange chanting, and they soon saw its source: a half-man, half-toad creature was approaching. He was bouncing around and repelling the cat-hornets with a metal ball attached to a rope that he twirled over his head. Modulated sounds and scented vapors emanated from the device. Matar guided Neria towards the life-saving fumes while Forg tumbled from the sky. Their savior jumped impressively far for such a frail being. He led them with a quiet confidence out of the labyrinth then toward a stretch of water on which a dugout floated, moored to a tree. On the way, they found Onyx, who was waiting for them, with Anaëlle unconscious on his back.

Matar had to cut the tangled mane from between the child's clenching fingers.

"Quickly, quickly! Hurry, I'm in a rush! You, put this one on the boat. You there, unload the donkey."

"What will happen to him?"

"He'll swim after us."

"I wouldn't count on it."

Exhausted and aching, they submitted to his authority. With a long bargepole, he maneuvered through the maze of passages between plant life like a city dweller through the streets of Alipaz. Onyx had resigned himself to following them and swam with vigor, but Matar had to get in the water to help a few times in the difficult parts.

Neria held the still unconscious Anaëlle in her arms, speaking to her, imploring her to wake up. The only task that Nephalie had ever entrusted to Neria, apart from staying alive herself, was to protect Anaëlle. She saw her mother again, alive with fear and courage, the evening of their escape. The strange trees of the marsh looked at her with contempt. She put her finger in the hollow of Anaëlle's fragile neck, on the blue line that snaked there. Her soft skin yielded and revealed a steady pulse that resounded from the depths of her inert body. Neria clung to the tenuous hope that sang in these soft beats.

"We're almost there. We can leave the donkey here. He'll be dry there and will be able to find something to eat."

He pointed to an islet with his spade-like finger.

"I'm not going to leave him."

"Anaëlle isn't waking up, she's going to die."

"No, honey, she's not going to die, not anytime soon anyway. Listen, I was informed of your little 'incident' and I have to say that I was somewhat reluctant to come to your rescue. As visitors, the least you could do is respect your hosts."

"That monster attacked us and we defended ourselves."

"Certainly, the Moguedon was rather foolhardy, but you were the ones who went into his territory. What did you expect? And, well, he's got to feed his young, hasn't he? The old paternal instinct... It won't happen again, I've made agreements with the main parties involved."

"What kind of agreements?"

"The sort a good neighbor makes. They don't hunt in my territory, and I respect theirs. You don't have to worry about anything at my place, not you or your donkey. But we must hurry."

Matar watched Onyx, who had arrived at the islet and seemed to be enjoying himself, and then nodded.

They came within sight of a gray, shingle-roofed shack that stood perched on many stilts, like a giant insect walking on the water. Fishing nets of all shapes and sizes were drying on the outside walls. The toad-man moored the boat, leaped onto the pontoon and rushed inside. He yelled a long cry of despair.

"Oh no! That's what I was afraid of, it got stuck on the bottom."

The Peddler and the Gargoyle exchanged a glance. Neria had not moved and was crying while rocking Anaëlle. When Matar approached to take her, she tightened her embrace and lifted her distraught face up to him.

169

"Don't touch her! It's your fault she's in this state. You stopped me from following the Gargoyles. Look at what happened!"

His wild tawny pupils fixed on her somber, moistened eyes. Neria hoped for a retort, but Matar remained expressionless.

"It's cold. Let me take her inside."

Neria finally yielded and gave him the child. He carried her into the main room and settled her down on the thick blanket that the toad-man had improvised as a bed.

"Don't worry yourselves! I've seen worse. Being unconscious for more than a couple of hours may be dangerous, but we can't do anything about it now, so it's not worth fretting over. Ah, good news! I've managed to rescue my soup so we'll be able to eat soon."

Neria clenched her fists and tensed her jaw but stayed silent. Forg crouched down near the child and pinched a muscle at the base of her neck. Anaëlle's face contracted and she groaned.

"She reacted! That's a good sign."

"Stop torturing the child!"

"A little water on her forehead..."

"Salts..."

"Rub her hands, she's freezing..."

"She's waking up!"

Neria felt the relief spread through her limbs like a stiff drink. If Anaëlle had succumbed... She forbade her thoughts from going any further and comforted the child, who was moaning and blinking. She marveled at the beauty of her large hazel eyes under her well-defined eyebrows, caressed her silky curls, pushing them away from her sweaty forehead before kissing her. Every breath of this exquisite creature was a miracle. She thanked Asoas for sparing her.

The toad-man left them and crossed the room. He chattered on and on and wore a cheerful look on his unsightly face: widely set and bulbous eyes, a stubby nose, a huge mouth, thin lips that drooped in the corners and from which massive, yellow, awkwardly set teeth protruded. He moved like the sway of a pendulum, his neckless and shoulderless barrel-shaped body swinging on slender legs. His long fingers glided over the furniture — table, cabinet, and mismatched chairs — which glistened, dripping with wax, and adorned with crochet work lending a festive appearance. He arrived in the kitchen area, cluttered with ceramic jars of various sizes, utensils, dried sausages, and garlic and chili braids hanging from the ceiling. An exquisite aroma wafted from a cooking pot on the stove.

"What's your name?"

"Sidehmoliomatch, at your service! But you can call me Liomatch."

"I prefer Sidehmo," said Forg. "Lamoitchy, or whatever, it's too complicated."

"Well, let's go with Sido then."

He opened several jars, smelled their bouquets, poured a few ingredients into a pot, which he placed on the stove. He mixed it diligently and finally obtained a thick, foul-smelling concoction, which he presented to the travelers with a wide grin.

"First, you need to see to your skin. Each bite has to be washed then covered with this salve."

"And why's that?"

"If you don't, the egg hatches, the larva develops in your skin, and when it matures…"

"Okay, okay, we get it."

The muddy poultice was then applied and held in place with strips cut from an old sheet.

"You need to replace the bandages every day for four days to kill the larva. Anyway, let's eat, otherwise, dinner will start burning. You need your strength to recover."

They gathered around the small wooden table and Anaëlle, still very weak, perched on Neria's lap. Their host, who had put on a floral apron that he said was a gift from another lost traveler, served them a thick fish soup with an appetizing amber color. Forg swallowed large spoonfuls, punctuating his greedy slurps with ecstatic exclamations. From time to time, the toad-man's long pink tongue would snap out like a spring, catch an unsuspecting insect, and curl back, carrying the saliva-soaked prey with it. The entire process was over in a split second and Neria had to see it again several more times to be sure that she had not imagined it. She looked at her bowl then wondered aloud about what was in the dish.

"Don't ask stupid questions."

She reluctantly dipped her spoon into the thick liquid, brought it to her lips, then began feeding Anaëlle, who, delighted by the flavors, asked for a chair and a bowl all to herself.

"It's ever so nice of you to pay me a visit. To my great regret, travelers tend to avoid this part of the forest. It does have some very attractive spots, though, well worth a trip. It's a good thing I heard you, I was polishing my floor, you see, a task that requires considerable concentration."

"How did you hear us? We got into trouble quite far away from here. Can you tell us what you did? And what about your agreement with this monster?"

"The Moguedon? There's some humanity in him, you know."

"Then he's a cannibal."

"Oh, morality, philosophy, and the arts aren't genetic. The Moguedon isn't exactly what we'd call very well educated, believe me."

Sido's explanations were always confusing. But days of calm passed in his home while he plied the travelers with foul potions, scalding soups, and droning incantations. In between meals, he would throw himself into making little culinary surprises: thin slices of smoked meat on cornbread, a variety of compotes, spiced vegetables, dried fruits and nuts, all washed down with fragrant herbal teas. He obtained his provisions during his solitary errands, during which he rejected all offers of company. One morning, Forg jumped into the dugout after him, but the toad-man refused to move until Forg went back on land. The Gargoyle had then pursued him by air and returned home in dismay, unable to understand how he had lost him. Matar shook his head.

"He's afraid we'll discover his secret ingredients. I've never seen anyone make such a fuss over a meal. I've been cooking myself for decades and I make perfectly fine stews in a tenth of the time."

"Your stews are edible, Matar, but Sido's cooking... If I were you, I wouldn't go badmouthing his art."

Matar went to visit Onyx at least twice a day, most often accompanied by the other members of the group. There, they would find grassy patches, tamed by the keen attention of the donkey, along with fruit trees, flowers, and most importantly a little space to stretch their legs. After these excursions, they were happy to return to the pleasant warmth of the shack.

When he wasn't cooking or cleaning his home, Sido listened to the tales of his guests. The description of the torment that the Humans inflicted on the Chimeras moved him.

"My, how unfortunate! What do we do next, may I ask? What if they come to our region?"

"Frankly, I doubt you folk would be first on the list."

When Sido didn't want to answer a question, he would become evasive and change the subject. He would describe the Edamur Marsh to them as a peaceful, bucolic place where wanderers could lose themselves in daydreaming and philosophical reflection.

"Such sublime nature here. Take the relationship between the cat-hornets and phlegmons, for example. The hornets, immune to the phlegmon poison, make their prey set off the gas, then lay their eggs in their bodies. The phlegmons then digest every last part of the corpses but spare the hornets' eggs and larvae. It's a perfect symbiosis! If only intelligent life like us could manage such a feat…"

He sighed and looked at the ceiling as if it held the solution to the trials of existence. The travelers, with their legs outstretched and palms resting on their strained bellies, acquiesced unconvincingly. Neria could not prevent herself from intervening.

"And what about the poor souls those vermin feast on?"

"Well, that's the way of the world. The strong eat the weak."

"I disagree. The Gargoyles have created a community that respects all of its members."

"Their system remains an exception."

"Not really. The Gargoyles and the Free Cities treat all their members as equals."

The others burst out laughing.

"You're still young and idealistic, you'll learn."

"But don't you mean to free Alipaz and establish an enlightened government?"

"I hope to free the slaves one day, yes, but I'm not planning on deciding who'll be in government after the More-than-Pure."

Neria concealed her irritation. Later, she refused to go to the islet to visit the donkey and remained alone with the little man. He stopped polishing the teapot with a rag for a moment.

"I rather enjoyed what you said earlier. Don't let Matar's cynicism get you down."

"What's the point of dreaming? The reality around us proves me wrong."

"Dreamers have the power to change the world, sometimes for the better, and other times... We can consider Elatek a visionary, can't we? Of course, his influence has benefited the few and caused a great deal of suffering for everyone else."

"While we're speaking frankly, I wanted to thank you for saving us and being so dedicated to looking after us... and without asking for anything in return. But sometimes I get the impression you think we're Elatek's spies. Don't worry... I

175

can't blame you for that when even my own friends are suspicious of me. It seems Demons have a bad reputation."

"Don't listen to those rumors. It's well worth getting to know the Pale Demons who live in the marsh, even if some do criticize them for being so cold and for their penchant for isolation. Many outcasts come to our region and while it's indeed true that some of them have rather disturbing customs, everyone has the freedom to change their own destiny. You're welcome here if you wish. No, I understand. Like many other young people with a highly developed herd mentality, you're looking for company. You think you need others. But as you get older, you'll realize the advantages of solitude. However, I have heard of a community of Urbane Demons living in the mountains. You might want to consider them as an option before you head to the city."

"And here I thought you'd be keeping me company for at least a month... This is the thanks I get."

"He's right," said Forg. "What's the hurry? Let's enjoy his hospitality for a few more days."

They were sitting down to a hearty breakfast: omelet with herbs, smoked meat, bread and preserves. Clad in his ever-present floral apron, Sido served them, with his brows furrowed and his eyes moistened.

"Why are you, who have already suffered so much, rushing into such an angry world? Make the most of the protection of our marsh a little longer."

"You've been fattening us up for six days already. It's decided, we're leaving."

Sido got up, snatched three small ceramic cups, and arranged them on a tray that he placed on the table, his movements marked by an out-of-place solemnity. He tipped the teapot and filled the cups with a rich garnet-colored syrupy liquid.

"I didn't think you'd listen to me. Drink this."

"What do you want us to drink this time?"

"I worry about you and I know you won't get out of the marsh alive without my help. I shall pass the Key on to you. The philter will guarantee your discretion."

Without any sign of hesitation, Forg picked up the cup nearest to him, drained it in a single gulp, and set it back down with a hard slam on the table.

"Not bad, well done, even your potions are deli…"

His eyes widened, he brought his hands to his stomach, his body slumped, and he collapsed to the ground. Matar and Neria rushed to his aid, while Sido remained seated at the table, the corners of his wide mouth raised in a subtle smile. Anaëlle stopped her game to watch the scene unfold.

"Talk to me!"

"Is he breathing? Is he breathing or not?"

"Put him on his side, try to make him throw up."

Forg's face tightened before he burst out laughing.

"You're evil, really!"

"You should have seen your faces! Come on, drink up. I survived it."

They complied and Sido asked them to repeat the hallowed words, "I swear not to reveal the secrets of the Marsh and not to give away the Key."

Then he took out a parchment from the front pocket of his apron.

"Contrary to what you may think, we do not live in total anarchy here. We have ancestral laws. This is the Key, the secret map of our land. See this line that runs through it? It's the path of the Breath of Life. A powerful spell protects the travelers who use it, even mosquitoes won't bite them. All you have to do is learn it by heart. But before you leave, I wanted to give you a gift."

The Peddler opened the tiny clay pot that Sido had given him. Inside glowed an ointment with a surprising fuchsia color.

"This is too much!"

"It's my pleasure."

"We can't accept this."

"Don't talk rubbish, I'd feel more confident about you making it out alive. Your refusing is out of the question."

The toad-man took out a spotless white handkerchief from his pocket, which he used to wipe his eyes and nose.

"Most importantly, don't venture into the areas marked with gray, they're the most dangerous. And now you know the way, feel free to visit me. I shall miss you terribly."

After a noisy farewell and multiple promises to meet again, they set off. The sun came out every now and then, warming their bodies and their spirits. They walked along an elevated path covered with short grass, like a bridge over a flooded land. The only living creatures on it, harmless insects, fled under their feet while the travelers strolled along it as if they were in a garden. Forg walked too as Sido had said there was no special protection in the path through the air. The danger had not gone away, but the magic kept it at bay. First, they noticed a swarm of hornets, then a giant bird of prey with a red beak and crest, cobalt-blue plumage, and wolf's paws, which flew over them before landing on a large bough, settling there to observe them at its leisure. Moving from tree to tree, it watched them for an hour before taking off and never coming back.

Later, the sound of splashing drew their attention. Indifferent to the arrival of the newcomers, the Moguedon was fishing with his son. The adult scanned the moving waters, harpooned fish with its formidable claws, and gobbled them up alive or threw them to his offspring, who devoured them with the same voracious appetite.

"You two wait here. If he attacks us, run away to find Sido. Stay calm, don't get hysterical, and don't provoke it."

Neria helped Anaëlle, pallid face and numb limbs, to get down from the donkey. The child at her side, her hand in hers, she looked at the Peddler and the Gargoyle moving away, while the monsters, with their tiny black eyes, observed their approach. Onyx stopped suddenly and refused to move any further. Matar pulled on the tether while Forg pushed the donkey's hindquarters, risking a kick from his hoof. They then resumed their journey as best they could.

The gelatinous mass and corpulence of the Moguedon would have been better suited to a more placid animal, but the size of its jaws indicated his ability to crush bones, while his hideous wound bore witness to their previous encounter. A wide band of cloth was wrapped around his loins, with these attempts at clothing making his appearance all the more abominable. His man-sized offspring, an outline of a horn on his skull, approached his father.

When Matar turned around to signal to Neria to advance, the little one plunged under the water and the big one launched his attack. He swam so incredibly quickly, in the manner of a salamander. Neria placed herself in front of Anaëlle and tightened her bow. She aimed at his good eye. Then, following an intuition, she lowered her weapon and waited. The Moguedon surfaced, opened his huge jaws, and let out a roar so terrible that she shook, terrified by the sight of his jagged teeth. She was struck in the face by a spray of saliva and the stench of foul breath. Anaëlle fell to the ground and clutched onto her leg.

This roaring seemed to last for hours. Then the beast closed his mouth once again. In his black eye shone a gleam of wicked intelligence. He let out another, weaker roar, followed by a whimper that sounded like a kitten crying. She wondered if they had been mistaken about the monster's intentions. Had he welcomed them like a boisterous dog that, excited to see his master once again, scratches against their skin with his claws? Yet at the moment of the attack, she had felt herself the target of deadly aggression.

Anaëlle still sobbed at her feet. Neria could make out the outlines of her companions, petrified statues, distant, and slender. The water shimmered all around the path as the breeze carried the fresh, living scent of damp vegetation. Time seemed to stand still. The young Moguedon had reappeared while his father still stared at her with his eye as motionless as a polished pebble. She could hear the sound of his breath, a little winded, and suddenly felt like a stranger in this land, an intruder similar to Valterone who sowed destruction in her path.

Without thinking, words escaped her lips.

"I'm sorry."

The Moguedon immediately submerged, moved away, and resurfaced beside his son before returning to his previous activity. Neria observed them for a moment before crouching down and removing Anaëlle from her leg. She took her in her arms and started to run to catch up with the others.

CHAPTER TEN

The path quietly died away, melting into the rugged terrain of the forest as one lump of clay sticks to another. After taking a ceremonial step across the barely noticeable border, Neria made her decision.

"I won't be coming with you to Roguelle, at least not right away. Sido told me about a community of Urbane Demons living in the mountains…"

"Sido..."

"I just want to find out, that's all. I want to meet my people."

"Sido doesn't know anything other than how to cook. Haven't our problems in the marsh been enough for you? Are you planning on dragging the little one into this madness?"

"Me? I'm going to stay with Newia."

Anaëlle jumped down from the donkey and ran toward her aunt.

The bubble that had been pressing down on Neria's chest for days immediately burst. She had feared Anaëlle would choose the company of Matar, more reassuring, or of Forg, more amusing. She crouched down, hugged the child, and kissed her on her plump cheek.

"I'm going with them," said Forg. "I'd rather not leave them alone on the roads, but you don't have to come. Your friends in Roguelle are counting on you. Don't worry, we'll be fine."

Matar approached the donkey and scratched him on the neck. His lips twisted in a smile before it faded away. He took his time to decide as the others followed his every move in hopeful anticipation.

"The kid would be better off in a city."

"You took us to the forest yourself when we escaped Alipaz."

"I was worried about your father's agents and I placed too much faith in the protection of the Corrie."

Matar's hand slid down before closing around the tether.

"I'll be going then. Good luck."

Without saying another word, he took two bags from the animal and dropped them on the ground before leading him away. They soon vanished into the dense vegetation and, before long, only the sounds of their footsteps attested to their presence. He had taken advantage of the first glimpse of independence, the opportunity to be rid of the unruly children that incompetent parents had entrusted to his care. And after all, who could blame him? Only a young love, a tenuous link like a spider's thread broken by the first breeze, had, for a time, bound them together. At this all-important moment, at the end of the path and its protective influence, Neria had made her decision. Matar had kept their interactions to a minimum from the beginning. He had undoubtedly planned on freeing himself at the first opportunity of the cumbersome responsibility that they seemed to represent for him.

Neria pursed her lips, stooped down, wiped away Anaëlle's tears, then lifted her in her arms and turned to Forg.

"Thank you."

He approached them and surrounded the young woman and the child with his powerful arms and wings of leather. Neria burst into tears.

She flew. Not just short bursts interrupted by catastrophic landings, but well-planned, skilled, and controlled journeys. The forced rest during their convalescence with Sido seemed to have broken her shackles of bad habits and fear. To take their minds off the departure of Matar, Forg had found a tambour pine with rippled boughs that Neria had stormed with a determination tinged with fear while her wings pulled her back with a will of their own. At the top, she had watched the night landscape and had felt the desire to curl up and fall asleep. But Forg was already showing signs of impatience and she had sighed in resignation. Her skin, barely healed from the hornet's stings, would soon be adorned with several new bruises. Comforted by the fragrance of the resin, she took a deep breath, spread her wings, and soared.

The miracle she had no longer expected to ever occur finally happened. Like a still faltering foal that suddenly starts to gallop, she glided, dived, and turned effortlessly and fearlessly. Forg criticized her style, but what does it matter what it looks like when you are as free as a bird, or rather, in Neria's case, as free as a bat. She had run away from a forced marriage, had fought in battle, had killed men, but all these trials seemed negligible compared to the one she had just overcome, and the fleeting pity she felt for Anaëlle, and the other creatures doomed to walk the earth, did not dampen her exhilaration. She dived sharply, then bounced off a branch to gain altitude. Birds startled wide awake by the noise flew away with an angry fluttering of their wings. A branch broke under her weight. Neria plummeted then landed on another before leaping up again, laughing.

When they set out for the east, Neria wondered if Matar had left them out of fear of slowing them down. The journey through the air avoided the arduous ascent of the rugged terrain but it did require an intense effort. Anaëlle missed the comfort of Onyx's back and complained about the harness straps cutting off the circulation to her legs and digging into her skin, while Forg carried her for long distances without protest. They all collapsed from exhaustion at the stops they deemed absolutely necessary.

They finally spotted the peak of the mountain, astonishing in its audacity, a hand outstretched toward the pale sky, oblivious to the trees it was crushing to rise ever higher. None of them had ever seen snow before and they were looking forward to having the opportunity to touch it. The wind, picking up now, slapped at them mercilessly as the girl complained about the cold that froze her fingers and tip of her nose.

During their conversation, Sido had indicated a general direction to Neria and had suggested she ask for additional information from the inhabitants they would pass on their way. But when they arrived at the foot of the Darelis Mountains, they discovered a desolate land where even the animals were silent in anticipation of the storm they could feel approaching. The travelers decided to look for shelter to regain their strength before daybreak. They found a kind of natural dolmen leaning against the mountain, under the shelter of which they lit a fire. Neria took advantage of the respite to take out the sewing kit and make a long scarf and rudimentary mittens for Anaëlle out of an old, tattered tunic. Her fingers were numb, making the needlework difficult and giving her a newfound admiration for the patient, unassuming woman who had taught her how to sew. If she had been able to return to her old study, she would have better appreciated the comfort it offered and the usefulness of the lessons she was given.

"This cold is worrying me," said Forg, "we need to find better shelter than this."

"You're getting as negative as Matar."

Each of them made do as best they could without the Peddler, and Anaëlle's rare attempts to evoke his memory were met with curt replies.

When they awoke, the snow had blanched the landscape and it was falling still. Anaëlle and Neria rushed outside and played until Forg told them to come back to the shelter. They revived the fire and nibbled on the provisions that they had made last since the marsh. Before leaving, Neria wrapped the child's head and neck with the long scarf, tied it under her chin, and then slipped the misshapen mittens onto her hands. She moved back a little to evaluate her work. The little girl looked... like she'd gone through a failed mutation.

"It's stwangling me."

"You'll thank me later."

The darkening sky seemed to close in around them and awe turned to incredulity and then to worry. The cold froze their exposed extremities, filled their eyes with tears, and burned their cheeks. They moved forward on foot as the bad weather made flying dangerous. Rough flakes crackled on Neria's skin and stayed clinging to her lashes. She tried to protect the child, all too silent. She desperately wanted to find some words of encouragement but only just had enough energy to keep herself moving through this white magma. She hoped Forg knew where he was going. Personally, she could no longer tell up from down and was afraid of crashing into something. She then recognized the familiar shape of the dolmen and realized that they had gone in a circle. Forg made a sign to her to go inside and rushed in after her. Neria warmed Anaëlle while the Gargoyle lit a fire with their meager reserves of dry wood.

The travelers would die with their fire. The heat would leave their limbs first, then the cold would creep in deeper and deeper like a white worm eating away at their insides. When the sun finally came out and warmed the hardened earth, it would illuminate the darkness in which their frozen corpses would be lying. Anaëlle turned her fear-ravaged face toward her. Neria kissed her tender cheek and tightened her embrace around her body, which shook with uncontrollable tremors. What could she say? She hoped without really believing it that the storm would pass as quickly as it had appeared. Time went by, bleak and sorrowful, until they heard a noise. Forg and Neria looked at one another, checking that they had not imagined it: a beast was approaching. They drew their knives and waited.

The face of a tiger man appeared suddenly in the opening and, after the initial shock had passed, they saw it was Matar. He cried out in a fearsome roar that set them in motion and they went out after him to brave the storm. They put Anaëlle on the back of the donkey, his tether dragging on the ground. The tiger ran on ahead of them.

They first heard the faint sound of a bell being rung by the wind. Chilled to the bone, they came to a stone arch in the middle of which the instrument was hung, flailing in the storm. Matar straightened up and clutched at a rope with his clawed hands. As he tried to make the bell ring louder and louder, Anaëlle lay down on the donkey's neck while the other two hunched over her. The cold was tormenting them even more now that they were not moving forward. When Matar became too tired, Forg took his place, hoping that the Peddler knew something they didn't.

Suddenly, the snow condensed into three shapes that descended from the sky, immaculate and sublime creatures swirling the snowflakes with their white wings.

After sheltering Onyx in a stable reserved for the use of occasional visitors, the Angels turned their attention to Matar. They used a simple — perhaps excessively so — yet effective system for lifting him to the summit. A large, unfolded net served as a basket for the Peddler, who was hoisted up like a chicken in a hamper. This experience, rather enjoyable in good weather, proved horrendous in a snowstorm. Battered by the blizzard, Forg and Neria followed behind the white wings. They flew in unison, jostled by the wind, blinded by the snow, each of them worried the other would lose their way or crash into a craggy cliff. Anaëlle, harnessed against Forg's body, could no longer feel her legs as she buried her face in the comforting warmth of his hairy chest. They finally landed on a wall-walk adjacent to a tower. Forg and Neria helped Matar get untangled from his net while the Angels headed for a cavity and opened a guillotine door. They rushed one after the other inside the building. When the gate closed, a silence descended on them, for a moment just as deafening as the storm that had battered them. Forg removed Anaëlle from her harness and Neria rubbed the child's legs as she whimpered, tormented by the thousands of invisible needles piercing her skin. They then brushed off the snow that still clung to their clothes, their hair, and their fur.

"I'm not going back down like that," said Matar.

Two of the Angels had left them, but one stayed behind watching them with a sneering interest. Neria admired his athletic physique, his graceful white wings, his blond hair, his bright eyes, and his scintillating smile. This smile was intended for her, his dazzling gaze lingering longer than necessary. She felt herself blush.

"Welcome to Jenkala, the Blue City. My name is Kamau."

They followed him to a room furnished with a few seats, a table, and two armchairs.

"Have a rest. The two rooms across the corridor are yours. I will come back tomorrow to take you to the Hall of Words where Jabaury, our leader, will welcome you."

"We've met before, Jabaury and I," said Matar.

"My uncle will be pleased to see you."

His beauty shone through even from behind, his folded wings seeming to glow with an inner radiance. He left them with a pomp so natural it seemed all the more irritating. Neria threw a glance at her own wings, the color of dull mud.

A fire was burning in the hearth. Matar approached it, crouched down, and held his still trembling hands out toward the fireplace. Anaëlle ran to hug him with an enthusiasm that sent them both tumbling. They got up laughing.

189

"We weren't expecting you," said Forg, "but you made the right call to find us."

"I must be getting soft in my old age…"

"We're just glad your guilty conscience got the best of you. We would, of course, have eventually found our own solution to our problems, but I've got to say I was relieved to see your ugly face. Has anyone ever told you that your changes in appearance aren't always in the best of taste? By the way, how did you ever catch up with us?"

"You Fliers forget what you can do with a good pace."

Later, in a hushed voice, Matar recommended that Neria stay quiet about the names of her parents. She nodded and remembered Ellane, the slave who had retained the ethereal grace of her people in spite of her severed wings.

Three women brought in trays laden with dishes giving off enticing aromas. While Forg and Matar rushed to help these apparitions, Neria stretched a hand toward the back of a chair and leaned against it. A sudden weakness overcame her, and she sat down in exhaustion. She could not take her eyes off the Angels as they laughed, amused by Forg's enthusiastic thanks. Ellane must have looked like them before she had been enslaved. Neria ran her hand through the coarse hair that covered her head and regretted once again that her mutation had not transformed her into something more attractive, like these Angels, blessed with long hair that rippled around their faces and caressed their shoulders in such a graceful manner.

Famished, they sat down at the table without any further delay. Anaëlle devoured an impressive number of chervil pancakes, then let out a content sigh, before sinking into her seat.

She closed her eyes, resting her hands on her bulging stomach. Soon, her slow, deep breathing revealed the extent of her relaxation. Neria carried her into their room where a good fire, scented soap, and a large tub of hot water awaited them. She undressed Anaëlle and put her to bed. Despite her fatigue, and determined to make the most of the amenities, she bathed, then washed their clothes, before snuggling under the fresh sheets and thick bedcovers. Outside, the harsh winter was unfolding in all its splendor, making the cozy warmth of the room all the more potent.

She was later startled awake by screaming and immediately realized its origin, although it took her a few moments to recognize the room. She held Anaëlle in her arms, calmed her down, and asked her to tell her about her vision. She hesitated at first, but finally gave in to Neria's insistence.

"I saw you fall into the Souwce."

Anaëlle burst into tears.

"I don't want you to die, I don't want you to die, stay with me…"

Neria squeezed her and felt the tears flowing down her cheeks. She had been granted the questionable privilege of learning how she would die. But she had known that since she was a child. The Source, for some reason, demanded her sacrifice. The embers of the fire glowed in the darkness. Should she get up to stoke them? She breathed in the comforting aroma of the girl's hair and stroked it. Still locked in an embrace, they both drifted back off to sleep.

The next day, Anaëlle's antics on the bed awoke Neria who, instead of scolding her, sat up and stretched with a yawn.

"A little quieter, please. Try jumping like a butterfly, light and graceful."

At this, Anaëlle burst out laughing and eagerly played with even more enthusiasm. Her joy, her forgetting the prophecies of the night before, and the sun appearing between the clouds pushed aside thoughts of drowning and death. Matar then rapped on their door and told them to hurry out. They soon found themselves in front of a hearty breakfast. In response to a remark from Forg about her downcast expression, Neria reluctantly recounted Anaëlle's vision. As she had feared, the child's face stiffened, and her eyes grew misty.

"No, don't cry. You can see I'm doing just fine and that you don't need to worry."

"You were probably wrong this time," said Forg. "You were right about the attack on the Corrie, but that doesn't mean that all your prophecies are going to come true. Besides, I'm here to look after Neria. Don't worry, I won't let her down."

With a great deal of patience, they managed to take her mind off of matters.

At the end of their meal, Kamau arrived and offered to take them on a tour of the Blue City before their meeting with Jabaury. His fresh and luminous appearance made Neria want to get cleaned up and wash her clothes all over again.

Kamau explained the function of each building and gave them an important piece of advice: each floor had at least two doors fitted in alcoves that opened out into the void. These were larger and also differed from the interior doors due to them featuring an engraving of a sun. Neria shivered when she imagined Anaëlle standing on the edge of the abyss and felt he should have warned them earlier. She saw an Angel standing on one of these ledges, adjusting his cloak for a moment, and then leaping into the void. She spotted two others chatting away before a dizzying height like two gossips on their doorstep in Alipaz.

"The inhabitants here were stuck inside yesterday because of the bad weather so they're taking advantage of the respite to stretch their wings."

Neria, dreaming of returning back under the covers in the ever-so-comfortable room, was startled when Kamau addressed her.

"Come with me, the city's even more beautiful from above."

"Uh... Do we have time? Your leader..."

"Of course, it's just a quick tour. Come on!"

"I'll come with you," Forg grumbled.

In two wingbeats, Kamau was on the third floor. Neria knew that neither she nor Forg could ever accomplish such a feat, with taking off not being their forte. She spotted a window ledge, jumped up, and pushed off against it to leap off again. From one bounce to the next, she managed to gain speed and catch up with Kamau, followed by Forg. They glided together between the snow-covered pointed roofs, skirting the slate walls and the rock faces accompanied by other Angels, drifting under the convivial sun. Neria admired the sweeping and elegant flight of their guide but felt that Gargoyles and Demons were just as fast and even more accurate when changing trajectory in the air.

While Human villages typically clustered in the foothills, the Blue City defiantly perched itself atop the mountains. Rather superfluous posturing, perhaps, for a city that was insignificant compared to the peaks that surrounded it. No vegetation could survive at this altitude and at this time of the year, prompting Neria to wonder how these people could sustain themselves.

As they caught their breath on a terrace, a beautiful young woman joined them. She landed with grace and moved toward them with a confident pace. The fur collar of her cream cloak framed her enchanting face and accentuated her perfect complexion, barely pink from the cold and physical exertion. In this place, blond hair and bright eyes seemed common, almost boring in their ubiquity.

"What are you doing here? They're waiting for you in the Hall of Words."

Neria thought Forg looked like a fool, staring dumbfounded at the Angel.

"I'm showing our visitors the city."

The newcomer sized up Neria.

"I see."

Neria felt herself blushing once more. These haughty beings had a gift for making her uncomfortable.

"Well, thanks for the tour, I'm going to find Matar."

She left the others without waiting for their response. Matar and Anaëlle, sitting on a bench, were busy with a game of rock-paper-scissors.

"So," said Neria, "how do you know this place?"

"It's a long story, I'll tell you one day."

"Why not now?"

He crushed Anaëlle's scissors with his rock.

"Anaëlle, don't just pick scissors. If you want to surprise me, you have to change your strategy!"

"But I like scissows!"

"What do you know about these people? They're getting on my nerves."

"Yes, they do have that effect. Don't worry, we won't be staying long."

"So, are you going to tell me?"

"Not now."

Kamau and Forg joined them. They laughed in a conspiratorial manner and did not seem to have noticed her sudden departure.

"Let's hurry up, we've delayed too long."

The city was proving inconvenient for the wingless. They crossed a ravine over a narrow footbridge, entered a tower, went down a winding staircase, followed a dark corridor, barely lit by a few oil lamps, and climbed another staircase as steep as a ladder, leading into a large hall where groups of Angels were deep in conversation. Just when Neria thought they had arrived, they went out again. The sky was cloudy once more and a harsh wind swept through the square surrounded by slender buildings. Neria stumbled when she saw the Source waiting for her in its center.

"Is everything okay?"

Kamau held her arm. An exhilarating warmth emanated from his body, so close to hers. She lifted her face to his smiling eyes, then pulled away and took a step back.

"It's

just…"

How had the black water managed to creep up here? Snowflakes drowned within as the wind glided over its polished surface without even a ripple. An image formed in it of a magnificent Demoness smiling at her. Neria knew that this smile was intended for her and she wanted to rush toward it, but Forg's grip held her back.

"Let me go, you're hurting me."

"Come on, it's just a trick."

But Neria wanted to join this goddess who — she was sure of it — would understand her and accept her without hesitation. She tried to push aside the hand and free herself from the cruel grip that kept her from her destiny. Then, like a stick snapping underfoot, the enchantment stopped. Neria ignored the worried glances of her companions and let herself be dragged toward a door.

Jabaury was sat at a great stone table. The assembly was attended by dignitaries, some standing, others sitting on benches arranged in a semicircle. The opulence of her father's chambers had amazed Neria in the past, but this elegant austerity seemed more refined. The bare stone and rough wood accentuated the solemnity of the place and the beauty of the Angels.

"By Asoas, I thought I would never see you again. To what do I owe the honor of your visit?"

"We're looking for a home for these two young girls and we're hoping a community of Demons we've heard about will take them in."

"And I was afraid you were going to try to convince me to

join your rebellion."

"In all honesty, the rebellion needs your support more than ever."

"I have no desire to meddle in the affairs of strangers. Besides, you have a nasty habit of picking battles you can't win... Anyway, we don't go anywhere near the Demons living on the dark side of the mountain. An ancient treaty binds us: they don't come over here and we don't bother them. I recommend you follow our example; there are rumors of cannibalism. The Demon girl might survive, but the others will surely perish."

Back in their living room, Neria took the first opportunity to make her case to Matar.

"Jabaury doesn't know what he's talking about. He said so himself: the Angels haven't even met any Demons for decades."

"That's not true, they do occasionally take in defectors."

"And where have these refugees gone? Why didn't they settle here? Jabaury's hiding something from us."

Neria approached the windowed doors and rested her face on the icy pane. Possessed by a sudden impulse, she threw open the panels. A gust of cold air rushed into the room and, without paying any attention to the protests of her companions, she threw herself out. Although the spectacle of the casually falling snow was spellbinding for Neria, she hated this cold that seemed to pierce her skin and seep into the very depths of her being. She increased her velocity, delighted to feel her muscles at work, her heart hammering in her chest. She grew intoxicated with this energy, driving out her frustration and anger.

A noise interrupted her train of thought... Those wings

chasing after her weren't those of a Gargoyle. She turned around and headed straight for the Angel.

"What do you want?"

"To talk to you. Let's take a seat over there, on that outcrop, it'll be more comfortable."

Without waiting for her answer, he moved toward the indicated spot and landed there with an elegant rustling of his white feathers. Neria wondered if she had made a mistake by going out alone but decided to join the Angel and his abundance of charm.

"I wanted to offer you my services as a guide."

"Is there anything to see around here?"

"How very condescending! Now, there aren't any boutiques, but we do pride ourselves on having some areas of astounding natural beauty."

"The bad weather's coming back and the others will be worried."

"Come on, just for an hour, you won't regret it. They won't even notice you're gone."

Every time their eyes met, she felt an uncomfortable weakness come over her. She smiled at him.

He showed her peaks of strange shapes that had names laden with imagery. They admired a waterfall that fell into a playful stream, with rounded rocks like sugar-dusted donuts. He then took her to a cerulean lake, a translucent eye in a pale face. They flew over it so close that she could touch the icy ripples with her fingers. She watched their reflection, black and white: she, like a stain on the landscape, and he...

They landed at the entrance of a cave.

"You've convinced me! This place is better than all the boutiques in the world."

"And yet I envy your travels. Our life here seems so monotonous to me."

"If I'd grown up here, I would never want to move."

"One day, I will leave this place."

"Why?"

"It's hard to explain... I don't always feel at home in Jenkala. It's like something's in the way of my future."

"I know what you mean. I would have invited you to join us, but I'm planning on going to the Demons, and their land doesn't seem to be a very popular destination."

"If I left, I'd like to see the sea."

Neria burst out laughing. Then she remembered the landscape she had contemplated during her final visit to the Temple. The golden city that tumbled down toward the waves of the azure waters, inhabited with monsters that the civilians endeavored to hold back using dikes and nets that constantly needed repairing.

"I grew up next to the sea. Its beauty seems overrated to me."

"Is it? I want to hear all about it! What was it like living down there?"

"Oh, I had a very normal life, a typical family, you know... A father, a mother..."

"You're lucky."

"I am?"

"My mother, a distant cousin of Jabaury, died in childbirth and my father abandoned me. A bad guy, no doubt. Yes, my uncle treats me like one of his own children, but there's always the circumstances of my birth... I sometimes toy with the idea of going to live somewhere where no one knows who I am."

"I understand. I'm sorry..."

"It's not your fault. On the contrary! Your very presence evokes dreams of distant lands and exotic landscapes."

"You're being ridiculous. Have you seen what I look like? This repulsive mutation..."

"I don't understand what you're talking about. All I see is a captivatingly charming, young, and beautiful adventurer. Big black eyes, full lips, a smile..."

"You must be going blind young."

Kamau burst out laughing.

"I don't have any problems with my eyes and I can prove it."

He moved over to her and held her hand.

"I was right, you're even more beautiful up close."

"Where have you been?"

"I told you, I went to get some air."

"What? You go out for a moment, supposedly to calm your nerves, and then you disappear for hours on end. We were thinking of going to look for you."

The Gargoyle's amiable, clownish appearance cracked at

that point to reveal the aggression that had been shown during the battle at the Corrie.

"Sorry."

"What have you been doing all this time?"

"I bumped into Kamau and he offered to give me a tour of the area."

"I see. The young lady went sightseeing with a handsome dandy. Look, I love your niece, but I'm not her nanny. So next time, I hope you'll check to see if I've got any plans of my own."

"What plans? Like napping?"

"And whyever not?"

Matar poked his needle into the tunic he was darning and stretched.

"They're only tolerating our presence here for now. We'll be leaving as soon as the weather permits."

Anaëlle, sitting by the fire, was playing with her doll. She paused and announced, "In thwee days, the weathew will be nice and sunny."

"You're doing weather forecasts now?"

CHAPTER ELEVEN

Her clothes were not meant for these temperatures. She struggled against the violent gusts of wind and tried to ignore the shards of ice that scratched her face. She wondered why she had ever agreed to leave the comfort of her room. Before her departure from the Corrie, Neria had spurned the timid advances of a male Gargoyle with tawny hair. What was his name again? But a primal link bound her on a profound level to Kamau, a name that she would never forget. She tried saying it in different ways, whispering and shouting it, despite the snowflake-peppered wind blowing into her mouth in a bid to silence her. She made out their meeting place, an old building left uninhabited since its owner, an eccentric who preferred a life of isolation, had died some fifty years earlier. Like all the dwellings of the Angels, it clung to a rocky spur. Neria opened the door and rushed inside. Kamau, crouching down in front of the fireplace, rose to welcome her while she continued struggling to close the door. When she finally managed to get it shut, the relative silence grew heavy, the presence of her host seeming to fill the entire room.

"You came."

"Evidently."

"What did you use as your excuse?"

"Same as yesterday. 'I need to go out.' They thought I'd gone mad, but I got away before they could do anything. This weather's so bad! I've never been this cold in my life."

"I've brought blankets and we can start a fire."

He had pushed the broken furniture into a corner. Despite a hole in the roof through which snowflakes and wind swept in, the shelter provided welcome protection. He took flint, steel, and a piece of tinder fungus out of a bag, handed them to her, and laid out the required kindling in the hearth. She usually preferred to leave this task to others but dared not refuse. She crouched down and hoped he would not notice her trembling hands. She fashioned a nest with the twigs, placed the fungus in its center, and rubbed the flint on the steel striker. The sparks jumped onto the fungus and blackened it. She blew. Softly at first, then harder and harder. When the flames reached the twigs, she settled her bundle of fire in the hearth, adding small branches which in turn caught fire. She arranged the remnants of a stool around it and then sat down on a thick blanket. Kamau unfolded another one, placed it over Neria's shoulders and sat down. He moved with a quiet confidence that gave away his experience.

"Why did you want to meet up with me?"

"You intrigue me. The girls here are all the same, predictable and perfect."

"I understand. I'm unpredictable and imperfect."

"That's not what I mean, you're unique… fascinatingly unique."

"You mean fascinatingly hideous."

"I'm sorry, but… why do you say things like that? I think you're beautiful… your eyes, your mouth, your figure… and even your ears!"

Neria placed her hands against her ears.

"By Asoas! They're enormous!"

"They're elegant and distinctive, rather like you. Unlike most people, you aren't satisfied with a mundane life."

"Living here in this incredible place, surrounded by beautiful people, it should be enough to make you happy."

Neria recalled her journey: the crude meals, the uncomfortable camps, the long grueling treks, the unforeseen dangers, the fear, the cold, the heat, the hunger. She would have swapped lives in an instant.

"You don't see many outsiders around here, do you?"

"Sometimes the odd renegade Demon finds their way here. They turn up in a sorry state and leave soon after. But never has a visitor as lovely as yourself graced Jenkala with her presence."

He leaned in and brushed aside a lock of hair on her forehead. Neria felt her throat tightening and a wave of heat coursed through her. She blushed and turned her head away.

"Why... it's just... I don't know... sorry..."

"It's okay."

Tilting slightly toward him, her legs tucked to the side, she leaned on her hand, which he covered with his own. She grew intoxicated from his exquisite tenderness to the point of it becoming unbearable, then freed herself, changed position, cleared her throat, and invited him to join her under the blanket, large enough for two. He accepted with a knowing smile. Women liked him and he knew it.

Snow was still falling through the opening in the roof. The wind whistled, shook the shutters, sneaked through the cracks, but Neria did not care. He drew nearer and she closed her eyes.

She breathed in his scent of leather, resin, and smoke, trembling at the touch of his lips on hers. He held her and she returned his embrace. He lay down and pulled her close, enveloping her with the quivering warmth of his wings. She kissed him. She wanted to remember the caress of his skin and his feathers, the perfection of this moment, for later, when she was on the road...

She broke away from him and sat up straight.

"Are you okay? You seem upset."

"I can't stop thinking about when I have to leave you."

"Then stay here with me."

"Your leader can't wait for us to go away."

"Jabaury? I'll be able to convince him."

"Anaëlle can't fly..."

Neria did not dare say she thought the Angels were less welcoming, colder, or more reserved than the Gargoyles. Would Anaëlle find a playmate here similar to Kloups? Neria had to admit that they missed that unruly child a great deal. And then, who was this magnificent Demoness she had seen in her vision? With his clumsy enthusiasm, Forg had disturbed her before she could understand. Was she really going to give up on finding her own people?

Kamau leaned in and kissed her.

"Don't worry about it for now. Let's start by extending your stay here. And if my uncle refuses, which I doubt he will, I'll come with you."

Anaëlle hated having her hair combed and Neria often felt too tired to tackle a job made even more difficult by her protests and cries of pain. But the clump that had formed above the graceful nape of her neck required urgent attention. With one hand, she grasped each strand close to her scalp to avoid pulling on the roots, and with the other, she began by untangling the ends, then progressed upwards. The satisfaction of seeing the tangle reluctantly unraveling dampened her irritation.

"We should stay here longer."

Matar looked up from his book.

"Why?"

"I don't know. I'm comfortable here."

"I see, still enjoying your life of luxury. But I doubt the Angels would agree to keep on providing for us or serving us. They work hard to survive here and have little patience for visitors."

"We could work too, like with the Gargoyles."

"Trust me, the Angels may be tolerating us for now, but they'll be relieved when we leave their city."

"We could at least try."

"What's the matter? Have you found something to replace your obsession with the Demons?"

"I'm just considering all our options, that's all."

Forg entered the room.

"Jabaury's summoned us."

Matar nodded to Neria.

"You see? No doubt he wants to know when we're leaving."

Her hand shook for a moment upon hearing this news, then she resumed her task while trying to calm her breathing. Matar would notice her racing heart and sudden flushing. So Kamau had kept his promise and had pled their case to his uncle. She imagined living in this wonderful place, welcoming her mother here one day, showing her father what a mistake he had made, and proving to him the true value of the Chimeras. She followed the others, walked through the corridors, refrained from turning her head toward the Source in the icy square, and suddenly found herself in front of Jabaury, who was as motionless as a stone statue, watching them advance. Sitting in the front row of the assembly, Kamau reassured her with a smile.

"On the agenda," began Jabaury, "is the decision to welcome a new member among us."

Neria clenched her fists. The Peddler and the Gargoyle threw questioning glances at one another.

"What does this decision have to do with us?"

"Did you know that this young woman and my nephew have fallen in love?"

Before lowering her eyes, Neria noticed Matar's incredulous and Forg's miserable expressions.

"That's ridiculous! They barely know each other. Neria? Neria, say something! Were you going to tell me about this?"

"Well, there you are then, now you know."

The Peddler's jaw clenched, and she regretted her words immediately. He gave her a look of contempt, a look she hadn't seen since the first weeks of her metamorphosis.

"I was going to just keep my mouth shut… Since we were just passing through, what's the point of bringing up bad memories? But under the circumstances…"

He drew his breath as if preparing himself for physical exertion.

"Neria is Valterone's daughter."

"How dare you bring her here?"

Neria took a step closer.

"Don't judge me by the crimes of my father. I'm not the same as the spoiled child who lived in Alipaz. If you accept me, I will adapt to your customs. I can work and fight. At least give me a chance."

The effervescence of the crowd contrasted with the rigid immobility of their leader, and Neria wondered how a creature of such stature, who exuded strength and self-control, could be stripped of it all in an instant. Jabaury finally stood up and dismissed the assembly with a few curt words. The room emptied and he turned to Matar, his face pale.

"How is Ellane?"

Kamau leaped to his feet and approached the throne.

"I thought my mother was dead!"

"I lied to protect you. She is living as a slave of Valterone's."

Neria could see the resemblance... the eyebrows... the smile perhaps... but Ellane smiled so very little. He was going to hate her, hold her to blame.

"I apologize on behalf of my family. I was not yet born when the More-Than-Pure took over..."

"Don't say another word," said Kamau, "I forgive you. Neria isn't to blame for the crimes of her parents. We must give her a chance."

"Sit down," Matar interjected, "there's more."

"I don't want to sit down, I just want the truth."

"Ellane had only just married Jabaury when the land of Gashom fell to the More-Than-Pure."

"We got married in Opheck. A small, spontaneous wedding that my family wouldn't have approved of. On the way home, Ellane insisted on going to Alipaz. She'd grown up there and missed the city. I let her go. She flew... so well... she was fast, so very fast... I thought she would be safe."

"I don't understand. Are you saying you're my father?"

"No, Valterone is."

Arhel's features were superimposed on Kamau's face: his high forehead, his long, full eyelashes, the shape of his jaw, a pout of anger. An ephemeral reflection disturbed by the concentric waves of a stone dropped into the water.

"Are you okay? Neria, can you hear me?"

With the rising tide, the waters of the Source, as black as Valterone's eyes, would lick at Neria's feet, reaching, wave after wave, her ankles, her knees, her waist, her chest, and then her neck. She opened her mouth and breathed in before allowing herself to sink. Forg grabbed her and she put her head on his shoulder. He guided her toward the bench, helped her to sit down, and then abandoned her as if her touch repulsed him. The wood held the memory of Kamau's warmth. She ran her fingers over a groove in the grain and imagined the crack widening until it became a crevice and cut the sturdy piece of furniture in two.

"This is one of the reasons for the lack of female Chimeras in the cities," Matar continued. "How can the Chimeras be

209

prevented from proliferating if everyone just acts on their urges? At least, that's the explanation the More-Than-Pure came up with.

"However, Valterone managed to keep Ellane close to him, even after he got married. Nephalie took great risks to save her and to conceal her pregnancy. It's a miracle you survived.

"I was there for one of the few happy moments in Ellane's life, when she held you in her arms as she lay on the hay in the barn. While she was marveling at how you looked and felt, I thought about killing Valterone. But I decided to save the life of a child rather than murder a More-Than-Pure who would just be immediately replaced.

"So I took you from your mother's embrace and carried you away, before hiding you in a false-bottomed barrel. The hardest part was finding something for you to eat on the journey."

Jabaury stood up and approached Kamau. Though of equal stature, the elder seemed to be bowing down to the younger.

"I loved Ellane so much that I wanted to adopt you, but I was afraid of the problems of inheritance. I felt joy and pain seeing her through you, her memory resurrected by the features of your face. How many times did I wake up at night, having dreamed she was calling out to me and begging me to save her? I wanted to prevent you the pain of knowing that she was enduring an ordeal from which you could not rescue her."

Kamau turned to Neria.

"How is my mother?"

"Good... I mean... she lives with us, but her life as a slave... I didn't know, I couldn't imagine..."

"I have to go. I need to be alone."

"Don't go out in this weather," Jabaury intervened, "not like this…"

"I will do without your advice, *uncle*."

Matar approached Jabaury and rested a hand on his shoulder, "His anger is natural, but he'll calm down and understand."

"You are all to leave as soon as the weather permits."

The poor visibility, the muffled sounds, and the gale-force wind decreased the chances of finding Kamau. He must have sought shelter or else he would die from the cold. Neria found him in the old, abandoned building, the theater of their last encounter. When she burst into the room, he ignored her and continued to stare at the barren hearth.

"I need your help."

"What can I do for you, little sister?"

She shuddered. Adamek had never called her that, but Kamau had said the words with his violence. She crouched down beside him.

"I want you to show me the way to the land of the Demons."

"Jabaury has told you not to go near them."

"He doesn't know what he's talking about."

"The 'adults' are only looking out for us, aren't they? Without asking what we think…"

"So you'll help me?"

"Yes. Go away."

"I still love you... like a brother. I could stay here, we would have some time to get to know each other..."

"Your father's actions don't give you any right."

"Besides, Anaëlle is your niece too and, in a way, is as much your responsibility as mine."

"How can I be responsible for a child who was just a stranger to me only yesterday? You've got some nerve!"

"Anaëlle's a Chimera."

"She looks pretty Human to me."

"In appearance... She has visions... She's a Dreamer."

"Really? Has she ever seen the future?"

"Yes. She warned us of Elatek's attack on the Corrie."

She said nothing of Valterone's role in it. She couldn't tell him about it, not right now... as he took in this new information... information that might give them the right to stay in the Blue City for some time to come.

But he turned away.

"Leave me alone."

"I've never done anything to hurt Ellane... other than losing my temper with her sometimes."

"Like your entire family, you used her, and now you're only thinking of yourself. You humiliated me in front of the whole Assembly. I'm the bastard son of a Human who forced himself on my mother!"

"My niece and I are not to blame. Give us a little peace, talk to Jabaury."

"Go away."

After this exchange, she had joined the others in their living room. The air was filled with the fragrant warmth of the fire, the spiced aroma of a peppery brew and cinnamon cookies. At least the cook didn't seem to hold the revelations that had now spread throughout the Blue City against them. Matar was reading in an armchair while Forg was drawing on a piece of parchment. The latter raised his hurt glance up to Neria. His drooping ears, his pursed mouth, and his shaggy hair revealed his distress.

"I don't see why you're making that face, I've got the right to love whomever I please."

"Your brother, really?"

"I couldn't have known."

"A flutter of white wings and the lady swoons... tacky feathers and a little bit of glitz and glamor..."

"I admit his beauty took my breath away, but I think, unknowingly, our shared family bonds drew us to each other."

"Of course."

Neria took a place at the table, poured herself some tea, and nibbled on a cookie. Anaëlle, crouching near the fireplace, oblivious of the presence of the adults, scolded her doll in a quiet, but distinctive voice. The imaginary quarrel forced a smile from Neria. But the tone escalated suddenly and Anaëlle struck the soft underbelly of the toy with her fist, again and again, insulting it, then in a burst of rage, picked it up and hurled it to the ground. The doll lay with its arms and legs splayed out, a sewn-on smile on its blissfully happy face.

In a loud and determined voice, Neria announced her decision to join the Demons. Matar closed his book with a sudden slap.

"Jabaury's warned us against them. You're going to walk right into the dragon's den!"

"Everyone's just making up their own theories and talking about them as if they were true. There are all these vague rumors about these Chimeras, but no one's actually verified them."

"And you want to take that risk?"

"Why not? Since I'm one of their kind myself..."

"And what about your niece?"

Did Neria really want to give up the warm and welcoming Roguelle for the shadowy threat of the Demons? In Ellane's arms, still young and beautiful in spite of her mutilation, had rested a sleeping child who, barely pushed out of her nourishing womb, had gone away from her forever. She looked at Anaëlle, now busy forcing imaginary gruel into her doll's mouth; she seemed oblivious to the conversation. This child had also known escape and the false bottom of a barrel.

Was it a family curse or rather the nature of her metamorphosis? Neria carried misfortune with her. Discord and sorrow flourished wherever she went, first in the Corrie, then among the Angels. Only Sido had been spared. Was it because she had never considered moving to the marsh? She had to free her friends from her perilous presence and give her niece a chance to find somewhere to live in peace.

"I can't risk putting her in danger. I'm entrusting her to you. She'll be safe in Roguelle, and I'll join you later."

"I want to stay with you."

"It will only be for a little while. I'll come back for you no matter what. Don't worry, sweetie, we won't be apart for long."

Forg pounded his fist on the table.

"How can you make such empty promises?"

"And if your Demons accept you, will you stay in your own little corner, waiting for the danger to pass or for Elatek to come for you? Don't you care about those who are fighting and suffering for our liberation? When will you understand? You will never find peace as long as people like your father hold power."

Matar had prevented her from following the Gargoyles and had shattered Kamau's love for her. She was sick of these secrets and lies that, under the guise of protection, concealed a cowardly desire to avoid confrontation.

"You're acting as if I'm supposed to be the one to start it, this fight against oppression. Who says you're actually going to do it, this rebellion? Nobody cares about your cause. And what are you doing, anyway? I know. you saved my life, and others before me, but you've got no chance of success. I'll listen to you when you actually have a plan."

She knew she had won when she saw Matar's face turn pale and his eyes change color. He got up and left without saying another word.

Anaëlle whimpered and threw herself into her aunt's arms.

"Stay with me! Don't go…"

Under Forg's disdainful gaze, she tried to calm her down, telling her that she wasn't leaving for the time being, that the city would be better for her, and that she would come for her no matter what once her mission was accomplished. Then, in desperation, she raised her voice and threatened to leave immediately if she continued.

"Besides, you could have warned me. You can predict the weather, invasions, and even my death, but you don't tell me that Kamau's my brother! What a funny power really! I wonder what goes on in that head of yours! Do you want to help me or not?"

She managed to shut her up. Later, lying next to Anaëlle in the big bed, she listened for a long time to the child's steady breathing. Then she pushed back the covers, put on her cloak, and went out into the corridor. She hesitated before knocking on the door of the room that Matar shared with Forg. The latter opened it. The moment he recognized her, a glimmer of hope lit up his eyes. With his ears pricked up, he looked at her with a questioning expression.

"I'd like to talk to Matar."

The glimmer faded, his ears drooped, and he went back into the room. She felt the urge to call him back, but what more could she tell him? He, too, had to learn to accept her decisions.

Matar appeared, shut the door behind him, and leaned against it. He crossed his arms and watched her with his yellow eyes.

"I shouldn't have spoken to you like that. You saved my life and I guess you could say that you trained me... sometimes in a brutal... but necessary way. You're not easy to get along with, but I've always been able to depend on you. Still... you could have told me before we came here about Ellane and my father. All these secrets... they're dangerous. I'm convinced that the solution to my problems lies with the Chimeras who look like me — after all, the Gargoyles have a good life together — and I won't feel satisfied until I've looked into them personally. I tell myself that without facing the Moguedon, we wouldn't have ever met Sido."

"So you're going to risk your life in the hope that someone will come to your rescue just in time."

"I don't want to go anywhere near Alipaz and end up drowning in its Source."

"This world is riddled with Sources, even the smallest villages have them. One of them may be waiting for you with the Demons."

"I won't be able to convince you. I'm sorry, but I've made up my mind."

"Have you said sorry to Anaëlle?"

"I plan on coming back for her as soon as possible. You left us too, outside the marsh."

"And I've realized my mistake. How many people have died in Alipaz while I was trying to help you, when I could have saved them? What was the point of helping you if you're just going to die now? I will accept your apology if you stay with us."

"I can't."

His face took on the callous, scornful expression she hated. He went back into the room and left her in the corridor.

Anaëlle slept while Neria paced around the room, unable to calm herself. She eventually settled down in front of the hearth to stare into the flames. She felt the urge to leap up, to destroy something, and to scream, but did not wish to wake Anaëlle and, instead, simply clenched her fists and tensed her muscles. The alternation between tension and relaxation provided her with a sort of outlet. When a quiet knocking came at the door, she rushed to open it. Kamau stood in the doorway and, except for the absence of his smile, he had regained his confident demeanor. The tragedies of life seemed to harmlessly pass him by.

"Come in, Anaëlle's sleeping, but..."

"I just came to give you this."

He handed her a piece of parchment on which he had drawn a crude map.

"You should be able to find those Demons of yours with this."

He spoke in a pleasant yet dispassionate voice, pointing out the landmarks he had marked with his finger. Although he kept his distance and did not touch her once, not even by mistake, Neria felt as if he was putting his hand between her shoulders and pushing her toward the exit. He then gave her a package: a carefully folded cloak and leather shoes, tied together with twine.

"A friend's daughter had grown out of these, so she wanted to get rid of them. They're second-hand but could still be of some use."

The boots seemed of better quality than hers. Neria caressed the soft wool, admired the embroidered patterns, and thanked him with barely restrained enthusiasm.

"It's nothing. Have a good trip and I hope you find what you're looking for."

She thought he was going to say something else, but after giving her a thin smile, he turned and left. She watched him walk away until he disappeared around the corner.

Lying on her back in bed, she closed her eyes and saw herself standing on the edge of the precipice, with no confidence in her flying and Imri giving her incomprehensible instructions. Anaëlle had proven her courage and shown her a good example. Without wings, she had thrown herself into the void with blind faith in that unruly boy, that classmate she had met so shortly before. Neria asked herself if she was wrong to be so stubborn. Wouldn't it be better to submit to the will of Matar, more experienced and wiser than her? Or to trust Anaëlle who, in spite of her young age, seemed to have an intimate knowledge of the intricacies of their destiny? Or should she emulate Forg, who welcomed the unexpected events that came his way with equal enthusiasm? How could she know which of these was truly best for her?

CHAPTER TWELVE

She would have liked to eat alone with Anaëlle and savor the few moments of tranquility that remained before her departure, but their last breakfast with the Angels took place in a tense silence accompanied by the others. Matar ate methodically, a sullen disapproval written on his obtuse face. Anaëlle nibbled without taking her eyes off her, as if she feared she would disappear at any moment. And Forg... Forg was not eating anything for once. With his head down, he simply used his spoon to stir fleeting grooves in his gruel. When he straightened up for a moment, she saw his eyes... glistening? He bent down again too quickly for her to be able to see clearly, but this eventuality — the possibility of Forg crying because of her leaving — was almost enough to make her give up on the idea.

Just as Neria got up from the table, Anaëlle rushed over to her, clung to her leg, and began to sob, begging her to stay.

"You can't leave us! The Souwce is waiting fow you."

She repeated this over and over again as if possessed by some entranced gnome. "The water's waiting fow you... but I would be thewe and I would help you..."

Neria tore the child from her leg, flung her into Matar's arms, and left the room. She just had the time to grab the light bag she had prepared the previous day before heading for the nearest exit. The sun engraved on the door had large, startled eyes and an excessively thin mouth. She opened the panel, closed it, and found herself standing on the outside ledge. Her eyes glanced over the now-familiar city, shimmering under the blue sky. Matar had advised her not to travel during the day, but she wouldn't listen. He was wrong, of course, such a faint sun in this icy land would not trouble her.

Had Anaëlle wanted to hurt her? Neria could not forgive the girl's last words to her. This, possibly a childish temper tantrum, meant her farewells had been botched, like all farewells perhaps. Anaëlle had changed, the laughing girl from Alipaz had transformed into... Into what? Neria could not say.

Except for the brief episode that had led her from her home in Alipaz to the hovel with the blue shutters, she had never been solely responsible for her destiny. And even then, Matar had saved her from the drunken guards. Feeling through her clothing, she checked for the parchment tucked under her belt. She would follow its directions and reach the land of the Demons.

She took a deep breath, then exhaled, watching her breath form a faint cloud before disappearing. She forced herself to repeat this process several times, now a little calmer, turning her attention to the spectacle of the Angels twirling in the sky. She could not get used to the idea that these beings also worked, as if their beauty should have preserved them from any material need. In any case, one of them could open the door at any moment and ask her why she was blocking the way. This thought was enough for her to make a decision. A dark stain on an immaculate landscape, she sprang forward, determined not to look back.

If Matar hadn't come back to them, she would be living happily ever after in the arms of a beautiful creature. Or she would have frozen to death beside Forg and Anaëlle. She told herself to stop daydreaming and to concentrate on the current journey and the encounters to come.

She spotted the stream Kamau had marked out, which ran east, away from the land of Angels, the Marsh, and Alipaz. She took this first success as a good omen. At least Elatek's soldiers would not venture into these distant lands. But perhaps other unknown dangers awaited her. Starting with the climate. She was quickly overwhelmed by the sun's rays and sought shelter in the hottest hours. Most of the caves gave off the scent of beasts she would rather not disturb, and she lost a lot of time on the rocky scree. She settled as best she could in a recess, lit a fire with damp wood that smoked heavily, curled up in her soft cloak, and, despite the discomfort of the stony ground, fell asleep right away. She awoke later, her muscles tense and her body aching, as the sun was already beginning its descent in the sky. The flames had gone out and she was shivering.

She had to find the next landmark. The cold had infiltrated the shoes Kamau had given her, and she kicked her icy feet against the ground before taking flight. Her muscles gradually regained their suppleness, she flew more easily, and, without stopping, she surveyed the landscape. At these altitudes and at this time of year, life seemed to have disappeared; even the plants that could have survived this climate were buried under a thick layer of snow, marked nonetheless by the footprints of a few hardy animals. Only the wind, brazen as it blew, played its melancholic song among the motionless mountains. It buffeted her clothes, ruffled her hair, and intoxicated her with its harsh bursts. She caught sight of the Darning Needle and, through its eye, as Kamau had described it to her, she recognized the Little Fork. She turned in its direction.

The time for showing off her newfound aerial prowess was over and she was happy to just be moving forward, cubit by cubit, in the endless sky. She had never covered such a long distance in one go. The Little Fork seemed to be taunting her and dancing around like an unruly child, running away from its tutor's beatings. She finally reached it but, tormented by a sense of urgency, she didn't dare stop and set off again without waiting to find the next landmark. She got lost, turned back, and stubbornly continued. The rays of the setting sun cast yellow hues on the snow. She moistened her cracked lips, blinked her sore eyes, and forced her exhausted body to keep moving. She blinked back a few tears when she finally found Elaneau's Head, which looked more like the skull of a moray eel.

Before turning north, she landed on a rock, ran her hands through her hair, dusted off her clothes, and calmed her breathing. The fault — "a canyon so narrow that the sun's rays never penetrated it" — was not far. She had managed to find her way without help but could still give up and turn around. Her fellow travelers, who she missed already, would gladly welcome her back. She toyed with this idea for a moment before taking to the skies. Her next stop would be in the land of her kind, her equals, free and wild beings.

As if in response to her anticipation, black specks appeared on the horizon: five Demons were approaching. Two of them circled around her, while the other three inspected the surroundings. After making sure she was alone, they escorted her to a narrow crevice with a river coursing through its depths. They followed it for a while, then the sides parted and revealed the grand entrance to the kingdom. Unlike the Gargoyles, the Demons, sure of their power, were not in hiding: bas-reliefs, embellished with ocher paint, decorated a gigantic opening. Around this gaping maw fluttered a cloud of flying creatures.

Following her guides, Neria burst into an immense hall the magnificence of which exceeded that of the Temple of Alipaz. Five rows of massive columns embellished with spiral motifs supported the ceiling and complex bas-reliefs adorned the walls. The art of the Gargoyles — a lattice of lines that scampered and tumbled — invited attention without imposition, while here the dense, brutal sculptures stunned Neria. They crossed the hall without hesitation or slowing down, reached a junction formed by three avenues, and took the path to the left. A large crowd wandered around the place, indifferent to the presence of the newcomer. The humbler Demons wore simple garments, tunics of linen, cotton, or wool, in natural hues, but others strutted about, clad in dark leather, embellished with metallic finery and colored stones. Among them, some sported elaborate hairstyles that defied gravity and no doubt required extensions whose true nature was beyond comprehension. The more sophisticated of them flew with ostentatious grace and great care to preserve the scaffolding balanced on their heads.

They turned into a passageway and continued down a series of corridors that became narrower and narrower. She recalled the disorientation and vulnerability she had felt when she arrived at the home of the Gargoyles. This time, she could have found her way out with her eyes closed, or she could have seamlessly blended in with this darkly elegant community. But her attempts at conversation were met with a wall of silence. With a scowl, her guides led her into an empty room, a solid wooden door slamming shut behind her. A Demoness with a triangular face and hair with scatterings of gray rose from her chair to acknowledge her arrival before unleashing a stream of words. She could not express the joy she felt. She had been waiting for her meeting with the Queen for over a week and hoped they would let her see her now that she was no longer alone. Her name was Passoa and she came from Roguelle, the Free City. Her husband, an open-minded man, but older than her, alas, had loved and protected her. Thanks to him, she had enjoyed a comfortable and peaceful life. But after his death, the demeanor of their friends and neighbors had changed, and rather than continuing to endure their scorn, she had decided to try her luck among her own kind. Such wonderful people, aren't they? When she saw what they had achieved, she wondered why people resented Demons. They did, wasn't that so? She was looking forward to meeting the Queen and participating in the Acceptance ceremony.

"What are you talking about?"

"As you've seen, our brethren are doing just fine without us. I don't know all the details, but we're supposed to go through some kind of hearing that will test whether we're acting in good faith. Don't worry, they'll take you in no problem. I'm afraid I'm a little old, but I can contribute a lot to the community. I actually started my own small business, yes, I developed a line of potions and beauty creams that are very popular among the high society of Roguelle."

Why was this hearing required? What did it consist of, for that matter? The Gargoyles had accepted Neria without any kind of preliminary examination... Of course, Matar had spoken in her favor back then. And here she was lost once again in an imbroglio of convention and prejudice on which she did not exert any influence. These Demons, with their ridiculous hairstyles and trinkets, did not impress her. She had not come all this way to suffer their humiliations and was going to prove to them that she was no longer the ignorant girl who had left Alipaz. Did she have to hide her father's name? Had she joined her people to live a life of deception? She would wait until she knew the nature of the test first and would not speak of Valterone right away, but she would not hide it either. She just needed time to show her worth and goodwill.

Passoa was now describing her old home: the high-quality furniture — she appreciated esthetics as much as the next person but did not overlook durability or comfort either — the tapestry she had managed to import from Opheck despite the poor connections between the two cities, her valuable tableware... She had sold everything to finance her trip and the beginning of her stay.

The room in which they waited did not offer any appeal, just another stage in an all too long journey to hosts with dubious intentions. Neria assured Passoa that, without any doubt, their kin would appreciate her taste, her ingenuity, and her courage. Yes, this woman had shown daring. She had left behind a safe and quiet life, while Neria had abandoned faithful friends.

Matar, Forg, and Anaëlle... She missed them so very much... This trial, she would overcome it for them, and also for Nephalie, Paz, and Ellane. And for Elinor. She would make it... and they would welcome her with glee when she came back to them. She imagined Matar's subtle smile and Forg's excitement. She would lift up Anaëlle and twirl her around and laugh... She reached for her knife, grateful that her escort had left her bag and weapons. Who knows? Gargoyles and Demons could join forces against Human hegemony... and free Alipaz together.

She could see her mother and sister again. She took out her provisions and offered to share her meal with Passoa. She refused and plunged into a detailed description of all the refined delicacies that she had been served up to that day while Neria nodded from time to time, glad of the stream of words to take her mind off matters.

Afraid of coming across as lazy, Neria had not dared lie down on one of the straw mattresses. But overwhelmed by fatigue, she fell asleep, sat on a chair, her arms framing her head resting on the table. When the door opened, she awoke with a start and used her sleeve to wipe away a trickle of saliva that had run down her chin. Two women appeared bearing bowls, jugs, and towels. The elder of the two announced, "You shall soon be presented before our Mother Supreme, Queen Analour, Soul of Cambolae. Please wash yourselves and put on your finest attire. You may leave your weapons and other possessions here; you can retrieve them later."

The woman's glance lingered on Neria. She felt the urge to explain her unkempt clothing, to announce her aristocratic origins, but Passoa talked incessantly and the maids left before she could say anything. Neria examined her reflection in the water. Kamau had liked this face, flanked by sharp-tipped ears. No, her ears did not seem as enormous to her as before. The big problem — even Anaëlle had noted — was the black mane that had replaced her brown curls. She had hoped that it would become less coarse and longer with time… In all honesty, the Gargoyles were not much better off in this regard, but it suited them. Reptile women adorned their bare heads with little hats. Such a shame she didn't have one. Angel women not only had silken feathers but magnificent hair as well. And these

227

Demonesses had found a way to make their hairstyles more...
interesting. Neria sighed and plunged her hands into the water.

"Hey! What are you doing?"

"Don't worry. I'm going to take care of this bird's nest
you've got on top of your head. I know what I'm doing, I've
worked in this field for many years. My clients used to come to
me from all over the land for beauty treatments. So don't panic
and let me show you what I can do."

"No, no! Stop it! It's already too short!"

"Don't move, I mean it. I'll sculpt this fuzz of yours, give
it a little shape."

"Look, I appreciate it, but..."

"I assure you that in your state, you've really got nothing
to lose. I am your only chance of salvation, so put your hands
down and keep quiet."

Neria refrained from intervening and watched her hair fall
to the irksome rhythm of the scissors.

"Don't overdo it though."

"I already told you, I know what I'm doing. And I think we
ladies need to help each other out because men will never
understand us, they're too unsophisticated. As powerful as they
may be, they will always fear our creative power. Unfortunately,
I've not had the good luck of being blessed with children..."

She fell silent and the quiet that followed seemed
melancholic and laden with danger. Neria searched for some
words of support, but Passoa resumed her monologue before she
could think of anything to say.

"I look forward to meeting Queen Analour. To me, she

embodies our energy and strength…"

The maids returned and Neria smiled at them. Sure, her clothes, only dusted off a little and scrubbed with a damp towel, left something to be desired, but the sheep's wool that had crowned her head had turned into a halo of playful curls that framed her face with flair. The long madder-colored belt that Passoa had fastened — "you can give it back to me later," she had said — distracted from the pitiful state of her old rags. Its ends waved with her every move and the bulging knot accentuated her slender waist. The two women, meticulous and efficient, their gaze still lowered, simply cleared the room of the toiletries before leaving. Neria was not able to enjoy their surprise at the sight of her metamorphosis. Then a guard, a middle-aged Demon who wore his leather uniform frayed from use with seductive abandon, entered the room and closed the door with care. An old scar ran from the top of his cheek to his lips. He had the same short haircut as the other soldiers: they did not care for the extravagant hairstyles reserved for dilettantes. He told them that they were soon to be presented to the Queen. Passoa let out an exclamation of joy that seemed to irritate the Demon.

"I'm sorry," she said, "I didn't mean any disrespect."

"I don't know what you are expecting, but I must warn you. After a degrading ceremony, you shall be thrown into slavery. Many Demons here disapprove of how the thralls are treated. Why harm them when they would be far more useful if they remained healthy? Some think I'm an extremist, but I consider first-generation Demons to be our equals and I believe we should obtain our slaves from the other Chimeras. Anyway, time is running out and I wanted to urge you to stay hopeful. Try to get through this as best you can, and we will do our best to improve your lot afterward."

The man had spoken in a monotonous way that contrasted with the content of his words.

"What are you talking about? But you must be mistaken! A woman, I remember her name, Ouliane, you know her, don't you? She came to see me one day and told me about the wonderful life you had here. Helping each other, sharing..."

He pulled a chair toward him and sat on it. His face had taken on a weary look and his body had lost its military rigor. His shoulders drooping and his legs sprawled out in front of him, he looked at them for a moment in silence before resuming his explanations.

"A tout. We like to lure our brethren and then use them as we see fit. I used to look forward to my meetings with Analour; she had a lively temperament and a lot of spirit. A little too short-tempered, no doubt... We thought that this trait would subside with time."

He stared into space and seemed to be talking to himself.

"Instead, her fits of rage got worse, and she couldn't take any form of criticism. The growing discontent fueled her delusion. She saw enemies everywhere and surrounded herself with advisors who made her even more alienated and easier to manipulate. She got it into her head that she wanted to become immortal... You, the young one, I advise you not to resist if the Queen decides to drink your blood."

He slowly got to his feet and remained motionless for a moment.

"Keep hope. There are those among us who yearn for

change. Above all, don't even think about turning me in as you would share my punishment. I must go. I know these revelations must have shocked you, but I urge you not to be discouraged. The life of a slave is a life all the same."

Once the door was closed, no sound broke the silence.

Stupid gullible Chimera! Had Elatek drawn his inspiration from the Demons? The repulsive ideas of the More-Than-Pure were spreading everywhere. Drinking blood! Neria imagined a yellow straw stuck into her bleeding elbow crease and a woman bent over it, drawing the liquid with relish. Out of the question. She would not let herself be reduced to slavery like Ellane and so many others before her. She had to find a way to escape. Anaëlle, who loved dolls, card games, and chervil pancakes, was waiting for her.

Passoa, frozen in her sorrow, was still staring at the door without moving. Neria turned toward the meager possessions that she had arranged on a chair. She turned her back on her companion to make sure she could not see what she was doing, before taking the knife out from its sheath and putting it in her lavish belt. She arranged the knot to conceal it as much as possible. A keen eye would notice, but she hoped the Demons would prove too arrogant to search their prisoners. Then she walked over to Passoa and put a hand on the shoulder of the still motionless woman.

"It's okay, we'll make it through this."

"He's insane… I don't believe a word of his lies."

Neria did not have time to answer because the guard returned accompanied by five others and they left, flanked by this escort like esteemed guests or dangerous criminals. The corridors widened as they continued. They arrived in front of enormous doors, staffed by two halberdiers who opened them. They entered a huge hall where a bustling crowd of Demons was standing, hung from the walls, or suspended from the ceiling like bunches of grapes. The two prisoners and their escort walked down the central aisle, lined with columns carved with winding patterns. They halted several feet from the platform on which stood the most beautiful creature Neria had ever seen, the one that she had seen among the Angels in the reflection of their Source. The stone of the throne highlighted the paleness of her complexion, the refinement of her waist and her limbs, the lustrous opaqueness of her hair arranged in a skillful scaffolding, and the glittering of her almond eyes. Her graceful fingers were adorned with long silvery metal nails. At the bottom of the platform, a stolid Source reflected the watchful crowd. Neria turned her glance from it. A master of ceremonies, equipped with a heavy ornamented staff, ordered them to declare one after the other, their names and the purpose of their visit.

"Let me take care of this," Passoa whispered.

She stepped forward, upright and graceful, a brave smile spread across her face.

"My name is…"

A sharp blow crashed down on her skull.

"Lower your gaze before Analour, the Mother Supreme, the Soul of Cambolae."

Passoa's figure seemed to slump, and she obeyed, hastily imitated by Neria. She gave her name and, with a trembling voice, explained that she wanted to join the glory of the Demons.

The Soul of Cambolae rose with a languid grace and,

hindered by her long narrow tunic, descended the steps. She approached Passoa, studied her, smelled the fragrance emanating from her body, and then ordered, "The Assessors shall come forth for inspection!"

Five Demons wearing pointed hats appeared and proceeded to conduct a detailed examination. Passoa let herself be manhandled while they measured the size of her limbs, the circumference of her skull, studied her nails and fingers, and forced her to open her mouth. One of these austere figures, with gray hair and a prominent Adam's apple, turned to the Queen and announced, "She is one of us!"

With these words, the crowd applauded in a sinister manner, following the dreary rhythm imposed by the staff of the master of ceremonies. Neria swallowed with difficulty.

The Assessor raised his hand to ask for silence, "Yet her birth did not result from the union of two parents belonging to the Night People but from a recent and poor-quality mutation."

The dirge-like pounding had resumed. The Soul raised her hand and restored silence.

"Pity… She would have made a thoroughly presentable maid. Please proceed with the Disposal of the waste!"

The crowd chanted these words with delight, as two guards led Passoa toward the Source. Head bowed and limbs limp, she allowed herself to be led at first without reacting, then suddenly straightened up and began to beg the Queen and the crowd to let her live. She struggled, her feet dragging on the ground, unable to stop the relentless march. The condemned, who resisted so desperately, made the spectacle of their executions even more painful. However, until the end, Neria followed her new friend with her eyes. At the last moment, Passoa looked for her and managed to find her, the only friendly face in a heinous assembly. They stayed connected by this tenuous link for a few seconds, which was suddenly broken before Passoa disappeared, swallowed by the dark water. Neria swore to preserve the memory of this pointless death forever.

Was her life going to end like that, alone in the middle of these longed-for siblings, brutes as malicious as the More-Than-Pure? A ludicrous and untimely death, devoid of even the slightest meaning. Anaëlle and Matar had warned her. Neria did not even have the excuse of having come across a tout. Patient and silent, the Source was waiting for her and would soon open its gaping mouth to swallow her whole.

When the crowd grew quiet, the young woman was pushed toward the Queen. Disgusted by the heavy perfume that fluttered in the trail of Analour like a heady fog, Neria, head lowered, admired the elegance of her leather slippers. The Assessor then proceeded to his inspection and pronounced his First Generation verdict. Neria could have told him and saved some time, but what for? These people held to their ceremonies and she was in no hurry to die. The Demon with the pointed hat took advantage of the restored silence to add, "A mutation of exceptional quality this time…"

"I demand an Energy Transfer! This girl has plenty to spare."

The audience seemed elated with these words.

"Do it," whispered a voice behind Neria, a weapon pressed in her back to emphasize the point.

Analour approached, swaying with her steps. A smile

raised the corner of her lips, the same smile that had bewitched Neria and had drawn her toward the black water.

"One second!"

The weapon pressed in a little more and Neria held back a cry of pain.

"I agree to sacrifice myself to the Queen of the Demons, the Soul of Cambolae, our light in all. I, Neria of Alipaz, ask to serve the Mother Supreme as she wishes."

The smile widened and revealed yellowed teeth, weathered by the years. Yet her skin and appearance had retained their youthful aspect.

"You seem smarter than the others. Rest assured that you shall progress quickly, for we know how to show our gratitude to faithful servants."

The guards moved aside a little, but the threatening spike still persisted. Neria understood that she would have to succeed the first time. She tilted her head and offered her neck; a barely visible blue vein snaked across her golden skin. A gluttonous expression spread across Analour's face. She approached the willing victim, her mouth opened to savor the throbbing vein. At this very moment, Neria's body tensed and struck back. She put all her cumulated rage against the cruelty of this Demoness, the scorn of Kamau, the savagery of the Moguedon, and the arrogance of Valterone into this blow. Her head crashed against her all too perfect nose, then she took the knife out from under her belt and, with a precise back and forth, cleaved a new smile across the queen's throat. She suddenly found her less beautiful. The Soul of Cambolae lost her balance and fell back on her rump, looked for a moment at her murderer with a bewildered expression, and then collapsed to the ground. She had not suffered too much.

Surprised to find herself still alive, Neria took flight and spun around. She drifted in the center of the hall like a monstrous fetus floating in a rotting uterus. The man who had warned them gazed at her, mouth agape and arms dangling by his side, the knife still in his hand, a red scar on his pale face.

Anaëlle! Anaëlle was waiting and she would not disappoint her. She would fight to join her, escape the Source, go free, or die at the hands of her so-called brethren. With a motion, she loosened her belt, which dropped to the ground like a rose petal. At this signal, the trance shattered and a destructive fury swept through the crowd. Cries of joy and rage resounded: "The queen is dead... Freedom... Kill the traitor... Kill them... Vengeance... Mine..." Three Demons threw themselves at her, coming from different directions. One of them screamed and fell, impaled by a spear intended for Neria; the other two crashed into each other when she dodged them at the last moment.

The death of their queen had shattered the façade of civility and the Demons were slaughtering one another with a ferocious hatred fueled by years of repression. With knife and heel, Neria carved a path through their murderous rage. Like Forg had taught her, she changed the trajectory of her course to disorient her pursuers. Another spear barely missed her. She reached the doors, which had just opened. The men stationed there gazed at the crowd for a moment with a dumbfounded expression.

She shouted at them, "The Queen's been attacked! Come quickly!"

She almost collided with Scarface, who was surrounded by

four men and was on her heels. He whispered, "Come with me."

She looked into his unblinking black eyes and nodded. He barked at the halberdiers, "Go to her aid, we'll find a doctor."

The halberdiers continued to hesitate to throw themselves into battle as the fugitives flew past, the soldiers lacking the intelligence or the courage to stop them. Neria turned around. The Demons were still tearing each other apart in the glorious hall. While the outcome of the fighting still seemed uncertain to her, she would not place any bets on the wigs who appeared to have forgotten the art of handling a weapon.

They reached a main thoroughfare and mingled with the stream of passers-by. Clothes soaked with another's blood, Neria hoped that nobody would be alarmed by her state. She concealed her knife, now without a sheath, in her sleeve. When Scarface veered into a side corridor, which moved away from the only exit that she knew, she decided to trust him and followed. The news of Analour's death had not yet reached these outlying parts and the people they passed seemed to belong to a more serene past. They went into a poorly maintained tunnel. Scarface moved forward without hesitation and soon led them into the open without any further incident.

The Demons dissuaded her from going to Roguelle; they knew a safe place where they could hide. She put aside her eagerness to find her niece and her friends. If the Queen's supporters won, the new ruler would send soldiers after the murderer. They came to another ravine and proceeded for a while between two stone walls, then her guide rushed down a narrow opening she wouldn't have noticed. After a short corridor, they came to a spacious hall and landed. Crates and weapons were piled up against the walls, amphorae leaning against them. Neria understood it to be a hiding place supplied with provisions.

The five men, seasoned soldiers, formed a wall in front of her. Their unrefined attention, like that of an animal following its prey with its eyes, made Neria aware of her vulnerability. She assessed their weapons, their size, and touched the handle of the knife still hidden in her sleeve with her fingertips. Scarface stepped toward her. She breathed in and prepared herself for combat. She watched her opponent's chest so as not to be distracted by the expression on his face while also keeping a close eye on the others. He fell to his knees.

"We shall never be able to thank you. You have done what no one has ever been able to do. I swear to serve you until I die."

"Come on, come on... Get up, it'll be easier to talk. Get up! I'm telling you to get up. If you want to serve me, you can at least stand up! That's better."

"Queen Analour is dead! Long live the Queen!"

Stunned by their exclamations, Neria suddenly imagined herself sitting on the stone throne, her back straight, her hands resting on the armrests, dignified, a benevolent and gracious smile on her lips. This man offered her the unthinkable chance of influencing the lives of thousands of people. She still had battles ahead of her, but once peace was restored, she would be able to bring in Anaëlle and Nephalie. She laughed at the thought of her mother in the dark maze of the land of the Demons. The others exchanged confused glances. After some time, Neria calmed down, wiped her eyes, and sat down on a crate, still shaken by sudden bursts of uncontrollable laughter.

"The queen of what? This cave?"

"Analour's minions are being slaughtered by our allies as we speak. They shall inform us when they have secured power."

Neria jumped to her feet.

"Who knows about this place? How many allies do you have? Can we trust them?"

Without waiting for their answer, she moved toward the opening, the others on her heels. Before leaving, she checked that no one had followed them, then flew out.

They found shelter under a stubborn tree that clung to the rocky ground. Daylight was breaking and the sun's rays soon radiated a welcome warmth. They took turns keeping watch and managed to get some sleep. But the wind picked up and the night left them feverish and hungry. If deep inside, the men were critical of the decisions of their new "queen," they did not complain. Neria found hardship to be a habit of hers and wondered if the solution to her problems lay in a nomadic life. Searching for a home, she had found it the day she had set foot on the welcoming, serpentine, and never-ending road that fled Alipaz.

"I hope my humble contribution will give your country a new start and that you'll be able to put someone worthy of the position on the throne."

"We shall always consider you our queen. How can I convince you to come and sit among your people and agree to lead them?"

Undoubtedly due to the hunger tormenting her stomach, Neria felt like a beggar who had been offered a platter of fine foods. Once again, she imagined herself on the stone throne, endowed with a power that she never could have expected to enjoy before. A comfortable life, luxurious clothes, extravagant hair, servants… She would bestow her blessings… abolish slavery and privilege. Would they let her? Thrilled by the feat — a stroke of luck really — she had just achieved, they would promise her anything she wanted. But could they keep their promises? Did they have the same desires as her? Scarface approved of servitude if it was limited to other Chimeras. She knew so little about them, nothing of their aspirations, their desires, or their weaknesses, while deep down she was suffering from the void left by the absence of Anaëlle, Forg, Matar, and those left without hope in the vast prison that Alipaz had become.

"I'm leaving for Roguelle to find my companions."

"Our queen cannot travel without an escort. Grant us the honor of serving and protecting you on this journey."

They left two men behind, tasked with spying on their behalf, and headed for the city. After one night of uninterrupted flight, Neria felt such a pain — like a tearing where her wings joined her body — that she decided to stop.

In the valley, the milder temperatures made it possible to bivouac in the open air. The soldiers lit a fire, then left to find edible roots and game. Meanwhile, Neria rested. With her hands stretched out toward the flames, she imagined how Matar would react if he saw her once again indulging in her habits of laziness and luxury like this. She pushed these thoughts aside and allowed herself the guilty pleasure of enjoying these unexpected privileges. When the Demons returned, she insisted on helping with the meal and made them sit and eat with her. She asked them questions, and gradually the initially forced conversation became more relaxed. When he noticed her nickname for him, Scarface laughed. He asked her to continue calling him that.

"I am honored to be the first one you have seen. Analour often used this method to show her displeasure. If you had been afforded the opportunity to walk around the slums, you would have encountered many other disfigured men or women like myself."

He had displeased the Soul of Cambolae, who had scratched him with her sharpest nail at the end of a public humiliation session. Stripped of his rank and his fortune, he had embraced a military career to ensure his livelihood. Neria tried to imagine him with scaffolding on his head but failed. Those follies did not suit the austerity of his manner any longer. Had he ever worn one? Would he have wanted a change of power if he had not lost everything? Before falling asleep, Neria thought of Forg's surprise when she would appear, preceded by her courtiers and her new title: Queen of Demons in exile.

CHAPTER THIRTEEN

After a long night of travel, the Demons discovered Roguelle, huddled at the foot of verdant hills, under the timid rays of the rising sun. Memories flooded in at the sight of the city, different yet so familiar: the brightly colored houses reminded Neria of a building set Arhel had once had. With the help of these wooden blocks and a handful of dried beans reluctantly given by the cook, the brother and sister had spent hours imagining wonderful adventures. A new game unveiled before her and Neria wondered which role she would be allotted: a powerful and temperamental hand or the rather more sallow part of a bean tossed about at the mercy of the circumstances.

As they approached the stone walls, winged watchmen intercepted them and ordered them to land on the wall-walk. The soldiers inquired about the purpose of their visit and Neria explained that she was going to meet some friends.

"We know all the Demons who live here. What are their names?"

"They're not Demons, but a Gargoyle and two Humans, travelers like us."

"How long will you be staying?"

"We don't know yet."

"Roguelle's a peaceful city and we intend for it to stay that way."

Neria stopped Scarface with a gesture before he said anything unwise.

"We're not looking for trouble."

The patrol let them leave and they began their visit with a swift flight over the mud houses and the crowded streets. Although Neria noted the worrying presence of the soldiers of Purity, who wandered around the city in red clusters, she mostly marveled at the diversity of the Chimeras who rubbed shoulders with the Humans as equals. Dressed in the ocher-yellow uniforms of the Guards of Roguelle, the vibrant clothing of the rich, or the duller attire of the common folk, they practiced all types of trades: merchants, scribes, blacksmiths, masons... Neria saw Gargoyles, Lizard Men, Centaurs, Tiger Men and so many others going about their business in a carefree crowd.

Attracted by tempting stalls, Neria landed in a market that reminded her of the shopping trips of her childhood: the constant noise punctuated by the cries of vendors, colors intense or subdued, a cacophony of smells, packed bodies, fresh bread, fish, fruits, vegetables, and spices... A Centaur was busy making donuts. He grabbed the dough with his glistening hands, shaped a perforated disk in a few swift movements, dipped it first in hot oil, then in a syrup that seemed to diffuse around his stall, enveloping it in a honeyed mist.

"If you're not buying, beat it! You're scaring my customers away."

Neria turned toward the Demons, asked them with little hope if they had any money, then moved away with a shuffling step.

How could she find her friends in such a sprawling,

crowded place? As naive as ever, she had hoped to track down her companions as soon as she had arrived, and then, after a long heart-to-heart, getting some food and sleep. Or conversely, sleeping before eating, it didn't matter... She would fly over the city, knock on the doors of the humblest inns, and if she failed to find them, she would sleep outside once again, before resuming her search.

A passerby spat on the ground and grumbled insults as he walked past them without even slowing down. They were too taken aback to react as he nonchalantly strolled away.

"We've got to get out of this city as soon as possible."

Rattled by hardship and uncertainty, the Demons gave up on their tedious deference. It would not be long before the escort left this unfit and unruly queen.

"Just a little patience. I know you're tired, but first..."

"What's going on?"

"Shhh!"

Neria closed her eyes and listened. The echo of a thunderous laugh had caught her attention. But she had lost it... There! In that direction... She weaved through the dawdling crowd, complaining about the obstacles slowing her down, scanning the faces of all the Gargoyles she passed. She grabbed the arm of a stranger, apologized, resumed her search, and suddenly found him standing in front of a strawberry stand. Strawberries... already! She approached him in silence. He was talking with the vendor and not paying any attention to the pandemonium around him. Would he notice her? She brushed against him, then shoved him a little...

"Hey, there's enough for everyone, no need to push!"

He barely glanced at her and continued with his conversation.

"Let me try another one. I'd like to be sure of the quality, you see, personally, I don't think good strawberries should need sugar or cream, and those that do…"

He swiveled around to look at her but remained silent.

"Are you still angry with me? How ru…"

He took her in his arms and squeezed. She put her head on his chest, felt the softness of his fur, his familiar smell.

"I've not stopped thinking about you since you left."

He was still holding her. A tender yet firm embrace that she wanted to continue despite the unusual setting and the bewildered looks of the onlookers. But a slight change in his breathing or a twitching of his body alarmed her.

"What's wrong?"

He let go of her and hid his face for a moment.

"What's the matter?"

He signaled for her to be patient. Then he straightened up, took her by the hand without looking at her, and led her away.

"Come quickly! What would Matar think if he knew we were making a spectacle of ourselves? He's been harping on at us about how we need to keep a low profile. I think he's going senile. Say, do you know these strange people following us?"

"My escort."

"Rather conspicuous for an escort… Don't they ever smile? You can tell us all about it. I can't wait to see Anaëlle's face. And Matar's… But first, I want to show you something."

Forg navigated the bustling streets with ease.

"I hated this place at first, too many bodies packed in together and not enough space, but I got used to it. I do miss the trees though. See that building over there, higher than the others? That's the city hall."

He advised them not to stop and to look indifferent as they passed by. The soldiers posted at the entrance seemed bored and Neria wondered why Forg had brought them here, before noticing the wanted notices posted on a wall. She forced herself not to stare.

"It is quite a resemblance."

"Pretty close. Except for the ears and the hair, it's definitely you. By the way... I really like your new hair. What's the matter? Is something wrong?"

"No, no, I'm fine. Thank you."

Neria sighed. She would never find another person so skilled at taming her mane. Passoa had lived in this city, had walked these streets, and some of the women who surrounded them had undoubtedly bought her creams. Neria wondered if she should pay her respects in front of her former home. She had not known the Demoness well but knew that she valued beauty. Neria wanted to learn how to engrave stones before choosing a peaceful spot in Roguelle where she could place a rock, a small one that would not attract too much attention, visible yet not in the way, humble enough that no one would want to move it. And then she would go into the forest to replace the hastily painted stone that lay on Imri's grave.

Young wild sage leaves unfurled at the foot of a wall, the first signs of the spectacle of months to come when spikes of scarlet blossom would burst forth from their velvet green crowns.

"Dead or alive... I don't like the sound of that. And that reward seems far too high."

"He must really want to see you again."

"Yes, my father's very creative in showing his affection. 'Accompanied by a child...' At least there isn't a portrait of Anaëlle."

Neria suggested buying a scarf to hide her face, but Forg dissuaded her. The crude disguise would expose more than it would conceal and he hoped her ears and wings would be enough to blur the resemblance.

They arrived at an inn. Once inside the perimeter walls, they entered a large courtyard divided into three rectangular sections: the one in the center open to the heavens and the other two with flat roofs supported by beams, onto which thick woolen coverings had been attached, like those woven by nomads to make their tents. To the left were the kitchens and to the right the common room, the sounds of conversation and laughter coming from within. Forg pulled open a partition. Neria barely had time to get used to the half-light when Matar appeared in front of them, Anaëlle in his arms.

"Get out of here this instant."

He headed toward the main building taking great strides. Following a moment's hesitation, the others trotted after him without argument. Anaëlle, her chin resting on the Peddler's shoulder, her arms around his neck, looked at Neria with a stone-faced expression. They climbed the staircase and took a dark corridor into a cramped room, furnished with three straw mattresses and stools. A narrow skylight provided the only source of sunshine.

Matar put Anaëlle down on the floor. Neria moved toward her and crouched down.

"I missed you..."

Anaëlle pushed her away with such a force that Neria fell over. Scarface rushed to her aid and helped her back up.

"I'm fine, I'm fine, thank you... let go... everything's fine."

He threw an incensed glance at the child but remained silent.

"Why did you leave me?"

Neria looked at her accuser, so small and frail, her eyes glistening, her face red and her hair a thicket of thorns. She remembered her prophecy of "the Souwce is waiting for you" and how it had terrified her when she had been saying goodbye. She had felt the icy water running down her throat, spreading to her fingertips, and then, without thinking, she had pulled Anaëlle off her leg like a leech. But she had since confronted the Source in the land of the Demons and fooled it. Anaëlle was nothing more than a child with a powerful yet fallible gift.

"I apologize, I shouldn't have left you like that, but I couldn't calm you down and I lost my temper."

"You promised to stay with me."

Her high-pitched voice chirped yet the speech impediment that Neria had found so charming had vanished. She almost wished she still had it and felt the sensation of having lost a game. As if playing statues, she had barely turned away before Anaëlle had reappeared, transformed. She picked up the discarded doll, dusted it off, fixed its hair, and handed it to her niece.

"I'm sorry. I thought I'd found the answer to our problems among the Demons... it might actually be there... Anyway... I always planned on coming back to you, you know... but you're right, I shouldn't have left you like that and I'm really sorry... Everything worked out fine and here we are together again. Can we be friends?"

The child burst into tears and threw herself around her aunt's neck.

"Anaëlle, I can't breathe..."

"I don't want you to go."

"I don't want to go. Come down from there so I can talk."

"No, no way."

The girl still clutched onto her, Neria let herself fall back on a stool and recounted her adventures. At the end of her tale, Matar grumbled, "You managed an extraordinary feat, but you could have been stuck there."

"I was very lucky. I did think that for a moment... All in all, I made the right decision."

"You were wrong! And you should have listened to me. But you did fine in the end."

He assessed the escort with a disapproving eye.

"Three more mouths to feed, big strong lads who won't go unnoticed."

"I'm not surprised you live alone. Who could put up with such a crank?"

Matar finally revealed a smile.

"You, no doubt, since you came back to us instead of lounging around there playing at being a queen. You arrived just in time, by the way, we're leaving tomorrow. I don't like this city. Something about it worries me."

"I've got to admit the room could be a little more comfortable," said Forg. "I'd rather sleep in the fork of a tree than on these flimsy mattresses."

"Onyx, now he knows how to show gratitude. He appreciates his stable and his daily meal, unlike some others who constantly complain."

"Why are you leaving so quickly?" asked Neria.

"The mayor, Yourk, has opened Roguelle's doors to all travelers. The streets are teeming with spies sent by Valterone and snitches in the mayor's pocket. My informants tell me this is the case in all the Free Cities of the region. Valterone's preparing another offensive, I'm sure of it. We could try Tarkoya, it's on the edge of the forest and things seem to be better there."

"Our choices are getting narrower. We will never find a quiet place to settle down. Why not just kill all the More-Than-Pure?"

"Your father, however powerful and dangerous he may be, is only a small cog in the machine that Elatek's built."

"But if we destroy several cogs…"

"Others will replace them. Alipaz society seems too united in its love of slavery and its sense of superiority. Then again, if word got out that Valterone's own daughter had joined the rebellion, perhaps we could rattle the beliefs of the majority."

"A pretty weak weapon compared to the fear imposed by my father."

"Forgive me for speaking out, but I do not see any reason why our queen would fight for these people when her own land awaits her. But I can assure you that the friends of the Soul of Cambolae shall always be welcome among the Urbane Demons."

"Really? We don't even know who's won power."

Forg snickered.

"The Soul of Cambolae... What a dumb name! Let's go back to the forest instead. We can find wild and rugged country there..."

"Like vermin hiding in a hole..."

"It's just a suggestion... no need to get upset. There was a time when you wanted to stay with the Gargoyles too."

Several years earlier, at the end of a visit to the market, Rona had, under the veil of secrecy, dragged Neria into a tannery to visit the owner. Her tutor had hoped to marry this burly man with a booming voice. Within the unspeakable stench, slaves pounded skins to produce a soft and supple leather, pliant to the touch. The sight of these fermented, scoured, and beaten skins had so revolted Neria that she had threatened to report Rona if they ever returned to that place.

She stroked Anaëlle's hair, who was still perched on her lap, muttering inaudible commands to her doll. The day would come when no one in Alipaz would remember that Chimeras and Humans once lived in harmony.

"I'm sorry I lost my temper. You're right, I did want to hide too, but I've changed my mind. I need to return to Alipaz."

"Yes, the Source is waiting for you there."

"It's waiting for me and will be for a long time to come, I guarantee it. Stop going on about it, I don't want to hear any more."

"And I'm going to see Mommy."

"You're going to see Paz?"

"She's my mommy."

"When?"

"I don't know, soon."

Anaëlle resumed her conversation with the doll and Neria resisted the urge to throw the repulsive thing through the skylight. One after the other, the companions tried to get further clarifications, but the child's explanations remained vague and brief. Neria finally exclaimed, "On behalf of everyone's stomachs, how do we get food around here?"

"This stay's going to cost me a fortune. Go down to the common room but watch what you say."

"Tell her about her sister."

Matar shot Forg an angry glance.

"What do you know? Tell me!"

"I'm warning you we're leaving tomorrow."

"Talk."

"First promise me you'll act responsibly."

"I'm not stupid."

"I saw Elinor."

Neria jumped to her feet.

"Where? Let's find her."

"I'll go and find her. You are to stay here and wait for my return…"

"Do you know why she's here? Have you talked to her?"

"No."

"Why not?"

"What would I have told her? That I saved you and then lost you?"

"She would have understood."

"She wouldn't have understood a thing."

While the others went to the common room, Matar left them to look for Elinor, saying, "I've still got a few friends in this city, you'd only get in my way."

A fire burned in the fireplace and the woolen blankets that served as walls insulated the patrons from the cold. As they entered, the newcomers were greeted with stares. Some turned away with indifference, while others lingered, filled with curiosity or outright hostility. With a tray in her hand, a Reptile Woman weaved between the tables and swung her long tail from side to side. She wore a small orange hat with confidence, resting on her smooth scalp and flattering her bluish complexion. When she recognized Forg, her mouth widened in a large smile that revealed two neat rows of sharp white teeth.

"Hello, Forg, same as yesterday?"

"Yes, please! Good, healthy, nutritious, and affordable, what more could you ask for? My dear Livia! How are you today?"

Forg and the waitress continued their conversation without paying any attention to the sullen expressions of Neria and her

Demons. After the young woman left, Forg declared, "I don't want to live in this city, but I've got to admit it does have its advantages. If the journey didn't take so long, I'd consider making an annual pilgrimage."

Neria looked for a moment at her dirty nails, quite different from those of the Reptile Woman.

"Gargoyles are very popular around here."

The waitress returned with a heavy tray that she carried with great care. She weaved between Forg and Scarface and placed a pitcher of water, glasses, and a basket of flatbread on the table. She left again, then came back and, after having set down plates laden with puréed chickpeas, bent down closer to Forg. Her tunic slid down to reveal a firm, round shoulder.

"And here's a little gift from me!"

She flourished a small bowl of green olives, placed it in front of the Gargoyle and added, one hand on his shoulder, "Let me know if you need anything else."

He watched her walk away, swaying as she went.

"I love this city!"

Neria felt as if she were watching two butterflies coming together and parting, then reuniting to leave one another once again in a swirling dance: a phenomenon of intimate and secret significance, for which the way of the women in her family — the demure Ellane, the ever-dignified Nephalie, and the excessively beautiful Elinor — had not prepared her. In Alipaz, such brazen behavior would have tarnished the waitress's reputation and earned her several lashes. Kamau's advances had left no room for doubt nor for this strange choreography the rules of which were a mystery to her. Neria shrugged her shoulders and concentrated on the flavors of the simple yet delicious food.

When she straightened up, full, she noticed a brown-haired, tall Human was watching her. But he immediately turned his face away and resumed his conversation with his shorter, blond companion. She examined them for a moment before leaning toward Forg.

"Let's go. Those two guys... don't look... they look shifty to me."

"Not you too. Matar already sees spies everywhere..."

"I'm going back upstairs. You coming?"

"Go ahead. I'm going to stretch my wings and legs. I'll catch up with you later."

Neria did not insist any further. She had no authority over him and he could make as much a fool of himself as he pleased. Barely having arrived in the room, the Demons, too exhausted to maintain their decorum, collapsed on the straw mattresses and fell straight to sleep.

"I'm going to lie down for a few moments because I'm feeling really tired. Then we'll play together or maybe I'll tell you a story. Okay?"

The child, busy with her doll, nodded absentmindedly.

When she awoke several hours later, Neria found Forg and Anaëlle absorbed in a game of dice, sat cross-legged on the floor, a dish of red berries beside them. She joined them.

"How long have you been back?"

"Long enough."

"What have you been up to?"

"Nothing much."

Forg put three dice into a cup, sealed the opening with his hand, and shook. The cubes rattled in their wooden prison.

"Take a look at this. I think it's amazing."

He flipped the cup over. Its rim slammed against the floorboards and the dice fell silent.

"Well?"

"Hmmm... three, seven, and eight."

Forg lifted the cup.

"Three, five, and eight. Not bad. Go ahead, you can eat two... no, only two... Well, okay... Let's try again."

"Anaëlle," intervened Neria, "what do you see if you think of Alipaz?"

"Hmmm... Grandpa is happy... but Granny is sad."

"Why? Why's she sad?"

"I don't know."

"And your mommy?"

"Mommy is okay. She feels sad sometimes too, but... she's okay."

"Elinor?"

"Hmmm... Elinor isn't in Alipaz. Go on! Roll the dice."

"Anaëlle, stay focused just a little longer."

"Leave me alone! You think this is easy?"

"Judging by the dice, you..."

The door opened and Matar appeared.

"Clean this room for me, they won't be long. Neria, get

your squadron up. Strange escort, honestly... And then get Anaëlle ready, look at the state she's in."

"Who's coming?"

"Your sister and brother-in-law. I managed to find and convince them. They didn't believe what I was saying for a second, you'll have to explain it all to them again. Shake out those straw mattresses for me, get some air in here. You, there, fetch a broom."

Neria jumped to her feet and opened the skylight. A draft of cold air swept into the room. She thought she could detect the smell of the sea, fresh and salty. But it was impossible, they were too far inland. Your brother-in-law... So they'd gotten married. But what were they looking for in Roguelle? Valterone would never have let them leave without good reason. Neria grabbed a straw mattress, shook it out, put it on top of the others, then watched the dark shapes bustling around her.

"Forg and the Demons should leave."

"Good idea! Forg, take the squadron with you. Wait downstairs until you're called."

"Why? I want to meet Neria's sister."

"You'd only scare her away. Get out of here! And no wasting money!"

Neria smoothed down her clothes and found herself missing Passoa's red belt. Anaëlle's hair! Where had they put the brush?

Knocking on the door startled her. She froze, her eyes wide open, her mouth half agape. Draz appeared in the doorway, standing taller and more upright, a sword hanging from his waist.

Did he even know how to use it? He gave way to let Elinor pass. Neria moved back a step. Not only did Elinor seem radiant, but her clothing was also elegant and immaculate. She wrinkled up her nose and seemed to be suffering from nausea. Her gaze settled on Anaëlle.

"Anaëlle? Is that you? Oh, my darling… How thin you've gotten… and dirty. I'm going to take you home… Are you okay? How have these people been treating you?"

"I'm fine, Neria's taking care of me."

"Neria? Where is she? These people kidnapped you…"

She straightened up and turned to Matar.

"You want a ransom, is that it?"

"Elinor, it's me."

"How much do you want? My husband will handle the transaction…"

Draz grabbed his wife's elbow.

"Look… look at that creature."

Elinor threw Neria a look of contempt mixed with repulsion. Then her expression changed and she drew nearer to examine her more closely.

"Neria? Is that you?"

She brought her hand to her lips.

"How you've changed…"

"For the good, I hope. I'm a little older…"

Elinor's eyes grew misty.

"I didn't think I'd see you again, I thought it was a trap."

Matar grumbled disapprovingly.

"This man claims to know our mother... I didn't believe him, but Draz convinced me to come... Oh, Neria!"

Elinor took a step toward her sister then burst into tears.

What a pitiful being, swaying hesitantly, wringing her hands, then letting herself fall into the arms of her husband who had come to her rescue. Their mother had protected her overly sensitive and fragile older sister throughout their childhood. To her credit, Elinor had not abused this preferential treatment but had been content to float above the fray like a pleasant apparition, a flag that folds and collapses as the wind calms, inert and pale, exhausted by the effort. To her great embarrassment, Neria felt tears moistening her eyes.

"Come on, now, stop crying. You can see I'm in great health. Why are you making such a fuss?"

Elinor moved away from her husband and took out of a pouch, which she wore on her belt, an embroidered handkerchief with which she tapped her face.

"Just blow into it!" cried Neria. "Stop making such a fuss! It's just you and me!"

"Oh, Neria! How can you be so irritating! You're just the same as ever."

She rushed over to her sister and embraced her. Neria tensed up at first, then relaxed and patted her on the back, which was still shaken by tears.

"Everything's fine..."

Her face flushed and wet, Elinor stepped away, holding her sister by the hands.

"Draz, look! She has wings."

L. M. RAPP

"Hello, Draz."

"Hello, Neria. Glad to see you in good health... and good company."

"Congratulations on your wedding, you finally made up your minds. But you could have waited for me... I was supposed to be the maid of honor."

"Don't worry, you didn't miss out on anything, we gave up on our dream wedding. Elinor will tell you about it."

"My big sister, always so beautiful and perfect, as usual."

"How can you say that? You're stunning... wild, beautiful, and dangerous. How I envy you! You'd know how to defend yourself if anyone ever attacked you."

"Let's leave them in peace," Matar suggested, "and head downstairs for a drink. They serve a perfectly acceptable wine."

"Excellent idea!" said Draz.

Neria looked at Matar moving away. He was going to join Forg and would keep that Reptile Woman with the supple waist and charming smile at bay. Before the door closed, she heard him ask Draz, "By the way, what are your finances like?"

In a hushed voice, the two sisters told each other about the twists and turns of the past few months. They laughed a great deal and cried too. Neria described her adventures among the Chimeras, Elinor related the murder of Adamek, the imprisonment of Nephalie, and the treason of Zelimo.

"What a creep! No wonder he gets along with Valterone. You should have got married earlier."

"Draz thought he was protecting me. You see, he's leading the rebellion."

"Draz? That bore…"

"He thinks our fathers will forgive us. He wants to go back to Alipaz."

Later, Matar returned, followed by Draz, Forg, and the Demons.

"You've been drinking."

"Draz offered us a sum of money that'll be enough to cover our expenses and, to celebrate, we ordered a couple of bottles of a remarkable wine."

"A full-bodied but generous wine that'd be at home in the Queen's cellars, alongside the most renowned vintages."

"And Maznar here knows what he's talking about, once a member of the upper echelons of Demon society."

"Maznar?"

"I don't intend to call him by a ridiculous nickname."

"I didn't know you were so sensitive."

"You and your pompous airs…"

"But that doesn't bother… uh… Maznar. He assured me he felt honored by that nickname!"

"And you believed him! Your sense of superiority is so deep-rooted that…"

"You're making a big deal out of nothing! How can I know what he wants if he doesn't say anything?"

"Scarface here, Scarface there, make my bed, serve my food."

Forg and Draz managed to calm Matar down and encouraged him to take a seat. As soon as he was sat on a stool, the Peddler began to gently nod his head before finally sprawling out on the straw mattresses. It wasn't long before he began to snore loudly.

"Sorry about him, he's not used to drinking."

Draz walked over to Elinor and put his hand on her shoulder.

"We should go."

She grabbed her husband's hand and squeezed it.

"I'm afraid."

"We've talked about this before."

"I'm afraid of what's waiting for us there. I wish we could go away and live in a faraway land where no one would know anything about us."

"Your father will never leave us alone. If we stay here any longer, he will send his soldiers after us and there will be a price on our heads."

Neria tried to imagine the family home without Nephalie. Just Elinor, so wise, the evanescent Ellane, and the belligerent Valterone.

"Will Mom come back soon?"

"At first I hoped our father would bring her back, that he was waiting for the scandal to die down, but I don't believe that anymore. He told me a few days before we left that he'd decided to get married again. Our mother's presence there would force him to move."

"Don't go back to Alipaz, stay with us."

Elinor looked at her with a distraught expression. Neria imagined her in the forest, a Human without wings, nor claws, nor fangs, so fragile and sensitive…

"You'd adapt too if you didn't have a choice."

"I'm afraid it's too late for me."

Draz wanted to get back to their inn before nightfall, and the two sisters parted without knowing if they would ever see each other again.

Neria, still exhausted in spite of the few hours of rest she had enjoyed earlier, forced herself to go to the public baths and made Anaëlle accompany her. The place, austere but adequate, did not have the magic of the pools of Gork's Corrie. They washed and put on clean clothes, their fabric all too glossy and darned in places. Before they left this city, she would ask Matar to stop at the market to buy new ones. She started combing Anaëlle's hair but soon realized she would not be able to untangle all the knots in one sitting and postponed the rest of the task until the following day. At the child's request, they stopped at the stable to see Onyx. The donkey cheerfully greeted them and eagerly allowed himself to be petted. Anaëlle said that he was getting too bored and that he wanted to sleep in their room. Neria refused and finally managed to get Anaëlle to say goodbye to him.

When they returned to the room, she found her companions settled down for the night: the Demons to the left, Forg and Matar to the right, and free bedding between the two groups. Scraps of conversations lulled a silence barely illuminated by the moribund moon. Neria lay down near Anaëlle and hoped never to forget this moment, the regular breathing of the child, her familiar smell, and the gentle warmth of her body. She unfastened her knife from her thigh and attached it to the other.

After having lost her sheath in the land of the Demons, she had improvised this solution, less practical, but more discreet. She listened for a moment to the echoes of laughter coming from the common room, to the quiet breathing of her companions, and fell asleep shortly after.

A hand shook her by the shoulder and awoke her.

"Get up. I heard a noise," Matar said in a quiet voice.

She brushed his hand away with an irritated gesture. Noise in an inn, what could be more natural than that? Then Matar's concern seeped into her, spreading through her mind like a drop of wine in a glass of water.

"Leave through the skylight," said Matar.

"It's too narrow."

"We'll take the stairs."

Swinging a stool, she shattered the cloudy glass and latticework. She grabbed Anaëlle, already on her feet, by the waist, ready to hoist her out, but the appearance of two Gargoyles on the roof stopped her in her tracks.

The door crashed open.

"Don't try to run away, all the exits are blocked. Drop your weapons."

Soldiers had burst into the room and, among them, a blond man pointed his finger toward Neria.

"That one there, that's Valterone's daughter."

The tall brown-haired one that she had noticed in the common room backed him up.

Anaëlle, frightened, took refuge between Neria's legs. The soldiers restrained their prisoners one by one. Some of them held poles at the end of which dangled a lasso. They threaded them skillfully around the necks of the winged Chimeras. The coarse rope dug into her tender skin. Raising her bound hands up to it, Neria was brutally whipped, swearing to give her torturer a taste of his own weapon at the first opportunity.

The ocher-uniformed soldiers herded them onto the street with the end of their poles. Anaëlle had climbed onto Matar's back, the only one to retain some degree of freedom of movement. At this time, the few people still awake or not yet in bed watched them pass without reaction. Neria had felt as if she had slept very little, but a slight clearing of the darkness indicated to her that the day would not be long. They arrived in front of the city hall, entered the building, and began to ascend the staircase. The relentless poles steered them to the top. They came out onto a roof terrace and drank in the icy, tranquil air of starlit darkness. The soldiers then pushed them toward a cuboid structure on the flat roof, into a generously sized room, perfumed with incense and illuminated by a multitude of oil lamps. Intricately carved wooden furniture decorated the space like lace panels. Behind an imposing desk on a padded chair sat a Gargoyle, whose sparse hair indicated health problems or a fraction of Human blood. Neria wondered if his frail wings and his corpulence prevented him from flying.

"Take off their chokers. We'd rather our conversation be more comfortable, wouldn't you?"

He picked up the poster spread out on the table and held it up for them to see.

"Neria, daughter of Valterone, come forward."

The blond snitch rushed over to him.

"It's that one. Look at her face and the one on the poster. I recognized Elinor too, that's her sister, she came to visit her."

"The daughter of the most powerful Human in the land has turned into a Demoness... Interesting... And who is this child?"

"My daughter," Matar replied.

"I see. Neria, do you have anything to add?"

"My identity's nobody's business but mine. Roguelle is a Free City, where Chimeras can move around without being harassed. Unless you've pledged allegiance to Elatek? In which case, do you know the fate that awaits you?"

Yourk studied the portrait carefully once more, then cheerfully announced, "We shall contact the emissaries of Valterone and bring them the Demoness... and the little one too, since the poster says that the fugitive is accompanied by a child..."

"Don't you take my daughter away from me! I beg you..."

A blow to his stomach with a baton cut Matar's pleading short. He buckled and fell to his knees.

"As for the others..." said Yourk, "I am in a rather generous mood. I shall let you go on the condition that you never set foot in this city again. We have just concluded a series of treaties with Alipaz and are entering a period of openness and cooperation between our peoples. Adventurers like you could jeopardize our efforts."

"When can we collect our reward?" asked the tall brown-haired man.

"You shall receive your compensation after the identity of the Demoness is confirmed."

"I want to talk to you Chimera to Chimera," Forg interjected. "After all, we're on the same side by our very nature, aren't we?"

"That remains to be seen."

"Elatek's soldiers destroyed my home, killed my friends and family, without any provocation from us. Now they're walking the streets of Roguelle along with the scum of Alipaz, like these two rats, with total impunity. I fear for your future. Who will stop Valterone from enslaving Roguelle if he so wishes?"

"My dear fellow, I feel for your plight, but I suggest you stop worrying about us. Valterone, an ambitious but pragmatic leader, will honor our agreements. Besides, our army will protect us."

"Are you comparing it to Elatek's army?"

"Let me finish! The only problem here is your stubbornness. Every now and then, rebels come to beg for my support to free Alipaz, but I will always refuse to help them. These Humans, so physically weak compared to us," Forg looked doubtfully at the mayor's wings, "have legitimate fears and feel scorned. They have their own culture and their own values, no hasty judgments, please, which we must respect. If we push them away, the problem will only get worse! You want war. What a waste! We open our arms to peace, we accept all those who want to join us, and you will see that they will improve through interacting with us."

He leaned back in his chair and rested his hands on the armrests.

"My once insignificant city is growing. Construction sites

are springing up and more and more travelers are flocking here every day. And so what do the people want? When business is booming, everyone celebrates, no matter their beliefs, and..."

The sound of a body hitting the ground interrupted his rant. Stiff, Anaëlle stared at the ceiling with an icy gaze. Yourk leaped up from his seat and shrank away to the back of the room.

"This child is sick! Is it contagious? Get her out of here now!"

"It's all right. It's just a fit..."

Neria, kneeling beside her niece, held her hand as she waited for the seizure to pass. As soon as she regained consciousness, Anaëlle burst into tears.

"We're all going to die!"

"The child's delirious!"

"What did you see?"

"Fish are going to attack the city!"

Yourk laughed.

"The child is disturbed. Fish from where? We're a long way from the sea. The few schools of piranhas that do sometimes come near never do much damage, other than biting off the odd hand or foot from an unlucky fisherman. There's no point in trying to alarm us, we enjoy a peaceful existence here."

A panting officer burst into the room.

"Master Yourk, I request an immediate audience, Elatek's soldiers and Valterone's emissaries left the city during the night. We found two guards dead in front of the north gate."

An uproar of voices erupted. Neria and her companions were trying to pry more information out of Anaëlle while Yourk was questioning his captain. Shouting grew in intensity outside.

"Out of my way, let me through!"

With surprising agility, Yourk rushed outside, shoved aside the soldiers in his way, ran to the far end of the terrace, and pressed his stomach against the balustrade. The others, who had followed, gathered around him.

Illuminated by the slanting rays of the rising sun, an armada of enormous fish was floating around the city.

CHAPTER FOURTEEN

How can they even survive out of the water? How are they flying? Have you ever heard of such a thing?"

With his hands clenched on the guardrail, Yourk turned his head from side to side and questioned Yado, the commander of the troops. Alerted by the alarm sounded by dozens of horns, the city's inhabitants had rushed into the streets and were marveling wide-eyed and with beaming smiles at the sight of the fish, whose flamboyant colors stood out against the dark sky. Gargoyles in harnesses pulled them forward while baskets carrying red-uniformed soldiers swayed beneath their bellies.

"Can we shoot them down?"

"No, they're too high."

"Look at that one, the yellow one that's come over the walls, it's losing altitude. Is it wounded?"

"I don't think so."

"What is their plan? To bring troops in to attack us from the inside?"

"Then why would they evacuate the city just to come back by air? It doesn't make sense."

"What are you doing here anyway? Wouldn't you be of more use at the front?"

"I came to warn you. But you are right, my presence is no longer necessary and, with your permission, I shall join my men."

"No, stay."

"The lieutenant here can serve as liaison officer."

"You are not to leave here until we know the nature of the assault. What about catapults? Do we have any?"

"Catapults would do us no good.

"What about bows and arrows, you know, big ones? We have them, don't we?"

"Very few. You decided to develop a garden by the riverbank instead…"

"It doesn't matter! Stop dithering! We're under attack!"

"I request permission to join my men."

"Out of the question, I've already told you, you are to stay here until we know more!"

"Lord Mayor, I have no choice but to disobey your orders. I hope you understand."

Yado walked away, followed by his soldiers.

"You will hang for this! Deserter!"

The officer hurried over to the stairs and disappeared.

The sun continued on its journey and tinted the thinning clouds pink. Residents came out of their houses and watched in awe as the flying ships dotted the sky like flowers in a meadow, silently crossing the city walls to roost within. As the Roguellians waved their hands and handkerchiefs, the men in the baskets began to empty bags of colored balls that gave Roguelle a festive air. Hysterical laughter erupted, followed by resounding screams, as some fled and others fell to the ground, not getting back up. Like a swarm of locusts fleeing a fire, the flying Chimeras of Roguelle launched into the air and perished in droves as the red soldiers released their bolts.

"Let us go! At least give us a chance of survival."

With a bewildered expression, the mayor stared blankly into the sky, but a guard approached and began to cut the prisoners' restraints.

Yourk suddenly grabbed Forg's arm.

"Save me. I can't fly, I never learned. But the two of you could carry me over to the other side of the walls."

The guard who had freed the Gargoyle continued his task while his comrades, a dozen men who had stayed on the roof, watched them, uncertain. Her bonds cut, Neria grabbed Anaëlle and flew away. With a jolt, Forg released himself from Yourk's clutches and followed her. Neria skirted around the fish looming over the city hall and rose higher. Arrows whistled past her ears. Below, she saw Matar, transformed into a monstrous tiger, leaping away from the building, clearing a path, before disappearing into the crowd as people ran in all directions. Anaëlle screamed in horror.

Orange, blue, yellow, and green balls fell on the terrace around the abandoned mayor and shattered, releasing a scum-colored gas. Yourk burst into uncontrollable laughter and collapsed to the ground, his body writhing in agonizing convulsions. His lips, clenched in a demented grin, were smeared with a deluge of foam. Neria wished him a quick death. Surrounded by the Demons, she followed Forg toward the walls. They found them strewn with the corpses of Roguellian soldiers. A few pockets of resistance were still fighting, but their efforts seemed futile. Two concentric circles of laughing fish surrounded the city. They successfully made it past the first one, which was lower and more disorganized. Anaëlle's weight hindered Neria's movements and her arms, tightened around her neck, choked her.

Forg shouted, "I'm going to look for a way through. I'll be back."

The fish surrounded her. Dazed by their dance and that of the arrows, by the screams of the child and the soldiers, Neria redoubled her efforts, but understood she would not succeed. An arrow pierced her wing. A sharp pain, fleeting, bloody... She continued to fly. Another grazed the skin on her calf. One of the Demons screamed, fell, and disappeared. She ordered the rest of her escort to flee, but they stubbornly stuck by her side. They would all perish. Seized by a sudden inspiration, Neria dived down and took shelter under the lowest basket. She could not see the Demons anymore. Anaëlle was no longer screaming, but her body, stiff and shaking with convulsions, slipped in her arms. One of the ships was losing altitude. They'd soon be easy targets. Neria tightened her grip and took a deep breath. If she failed, a fall from this height would make their deaths quick. But she pushed back these thoughts. In a few moments, she would try to make an exit and find a gap through which to escape. The basket was getting closer and she prepared herself to leap out.

Neria noticed a yellow fish turning in a circle as if in an invisible fishbowl. The Gargoyles, all female, refused to obey their handlers and swept their flying carriage along in an infinite vortex. Some of them, dead or unconscious, dangled inert in their harnesses, their limbs shaking with the motions of the whole. The drunk fish pushed aside the one threatening Neria and she took advantage of the diversion to make her escape. She made it past the final circle and moved away toward the forest.

Forg appeared suddenly.

"Take her!"

They stayed face to face for a moment, their wings flapping in the air and keeping them upright. Forg took hold of the still unconscious child, held her close to him and flew away. When he realized Neria was not following them, he turned around, "What are you waiting for? Hurry up!"

"I'll catch up with you later!"

He shouted, called out to her, even insulted her, but she listened neither to his commands nor his pleas and headed back to the city.

In Alipaz, of all the jobs, fishing was undoubtedly the most dangerous — chance encounters with sea monsters could destroy an entire expedition — but also one of the most lucrative. The wealthy clambered to pay for the very dear privilege of tasting the exquisite flesh of these fish, supposedly having therapeutic qualities.

Neria had seen several of these expeditions set sail from Alipaz. The fishermen, made up of seasoned survivors, frightened new recruits, and unwanted slaves, organized themselves into a flotilla consisting of two or three large ships and a large number of small boats. The attitude of the women always surprised her. No crying or screaming, but a resigned and apathetic sadness that spread to the young children as well. The farewells undoubtedly took place in the intimacy of the home because, after the blessings were given and the religious ceremony completed, the men departed without looking back while their wives remained motionless and left only when the boats, reduced to a few dots moving in the distance, were no longer distinguishable from the birds floating on the sea. Neria, who was also leaving for a peculiar fishing expedition, thought of Anaëlle, abandoned once again.

She noticed a fish following an erratic course, moved toward it by taking care to maintain her altitude and landed on its domed back, its taut skin giving way a little under her weight. The soldiers in the basket could not reach her, but another ship was now approaching. She pulled her knife from the strap on her thigh and stabbed. As she had hoped, a wound burst open, and a hiss of air escaped from it. She struck again and again. The fish fell abruptly, dragging along its passengers and the Gargoyles harnessed to it as it plummeted. Neria headed for the next one. This time she only made a small incision; she wanted to stay unnoticed and leave any rebels a chance of survival. She did not wait to see the reaction of the passengers nor to see a possible landing and, moving from fish to fish, she reached the walls where she noticed a small island of resistance more organized than the others: Yado had positioned his troops in the shelter of a tower. She landed next to him and tried to get his attention. Without taking the time to even look at her, he pushed her away with the back of his hand.

"Not now!"

She stood firm before him, grabbed the collar of his tunic and shook him.

"Rally the flying Chimeras!"

Soldiers rushed to their commander's rescue and grabbed her, one of them putting a knife to her throat. She managed to add, "I know how to kill them."

He ordered his men to let her go. She launched up into the

air, landed on the nearest fish and pierced it in several places. It began to fall. She could now gauge the number of punctures needed to get the ships to the ground as quickly as possible without killing the shackled Gargoyles. She headed for another erratic blimp. Horns sounded a sorrowful bellowing. The Gargoyles and a few Angels who answered their calls flew, after a brief explanation, toward Elatek's troops, like sparrows attacking elephants. Their weakness discovered, the fish were run aground, one by one, and the inhabitants of Roguelle regained their courage.

Neria knew that once the last blimp burst and the last enemy soldier was killed or imprisoned, the survivors would be left with the painful task of cleaning the mass grave the city had become. She clung to the idea that her companions would not be among the dead to be buried. Her gaze skimmed over the corpses that littered the roads, stopped dead in their attempts to escape. Several months earlier, she had searched for Matar's body at the foot of the walls of the Corrie. Had he managed to survive once again, swept up in the stampede of terrified crowds in streets flooded with noxious fumes? As soon as she arrived at the inn, she realized that their arrest had saved their lives.

She landed by the entrance to the courtyard and held her sleeve against her nose to dull the stench of green apples. Suddenly, her stomach lurched with fear. She turned down the path that led to the stables and started to run. She knew what she was going to find before she opened the doors, but went in anyway, the crease of her elbow still pressed against her face. The sight reminded her of the tannery she had visited with Rona, only worse. The animals, with their bodies scarred by fresh wounds, littered the floor like the pieces of a grotesque mosaic. These animals had shared the fates of their masters, who had perished at the crack of dawn, without even understanding the reason for their deaths. She found Onyx lying on his side, his ears flat, and his beautiful eyes wide open. The same and yet different... The uninhabited remains of a beloved companion. Impelled by the urge to pet his rough coat one last time, she crouched down, her hand touching his strong neck and brushing it with her fingertips.

A sound of footsteps startled her and she rushed outside.

"Don't come in."

She blocked the entrance, spreading out her arms. She wondered if Matar would ever remain trapped in his beast form. Out of breath, hair standing on end, his canines protruding from under his lips, he spoke in a gruff voice.

"Let me through."

Imri's lifeless face often appeared to Neria at the most inappropriate moments and she regretted having ever seen it. But she moved aside. He entered the stable, slipped into the half-light, and fell to his knees in front of the donkey's body. His broad shoulders shook.

She was still hesitating about what to do when the sound of wings caught her attention. She looked up to the sky. Forg's feet had barely touched the ground when the Demoness pulled Anaëlle from him and squeezed her in her arms.

"How is Onyx? I want to see him."

"I'm sorry..."

Neria took the sobbing child away and went in search of a

place untouched by the poison gas. She found a small square where a fountain was trickling: a dragon-man, whose head and torso were sculpted into a wall, was spitting out a thin stream of water from his lips, pursed as if for a kiss. Neria sat down on the edge of the basin.

Unable to speak, she stroked her hair and listened to Anaëlle's wailing, suffering, but at least still alive.

"He was all alone. I don't want him to die... I love him... He's so sweet... I want to see him."

Neria hoped the donkey had been among the first to be afflicted by the poison gas, so he would not have had time for fear, to pound the earth with his hooves, to throw himself against the walls, his eyes wide, his mane standing on end, his nostrils flared... If the inn, far from the center, had been attacked at the very beginning and he had died at the moment the hostilities started while they had still been standing on the roof terrace of the city hall, she would feel less guilty for not having thought of him when she had fled and for not having saved him while she still had the time. She dipped her hand in the water, watched it flow between her fingers, then cooled her face. Death, which had followed her since childhood, at first punctuated by distant monthly executions, now manifested itself in a macabre succession accentuated by the deaths of loved ones.

Matar appeared and Neria thought he looked hideous, but Anaëlle ran toward him, unconcerned with his appearance. He lifted her up, squeezed her in his arms and wearily answered her moans, "I know... I understand... It's true..."

He approached Neria and sat down.

"I did everything I could to get to him, but the streets were filled with gas and I failed him... He didn't suffer... At least, not for long... He was a brave animal... who lived a good life."

Neria nodded. The elegant houses around the deserted square gleamed in the sunshine.

Three Demons landed in front of them. She thought for a moment that the wounded Demon had somehow survived, before realizing another was now in his place. She stood up and walked over to Maznar.

"Please accept my condolences for Tartello's death."

Since her altercation with Matar, she had made sure to call each member of her escort by their name.

"A needless death, surrounded by people who despised him... I know how you must feel, you wish you hadn't come with me."

"He fought well... and for a good cause. His family will be proud, I shall make sure of it."

After hesitating, he added, "I beg your forgiveness. I should not have doubted the abilities of my queen, Nerialour the Big-Hearted, the warrior of a Thousand Lives. When Your Grace disappeared, I thought you had been struck like Tartello and I lost hope. I apologize for my lack of faith. I am unworthy of serving Your Grace."

He dropped to one knee and bowed his head, followed by the other two.

"An emissary has just arrived from the motherland bringing us news of our side's victory. I beg Your Grace to accompany us. Return with us to the land of the Urbane Demons. Our brethren need a guide and you alone can fill this role."

Neria suppressed a burst of laughter. She, who had been struggling for months with doubts of her own, should show the way for other lost souls? Maznar looked at her, eyes filled with a sincere hope. She envied his gullible zeal. They were all lost and were going to kill each other to the very last in foolish fury. But with an almost maternal feeling for this older man, she made him stand up and assured him that she would consider his proposal. To her surprise, she realized she was telling the truth. She turned to Matar.

"Where did Forg go?"

"In the inn... Let him be."

Neria stepped out into the courtyard and walked around a series of corpses lying in strange positions. These people had initially gone outside to admire the spectacle, then, when they had realized the danger, had tried to flee back to the buildings. She approached the Gargoyle looking at a figure lying on the ground. Livia held her small orange hat between her clenching fingers. Her skin seemed to be pasted to the bones of her face, her gaping mouth revealing sharp teeth and a blue tongue. Neria turned her gaze away.

"Come on."

"We have to bury her."

"There'll be people taking care of that soon. Come with me, you can wait for them outside."

When he didn't move, she took his hand and pulled. He let her lead him to the fountain. She took Anaëlle in her arms and flew away. The dazed men watched her leave without question.

The attacks had left the wealthier districts unscathed; perhaps spies had taken refuge there or maybe the Humans had wanted to extort money from the wealthy Chimeras before enslaving them... In any case, if Yourk had stayed in bed, he would have survived, and they would have died. Elinor had planned to leave the city that day, but if she was still in her room when the assault had begun, she should be safe. Neria did not feel tired anymore. She flew over the beautiful houses, the Temple, the esplanade and its Source, located the Golden Phoenix, one of the rare stone buildings and the only opulent inn in Roguelle. Neria examined the passers-by who seemed to be going about their business without concern but could not make out her sister among them. She approached its façade and shouted Elinor's name. She circled the building, tried to see through the cloudy glass and continued her calls. A window opened and a man shouted at her to stop the racket. Another... and Elinor's haggard face appeared. Neria rushed over to her.

"Take Anaëlle... Get back, let me in."

The Demoness jumped into the room. Elinor stood behind the girl, hands on her shoulders. Both looked at her in astonishment. Neria threw herself at them for an embrace.

"I knew it... I knew you were alive."

Neria later parted for the battlefield to look for survivors among the Gargoyles harnessed to the baskets. She preferred this task to burying the dead. She feared that no one would come to the aid of these women who had slowed Elatek's army and whose sacrifice had saved the city. If, as expected, the fish had managed to be deployed before sunrise, Roguelle would have fallen with no chance of resistance. She first looked for those who had allowed her to escape. Intertwined bodies lay tangled in the harnesses that had held them captive. A cry caught her attention. A female Gargoyle, her spine shattered, was still moving. Neria approached and poured some water on her cracked lips. A grimace of pain contorted the hairy face.

"Your hand..."

She placed a tiny, blood-stained pouch made from a coarse cloth in her outstretched palm.

"All the women have one... find them... and give..."

Her head tilted back. Neria pressed her fingers against her neck, but failed to find a pulse. She opened the bag and found a piece of folded parchment inside. There were tiny symbols on both sides, which she deciphered: a letter to a husband, parents, a child, wishes, vows of love, farewells...

All the women have one...

Neria inspected the corpse of another Gargoyle. After several minutes, she discovered an identical pouch, sewn under her chest strap. She continued her search and collected a dozen more. While she was continuing in her search, an emaciated Gargoyle landed beside her. She must have been suffering from an illness, with her skin showing in patches.

"Give them to me."

"What?"

"Give me those letters."

Neria obliged without argument.

Once the pouches were in her possession, the woman placed them carefully in one of the bags hanging from her belt.

"We made a promise to each other to give them to the surviving families."

282

"Can I help?"

The Gargoyle wavered, then composed herself.

"I knew a Demoness once, but she didn't last. Demons and Angels aren't as resilient as we are."

"That's true. Female Gargoyles are just as strong as males."

"Maybe even stronger. Where are you from?"

"Alipaz."

"Ah, I've found three letters for Alipaz. I'll give them to you, maybe you'll have a chance to pass them on one day."

Her hands trembling, she carefully studied the papers stowed in one of the bags.

"You can give them to me later."

"It won't take long, I've got them organized."

After several long minutes, she handed over the three letters.

"Take good care of them."

"You're in no condition to carry on. Drink some water."

She gave the Gargoyle her canteen and some cookies she had brought with her. As the surviving Gargoyle left, Neria, who had already retrieved a sheath for her knife from a soldier's corpse, found a small canvas bag with leather drawstrings that she opened to place the letters inside. But she could not bring herself to do so. They remained in her palm, light and translucent, like the scales left behind by a snake after shedding its skin. The scrawled characters seemed to call to her. She sighed and began to decipher the first letter. It was addressed to an Angel in the service of a More-Than-Pure she had met before. The second was to a Reptile-Man. She recognized the name on the signature of the third letter.

Since she was very young, she had heard talk of Souphe, Bobka's wife who worked in a camp and whom Valterone, in his immense magnanimity, protected.

"Dear Bobka, your memory has sustained me through all these hardships. Our children are dead. Keep on living for us. I love you."

Neria fell to her knees and wept without anyone paying the slightest attention to her. Such scenes were now too commonplace to be of note anymore.

"I just wish I'd been there to see it."

"The last person who grabbed me like that," said Yado, "ended up unconscious for two days. I was ten years old at the time."

"So what happened? What stopped you from knocking Neria out?"

"She seemed to have lost her mind."

Forg burst out laughing heartily.

"I know exactly what you mean. I'm very familiar with that look she sometimes gets and it scares me too. Come on, Neria, try a little of this wine. I've never had anything like it!"

She was not used to alcohol and found the flavor unpleasant, but out of respect for Forg who had gone to a lot of trouble to organize this meal, she wet her lips in the goblet. The others exclaimed as if this were some great feat. She smiled at them.

Her gaze kept returning to Matar, who was even more

taciturn than usual, eating reluctantly. His cheeks were sunken and his clothes hung loose on his body. Anaëlle, sitting between them, was talking to him incessantly. One might have thought he wasn't listening to her if it weren't for the short answers he occasionally let slip. The two of them spent a lot of time together. They wandered the streets with their respective canes — people laughed at the girl masterfully mimicking the stride of her elder — and went on excursions into the forest. Exhausted after these adventures, Anaëlle would fall asleep at the table, while Matar lingered with a glass of wine in his hand. He had resumed his weapons training and the child was proving a diligent apprentice. She often repeated the same anecdotes and described Onyx's graceful physique and perfect personality in great detail. Although the Peddler never talked about his donkey, he seemed grateful to the girl for having undertaken the task.

Opposite her, Draz held his wife's hand between his own. He would leave the next day, alone, for Alipaz, where he would explain to Valterone the reason for their flight and beg his forgiveness. If all went well, Elinor would not return to Alipaz until the city was liberated. Maznar, at the end of the table, even quieter than usual, looked on disapprovingly. The Demons had capitulated to Neria's request for reinforcements, even if this arrangement did not exactly thrill them. Neria would become their queen after the coronation ceremony should she survive the battle to come. She doubted she would want to leave a newly liberated Alipaz, but no circumstances could free her from such a promise.

To her right, Forg and Yado were still making a great deal of noise. Under the control of the commander who had taken Yourk's place, and after much hard work, the city had returned to normal. Neria had protested at the sight of a group of shackled prisoners being branded, but Yado had dismissed her disdain. "I'm handling this crisis. We have to clear up this abattoir and need a larger workforce."

Neria turned to Anaëlle, sitting beside her.

"Eat your lentils."

"I don't like lentils."

"They're very good for you, eat them."

"I don't like them."

"You can't always get what you want, you know."

Anaëlle abruptly pushed her plate back and stood up.

"You never ask what I think. Any of you... Nobody cares what I want! But I know as much as you do, maybe more, and I want to be involved in decisions. I won't eat this disgusting food!"

Scarlet-faced, eyebrows furrowed, she pounded her little fists on the table and challenged the other diners with her eyes. When the laughter subsided, Neria responded to her, "Very well. We'll try to include you more in the future, but don't be surprised if we don't always follow your advice. You may be gifted and intelligent, but you're only six years old and you can't compare yourself to an adult."

"Says the sixteen-year-old," said Matar.

"Seventeen."

"Is that so?"

"Yes, I was born in the winter."

Elinor apologized for forgetting her birthday and everyone

wished Neria a long life, happiness, and prosperity. Forg left for the kitchen and returned with a platter of donuts in the middle of which he had placed a candle. Before blowing it out, she thought of the most appropriate wish. Her status as Queen of the Demons surrounded her with an aura that reached even the most remote corners of the land, with money and gifts already pouring in. She had even bought new clothes for herself and her friends and they had all moved into the Golden Phoenix. The innkeeper, initially uncooperative, had realized he could not afford to cherry-pick his customers in these troubled times.

The news of the fall of three Free Cities had stunned them, but Valterone's aggression had finally pushed the Chimeras to unite against their common enemy. Troops poured in from the spared cities and the land of the Demons. Against Matar's advice, Neria had also sent two emissaries to the Marsh.

"Why bother Sido? So he can supply us with onion soup?"

"Don't underestimate the importance of logistics," laughed Forg.

"You can make fun of him all you like, but without him, we'd have been gaseous phlegmon food. He saved us. Besides, he knows how to make powerful remedies."

Forg had applied the ointment the Toad Man had given them when they left to the wound on her calf. It had dried like a second skin and had instantly soothed the pain. On seeing the needle and thread, Neria had tried to avoid having her wing treated, but the Gargoyle had insisted so much that she had relented. As she had feared, the operation had proved painful, but the wound had not become infected and all that remained, as a souvenir, was a scar in the shape of a one-post ladder.

"In any case, Sido sent a very kind note back to me. He understands the importance of the fight against these fanatics and sympathizes with our cause."

"So what? Is he coming?"

"He's started his spring cleaning, but will try to join us."

"How reassuring."

A few emissaries had gone deep into the forest and returned with a troop of Gargoyles, led by the ill-tempered Barz, the first to consider her an adult. Other Chimeras had answered the call, some Centaurs, Dryads and Tiger Men. Neria respected their courage but was not under any illusions: they would need a great many organized warriors to defeat the vast forces of Elatek and these volunteers did not seem sufficient. She had only felt the hope of victory when the Angels — who Matar said had a military tradition perpetuated by their harsh life in the mountains — had agreed to join the assault.

She closed her eyes. After the fall of Alipaz, she would organize another meal. Her mother, Ellane, Bobka, and Kamau would be joining the current guests. She blew. The flame suddenly went out.

She pulled her head out from under the covers, looked out of the window and fell back. Afternoon already... The excessively rich food of the past few weeks was making her nauseous. She loathed the thought of another day of waiting, barely distracted by games of dice or backgammon, meals that took far too long, and weapons training with the Peddler and his renewed belligerence. The Angels were late and she wondered once again if Kamau would be among their ranks. Anaëlle had disappeared, probably off rambling with Matar. Neria got dressed and went to knock on her sister's door. Wrapped in blankets, her hair in disarray, she half-opened the door, then stepped aside to let her in.

"Get ready and come down to eat with me. I'll wait for you."

"What's the point?"

"You can't just stay here and wither away! Draz went to fight for you, for all of us. The least you can do is get out of bed."

"I won't be of any use."

"No, don't go back to bed! You'll have the most important task of all during the assault: looking after Anaëlle. You know how important she is to us!"

"This war terrifies me. If you would at least try to negotiate before…"

"Don't be so naive, you know what Father's like. He'll never listen to us. Get up! Okay, if you're going to be like that, I'll leave you to it then."

Neria opened the window, jumped on its ledge, ignored the grumbling of her sister, and leaped out into the void. The wind, blowing and gathering clouds, indicated a storm was brewing. But she had several hours beforehand to stretch her limbs. She flew over the city, spotted a group of Demons in the market, turned, and moved away before they could recognize her. She couldn't stand being constantly followed around any longer and had subsequently ordered a public holiday for all her subjects. Besides, the men could use a little entertainment. Roguelle looked so peaceful from this height, almost happy with all the warriors who had flocked there.

A Gargoyle came hurtling from a roof, Neria brought her hand to her knife, but recognized Forg.

"I wanted to take my mind off things. Follow me!"

She wanted to get back to the forest and burrow under its protective cloak, like an animal in its den. She would have been better off had she stayed wandering and free. They headed for a narrow lake, where gallinules abounded, busy in their peaceful and diligent routine. Their heads bobbed back and forth, following the rhythm set by their submerged legs. They were dredging through the mud, preening their feathers, and feeding their young, so endearing in their resemblance to disheveled adults. The heat had subsided and the water, barely disturbed by the ambling birds, shimmered like an emerald.

Forg nose-dived, his bow drawn. The birds fled in a rustling of frightened wings and two hens fell, struck. Neria landed beside a grove of ferns and Forg joined her, brandishing the fowl, holding them by the legs. Their heads dangled limply with their beaks half-opened. For these graceful creatures, death had taken the form of two black giants.

"I'll give them to our hotelier to prepare for us."

"Poor things."

"Well, we've got to eat."

"You may think I'm too sensitive, but these birds have built a nest, raised their young, taught them to fly…"

Her voice broke and she felt her eyes sting. She bit her lip to keep from crying.

"What's the matter with you? What's wrong?"

Neria picked up a fern and began to pull off its fronds.

"You're right," said Forg. "Only the weak take pride in destruction."

"My father being a good example."

"You're nothing like him."

"I hope not."

"You know, it's natural... I'm afraid myself."

She turned to him, "You? Afraid? But you take everything so lightly."

"My parents were artisans. They used to leave me with an aunt when they went to sell their goods in town. I had some great times there, having fun with my cousins... My last stay with them lasted until I was an adult because they just never came back. I can't even remember their faces. I feel like I abandoned them."

"You were very young..."

"I will at least try to remember Livia."

Although she'd hardly enjoyed this chore in the Corrie, which hurt her hands and sapped her energy, Neria felt the strange urge to chop wood. She picked another fern which she began to dismember.

Activity resumed in the lake once again. A family of ducks with black and white livery and piercing red eyes skated there with an elegance that contrasted with their terrestrial clumsiness.

"I won't forget her either. You loved her very much, didn't you?"

With a sudden motion that took her by surprise, he dropped the two birds to the ground and approached her. He grabbed her by the shoulders.

"Let's go! Deep into the forest, or the Marsh. We'll take Anaëlle with us, maybe Matar, if he insists... I'll protect you, I'll take care of you, you won't want for anything... Well, you'll always have something to eat and a place to sleep. Isn't that enough? Let's leave the others with their wars and their madness. I know you can never love someone like me, but..."

"Oh, Forg!"

"I don't want to lose you, you understand?"

She moved closer to him, wrapped her arms around his waist and rested her head against his neck. He held her tight against him. She felt his muscular yet soft body, his fleece caressing her skin, his musky scent of earth and crushed leaves. She, who for days had been brooding over battle tactics, could not fall asleep without fear of a nightmare, startled by the slightest sound, now felt as if she were floating in the sky on the warmth of an updraft... Or rather, that she had swallowed a bright, stirring melody, a huge pocket of air that fluttered in her chest and lifted her off the ground.

"I didn't think you loved me... well, not like this."

"I've been in love with you since the first stone you threw at me. Your rage and the accuracy of your aim blew me away."

"I was understandably angry after being treated like that..."

"When are you going to accept that I just saved you a long walk?"

Neria burst out laughing.

"Always the same argument! We'll never agree on this. But you should know I don't believe you. I thought I was so ugly at the time, nobody could have liked me..."

"No uglier than anyone else with Nymphosis... You were so annoyed with me... You finally got over it, but our arrival in the land of the Angels dashed all my hopes, especially since you decided to go off on your own. And now you've become the queen of the Demons..."

"I can just imagine the look on the faces of those socialites when we appear together. I could have you crowned too..."

"I'd like that, lounging around with servants and eating all day. But never mind... There are more pressing concerns that need my attention."

He leaned in and kissed her. She felt as though raindrops were fizzling on her skin.

"Are you sure I'm hairy enough for your tastes?"

"It's not all about looks. Don't worry, I'll make you a coat."

"And a mace, and a horned helmet, I can't go out without horns..."

They stayed by the lake for several hours, considered the possibility of running away together, gave up on it, and when they came within sight of Roguelle, noticed the unusual number of white wings gliding over the city.

CHAPTER FIFTEEN

The noise startled her. She felt afraid, but not as much as she had expected. After all, she had already seen this happen. She would have confided in Neria, but she had feared that her aunt would run away again. Sylophine, her doll, the one who knew all her secrets, told her not to cry because they would see each other again one day, if all went as planned. Anaëlle squeezed her, then kissed her, and managed to put her in a chair before the powerful arms lifted her up and carried her away.

Neria contemplated the broken glass scattered on the ground below the smashed open window, icy air rushing in. She approached the bed and the motionless figure lying there. Her pale face and blonde hair barely stood out against the light fabric of the cushion.

"Why haven't you asked for the window to be sealed?"

"I don't know… I haven't had the strength. I want to feel what she feels. Hungry, cold, afraid…"

"That's not going to help us find her."

Still wrapped in her blankets, Elinor sat up unsteadily.

"I went downstairs to give instructions for our meal, I thought she was safe, she was playing right here, I feel so awful, I told you, I'm no good at anything… They're going to find her, aren't they? I raised the alarm straight away. She can't have gone far…"

"Maznar's organized the investigation. There's a search party going around the city, groups of Demons, Angels, and Gargoyles have gone looking in all directions, others are searching the buildings and questioning local residents. I'm optimistic they'll find her soon."

The iron-tipped cane, which Anaëlle had been using to train for combat, was leaning against a chair. The doll sat on the seat, waiting for her playmate to return. She looked clean and tidy thanks to the bath Elinor had forced upon her a few days earlier, despite Anaëlle's protests, who, unlike her aunts, rather liked Sylophine's musky smell.

"You clearly don't know anything about the world we live in!" said Neria. "I've gone off without her sometimes, but I've never left her on her own."

Elinor burst into tears.

"Who could have taken such a young child? You told me about Arhel... but Anaëlle poses no threat to Father!"

"This city's swarming with spies. Some will have told Valterone about Anaëlle's abilities and where she lives. She's more powerful than she appears... And she can be used as a bargaining chip."

"But he'd never lay a hand on her!"

Neria shook her head.

"You don't want to see the truth..."

"Don't speak to me in that tone!"

Elinor got out of the bed and began to get dressed.

"I'm leaving for Alipaz, I'll go and look for her."

"Don't talk nonsense."

"You entrusted this child to me, and so I'm taking responsibility. As the oldest sister, I will talk to Father. He'll listen to me."

"If you don't die on the way there, you'll just be giving Valterone another hostage. You aren't going anywhere without my permission."

"How dare you?"

Even rage suited Elinor's complexion. Rosy cheeks, eyes glistening, she threw a shoe at Neria's head. She caught it mid-flight.

"You're attacking the wrong target."

"Listen to me now. If Father… if he hurts Anaëlle in any way, I'll demand you slaughter him and destroy that cursed city. I'll kill him with my own hands if I have to."

A few knocks on the door interrupted their conversation. Forg and Matar entered the room.

"The investigations are ongoing."

Neria dropped back on the bed and hid her face in her hands. She felt the urge to take the place of her sister under the covers and never get up again. Where was Anaëlle at this very moment? The pain of her absence ate away at her insides like a hungry worm. In this Free City, surrounded by friends and comrades-in-arms, she had relaxed in her vigilance. She could just as well direct the criticisms she had given Elinor to herself. More so because she had experience that her sister did not. She knew the extent of Valterone's power and had seen it in action. So far, she had avoided thinking about a possible confrontation with her father, but now a rage had come over her that made her want to beat him. To make his own body feel some of the pain he had caused others. She breathed in, exhaled for a long time, grabbed the doll, and held it close to her. Forg sat down and put his arm around her shoulders.

"All is not lost. The search is still ongoing. Someone seems to have noticed a child being carried by a Gargoyle near the inn. The kidnapper may be hiding in the city. He's been watching for the right moment to abduct her and is waiting to get her out. He must have accomplices nearby, perhaps even among our own people."

"The more time passes, the less likely we are to find her."

"I should have stayed with her," said Matar. "To think that I left her to train volunteers, rookies who are only going to die in battle anyway. I'm leaving for Alipaz."

The Peddler seemed to have thinned out, like a strand of wool stretching to breaking point under a spinner's fingers. Hurried footsteps announced the arrival of several people. Barz, Yado, Maznar, and Kamau rushed into the room, which seemed to have shrunk.

"We must call off the assault," said Kamau. "If we attack, Valterone could kill her."

Neria felt for a moment the desire to defer to the natural authority of the Angel. Let the fate of the free world cease to weigh on her shoulders and come what may! She could then close her eyes and not think of it anymore. When she had seen her half-brother at the head of his troops, she had hoped he would have mellowed somewhat, even smiled at her, but she had found him harsh in his demeanor and clad in battle armor. They had simply greeted each other coldly.

"It's clear you don't know our father. He'll kill her if her murder serves his plans, whether we attack or not."

"You can't call everything off for one person," said Yado.

"I'm leaving for Alipaz," said Matar. "I'll bring Anaëlle back."

"You're talking about it like it's a walk in the woods."

"Regardless, I won't just sit around here doing nothing."

Suddenly, a strange clamor sounded, with a tone so deep her bones vibrated. Matar and Yado rushed down the stairs while Forg and Barz flew out of the broken window. Neria turned to Elinor who, leaning against a wall, pale and wide-eyed, wept.

"Wait for me. I'll come back as soon as possible. You hear me? Answer me!"

"They're going to kill us all this time."

Neria agreed in silence and walked to the window, her limbs heavy. People ran in the streets while flying Chimeras crossed the sky in all directions. She pulled herself up onto the ledge awkwardly. She took a deep breath, jumped, and let herself fall. More out of instinct than will, she opened her wings — a Gargoyle yelled at her when she almost hit him — and then headed for the commotion. She found Forg and landed beside him.

She had long stopped calling Chimeras monsters, but that was the word that came to mind at the sight of the hopping, crawling, flying mass: hairy crocodiles, pallid Demons, hydras, dragons, griffins, and many others. An army of shadows, led by a giant rat and the Moguedon, a swarming horde that threatened to overwhelm them. Elinor had felt it, the end was approaching to the rhythm of those claws. They would never be able to overcome this onslaught without huge losses, and the survivors would never have the strength to free Alipaz. How had Valterone managed to convince these Chimeras to join forces with him?

The Moguedon moved with unsettling ease for its size as its gelatinous mass shook from the impact of its powerful steps. It shook its head intermittently, opened its mouth, and let out hoarse shrieks, sharpening to a piercing pitch. The bull-sized rat bared its teeth, as menacing as a tiger's, and shook its minuscule wings of uncertain purpose. A repulsive gnome was sat on the beast, directing it by keeping the reins short.

Neria suddenly felt the strange sensation of a gentle and familiar comfort. She was about to fly away when Forg grabbed her arm to hold her back.

"Have you gone mad?"

"I won't get near them."

"They're coming for us, no need to throw yourself at their claws. Don't move from here!"

She slipped out of his grasp and soared upward while Forg rushed after her. A few wingbeats from the procession, Neria shouted with joy and, without heeding the warnings of the Gargoyle, swooped down toward the giant rat. She slapped the hand of the Toad Man as she passed, then flew over the rest of the army just low enough to hit their hands of different shapes and colors, rising and falling like a row of dominoes. Surrounded by Pale Demons who looked so much like her, if it weren't for their total lack of pigmentation, and black-feathered and red-crested Chimeras of which she had been unaware until that moment, Neria was astonished by the diversity of these wild creatures and felt inspired by their ferocious energy. These Chimeras' support for their cause moved her even more than the support of all the others. She was still laughing when she rejoined Forg who had landed and was walking beside the strange mount. She called out to Sido, "So you've finished your chores then?"

"Don't talk to me about it! I dropped everything to come."

Neria's smile faded when her glance crossed that of the Moguedon. She had noticed other individuals of this species in the ranks, but this one had an unsightly scar that ran over an empty eye socket. He responded to her wave with a grunt that sent a ripple of shivers down the young woman's spine.

As merry as ever, Sido lavished them with details of his life back home as Neria said to herself that with such allies, victory would not be long.

They stood on the roof of the inn, their footsteps crunching on the hail-strewn ground, the questionable gifts of a brief but brutal storm that had been the last throes of winter's belated protest. The wind swept away the clouds and in its mischievous wake, there shimmered a brilliant rainbow.

"Don't you find it strange that Anaëlle's disappearance has coincided with the arrival of these creatures?"

Kamau's face had assumed an expression of revulsion at the sight of an exsanguinated humanoid perched on a rhynolion riding leisurely across the square. The perfection of the Angels likely made them all the more aware of deformities. Before leaving Alipaz, Neria had found most Chimeras repulsive. Even today, she was not fond of the bleached wings of the Pale Demons, while she marveled at Kamau's. However, the Gargoyles' appearance, full of energy, agility, and spontaneity, seemed just as attractive to her, if not more so than the cold and arrogant beauty of the Angels. Neria lifted her gaze toward her brother, still absorbed in his pouting contemplation. She did not want to pressure him; their relationship was beginning to relax a little and be tinted with a prudent cordiality.

"Sido only joined us after the kidnapping."

"Right after."

"Just because you think they're ugly doesn't mean they're traitors. I'd put my money on it being a renegade Chimera, a resident of an area spared from the attack."

After a pause, she added, "Let's not allow our enemies to take advantage of our divisions."

He smiled and ruffled her hair.

"You're right, little sister. Or should I call you Nerialour, Soul of Cambolae? We're going to be neighbors, aren't we?"

"In all likelihood, since I've promised to return to the mountains after Alipaz is freed. But you can still call me Neria. The bonds of blood grant you that privilege."

Neria had wondered several times if her new status had hastened the rallying of the Angels to their cause. A request from a neighboring kingdom carried more weight than that of a wanderer, and Jabaury had realized where his interests lay.

"I find your concern for Anaëlle very touching, but don't worry about Sido, I trust him."

Later, she wandered with Matar through the streets of the

city. She wanted to spend a moment alone with him, to distract him a little from the absence of the girl. They walked in silence, one lost in his thoughts, the other unable to find a suitable topic of conversation. When they reached the riverbank, she watched the miscellany of debris floating on its surface. In a city of this size, the water could not stay as clear as in the forest. She immediately scolded herself for this thought. Why make excuses for the morons who'd polluted the river? She cleared her throat before speaking.

"We'll attack soon."

"I know, Sido is in a hurry to get back to finish his housework."

Matar said the words in a weary voice, without looking at her. He bent down to pick up a flat pebble, then skimmed it across the water.

"Thanks to him," she said, "taking Alipaz will be nothing but a formality."

"Who would have thought he had such power?"

"Oh, he claims his lordship is nothing but an honorary title, but I think he's just being modest. In any case, if you end up getting captured, try to survive until liberation comes."

He turned and looked at her for a moment in silence before answering, "I won't get caught, I'm very familiar with the city."

"Still, getting Anaëlle out of the clutches of Valterone…"

"You know I might not have any other choice but… getting rid of him."

"I don't care about Valterone, it's you I'll be thinking of."

302

A cloud parted and revealed a round moon peering into the darkness. Its pearly glow rested on a clawed paw camouflaged by the undergrowth. When another cloud slid over the celestial body and covered it, the Tiger Man suddenly sprang up, reached the walls, began his ascent and, as a soldier approached, pressed himself against the stones like a puddle of ink on blotting paper. The man, whistling a popular tune through his teeth, stopped to observe his surroundings. If he had leaned over, he would have seen two shining yellow eyes, but he left without noticing anything unusual. The big cat resumed his journey. When he reached the top, he dropped down onto the wall-walk and lurked there to let a guard pass. Normally, only a handful of drowsy soldiers guarded the walls.

In a few leaps, he reached the garden of an adjoining house, then crossed it without drawing any attention. The trees protected him with their dark shadows. Armed men may have been preparing themselves, but the people were sleeping without any particular concern. He crossed the wall without difficulty and, going from garden to garden, eventually arrived at Nephalie's. He smelled the scent of the guards. Just as Neria had told him, some stood by the doors leading onto the esplanade, but others were posted inside: about ten by the main entrances and the same number in the living room, the scent of Anaëlle and Valterone wafting from within. A crude trap was being set for him. He would be better off turning back and getting out of this city. Anaëlle alone with her grandfather... Who knew what cruelty he had already inflicted upon her? He thought of Nephalie who, in her dungeon, thought she had saved her... He imagined telling Neria and the others about how powerless he had been...

He remembered their last outing in the forest, the way she had slipped her hand in his and he felt the intense longing to listen to her ceaseless babbling. He bared his teeth. Onyx would have run away. He'd had the gift of spotting danger and the intelligence to get away from it as quickly as possible. Onyx would have run away... But twenty or so soldiers... with a little luck, he might just make it. The leaves rustled and a cool breeze ruffled his fur. He lifted his huge head to look at the stars. He loved the forest and had felt intense regret and longing every time he left it. Whether he lived or died, the assault would soon begin, and this city would change forever.

He noticed some half-open shutters upstairs, climbed up the wall, lifted the latch, broke the glass, and entered the freezing, long-unoccupied room. He approached her vanity cabinet, picked up a comb, and brought it close to his face. He recognized Nephalie's smell, of her silky brown hair. During his convalescence, after having run out of subjects to talk about, he would sit with her on the divan to read and take advantage of these opportunities to steal a glance at her. When his deformities had finally faded and he had recovered his courage, he had dared to brush away a lock of hair that had fallen on her forehead. She had smiled at him and he had leaned in to kiss her.

Two guards were marching up and down the corridor. Matar listened to their monotonous, peaceful routine. He opened a drawer and found, in a finely crafted box, a thin golden ring. He took advantage of a moment when the men were moving away to slightly open the door and place the band on the floor, before carefully closing it again. He waited. As the guards approached, one of them slowed down and then stopped, while the other, who had not noticed anything, continued walking.

Matar opened the door and, before he could react, grabbed the crouching man's head, and snapped his neck. He carefully placed his victim on the floor. In two silent bounds, he reached the man who was still marching forward, wrapped his arm around his neck, and squeezed.

At that moment, Ellane came out of a room. She was carrying a tray laden with dirty plates and the scraps of a meal, which she almost dropped when she saw him. Her eyes widened and she shook her head from right to left. He smiled with a look that he intended to be reassuring and disposed of the motionless body. Scents were wafting up from the living room: those of Anaëlle and Valterone, clearly defined, and those of the guards, like a vague chattering. He would have to catch them by surprise and take the girl before they had time to react. He moved toward the first steps. Ellane whimpered faintly and shook her head again. He rushed down the stairs in two strides and ran over to the divan, where two people were sitting with their backs to him. He was about to seize the child when he noticed the blade resting on her slender neck, with this moment of hesitation giving the guards the opportunity to take aim at him.

Anaëlle was wearing a yellow tunic embroidered with floral motifs and elegant slippers of the same fabric on her tiny feet. Her hair was neatly arranged in a braid that ran down her back, leaving her face clear and composed. Matar thought she looked so sweet that it pained him. The blade shone like a heavy silver necklace.

"You wouldn't kill your own granddaughter."

"I wouldn't enjoy it, I'm not a monster. But if the circumstances demanded it… If, for example, a Tiger Man were to pounce for my throat, then I would rather kill her than have her fall into his hands. Let it go and she shall live."

Valterone was within reach of just one swipe of his paw. But if the arrows stopped him before he could incapacitate him... The unblinking black eyes stared at him. The Peddler straightened up and gradually assumed his Human form. The soldiers rushed toward him and shackled his hands and feet.

Valterone guffawed. He stood up and approached Matar.

"I suspected one of you would come looking for her and I'm delighted that it's you. After all these years, I wish I could flatter you and pretend you haven't changed, but let me tell you as an old acquaintance, you have well and truly lost your looks. You should take care of yourself. If Nephalie were to see you like this..."

He punched him so hard that the Peddler fell over backward and dragged the soldiers holding him down with him. Anaëlle began to cry.

"Grandpa, you promised me you wouldn't hurt him."

"I know, my dear, I know. I'm sorry, but I couldn't help it. You see, I'm very angry that this man took you away from me. He separated us. Because of him, I thought you were dead and there's no forgiving something like that."

He called out to Ellane at the top of his voice.

"Take this child with you, put her to bed, and make sure she doesn't leave her room. But, how forgetful of me... Look who came to pay us a visit. All that's missing from this school reunion is Nephalie. Well, we're not going to get her out of her cell for that. Ellane, do you realize just how lucky you are? No, don't thank me. Come on, get out of here, both of you. We men have more memories to reminisce over and plans to make for the future."

He picked up the napkin lying next to the teapot on the low table and meticulously wiped his bloodstained fingers.

"So, you managed to survive and spend all that time pestering me. But look at you, you're pathetic. You can't even hide your beastly nature anymore."

"Why disguise it? A Human shell doesn't seem any better than an animal. Or a plant, for all I know."

"Personally, I've always known you were worthless."

Matar wondered why Valterone insisted on humiliating him when he had, as the Star of Alipaz, amassed accolades, money, and power. This success was in danger of fading, even disappearing. What would be left of all his fighting, crime, and intrigue when the city fell? As for Matar, if he died at this very moment, he would have his regrets, but also the satisfaction of having saved Neria, of having taught her how to survive. He would still have the precious memory of a young love that he had not betrayed and that of a little girl who was more resilient than anyone had ever suspected.

"You're right, I never accomplished all that much, but I did know the joy of loving someone and of her loving me back."

Valterone, taking two steps, approached Matar and beat him to a pulp. When his rage subsided, he examined the motionless body. He was panting, covered in blood.

"Tiger Men don't make good slaves. Take him away and throw him in my wife's cell. It would be pointless for her to entertain the hope of ever being freed."

He then went up the stairs, opened the door to the room,

watched Anaëlle dozing and Ellane sitting on a wooden chair. The Angel dared a furtive glance, then looked away and absorbed herself in gazing at her hands clasped on her thighs. He closed the door and went to his room. He poured water into the basin and started to wash the blood staining his skin. He no longer felt any desire for this creature and had only spared her because of her temporary usefulness. She symbolized, along with Nephalie and the others, a bygone part of his life that he was eager to be rid of.

"Have some water."

Matar groaned. A woman with sunken cheeks, yellow skin, and drooping lips propped up his head. Her gaze bore into him like the icy water of a mountain stream.

"Nephalie."

"Don't talk, just rest. But, of course, you won't listen, as usual."

He was in a dark, cold cell. Draz, lying on the floor, moaned with his eyes closed. His mangled knee, inverted like that of a bird, gave off a putrid stench. Matar touched his burning forehead.

"Look," said Nephalie, "what a state Valterone's left him in. A son of a More-Than-Pure... He's not said a thing since yesterday, other than babbling in his delirium. They stopped bringing us food and I don't know how to help him."

From a secret pocket, Matar pulled out a handful of almonds and a few dates.

"I always take some with me on expeditions."

He split a fruit in half, tossed out its seed, and stuffed its flesh with two almonds.

She took the offering in her trembling hand and brought it to her mouth. She bit off tiny pieces and chewed them slowly.

"What about you?"

"Later."

He picked up a pewter cup, filled it with a little water and crushed in one of the dates with his finger. He worked diligently until he obtained the desired consistency, then approached the unconscious man. With careful and gentle movements, he lifted his head as the woman had done for him a few moments earlier.

"Draz, swallow this."

A few drops trickled between his lips, over his tongue, down his throat.

"Elinor, is that you?"

"She's fine. You'll see her again soon."

After swallowing the concoction with difficulty, Draz, exhausted by the effort, fell back into unconsciousness. Matar joined Nephalie. He leaned against the rugged wall, closed his eyes, and tried to imagine himself sitting on the sand. Despite or because of the inherent danger of the sea, they had enjoyed such outings in their youth. At the beach, they relished a tranquility only slightly disturbed by the occasional group of slaves busy collecting seaweed. They waited for them to move away so they could hold hands and kiss.

"Your husband's generosity amazes me. I didn't expect us to end up together."

"He considers it a form of torture, watching those you love

suffer…"

"So you do love me a little?"

"You know I do. Don't take advantage of my weakness to beg for flattery. The great regret in my life will always be that I didn't run away with you. I caused you nothing but trouble."

"Not at all! If anything good came out of your union with Valterone, all the credit goes to you. Anaëlle and Neria have done well."

"I'm so happy you're with me. I'm probably being selfish, but the solitude has been getting me down and I'm almost glad to die in your company."

"Who said anything about dying? Neria will free us."

"Draz told me, but I find that hard to believe. Tell me about it… tell me everything. We have time."

Matar told Nephalie about Neria's metamorphosis, the abilities she had developed, her rise to becoming a queen, her courage, her decisive actions in uniting the Chimeras and saving the city. Not wanting to worry her, he overlooked Anaëlle's kidnapping.

Bobka walked briskly and carried two full baskets in his hands. His blood pounded in his veins and his nerves trembled with a forgotten energy. The hope of revenge and freedom had erased the fatigue of servitude. His club, which he had carved from a large branch broken by a bolt of lightning, was waiting for him safely under the hay. It was finally going to be put to use. With a little luck, it would crash down on Valterone's skull. Draz had told him as soon as he had arrived in Alipaz an army was being prepared that was going to crush the More-Than-Pure and their minions. Nephalie had been right to have faith in the future. He would have liked to talk to her about it, to meet her like before, in the garden, under the pretext of taking her orders.

He was still being sent to the market twice a week. Even though the house had few people to feed, Valterone, curse his name, often entertained guests. Mostly men, but also women with loose morals ever since Elinor had left the city. Bobka was carrying fresh fruit and vegetables, four pounds of flour, two pounds of rice, two pounds of lentils, as well as dates and almonds in his baskets. While he had been buying olives, he had watched the merchant furtively and wondered how he would react to the attack. Would he choose the side of Rebellion or Purity? Unlike the grain merchant, who insulted him for no reason, the olive seller had always treated him well.

There was a sudden clamor. Had the fighting started? The cries were coming from inside the walls... The screams of a panicked crowd were getting closer. Soldiers were pouring in from all directions, letting the Humans through and holding back the Chimeras. The Gargoyle placed his wares under a stall and considered surrendering to slavery, as a helpless old loner. He hadn't heard from his wife in so long... he could give up and bow his head to the blows like a beast of burden and thus abandon any chance of seeing Souphe and his children ever again. People were shouting and jostling each other in a frenzied stampede, trampling on the unfortunate who had fallen to the ground, suffocating those pressed up against the walls. The walls... Bobka suddenly saw them. Not the walls of an enclosure, but ladders that could save him. He made his way to a window and pulled himself up onto its ledge. He had spent his youth in the forest, where survival had also depended on physical strength. Didn't he do the most difficult jobs in the garden, didn't he climb trees to pick the fruit from the very highest branches?

He was now crouching on the top ledge but knew that the hardest part was ahead of him. He moved slowly, checking each of his holds. His flexible, hardy toes searched for gaps between the stones. He had almost reached the second-floor window when an arrow struck the wall a cubit from his face. He looked down. Two laughing soldiers were shooting at him. He pushed back his panic and continued on. He grabbed onto the lower lintel and hoisted his body onto the window ledge. Through the frosted glass, he saw a figure crossing the room and tapped on the pane. The shadow fled. There was no other option but to carry on. One more push... The upper lintel of the upstairs window... He could almost touch it... the top... An arrow hit him in the shoulder and he almost let go from the pain. Hanging by one hand, he felt drained of all his energy. He was going to die, his skull cracked open. Or the fools shooting at him, however unskilled they may be, would eventually finish him off. He recited the prayer of the Elders. The shots struck the wall without hitting him. Was this a sign? He swayed and, with a last burst of his wavering strength, managed to hang his right foot onto the edge of the parapet. With a surge of effort, he pulled himself up and toppled over onto the terrace. The arrow snapped from the impact. A sharp pain twisted through his shoulder. Gasping for breath, he lay motionless on the ground for a few moments. As soon as his breathing calmed, he stood up, his legs wobbling. The Humans had abandoned the flat roofs, where they hung out their laundry and enjoyed the fresh air on summer evenings. They had shut themselves up inside their homes. He crossed the terrace, climbed onto the guardrail, breathed in and out deeply several times. He jumped, landed on the neighboring building, and continued his journey, from roof to roof. The terraced houses made his task easier and he took detours to avoid the main roads.

Underneath his debonair demeanor, Bobka had become experienced in stealth, dark alleyways, and secret passages. He knew how to carry messages for Nephalie all over Alipaz without being noticed. If he had hoped to get away from the danger by going to another district, he soon lost his illusions: the army had the whole city under surveillance. He thus decided to go home. He climbed several perimeter walls. Dogs, which he knew from having fed them during his previous excursions, came to meet him and greeted him by wagging their tails. Bobka finally arrived in the garden, which he secretly called "my garden" because he took care of it and spent more time there than anyone else. From the top of a tree, he saw the column of slaves entering the Temple to be locked up. All around the building were enclosures filled with colorful balls.

"You amaze me," said Barz. "On the eve of battle, here you are arguing over nothing! We met today to choose the commander of our troops, not to discuss linguistic nuances."

"If we can't agree on a name for ourselves, we won't agree on a leader either."

"I put myself forward for this role in any case," said Kamau. "We have extensive experience in the art of war."

Sido burst out laughing.

"Your theoretical scholarship pales in comparison to the wealth of expertise we have amassed. Survival in the Marsh requires constant battle."

"Don't think that life in the mountains is easy!"

"I think Maznar would be a good candidate," said Matar.

"I know what you need. You need a pragmatic man."

"Barz, if you believe being pragmatic is rushing in without hesitation, then I'll grant you that, yes, you are pragmatic."

"We have the most troops," insisted Sido, "and they include infantry as well as an air force."

"I hate to put myself forward," said Yado, "but I would like to remind you all of my military career. Our troops are also divided into different corps."

"Most of them are just inexperienced civilians."

"So what's your combat experience?"

"How do you think I gathered these troops?" Sido exclaimed. "With pies? Yes, I heard you laughing at me! Know that if Neria had not asked me, I wouldn't have left the comfort of my home for the rest of you."

The war leaders had taken over a room in the city hall building. Frustrated by the arguments, Neria studied the fresco that decorated the walls. In a lush forest, animals and flowers depicted in detail in a rather naive yet striking style frolicked merrily. She wondered why the artisans had chosen this theme for one of the most grandiose places in Roguelle.

"Wake up! This isn't the time, I assure you. We've got to organize our assault. And this person wants to send us to the front line while he takes all the glory of the victory for himself."

Sido stood on his chair and gesticulated. He pointed an accusing finger.

"Look at his expression. He despises us!"

"My feelings have nothing to do with our situation," Kamau replied. "We must win this battle. I recognize your numerical superiority and your uh… brute strength, but I feel we are better suited to lead the battle. And from a strategic point of view, our position in the rear will only be temporary."

What was happening to her? Since Anaëlle's disappearance, she had not been able to concentrate. Neria remembered the Temple square and those children she had been forbidden to join under the pretext of them belonging to a lower social class. They seemed to her today more mature and more agreeable than these enraged adults. At last, they took a vote and, not without further discussion, agreed to call themselves "The Forces of the Entente" and to assign Kamau the role of "Chief Coordinator," while leaving each war leader in command of their own troops with the recommendation that they abide by the general instructions.

Kamau seemed to have matured under the burden of the task that had fallen to him, and Neria felt reassured that she had voted for him. After all, they shared the same blood. And what was more important than family? She knew his ambition and thought she owed him her support after the humiliation he had suffered because of her. At the end of the meeting, Forg joined her. She noticed the look the Angel gave her and suppressed a smile. Some people were uncomfortable with her new relationship with the Gargoyle. Kamau, Maznar, and even Anaëlle, who, when she had still been with them, had slipped in between them at every opportunity. She held Forg's hand and pulled him along.

"No need to take the stairs."

An open window, a jump into the void, the cool, intoxicating air that supported their wings and caressed their faces. She wished she could spend these last few hours of tranquility in the forest, atop a tree, with him.

As the council members left the room, Kamau watched the couple depart, one thick and hulking, the other thin and elegant, both as dark as streaks of mud. No one asked to join him, but he paid no attention. He leaned his chest out of the window and breathed in. Even at this height, the stench of this city bothered him. Without Neria's support, he would never have succeeded in assuming leadership of the troops. If these savages could let themselves be led, which still remained to be seen. Poor little sister born into opulence... Legitimate parents, an aristocratic family, and now a growing political power. With a kingdom right next to that of the Angels and another that stretched from the Free Cities to the sea, this girl could dominate the whole land. She thought she was invincible, but it wouldn't be long before disappointment came. He would almost have felt sorry for her if it weren't for the humiliation she had subjected him to and the one she was imposing on him now by parading around with that Gargoyle. What could she see in him?

One thing would have amused Kamau, however: the reaction of the Demon court to this caricature of a prince consort. The hostility between the Angels and Demons had been built on centuries of bitter struggle for control over arable land and hunting. Once on the throne, Neria would soon understand the stakes and would hasten to use her power. He left the room, took the stairs, and burst onto the roof terrace. With the end of winter imminent, when the rains would no longer risk damaging the furniture stored away under a tarpaulin, this neglected place would come back to life. He personally liked it this way, quiet and deserted. From here, the city looked clean and elegant. Everything looked better from afar. He liked the highest peaks, where no tree or building disturbed his gaze, free to roam as he wished on the landscape purified by distance.

A little like with his parents, whom he almost regretted having met.

He had encountered his father on a hill, near Alipaz, in the middle of the ruins of an ancient fortress. Valterone, a stately Human, had told him the history of the region. He had described how the threats of the Chimeras had provoked a violent reaction and had led to their extermination or enslavement. Humans seemed so weak to him in general. But not his father. With his tall stature and posture, all he needed was a pair of wings and a lighter complexion to be transformed into an Angel.

He had seen him again the next day at the same place. Valterone had arrived accompanied by soldiers, like the previous time, and by an insignificant-looking woman. When she had walked up to him and called him by his name, he stopped himself recoiling in disgust. He had thought her gray; her clothes, her hair, her complexion seemed devoid of even the slightest glow. How could he have ever imagined that his mother had lost her wings? No one had warned him. These degenerate Humans, maddened by jealousy and hatred, had committed unforgivable crimes for which they would one day have to answer. When she had shown him her scars, he had tried to conceal his horror, and after examining her face — she looked so very much like him — he had become convinced of her identity. Yet he couldn't help but wonder where the allegiances of an Angel stripped of its wings lay.

Valterone had promised to free her after the battle. Kamau could not take her with him into the mountains — she could be a detriment to him, looking like a... slave — but he would see to it that she had a comfortable life in one of the nearby villages. They could see each other every now and then and, in time, develop a close relationship.

Before leaving him, Ellane had whispered, "Go back home..."

Valterone had grabbed her by the arm and guided her toward a group of soldiers, then returned to him and said, "The bitterness of defeat... Everyone sees things in a way that suits them. Ellane has no gratitude for what I did, and yet I saved her. She wouldn't have survived more than a week in a work camp. I'm sorry your meeting didn't go well, but I did warn you."

Kamau had then left to join his men and they had gone to Roguelle, where Neria was waiting for them along with her Gargoyle. When the Chimeras of the Marsh had joined them, he had truly believed his mission was doomed to failure and had sent a message to Jabaury to this effect, but his response had forced him to continue. Kamau sighed. He didn't like this job but accepted its necessity. The hardest part for him would be the Demoness. He had to guarantee her demise. They had considered letting her live, but as he had made clear to Jabaury, her popularity posed a threat.

The day would come when they would push back these rapacious Humans, but in the meantime, Valterone would complete the conquest of the Free Cities while the Angels would enslave their shadowy neighbors, taking advantage of the infighting and the loss of their queen. Thus would begin a period of peace and prosperity.

CHAPTER SIXTEEN

Neria flew over the Little Sister before finding the winged Chimeras who had landed in a black cloud on the summit of the Big Sister, the infantry assembled at its foot. In the cool night, ideal for war, Alipaz seemed to be waiting for them, hard and dark like a glistening stone.

Forg embraced her and kissed the top of her head.

"If you ever have enough and decide to leave it all behind, let me know. I'll come with you."

She returned his embrace then stepped back to study his tender face. She wanted to reassure him, but the arrests of Draz and Matar, which she had learned of earlier, worried her. He smiled and added, "Otherwise, meet me at the Market Inn. My treat."

Valterone knew their plans. He may not have known the exact time of the attack, nor the nature of their army, but he knew enough to be prepared. The Forces of the Entente would win, however. They outnumbered them and had the advantage of flying Chimeras in their ranks.

"That inn would bankrupt you."

"Money's the least of my worries."

Elinor, who had followed after the foot soldiers against Neria's advice, caught up with them. She had insisted on watching the fighting and celebrating with them in victory.

"And if you're defeated... I'll have nothing more to lose."

Surprisingly, the unusual austerity of her attire accentuated her youthful appearance. Out of breath from the ascent, made unrecognizable by her peasant clothing and her bun disheveled by the journey, Elinor carried a bag on her shoulder from which a doll's head poked out.

"Anaëlle will be happy to see her again," she said, leaning on the girl's cane. Neria had offered to provide her with another one, longer and sturdier, but she had refused.

"It's good enough for walking and I wouldn't know how to use it for anything else."

If true courage was overcoming your fears, then Elinor had proven hers. The two sisters hugged and wished each other good luck. Tears trickled down the older sister's cheeks. A grimace spread across the younger sister's face, biting her lip, and quickly stepping away before taking flight.

The full moon illuminated the landscape with a soft glow, intermittently veiled by clouds. The people of the Marsh, chosen to march in the front line, began to move, followed by the inhabitants of the Free Cities. Neria, Forg, Barz, and Maznar, accompanied by the other Demons and Gargoyles, to whom the task of traversing the walls and opening the gates would fall, flew over them in silence. Neria greeted Sido. Righteous and dignified on his giant rat, he noticed her in spite of the distance and responded with a friendly wave.

To her great disappointment, Kamau had decided to assign himself a less dangerous position. She thought commanding an army meant leading by example and going to the front, but the Angel had claimed this would allow him to communicate better with all the troops. He had finally silenced his critics with the excuse of having poor night vision. He would, therefore, remain at the rear with his men until daybreak, which would come soon.

As soon as the gates opened, the infantry would enter the city and, with the help of the rebels and slaves, eliminate all resistance. The Forces of the Entente would strike, dismembering Elatek's army, and scattering whatever remained into the sea.

Maznar to her left and Forg to her right, Neria tried to think as little as possible of her father. She returned to Alipaz supported by the Demons, or at least some of them, and by a love she had ignored for too long. She saw the many figures of sentries posted on the walls and realized they were expecting them.

The blast of a horn struck her. Had Alipaz already spotted them? Another call answered it, then another, and great fires were lit on the ramparts. The quiet night resounded with the piercing sound of the instruments and cries of war. Swept away by their contagious energy, Neria added her own voice to the chimes of the Angels, to the yells of the Gargoyles, and to those of the Demons. The red soldiers could do nothing against such an army and the pathetic efforts of Valterone and his spies would soon be reduced to nothing. The Chimeras halted their advance when they came within range of the enemy's arrows, while a flutter of uncertainty coursed through their ranks. Kamau, as clear and sharp as a shard of glass, suddenly appeared and, without hesitation, flew to the head of the assault.

Neria exchanged a glance with Forg, seeing in his expression a new and incredulous respect, realizing how much he had underestimated Kamau. The swarming mass of infantry waited while the Angels — illuminated by the glare of the fires, their fair feathers adorned with glints of bronze — guided the compact advance of winged Chimeras. Neria had never flown accompanied by so many, their presence enveloping her like an intoxicating song. She thought it made sense that Kamau had divided his forces and that some of his troops had remained in the rear, although she did wonder about the strategic advantages of a frontal assault. During the Battle of the Corrie, the Humans had been deployed to force a breach in the Gargoyles' defenses. But she realized that the situation was quite different here. How could the Humans stop them when all they had to do was fly over the walls to get into the city? They reached the walls and unleashed arrows down on the enemy soldiers. As vulnerable as newly hatched turtles, they protected themselves as best they could with their shields.

As they started their descent toward Alipaz, Kamau sounded a sustained blare on his horn, followed by three short blasts. Neria did not understand the meaning of this signal, not resembling any they usually used. The Angels ahead of her suddenly turned around and brought blowpipes to their lips, inoffensive-looking weapons that could be concealed in the folds of their clothing. Initially incredulous, Neria wondered about the purpose of such toys. This uncertainty lasted only for a moment. Around her, Chimeras scratched by their darts lost the use of their wings and plummeted down in free fall.

Terrified by this sight, Neria fled and dived down. She landed not far from Sido. Where was Forg? One of the Chimeras who, like her, had turned back crashed by her feet with a dull thud. Screams of rage and horror went through her, while her own throat made no sound. The portcullis lifted, the city gates opened, and a flood of red uniforms poured out. The cavalry charged. The surviving Gargoyles and Demons rushed to face them. Humans hit by their arrows fell and were trampled under their mounts. On the Chimera side, infantry armed with spears improvised a defensive line, on which the riders impaled themselves, sweeping their opponents along with them. Neria heard war cries and the hammering of hooves, saw the sneers on their faces and their brandished weapons, but her own limbs were no longer responding. A chestnut horse was charging right for her. The cavalier laughed in anticipation of the pleasure of trampling over her. But the hours of training had prepared Neria's body, which reacted without thinking. She dodged the first rider, jumped on the croup of the following horse, and slit its rider's throat. She flew away, sheathed her knife, and tightened her bow. She hit one enemy in the side, another in the shoulder, a third in the stomach.

The rat stood up on its hind legs; it dominated the mounts with its size and tore them apart with its long yellow teeth. The terrified horses reared up and fell down before it. It jumped on their heaped bodies and Sido, still clinging to its back, continued his carnage.

What had she done? How could she have known? No one could have imagined… Why? When she found Kamau, she would ask him this question before gutting him and burning his entrails. As if summoned by her thoughts, he appeared before her. He had a blowpipe in his hand and was circling her, while she tried to keep her distance.

"You're going to ruin everything!" she cried. "We were going to win. You're shattering the hopes of all Chimeras! You don't know Valterone…"

"I've met our father. His side of the story makes sense to

me."

He brought the blowpipe to his mouth, Neria dived, he pursued her. She twirled as Forg had taught her — where had he disappeared to? — while avoiding the friendly or enemy perils in her path. Poisoned darts whistled past her ears. Neria knew she could not continue at this pace any longer and that she had to take the initiative. She tightened her bow, made an about-face, and took her shot. He screamed. She let herself fall, rose suddenly, and nocked another arrow. He was still pursuing her. She repeated the previous maneuver, but this time he was ready. They shot at the same time. Neria's arrow slashed his cheek. She tightened her bow again. The arrow lodged itself in the hand holding the blowpipe. A scream... The weapon whirled away like a twig falling from a nest. They looked at each other for a moment. Kamau's face was tinged with pain. His forehead glistened, his eyes so bright under his furrowed brow, his mouth twisted into a malicious grimace. She found him ugly for the first time. He fled toward Alipaz and she went after him.

The sun had risen. Its rays caressed the golden walls of Alipaz, the jewel of the north, nestled on its rocky outcrop above the sedate sea. They glided over the blond stones, the flat roofs, the holy eminence of the Temple of Asoas and the disemboweled bodies strewn on the battlefield. Infantry emerged from the city in formation. Protected by their shields, they advanced, unconcerned by the arrows pattering down on them. *This battle will soon be over and victory will not be ours.* A strange joy overcame Neria. She had hidden herself away, had looked for a utopian home, then had returned to the city of her birth. But she would not flee any longer and would fight until the end. For the hope of a life with Forg, for Anaëlle and Matar, for her family, for the slaves, for the people she knew, and those she had never met.

After crossing the walls, Kamau turned back toward the battlefield, as if he had changed his mind. She noticed her father gesticulating atop the Temple and her heart beat faster. She gave up on her pursuit.

The tall white figure of Valterone stood out on the Superior Terrace. Around him, a handful of soldiers relayed his orders by blowing into conches, sounding unseemly harmonies over the cacophony of war. The Star of Alipaz thus towered over his city and the vile mass of slaves. A wave of his hand and the guards would throw balls filled with deadly poison through the openings of the Grand Hall. Leaning against the guardrail, he contemplated these vulnerable beings, Humans and Chimeras mixed together, inconsequential figurines dancing to his music. His powerful breath would control their destiny, cast his opponents into the catacombs of oblivion, and crush any thought of resistance. The mutations impaired the cognitive function of the Chimeras, making them more like beasts than Humans. Valterone once again lamented not being able to gas all the vermin, but his advisors had persuaded him against it. Some had worried about the presence of poison in the city. In any case, he would be safe from this height.

If his mother could have seen him at that moment, she would have understood how different he was from his father. He stretched out his arms. His open hands seemed huge compared to the tiny creatures scurrying on the walls. He stroked the ramparts as if to bless the soldiers, then lifted his arms toward the battlefield, fists clenched. His knuckles turned white and he burst out laughing, before he shouted to the dumbstruck soldiers, "We shall crush them."

Kamau, who had insisted on seeing his mother, had seemed revolted by her appearance. Despite their undeniable resemblance, he had expressed doubts regarding her identity and had demanded proof. She had shown him her long, swollen scars, dark in color and repugnant. After the gruesome presentation, Kamau seemed to have finally accepted who this all-too-Human-looking slave was. Valterone had feared the boy would rebel, shaken by this experience, but, too full of himself or too prejudiced to change his mind, Kamau had eagerly swallowed his explanations. He understood that to achieve his goals, he would sometimes have to look the other way.

Ellane had been right. Kamau would have been better off taking her advice and going back to his mountains. The weakness of the Chimeras lay in their diversity: Angels, Demons, Reptilians, Tigers, Dryads, Centaurs... So many different kinds and desires. Having almost succeeded in uniting them, Neria — no one was to learn her identity, even if she had to perish to keep it a secret — had, in the process, amassed a power that inspired envy. Kamau had been the first to betray her, but others would have followed. The Chimeras were very good at killing one another, with or without the help of Humans.

While he saw this assault as a testament to his success — his enemies had realized the extent of the threat he posed to them and were trying to evade it — he also recognized his own weaknesses. Without the intervention of the Angel, who had sold out his brethren in an illusive deal, Valterone would have had the utmost difficulty in repelling this attack. But Asoas guided him and would destroy any who sought to harm him...

327

even his own daughter. When Neria fell into his hands, she would realize her mistake. This sickeningly pathetic moth would finally cease to inconvenience him. Tearing the wings off a listless insect that writhed to escape the pain... One way or another, this problem would soon be resolved...

He had scattered the other More-Than-Pure in strategic positions. Ever good in front of a crowd, Zelimo, whom he had forgiven, for the time being, had outdone himself.

"With the secret goal of spreading their defective genes, the blood-sucking Chimeras are plotting to kill us, rape our wives, and tear our children to pieces. We must stop them! There are traitors among us who will try to free them. These fanatics trust them, but do not be deceived: your own slaves will slit your throats in your sleep if you give them half the chance. My brothers, citizens of Alipaz, you are the righteous arm that will avenge the Human race! While our soldiers fight on the battlements, you shall protect the city from traitors and renegade slaves. Down with the monsters! We shall crush these foul beasts!"

With enthusiastic cries, the crowd had applauded and chanted as Zelimo gave his speech. They had armed themselves with hammers, pitchforks, pickaxes, kitchen knives, or, for the more affluent, weapons of war, and were patrolling the streets in search of a slave to lynch. Each wore a red scarf around their necks as a uniform and a string from which hung a whistle, a wooden children's toy, which they used as a rallying signal.

Valterone turned to Anaëlle. She was still observing him with that calm and irritating air she had maintained since her arrival. He could not deny that the stay with the savages had strengthened her character. If anyone had found the presence of a little girl strange, no one had dared to question his decision. One of the soldiers had brought a straw chair and an embroidered blanket that now covered her tiny body like a shimmering wave. The child, who had been trembling earlier, had warmed up and seemed indifferent to the commotion.

Valterone leaned closer to her.

"Tell me again about your vision."

The child spoke in a monotonous tone while swinging her legs. The sounds left her mouth like a trickle of honey, and when she straightened up, Valterone felt satisfied. After this victory, the North would fall into his hands, the forest would be civilized, and he would gain Elatek's confidence. Then he would take his place. Nothing would stop him now.

At the far end of the garden, huddled on the bough of an oak tree, Bobka listened to the clamor of war. Except for a few aerial clashes between flying Chimeras, the fighting had not touched the city. The Human servants had left the house in the early evening and the soldiers had escorted Ellane to the Grand Hall, where they had locked her in with the other slaves. Bobka didn't understand the purpose of the cages leaning against the Temple walls and filled with balls but suspected they did not bode well. Valterone had been the last to leave and he too had headed for the Temple, with Anaëlle trotting after him. He had climbed the stairs as if he were on his way to a religious ceremony. A guard, who had hoisted the child onto his back, had placed her down again after a remark from Valterone. She had not been able to keep up with the adults and had fallen behind, but they had waited for her before closing the gates.

For the thousandth time, Bobka imagined the sound of a club striking Valterone's skull and changed position. His shoulder was hurting even though he had taken the time to remove the arrow and treat the wound in the deserted house. He had survived this far and had to hang on a little longer. If he made it out of the city alive, he would go in search of Souphe. The camps were said to be to the south. He would walk, or borrow a horse, and find his wife. He dared not hope to see his children again. How could such fragile beings have survived? Souphe would accept him, even if he was mutilated, and accompany him into the forest. Together they would find a new meaning to their existence.

No more pandering to the Humans under the pretense of sycophantic servitude! The time for revenge had come. He had chosen the wood for his weapon with care, maintained some of its most prominent features, polished and waxed it, and waited for the right moment. If he were to perish, he would make his death useful.

Like rain that begins with a few scattered drops then builds to a deluge, men appeared and gathered in front of the doors of the Great Hall. One of them spoke, "Dear neighbors, residents of Alipaz, free the slaves. Free your city from these tyrants who have usurped power. If you open these doors, you will not be troubled later for collaborating with them."

His proposal was greeted with mocking laughter. A guard brought a conch shell to his lips and sounded a signal. A whistle answered him, then another, and soon their ears were ringing with shrill whistling. Zelimo's troops burst out of the alleys, pouring onto the esplanade, as fighting erupted on the city's grounds. The rebels, though outnumbered, fought with a courage and skill that took their opponents off-guard. Some of the soldiers began to throw balls through the narrow windows of the Great Hall, from which hysterical laughter and howls of terror escaped. One man, having smashed a red ball on a wall by mistake, fell to the ground convulsing.

Bobka tumbled down from his bough and found his way to the esplanade. He was going to show them what carnage a wounded Gargoyle stripped of its wings was capable of unleashing. His club whirled. He stooped, leaped to avoid the blows, surprised his opponents by striking them in the knees, and, before they hit the ground, moved closer to his goal. The doors were waiting for him. After a bitter struggle, he managed to fight his way to the Temple. He crouched against the doors, placed his healthy shoulder under the heavy crossbar and pushed. The bar lifted a few inches. Several rebels were defending the rear. How long could they hold out? He gathered his strength. His legs shook with the effort. Finally, the bar fell to the ground and he jumped aside to avoid being crushed. Suddenly, the doors burst open from the pressure inside and threw him backward. He tumbled over a soldier's back, managed to regain his footing, leaped up and landed before the stream of slaves spared from the poison. Fur, feathers, scales and even the smooth skin of suspected Human traitors were visible. Bodies lay strewn across the tiled floor of the hall.

He saw Ellane, grabbed her by the arm, and pulled her aside. He wanted to lead her to safety, perhaps in the depths of the garden, but she stopped him and held out her finger, pointing to the top of the Temple.

"Anaëlle! Anaëlle's up there with him!"

The red-scarfed men surrounding them, ready to do battle

with an outnumbered foe, backed away from the angry mass of freed slaves. Bobka recognized Zelimo, who had been standing on the edge of the esplanade, and saw him running away.

With a few well-aimed arrows and surprising ease, Neria disposed of the soldiers and landed on the Superior Terrace, next to Anaëlle. She thought to herself that perhaps the Humans had good reason to fear the Chimeras. Had the child, frozen in her chair and unresponsive, lost her mind? Valterone approached them.

"What a bizarre transformation you've chosen! I didn't recognize you."

"Drop your weapon over the balustrade."

"What skill! You have truly impressed me."

In spite of herself, Neria felt proud. Then she pulled herself together. She had lowered her bow of a couple of inches for a moment and already, his big dark eyes and well-defined brow were looking for vulnerability.

"Such a beautifully crafted weapon. It would be a shame to lose it. It could be yours one day…"

Neria felt astonished to see him so unchanged after all this time.

"Drop it."

He sheathed his saber, untied his belt, approached the balustrade, stretched out his arm. The weapon dangled in the air.

"Is this what you want?"

She nodded and he opened his hand. From this height, the sound of the fighting on the esplanade was still audible, and she thought she could make out the sound of the leather-sheathed weapon as it hit the ground.

"Don't come any closer."

"I can give my daughter a kiss now that I'm unarmed."

"You have a strange way of showing your affection. Putting a bounty on my head?"

"I wanted to see you again."

"Dead or alive?"

"You could have sent news of yourself. I thought you had betrayed us, gone and joined the rebellion. And I was right."

"I'd have hoped you'd give me the benefit of the doubt or love me no matter what. Have you never felt even a little fatherly affection?"

"Such hypocrisy! You've brought an army to destroy my city."

"I've come to talk to you about a truce."

He burst out laughing.

"A truce? What for? I don't see any point. You're so adept at killing each other that we'll soon be back on a good footing."

"What price would you pay for this victory? Wouldn't you rather avoid all these deaths?"

"What's the point? A few more Chimeras gone from this earth... And soldiers should know how to resign themselves to the hazards of war, it's their job after all. But let's talk a little about you. You're my daughter and I wish you happiness. I'm afraid that reintroducing you to Alipaz in your condition will prove difficult... Would you agree to get rid of your wings?"

"No."

"I thought as much. Between us, I don't understand the interest if you've got a good horse. Well, to each his own."

"You talk about cutting off my wings like it's a haircut."

"If you think about it, it is just as simple."

"They won't grow back."

"I could put you up somewhere on the edge of the forest, in a quiet place where we can see each other without being disturbed."

"See each other?"

"Well, yes. I want to keep you safe so you can have a good life. Isn't that what a father wants for his daughter?"

"I don't know. You've never been... how can I put this... that sort of father."

Neria imagined a sheltered life... Her father who would finally notice her... She could while away quiet days with her mother. Elinor could come to visit her and...

"Why did you throw Mother in jail?"

"She was threatening to destroy everything I've built."

"She wanted to keep us safe."

"She acted like a fool. If she had told me, I could have found a better solution. Besides, she supported the rebels too. I advise you not to oppose me — no one gets away with it — and I urge you to surrender. Your wings will have to go, your ears... A good surgeon can fix them. A rather small sacrifice in exchange for your life. I can't make any promises to you regarding the rest of the Chimeras."

Was he really planning to spare her, when her very existence revealed the impurity of the family genes? What use could she be? Did he want to marry her to Zelimo? In this state? She saw Forg's mischievous smile, his long expressive ears, his sparkling eyes, and his muscular body... A simple but comfortable home, a quiet life... This dream would never come true under Valterone's tutelage.

Had he moved any closer?

"Don't come any further."

Her father watched her calmly and thought he had her under control, as usual.

"I refuse to hide," she told him. "Can't you ever just be proud of us? Your granddaughter's a Dreamer now. You knew that, didn't you? Stop the fighting and let's avoid these pointless deaths."

"Learning of Anaëlle's condition was rather bittersweet, being further proof of your mother's harmful influence on your genes. But her talents will be useful. Do you not want to see her grow up?"

She could still sound the retreat and save the Chimeras before they were slaughtered to the last. They could fall back to Roguelle or the forest. She would have to get rid of her father, take Anaëlle, find a horn bearer, and give the order to flee. An arrow straight to the heart...

"I would like to live in peace with the people I love."

"Really? How naive! Do you think there was harmony before Elatek took over?"

"People were free..."

"Bands of Chimeras pillaged villages and killed any inhabitants who tried to oppose them. I lived through this false harmony between peoples, and my dreams were shattered by reality, my efforts reduced to dust... And by whom? By depraved creatures, like that Matar who was always around your mother... These monsters would have destroyed the Humans. You are more agile, more resilient, and you are conspiring to exterminate us. Elatek opened our eyes and will preserve us from this Nymphosis that the Chimeras propagate. He is our savior. Asoas has sent him to guide us."

"A homicidal savior."

"That's the prophecy."

"And you're responsible for supplying the corpses."

"So, what do you say?"

"I don't understand you. One moment you accuse the Chimeras of contaminating you, on another, of exterminating you. Are you afraid of becoming like us or are you afraid we'll destroy you? Do you see me as a monster? And who are the monsters really? The Chimeras? Or those who spin and hide their petty, selfish interests in fine-sounding words?"

Tension spread through Valterone's body. Brow furrowed, eyes narrowed, face pale.

"How dare you speak to me like that? You and your mother have done well out of my work. You didn't complain when you were living your life as a spoiled brat and you're a little late to be lecturing me on morality! You've switched to their side since your metamorphosis. You're the selfish one. I've worked for my family..."

"What family? What's left of my family? Who killed Arhel?"

"I did. I wouldn't have wanted anyone else to do it. He had no idea what was going on and didn't suffer. I loved him. Do you think it was easy? I did it for him, to save him from a miserable life, for you, for the future of the Human race, and for those who have the courage to defend it. Stop your lectures on morality! You are my daughter and you will obey me!"

She drew her bow and shot. He dodged the arrow, pivoting like a dancer. She had just enough time to marvel at his speed before his fist slammed into her stomach. The impact sent her flying across the terrace. She flapped her wings to slow the speed of the impact, but her back and skull crashed against the sanctuary wall. Stunned, winded, she brought her hand to her head, felt the wet warmth of blood escaping from the wound, and heard Anaëlle's screams.

A childhood memory flooded her mind. Her father was throwing her up toward the sky and she was laughing. Had he really thrown her so hard that she touched the roof every time? Was it Nephalie who had caught them by surprise and screamed? She remembered a face distorted with anger. He had exceptional strength… inhuman… which he hid the majority of the time. He was approaching and was about to grab her. She said to him, "You're a Chimera, aren't you?"

He stopped suddenly. The wrinkles on his forehead faded and his body went limp like an abandoned corpse. Only the glint of his eyes remained. At what age had he first known? Did he really know or did he suspect it without daring to admit it to himself? She felt a pang of compassion for this man who had denied his true nature all his life, for the teenager who had hidden himself away during his illness. While Matar, accompanied by Nephalie, had undergone his transformation without shame… She got to her feet. In spite of the shock, her aching body still worked.

"You hid it well. Not even Mother suspected."

She took his hand, which, initially inert, gradually curled around hers.

"I look Human, that's all that matters. The Chimeras would have despised me and the Humans would have persecuted me. This secret strength's given me an edge."

"I understand you, you know… I've gone through this change, the fear of being different, the feeling of repelling others. You could have run away… We could have run away together. Why kill your own kind? Let's stop the fighting…"

Valterone's gaze, like water blasted by an intense cold, hardened. His mouth clenched and the pressure on Neria's hand increased. He could not take the risk of her revealing this discovery.

"It's too late."

"Why?"

"I cannot go back…"

She saw Arhel again, sitting on the window ledge. She had grabbed him by the shoulder as he had leaned over without fear, while she had barely dared to glance down.

A cry of pain escaped her. He wanted to break her bones, she tried to free her hand while he forced her to kneel before him. He leaned closer toward her like a father scolding a wayward child.

"I will not abandon everything I've built. You're going to help me win this battle and all the others to follow."

"Okay, I'll help you... Father, no... Not in front of Anaëlle."

A shadow hovered over them and she suddenly heard Forg's voice.

"Let her go."

His bow drawn, he took aim at Valterone. But before either of them could react, Kamau swooped down on Anaëlle and carried her away.

"Save her!" cried Neria. "I can handle this, don't worry about me. Go!"

Forg left to pursue the Angel.

Neria turned her face back toward her father. He had not moved during the interruption. His black eyes were fixed on her, a smile on his lips.

"There will always be someone willing to assist me. And if you don't, your brother will."

The pressure increased again and the pain intensified. She struck him in the face. He parried with ease and continued moving forward. His hand wrapped around her neck and cut off her breath. He was going to kill her. She frantically flapped her wings and managed to lift herself up, hauling the overwhelming weight. She flew away, turned back, picked up speed, and with all her momentum and remaining strength, went to hurl Valterone at the corner of the building. He yelled, slipped, but caught hold of Neria's ankle. She drank in the air in great gulps.

He jerked up to snatch the knife from his daughter's thigh, but she grabbed it before he could. She whirled above the Temple, Valterone still clinging onto her, like a kite with a vast tail. Blinded by fury, he didn't realize that he was putting them both in danger, that his movements were throwing her off balance, and that they risked plummeting down together.

Neria suddenly saw Arhel's smiling face. She felt her strength fading. She used her free foot to kick the hands clasping onto her as hard as claws of metal. She thought of Forg waiting for her, bent down, and, in one blow, slashed Valterone's wrist. Blood spurted out, but his hands seemed to crush her ankle even harder. They were spinning and losing altitude. Too fast. Again the knife came down. This time she aimed for the knuckle of his thumb, managing to sever it. The hand let go. Another blow. He screamed. The seemingly eternal fall came to an end on the ridge overhanging the Temple. She then saw Valterone move and thought she was going mad, before realizing he was sliding down the slope. He fell once again, hit the terrace balustrade, and finally crashed down onto the forecourt.

CHAPTER SEVENTEEN

The sound of a set of keys, quite different from Draz's constant groaning, woke Matar with a start. His insides contorted with hunger, but there was no smell of food preceding the guards and Matar wondered why they had come. Nephalie stood beside the gate.

"This is the end."

"Why do you say that?"

"I know them. Valterone's won, or perhaps he senses danger, but he's taking the opportunity to clean out the dungeons."

"What's the point of finishing off the dying? Sorry... I didn't mean that... I think you're being pessimistic."

"Me, pessimistic? This is the best day of my life. Elatek's evil project is crumbling... Who knows? No matter what happens to us, the More-Than-Pure may lose this battle."

She walked over to him, crouched down, and brought her hand to his face.

"And then I was lucky enough to see you again."

He embraced her.

"We'll get out soon and go to look for Anaëlle, Neria, Elinor, and the others together."

At that moment, they heard the sound of a lock, then screams followed by pleading that suddenly stopped.

The Peddler heard an altercation between two guards.

"I don't understand why we have to kill them."

"We don't question orders. If you open your mouth again, you'll share their fate."

The men approached with a slowness that added to the torment, their advance punctuated by metallic sounds mixed with prayers and cries of agony Nephalie grabbed the bowl, the only object in the room that could be used as a weapon, and positioned herself in front of Draz as if to protect him. The Peddler lurked behind the door in the darkest corner of the cell and began his metamorphosis. Seized by a strange modesty, he wished he could have been alone. He would have preferred to die out in the open — this dark cell already resembled a tomb — but no one can choose the time or place. He let rage overcome him. This feeling had always helped him to complete his transformation. No one seemed to have warned these soldiers of their prisoner's special abilities, and he hoped he could thank Valterone in person for this oversight. Guards armed with spears arrived at the gate. As soon as it opened, Matar pounced and ripped open the throats of the first two. But a blade slashed his side and his shoulder was wounded by another. The group had him surrounded and threatened him with the tips of their spears.

He heard a shrill scream and the sound of a bowl hitting a man's skull. The man swore and hit Nephalie with the butt of his spear. She fell. Matar, taking advantage of the diversion, disemboweled the nearest guard and grabbed his weapon. He maneuvered, parried, maimed, and ripped open throats as he went, fighting his way toward her. In the midst of the turmoil, he heard another cry escape Nephalie's throat, a cry that had lost its bellicose quality and bore witness to a terrible pain. One by one, he slaughtered all the guards, except for one who had dropped his weapon and kept saying that he did not mean any harm.

He knelt down beside Nephalie. She lay lifeless, a spear thrust into her chest. He took her hand and brought it to his lips. Her beautiful eyes stared at the ceiling yet could not see it, a little blood staining the corner of her mouth. If he closed his own, he could imagine she was still alive. She had loved him and had never given up on him... and the years she had endured in Valterone's company had not changed a thing. He remembered the time when, bedridden, he had looked forward to her visits... the coolness of her hand on his forehead while, burning up with a fever, he could not believe his luck. Why had she chosen him, then, weakened and incomplete? It remained a mystery. And then one morning, he had got up exactly the same as he had once been, as if never struck by Nymphosis, and had rejoiced at having become Human once again, like her. She had not abandoned him either later when she had witnessed his first involuntary transformation.

Matar stopped the retreating guard with a roar.

"I wanted to fetch some bandages," he said.

"We'll get them together. First go and open the doors of the other cells."

They freed the unfortunate inmates who had been locked up for far too long, a pitiful lot of prisoners who moved with great difficulty but hurried to leave this place of torture. Matar then approached Draz and, with the help of the guard, carried him and set him down on a table at the entrance to the dungeons.

L. M. RAPP

The man fetched a first aid kit then bandaged their wounds with a certain degree of expertise.

"Why did you join the army?" asked Matar.

"I didn't know how to do anything else."

"Not a very good excuse. In any case, you've been promoted to nurse. See this man? If he dies, you die too."

A look of distress spread across the guard's face.

They heard hurried footsteps and a young woman appeared in the doorway. She recoiled at the sight of the Tiger Man, then pulled herself together and walked toward him.

"I have come to find Nephalie. You're Matar, aren't you?"

He grunted in affirmation.

"Oh, it's Draz! Whatever happened to him? I'm Paz, Anaëlle's mother. Where is she? Did you get her to safety?"

Forg tried to intercept Kamau without hurting Anaëlle. He managed to catch up with him, positioning himself overhead. He dived, grabbed his wing, and pulled. He heard a sharp crack followed by a cry of pain. Kamau spun through the air but managed to regain his balance without letting go of the girl, before making a crash-landing. He jumped onto the edge of the Source and held the child in front of him. Her tiny toes touched the dark water. Anaëlle was sobbing silently. Fat tears rolled down her cheeks as she stared into the gaping abyss.

"Don't come any closer or she goes under. Drop your weapons, the knife too."

He held Anaëlle by the hair and pushed her forward. She teetered on the rim, one foot on the edge and the other over the chasm. Her tears were suddenly suppressed by terror. Slowly, Forg got rid of his bow, followed by his knife. Kamau then set the child back on her feet. Pale, her eyes wide open, she looked at Forg with a distraught expression.

"Go away!" she shouted at the Gargoyle. "Don't stay here."

"Listen to the girl, she knows what she's talking about."

Around them, the fighting between freed slaves, rebels, and supporters of the More-Than-Pure continued.

"She's just a child, let her go."

"A child with invaluable powers."

Suddenly, Kamau threw a knife in a deft and precise motion. Forg, after a brief daze, touched the handle of the weapon embedded in his chest with hesitant fingers, then fell to his knees. He gasped for breath or perhaps even wanted to say something, choked sounds escaping from his throat. Kamau burst out laughing.

"You should have listened to the girl. But don't worry, I'll take care of her. Aargh..."

An arrow pierced his thigh. Anaëlle jumped to the ground, snatched a spear from the hands of a dead soldier, and struck Kamau's legs with all her might, sending him tumbling over the edge. The water swallowed him up in an instant.

Neria landed beside Anaëlle. She checked her over.

"Are you okay? Are you injured? Did he hurt you?"

"I'm fine... Stop! I'm telling you to stop. Just look, look in the water."

Neria approached the Source but could not see even a ripple on its polished mirror surface. Before the dance of visions could begin, she suddenly received a terrible blow to her head, and when she turned around, another in the stomach, so well delivered that she fell backward. Her flapping wings touched the surface of the water. She thought she was going to be able to regain her balance, but Anaëlle, in a masterly demonstration of Matar's lessons, dealt her even more blows, and Neria sank, carrying away with her the image of a childish face frozen in a wicked sneer. The violence of her father, his murder by her mother, the battles among the Gargoyles, the attack of the flying fish, and then, of course, the terrible visions had finally pushed Anaëlle into madness. She did not dare confide in anyone anymore and had abandoned the role of messenger in favor of making her premonitions come true. Neria regretted not having shown her more patience or love. All this mess could have been avoided. Their family, whose members had perished one by one, would disappear soon: Arhel, Adamek, Valterone, Kamau, and now Neria, who had only succeeded in bringing the Chimeras to their doom. She thought of her mother who was perhaps waiting for her, locked up in a dungeon.

She had prepared herself for a biting cold but found the temperature pleasant. She felt the sensation of dissolving like a spoonful of sugar in a glass of tea. Her body stretched in all directions, to the Sources scattered throughout the world, which claimed her eagerly. Motionless in the liquid element, she traveled from one to the other. Then she contracted and returned to her starting point. She recognized the quiet Source in the middle of the forest, the one in the courtyard in the heart of the city of Angels, and then the one in the throne room of the Demons. One of them, leaning over the water, seemed to hear her call. But, after a moment of hesitation, he had straightened up and moved away.

Then she felt presences surrounding her. First, that of Kamau. She understood his motives and fears, his ambitions, and doubts, and grieved with him for his defeat, but also rejoiced. Then she encountered a crowd of strangers, welcoming them as old friends. These condemned people had come to a place which, though different from life, had placed them in pleasant suspense. She recognized the young woman with the deformed feet, the one from the last execution she had attended.

But a being was looking for her and approaching, a being long gone… She suddenly burst out crying and her tears blended with the black water. Arhel was smiling at her. She could not see him with her eyes but knew he was there and held him close in an ethereal embrace. Valterone had not killed Arhel with a knife or poison but had thrown him into the Source. She was almost grateful to the man who had spared his son without intending it. Was this death? If she had known, she would not have feared it. She thought of Forg. She wished she could have sent him a message, telling him not to worry and that she would always love him.

Then she felt a disturbance in the suspension, at first infinitesimal, like the breath of a child, which grew and drew her toward the living. She refused to part with Arhel, took him by the hand, and dragged him with her. Her face broke through the surface. The frigid air made her want to return to the depths of oblivion. She clutched the stone ledge and pulled herself up, shivering with cold, and began to cry. She had found her brother, as helpless as when they had last played together and had lost him again. Anaëlle, with her hands in the water, muttered through her teeth, as if she were whispering a story into her doll's ear.

Suddenly, ripples disturbed the mirror. Arhel emerged and paddled to the edge. He was panting and squinting, dazzled by the light. She grabbed his arms and pulled to help him out. He stood before her, dripping wet and shivering, almost exactly as he had been, but even more beautiful than she remembered. He had struck an ideal balance between his father's poise and his mother's charm and looked like no one else.

The sound of soup simmering on a fire caught their attention. Chimeras were emerging from the Source: two Gargoyles, a Centaur, a Dryad... males, females, and children, each perfect in their different forms with completed mutations. They came out one after the other in a continuous stream. In the square, stunned by this phenomenon, the adversaries ceased hostilities. A flood of survivors poured out like flowers opening on a spring day, a bounty all the more poignant because it was fleeting. Rested after such a long slumber, they took weapons from the corpses and left without delay to fight those who had condemned them.

Neria took Arhel by the hand and led him toward Anaëlle, still bent down in her toil. The two children looked almost the same age.

"This is your niece. Stay with her, I'll be back."

Neria rushed to where she had seen Forg fall. His fleece sticky with blood, he breathed with difficulty and seemed exhausted.

"I'm here. It's going to be fine, I'm going to take care of you."

"Don't be sad... I die happy... because you love me."

"You're not going to die, not today. It's a tiny wound, just a hole two fingers wide…"

"You're here."

"Yes, I'm staying and I won't leave you again. We've won, we've defeated the More-Than-Pure."

Neria's announcement of this preceded the actual event, but behind her, an army of Chimeras was still pouring into the forecourt. The good news did not cause the hoped-for reaction. A grimace distorted the features of the Gargoyle and faded at once.

Forg tried to lift himself up to hold her in his arms, but he didn't have the strength anymore. He looked at her face, usually so animated, now frozen in confusion. He was leaving alone, but with her love and not lonely. They had shared moments together as rich in emotion and adventure as many lifetimes. He had taught her everything he knew and believed she was well prepared to go on without him. He saw her lips trembling. He didn't want her to suffer, not when he died or later. He was bowing down after reaching his peak and considered himself lucky to be doing so.

"Well done…you did it," he told her in a hoarse voice.

"Oh, I didn't do anything special. It was Anaëlle who…"

She took his hand, dark and hairy, in hers, squeezed it, and brought it to her cheek. Forg's hand tightened for a moment, then relaxed. He closed his eyes. He always fell asleep so easily. Neria found his weakness contagious; it spread to the depths of her being.

"Are you sleeping?"

His fur had turned a dull shade, his eyes had sunk back in their sockets. He, who used to have such a big presence, with his loud voice, his energetic body, and his incessant jokes, seemed to have shrunk.

"Open your eyes."

"I'm tired."

"Look at me. I'm scared, don't fall asleep."

His hand lay in hers. When she let go of it, it fell onto his lap, inert, incongruous, and sorrowful like a bird struck in mid-flight. He didn't know. On this day of miracles, the Source was going to heal him, grant him a second life, as it had given to the others who had drowned. She put her arms under his body and, gathering all her strength, lifted him up in one motion. He groaned. Wavering under her load, she advanced step by step in the direction of the black eye from which dazed Chimeras continued to spring forth. A hand, painful as if clasped by a crab claw, grasped her elbow. She heard Arhel's childish voice.

"No, don't do it. She told me to stop you."

Arhel, unchanged in appearance, had inherited his father's strength. Neria lifted her eyes from the other side of the pool, toward Anaëlle who was calling back a condemned people.

"Let me go! You must not have understood properly, the Source..."

"Look... it's too late."

She gently laid Forg on the ground.

"Wake up. Don't leave me! Forg!"

She had inflicted death on others, had seen corpses strewn on the ground, and yet nothing had prepared her for this moment.

She did not want to part with him. She could have loved him better and sooner, but it was over. She would never again be able to fly beside him, hear his laughter, listen to his advice, or feel his reassuring presence. She remembered the time he taught her to make those modulated sounds and realized he had revealed to her much more than this wondrous sight, and that since her first day with the Gargoyles, and despite her rebuffs, he had been by her side and unfalteringly supported her. He had claimed to die happy, but she could not believe it. They could have had so many new experiences that she would now have to discover without him. She would have liked to cry but found nothing but a great emptiness inside her.

Brilliant in its cruelty, nature was taunting her with its blue sky, its fragrances, its flowers, and its birdsong. She walked at the head of the procession, behind a wain pulled by the giant rat where, wrapped in a shroud, Forg's body lay.

The city had returned to the way it must have looked before the rise of Elatek: Chimeras and Humans mixed together, roaming its streets freely. Families had reunited and spontaneous celebrations were being held almost everywhere. To the great relief of the public, most of the inhabitants of what they called the Mists had returned to their homes, but Sido had lingered with his court, "Me, a king? I consider myself more of a kindly uncle. My people listen to my advice and sometimes choose to follow it."

At sunrise, Nephalie's body had been laid to rest in the family tomb. Elinor, Arhel, and Matar had shed tears. Neria, struck by a vague jealousy, had simply lowered her head. Valterone's corpse had been buried in one of the common graves dug for Elatek's soldiers. Neria had not wanted to know its exact location. Fate once again more generous to the elder sister, Elinor had chosen to remain at Draz's bedside, having survived his leg being amputated thanks to Sido's care.

They would soon reach the place she had chosen for the grave. This site lacked the mysterious beauty of Barham Forest, yet Forg would have been pleased with this peaceful spot in the shade of a carob tree. Among the people following this strange hearse, Bobka, his shoulder bandaged, looked with a devastated expression at the Gargoyles gliding overhead. He had collapsed the day before when Neria had told him of Souphe's heroic actions and tragic death during the Siege of Roguelle. Ellane walked beside Bobka. Freedom suited her well. She didn't seem to be concerned about Kamau, who had been captured by a group of slavers on their way south as he tried to flee with his wounded wing. Paz did not take her eyes off her daughter. Anaëlle walked with a confident stride, her mother on one side and the Peddler on the other. She was back to her old ways, chattering away while Matar nodded absentmindedly. Her doll, which she was holding carelessly, was dragging along the ground.

Questions swirled in Neria's head and irritated her, unable to get rid of them. Would she have fled with Forg if she had known what awaited them? If Anaëlle had not hit her, would she have fallen into the Source one way or another? The girl had not only predicted the future but had influenced it. Neria still bore on her body the bruises of the blows this obstinate little pest had inflicted on her and, in her mind, the regrets of not having submerged Forg when he had still drawn breath. She had not dared to enter the Source again. It held many mysteries. It seemed to facilitate mutations, but could it heal wounds? Or raise the dead? Forg, wrapped in his shroud, moved toward a grave dug between the roots of a carob tree. In spite of everything, Neria held on to the hope of seeing him again one day in the bosom of a still unknown Source, matured perhaps, but endowed with the same humor that she had learned to love.

What was going to become of the tyrants of yesterday and their henchmen? Some of the perpetrators would be tried and punished. But could they thwart the nefarious influence of the supporters of Elatek and put an end to the divisions between former enemies?

Sido joined Neria. He answered the questions she asked with his customary cordiality.

"No, he can't fly. His wings help him regulate his body temperature. This is a very intelligent and rather rare animal, endemic to our area."

"Was it worth it? All this death and suffering..."

She could have accompanied Forg into the forest, the mountains, or the Marsh and let the madness of the world take its course.

"We fought for the hope of a better life... for the survivors and our descendants. This war shall never end, but at least we will fight it together."

She held Arhel's hand, and he occasionally looked up at her, as if to check she was still there or to marvel at her appearance. She couldn't imagine how he had felt; he had awakened from a long sleep only to discover both his parents were dead and his sister had been transformed. She never imagined she would see him again unharmed, preserved in his innocence, that of a time when Nephalie had been beautiful and merry, when Valterone had sometimes given in to moments of tenderness, a time when she had believed in the future and when death had only struck others.

LIST OF CHARACTERS

In order of appearance

Neria

Ellane, slave

Arhel, Neria's younger brother

Nephalie, Neria's mother

Elinor, Neria's sister

Adamek, Neria's older brother

Valterone, Neria's father

Paz, Adamek's wife, Neria's sister-in-law

Anaëlle, Neria's niece, Paz and Adamek's daughter

Draz, Elinor's fiancé

Elatek, Supreme Leader, the liberator of Humanity

Zelimo, Valterone's friend

Bobka, Gargoyle, slave gardener

Rona, children's tutor

Matar, the Peddler

Forg, Gargoyle

Isk, elderly Gargoyle

Imri, female Gargoyle

Kloups, young Gargoyle

Barz, male Gargoyle

Fylis, female Gargoyle

Shorka, female Gargoyle

Mavom, infantryman

Berdomy, Valterone's friend, emissary of Elatek

Moguedon, swamp monster

Sido or Sidehmoliomatch, toad-man

Kamau, Angel

Jabaury, leader of the Angels

Passoa, Demoness from Roguelle

Scarface or Maznar, Demon

Queen Analour, Mother Supreme, Soul of Cambolae, Demoness

Livia, waitress in Roguelle

Yourk, Mayor of Roguelle

Yado, commander of Roguelle's troops

Tartello, Demon

Sylophine, the doll

ACKNOWLEDGMENTS

I would like to thank everyone who contributed to the creation of this book. To begin with, the first readers who endured it in its embryonic state: Morgane Azilis, Sybille Charbit, Sylvie Loubes, Thierry Loubes, Romaine Loubes, Ariella Chetboun, Carine Rapoport, and Pascal Rapoport.

I would also like to thank my literary advisor, Thibault Malfoy, who has shown me the way in becoming a writer, and Luke Owain Boult for his wonderful work on the English translation.

I would like to thank my family, my parents, my husband, and my daughters, who have supported me throughout this project.

Made in the USA
Monee, IL
21 November 2022